"Hey, is there some kind of theatre doing a nineteenth century play, some Jane Austen story or something?" Darrell turned and asked the bartender who passed, delivering two beers to a couple down the bar. Darrell hoped his question sounded simply curious but was afraid it came out desperate.

After he dropped off the drinks, the guy stopped in front of Darrell and picked up Kurt's empty bottle, using a towel lodged in his apron string to wipe off the wood. "Oh, you mean Margaret?" The server grinned, showing a few missing teeth.

Darrell swerved in his seat to point out the woman sitting at the second booth down the row. But she was *gone.* "She was right there." He pointed to the now empty table in the center of the room. "She wore this gaudy makeup and this fancy, old-time, flowing red dress. I saw her there a few seconds ago."

The barkeep chuckled and pointed at the inked snake on his neck. "With black ruffles on the collar?"

Darrell nodded.

"Oh, that was Margaret. She…um, you might say, she floats in here from time to time." He tucked the towel back into its place. "She's one of the ladies of the evening from the House of Royals. And…she's pretty much a regular round here."

"The House of Royals?" Darrell asked.

"Yeah, they tell me one of our hotels housed a famous bordello about a hundred years ago."

"A hundred years ago? You mean…?"

Crimson
at Cape May

by

Randy Overbeck

The Haunted Shores Mysteries,
Book 2

This is a work of fiction. With the exception of a few historical individuals, locations, and businesses; the characters, places, and incidents are either the product of the author's imagination or are used fictitiously.

Crimson at Cape May

COPYRIGHT © 2020 by Randy Overbeck

Cover Art by *The Wild Rose Press, Inc.*

The Wild Rose Press, Inc.
PO Box 708
Adams Basin, NY 14410-0708
Visit us at www.thewildrosepress.com

Publishing History
First Mainstream Fantasy Edition, 2020
Trade Paperback ISBN 978-1-5092-3163-8
Digital ISBN 978-1-5092-3164-5

The Haunted Shores Mysteries, Book 2
Published in the United States of America

Acknowledgements

My journey to create this narrative was aided and supported by a range of individuals and I would be remiss if I didn't acknowledge them. The unwavering support from my wife and family kept me going even when I doubted myself. I was grateful to have the input from my beta readers, who reviewed the manuscript in process and the story evolved as a result of their feedback. I believe the contributions of the Dayton Tuesday Writers' Group were most critical to strengthening my writing. Also, I don't want to forget the help and advice (and corrections) of two talented editors, Jaden Terrell and Dianne Rich.

I also want to acknowledge the interest and support of a different group of folks. Even though the character of the ghost bride I created for this story is entirely fictional, I found the research on the documented ghosts completed by Craig McManus in his series, *The Ghosts of Cape May,* very helpful in crafting my new ghost story. Also, even though this story is fictional, Cape May is, in fact, a very real place and most of the places mentioned were and are actual locations and businesses. (Yes, there really is a Poverty Beach with palatial, rich homes along the shore.) I'm especially grateful to Doreen Talley of the Cape May Chamber of Commerce for her help in navigating this wonderful town and in making sure I got the details of 1999 Cape May right. Also, thanks to the many merchants of Cape May for allowing me to include these real places of business in my narrative.

Author's Note

This novel is a work of fiction. With the exception of a few historical individuals such as Christie Todd Whitman, all the characters are products of the author's imagination and used fictitiously. However, the locations and businesses mentioned in the narrative are actual and specific to the incredible resort town of Cape May, New Jersey, though they are portrayed as they existed in 1999, not currently.

The primary offense depicted in the story, human trafficking, was and is a horrific and widespread crime that preys on the vulnerable, young population—primarily immigrant, but also local—and is vastly underreported, though the numbers represented herein are intended only as estimates. It is a stain on the human culture that has only grown worse and wider in the two decades since the time of the narrative. It is stunning that, today, there are more individuals being trapped in some kind of slavery, such as human trafficking, than at any time in our history. My hope is that this novel raises a little attention to this blot on humanity.

Chapter One

Cape May, New Jersey
June, 1999

"Of all the ghosts, the ghosts of our old loves are the worst."

~Sir Arthur Conan Doyle,
The Memoirs of Sherlock Holmes

There was something *off* about her.

Darrell Henshaw had first spotted the woman on the Promenade near the corner of the Cape May Convention Hall. Huddled in the shadows, her long white dress soiled and torn, she stared at him with sad blue eyes that might have once been enchanting, but now seemed haunting. With her dirty blonde hair, a pallid face, and ragged clothes, he thought she was simply another homeless person. He'd heard panhandlers like to set up under the shade of the Convention Hall, on the famous beach and across from the meticulously restored Victorian houses. That is, until the cops ran them off.

After he used the faucet to rinse off his feet from his walk in the surf, he dried them with a towel he'd brought along. Between the water and the cloth, he fussed to make sure not one grain of sand clung to his feet. He'd had another full day at the junior high football camp where he was assisting, and he only wanted to get to his room and collapse. After losing his teaching and coaching job in Wilshire, he was glad for this gig. He shot another glance over at the woman. He didn't need any complications.

He slipped his shoes back on and started walking, keeping the woman in his peripheral vision. Unlike other homeless he'd seen, she held no sign or bucket to beg for money. Instead, as he passed, she extended small, bony hands and said, "Please help me," the words so soft he could barely hear them. Darrell pretended he didn't see her. He didn't feel good about it, but he kept moving anyway.

As he made his way around the front of the Convention Hall, Darrell sensed movement behind him and glanced back. The woman rounded the corner, coming his way. He ambled across Beach Avenue, strolled past a few stores and then ducked into the alcove of a gift shop. He knew he was being paranoid, but with his experience back in Wilshire, he couldn't help it.

Stopping beside the glass window, Darrell chanced a look back. Across the avenue, the Convention Hall loomed to his right, its scrubbed gray stone and blue windows looking almost like some Greek temple. It was flanked by the wide stretch of a white sand beach, still populated by tourists in colorful swimsuits. He craned his neck and examined his side of the street, studying the restaurants, beach shops, and bars that fronted the road. The woman stood, about four shops down, waiting. Did she see him? He yanked his neck back inside the alcove.

A small bell tinkled and he jumped. As the door

opened, the aroma of homemade fudge wafted out. His stomach growled in response. He'd worked hard at football camp today, running drill after drill with the teens in the blistering Jersey sun, and hadn't had time to eat. An older woman with a tight bun of brunette hair exited the store and walked around him, giving him a wide berth and raised eyebrows. Darrell ignored her and peeked his head around the corner again, careful not to touch the grimy glass. *She* was still back there, not more than fifty feet down the walk—he caught a glimpse of her disheveled, shoulder-length blonde hair—just standing there, watching. Waiting for him? Working hard to not glance behind, Darrell headed out again. As soon as he stepped out of the alcove, the salty breeze off the water hit him.

He hurried on, his feet stumbling on the sidewalk. When he stole another glimpse back, she was keeping up with him.

Darrell couldn't believe he was being followed.

Picking up the pace, he turned up Ocean Street, trying to figure out where he was. On the right, he recognized the distinctive pink architecture of another Victorian. He remembered it. He was heading toward his boardinghouse and didn't want her to follow him there. In the middle of the block, he started across, dodging between passing cars, and turned onto Carpenters Street. Both drivers hit their horns hard, making Darrell dart across. He grabbed a quick breath and glanced back again. A few houses down, his shadow stepped out between the cars and eased across the street, apparently oblivious to the traffic.

He cursed aloud, his paranoia full tilt now. Staring at his feet and counting his steps, he hooked a left onto

Decatur.

Why would this woman pursue *him*?

Now a safe distance away, he studied her. She was thin, with a small, drawn face of pasty skin, and he would've guessed her to be about his age, mid-twenties. But there was something about her, something that made him shiver. Did she have a black eye? Were those cuts on her cheek? Why hadn't he noticed those before, when he passed her on the Promenade?

He sped up, the street crowded, congested with tourists. Normally, the jostling bodies would've given him the creeps, but today he was grateful for the numbers so he could blend in.

Not sure where he was headed—except away from his boardinghouse—he kept up a brisk pace. He hurried past the legendary Inn of Cape May, with its ornate, white period architecture and four stories of ancient rooms facing the beach. Any other time, he'd be thinking about taking Erin there. The place had an interesting old-time vibe. That is, if she still wanted anything to do with him. But he didn't have time for that now. He kept moving.

As he turned back onto Beach Avenue again, the sight of the beautiful blue ocean across the road struck him and he stopped for a moment, then chanced a peek back around the corner. No sign of his stalker.

He reduced his pace, easing past a beach shop, and saw his reflection in the store front. That gave him an idea. Ahead, he spied a coffee shop with two long windows facing the street, the panes so sparkling clean he could see the image of the sun hanging over the ocean in the glass. As he walked along, he turned his head to catch his image and, when he was far enough along, he glanced sideways at the window. Trailing behind him, he could make out, reflected in the glass, only two people, a gray-haired couple. No one else. He took a few more steps, watching and slowing a little, and exhaled. He'd lost her.

He turned and studied the man and woman, who'd paused to examine the restaurant menu posted next to the door. A few feet beyond the couple stood the woman. Darrell's gaze darted. The couple. The woman. The coffee shop window. Back to *her*. The petite young woman in the tattered white dress stood hunched not more than ten feet away. Darrell searched for her reflection in the glass. There was not even a shimmer.

Oh no. Not again.

The side of the young woman's face was beaten and bloodied. Her exposed neck bore a long, ugly purple bruise. The torn dress now had blood seeping across her torso and down her right leg. He looked back. Still nothing in the window. The hairs on his neck stood up.

"What the hell?"

Hearing Darrell, the couple turned and the woman asked, genuine concern in her voice, "Sir, are you okay?"

Darrell ignored the question and blurted, "Why are you following me? What do you want?"

The man pulled his wife close. "Son, I don't know what you're talking about. We aren't following you."

Darrell shook his head several times. "I wasn't speaking to you." Taking a step to the side, he pointed beyond them. "I was asking *her*. What do you want?"

In unison, the pair turned, peered behind and then back at Darrell. The man said, "Son, there's no one there."

Darrell kept staring and as he watched, the young woman walked *through* the older couple and stopped in front of him. This close up, her one deep blue eye—the one not blackened—seemed vacant and carried an emptiness that frightened Darrell. She again extended both pale hands, blood now covering them and dripping off her fingertips. Mesmerized, Darrell watched as fat crimson drops splattered red onto the gray sidewalk.

In her soft voice, she said again, "Please, help me. Help us."

Darrell shook his head violently. "No. Hell, no. Not again." Last time almost killed him.

He turned and ran full out, ignoring the aches in his calves and the people yelling at him. His Nikes slammed onto the concrete as he bounced off pedestrians, cut across streets, and ran between cars. Pissed off drivers honked at him. He didn't look back. Twice he stumbled and fell, scraping both knees. The pain didn't register. He picked himself up and sprinted. Up Jefferson, onto Lafayette, all the way to Jackson Street, the entire twelve blocks. He didn't quit until he made it safe inside his room, gasping with ragged breath. He threw the lock on the door.

As if a deadbolt could keep out the dead.

Chapter Two

"Darrell, stop pacing or you'll wear out my linoleum."

Darrell glanced over at the speaker, Sara McClure, who wore a blue tee with "Nurses call the shots" across the front. She arched one eyebrow at him, and he shot a look at his feet. He didn't stop moving, though. He kept walking the same precise line of designs on the white and blue flooring, back and forth, back and forth. He couldn't help himself. With his stalker in Cape May and his problems back here in Wilshire, his OCD had come roaring back.

Though almost a generation older, Sara and Al McClure had been—were—his best friends in Wilshire. Ten months earlier, Al, the fifty-something band director with a short, athletic build, had welcomed Darrell to Wilshire High School on Darrell's first day. They'd hung together ever since. His wife Sara was an OB nurse, kind and smart and, most importantly, had introduced Darrell to another hospital nurse, Erin Caveny. Erin and he had been a couple—Darrell had hoped for more—until…until everything. Tonight, he was here, at his friends' place and at their invitation, to try to do something about that.

After Friday's football camp and a quick shower, he'd headed out, realizing the trip to Wilshire would take at least three hours. Even with the ornately painted

Victorians of downtown Cape May in his rearview mirror, he couldn't get the ghost off his mind. Maybe his appointment later tonight would help.

He drove his car onto the large Cape May-Lewes Ferry and got out. Standing at the rail, he watched the small whitecaps as the boat bounced over bumpy, blue-gray waves. The rolling waves reminded him of his earlier trips on the water—including the time his investigation for the Wilshire ghost almost got him drowned. He took long, slow breaths, inhaling the salty tang off the water. Remembering the sails with Erin in her dad's boat, he smiled. Tonight's plan had to work.

By the time the ferry hit the Delaware shore and lowered the gangplank, he'd decided there was little he could do about his strange visitor in Cape May—at least for now. He needed to focus on Erin.

Heading west into a slowly setting sun, he drove the hundred miles of winding back roads across rural Delaware and Maryland, using the visor to keep the sun out of his eyes. He needed to make things right with Erin, or at least try. As wooded scenes and small towns flew by in the dying light, he rehearsed some possible lines. *I'm sorry I had to leave without talking with you* seemed way too feeble. *None of the accusations are true* sounded whiny and defensive. *Please forgive me for disappointing and embarrassing you* might make a difference, if she wasn't too hurt to listen. Not to mention Sara was planning on ambushing his girlfriend. She'd invited Erin over after work for another of her famous recipes—a slivered almond chicken salad this time—but she hadn't been told Darrell was the appetizer.

What could he say to convince her? To win her

back?

McClure's kitchen door flew open, followed by the flurry of paws across the linoleum. Two seconds later, a brown torpedo collided with Darrell's legs.

"I missed you too, Pogo, even though it's only been a week." Darrell stopped pacing and reached down to scratch behind the pug's neck, and the small dog settled on the floor, lying across Darrell's sneakers. The pug always was good at helping Darrell soothe his anxiety. "I'm glad to see you too, boy."

Sara said, "Hey, Pogo, how about a snack?" Reaching into a kitchen drawer, she pulled out a dog biscuit, waving it in the air. Pogo rose to all fours, his mouth hanging open. "Okay, go bother your Uncle Al." She pointed toward the door and threw the treat in that direction. The pug caught it in mid-air and barreled through the door.

From the family room Al said, "Hey there, boy. I see you got a treat. Yes, you do. How about I give you a little something smooth for your ears." Al started in on a song on the piano, sending notes flowing throughout the house.

"Hey, thanks for looking after Pogo," Darrell said.

"He's a sweetie. No trouble at all. But we're trying hard not to get too attached."

"I'm grateful you're taking care of him, and I hope I get him back soon. I'm just not sure how. Not in Cape May. The boardinghouse there can't handle animals." Darrell remembered, though, Pogo had helped him cope with his Wilshire ghost.

"You two will be back together here in Wilshire soon. I'm convinced," Sara said, her voice confident and optimistic.

"I wish I had your confidence."

From the family room, the dying strains of a sad blues song drifted in and Darrell recognized the melody of "You Lost That Loving Feeling."

"Hey, I don't need your musical commentary, Al," Darrell called out.

The piano keys stopped. "Oh, you caught that, huh?" Al pushed open the kitchen door, the pug now at his feet. Al tilted his head up, brown hair trimmed tight and edging toward gray, and did a poor imitation of Bill Medley's crooning.

When Darrell shook his head, Al switched. "Well, maybe you'll like this. Do you know what it means when you come home to a woman who'll give you a little love, a little affection, and a little tenderness?"

Darrell knew he shouldn't bite, but old habits die hard. "No, what does it mean?"

Al grinned. "It means you're in the wrong house."

Sara threw a spoon at him. Al ducked back into the family room, releasing the swinging door, which the spoon smacked. "Alan Raymond McClure, you're terrible." Shaking her head, she picked up the spoon, but she was grinning.

Within a few seconds, Darrell heard Al tinkling out another tune on the ivories and finally stopped pacing in front of the oven. He caught the scent of fresh cut apples but, glancing around, didn't see any. Then he remembered, Almond Chicken Salad.

"Sara, I'm not sure this is a good idea." He pulled the kitchen towels from the handle of the stove. "I might scare her away. I mean, for good." Without thinking, he found himself laying the towels on the counter and folding each one, aligning the cloth into perfect halves. After ironing each with the palm of his hand, he replaced them over the stove handle.

After he'd arranged the second one, Sara came over and placed a hand on his. "Al and I decided we had to do something. I don't believe Erin thinks you did what they claim. Not really. I mean I know what the medical records say, but she knows you." She shook her head, her short blonde hair swaying with the motion. "We know you didn't give those boys anything. Earlier this week when I mentioned you, she said she didn't want to talk about it. But yesterday, when I brought it up again, I could see her faltering…I think." She grimaced. "She's miserable, and you don't look so good yourself. It kills me to see you two apart."

"I don't know how to convince her I'm innocent," Darrell said. "I can't really blame her. If I heard what they said about me and saw the hospital records, *I'd* have trouble believing I didn't give my kids steroids." He stared down at Sara. "Every time I've tried to rehearse what I want to tell her, I get so nervous, my OCD goes crazy and I can't even think straight." He broke away and started pacing again, his feet following the same floor pattern.

"Well, maybe that's your problem," she said.

He stopped, facing her. "What do you mean? My OCD?"

"No, silly." She shook her head again, smiling. "That's not a problem. That's part of what we love about you."

"Then what?"

She moved in close to him and placed her hand on his chest. "You need to speak from your heart. I don't know. Maybe tell her you love her? Remind her you're still the same guy she fell in love with and not some manipulative, self-centered coach who'll do anything to win."

He glanced down at her fingers. "Is that what folks are saying?"

"I'm sure she's heard that." She withdrew her hand and looked up into Darrell's eyes. "You need to remind her you're still the same crazy, caring guy she knew."

"I don't know if I can—" he started, when the doorbell interrupted him.

Chapter Three

Al called out from the family room, "I'll get it."
After a few seconds, he said, "Great to see you, Erin.
Come on in. Sara's in the kitchen. She'll be right out."

Darrell's heart rate spiked.

Sara whispered to him, "Give me a minute, then
come in."

He stayed, but after the door swung closed, he held
the door open a crack to watch.

"Well, if it isn't the hardest working nurse I know,"
Sara said.

"Hey, Sara," Erin said in a weary voice. "Oh, hi,
Pogo. I'm glad to see you too." The pug gave a short
yip.

"Well, how was OB today?" Sara asked.

"Busy. Non-stop. You know, the usual.
Exhausting." Her tall, graceful figure was slouched and
she looked beaten.

Sara spoke up, "Well, I have a surprise for you.
Something that will help, I think."

"I've had enough surprises for one day." Erin
sighed. "Had an overweight woman admitted to the ER
this morning with stomach pains. During the exam, they
discovered she was nine months pregnant. Delivered
three hours later, screaming obscenities so loud, I'd
swear the entire hospital could hear." She pointed to
herself. "Of course, my patient."

Sara grinned. "I believe it. I've seen it more than once before. I'm pretty sure my surprise will make you forget your whole day." She cleared her throat. "Someone came to see you."

"Who?" started Erin.

Darrell nudged open the door and strolled into the living room, though his hands were balled in tight fists behind him. Sweat dripped down the side of his face. He wiped it with his arm and tried his brightest smile. "Hi, Erin."

Erin's emerald eyes grew huge, then turned hard as stone. She whirled toward Sara. "I don't need this. Not tonight." She shook her head, the long red strands flying with angry purpose.

Sara laid a hand on Erin's arm. "Simply hear him out. Please. For me."

For a long moment, no one spoke, the silence almost choking Darrell. He stared at Erin, *his* Erin. Her smile was gone. That beaming, innocent, heart-warming smile he fell in love with no longer lit up her face. His heart broke, seeing the scowl that replaced it, and realizing it was his fault. He examined the sprinkling of freckles on her neck as they seemed to pulse. Darrell always thought Erin's shape was beautiful, with a lithe, athletic body and curves in all the right places. Tonight, though, she looked thin and pale.

Because of him?

Tonight, Erin wore a different scrub top. Not like the ones she favored with an explosion of summer flowers or a picture of colorful balloons, but this one in institutional blue. As if reflecting her mood.

Her shoulders stiffened, the same soft shoulders

he'd kissed. The pit in his stomach grew harder. Her gaze flicked from Darrell to Sara and back to Darrell again.

Oh God, this was a terrible idea.

"I'm, um, sorry—" Darrell started.

"You're sorry," Erin yelped. "You're *sorry*. For what? For giving drugs to your students? You know my history. I told you about my problems in school." She released a short bark. "Sorry? For deceiving me? I believed in you. Thought you were different." She shook her head harder. "Sorry for making me think you were the kind of man I was looking for, when all you cared about was winning stupid football games?"

She spit out the words rapid fire, wounding Darrell like bullets. "How could you do this to me? To us?" By the time she finished, she was crying, the final syllables collapsing into sobs. She dropped her head, wiping her tears with her arm.

"Come and sit on the couch." Sara put an arm around the younger woman's shoulder, guiding her.

He took the chair by the fireplace, studying her, wishing against hope.

Al said, "I bet you could use a beer. One Dogfish Head coming up."

Darrell said, "Thanks."

"I was talking to Erin, but I'll get you one too." Al disappeared into the kitchen, only to reappear thirty seconds later with two longnecks.

Darrell watched as Pogo trotted over to Erin and arranged himself around her legs. Jeez, even the pug thought he was guilty.

Sara, sitting to the right of Erin, nodded her head to the left. Darrell got the message.

Taking a deep breath, he tried again. "Look, Erin, I know what they're saying, but I *never* let my players take anything other than aspirin. Or Tylenol. Never." He picked up the beer bottle and wiped off the ring it left on the hearth. "And I never saw them take anything else either."

"Well, either they deceived you, or you're lying." One small tear squeezed out of each of Erin's eyes, but they remained hard as green marbles. "I wanted to believe you. Hell, I believed in you completely. I told everyone they were wrong. Said there had to be some mistake."

"You did?" Darrell said.

"Yeah, that's why I got Stephanie in records to pull the actual ER test results. I wanted to see for myself. You know, the ones they ran when Seth and Jason were in that car accident. In *October*. No alcohol or marijuana in their system, but both tested positive for steroids."

Darrell shook his head harder. "There has to be some mistake, some mix up."

Sara broke in, "But Seth and Jason had this car accident in October, so how come it's only coming out now, eight months later?"

Erin shrugged. "Maybe they missed it then, I don't know. Or, knowing this town, they gave them a pass because they're *athletes*. Anything to win another game."

Darrell could see how that could happen, but he was certain it hadn't. "I worked with those kids, day in and day out. They both played football and basketball. If they were taking steroids, I would've noticed. And I would've done something about it."

Eyes brimming with tears, Erin choked out, "Okay, but if you were so innocent, why didn't you stay and fight? Why didn't you talk with me? Why'd you duck and run?"

Darrell hesitated, unable to meet her gaze any more. "I was trying to save the boys."

"What?" Erin sniffed.

Darrell got up from his chair and knelt in front of Erin. "Everything happened so fast. They gave me no time to decide or even talk with you about it. You were on shift, and the next day, I had to leave to start football camp in Cape May."

Erin stared at him, waiting, emerald eyes still hard. "Okay. Explain now."

Erin's name badge was crooked, turned to the left. He started to reach out to straighten it but stopped himself and hurried on. "Well, you know both guys had scholarships, full rides. Jason to Georgetown and Seth to Duke."

"So?" Erin asked, but her single word had lost its edge.

"If the colleges got wind of any drug charges, even in June, they would've pulled both boys' scholarships." He reached out and wrapped his hand around her long delicate fingers. He met her gaze again. "If it got sorted out later, when it all got sorted out, the colleges could have dumped our guys and offered the scholarships to other students. Seth and Jason would have lost their chance."

"Okay, but how did this become your fault?"

"The Board was somehow convinced I'd given them the drugs."

"Why you?" Erin asked. "Couldn't the guys have

gotten them on their own?"

"Because I was their coach? They said they had a tip. And they wanted a scapegoat, I'd guess." Darrell sighed. "I don't know, maybe somebody framed me."

"Who would do th—?" Erin started.

Sara interrupted her. "I heard it was Remington."

"Dr. Remington?" Erin turned to face Sara. "He's not on the School Board."

"No, but he knows every board member. He told them he knew about the drugs when he examined the players, after the accident in October. Said the boys told him Darrell had given them the steroids. But he kept quiet about it at the request of his friend, the coach."

"That's a lie," Darrell blurted. "I never asked him anything of the sort. He never talked to me about it."

Sara raised both palms. "That's what I got from my friend."

Darrell said, "That might explain why they seemed so sure." He turned back to Erin. "Anyway, the Board said if I took the heat and left at the end of the school year, they'd keep it quiet. Say nothing to the colleges. And if the boys' drug tests were negative this week, they'd be in the clear. So I did. Hoped I'd have a chance to straighten it out later."

Sara said, "And the results came back clean today for both guys, so they'll be able to keep their scholarships."

Erin pulled her hand away and looked at Darrell, both eyes wet. "I know you care about your students, but how could you throw away everything? Risk our future here in Wilshire?"

Darrell had no good answer and slumped back on his haunches.

18

While the other three had talked, Al had sat silently, sipping his drink. He set his glass down, the thin amber slice sloshing. "Erin, I believe this sad sack." He pointed to Darrell. "I've been around him way too much not to notice something like this. I've been in the locker room every week. The only pills I ever saw were aspirin."

Erin started to say something, but Al held up one finger. "The first question I have for you two," he looked at Erin and his wife, "is who could get into hospital records and change them. Say, add test results?"

Sara said, "The charge nurse and the nurse assigned to the case."

Erin added, "And a few doctors. The ER physician and any specialists called in…like *Remington*."

Al turned back toward his wife. "Right. And Sara, your friend told you Remington put a bug in the Board members' ears about Darrell?"

"That's what I heard," Sara said.

"Let's assume Darrell is telling the truth. The question we have to ask is, why would Remington go to all this trouble? What does he have to gain?"

Sara nodded at Darrell. "Well, Darrell did kill Remington's best friend."

Actually, the ghost had killed Williams, but Darrell didn't bring that up.

Sara continued, "I've heard Remington's like a lot of the locals who are none too happy with this *Yankee* exposing our town's dirty little secrets."

Al raised his eyebrows. "Or maybe the best question is, who turned in the anonymous tip about the boys using steroids in the first place?"

Chapter Four

Well, that wasn't a total wreck.

Al and Sara, Erin and he had discussed the whole situation for more than an hour. They started from the assumption of Darrell's innocence—thank God—and examined possible answers to Al's questions. They took turns discussing motives and tossing out possible schemes. After ninety minutes, they decided they were closer, but not there yet. Still, Darrell felt better. The McClures' unwavering faith in him buoyed him, and Erin seemed almost convinced.

By the time they all called it a night, Erin let him walk her to her car and even kissed him goodnight. And she left him with a smile, a little weak, but it was there. He'd take it. She'd said she had to work another twelve-hour shift Saturday, so they made plans for a run and brunch Sunday morning. Just like their first date. Definitely not the disaster he feared. And best of all, they'd set tentative plans for next weekend. Since she'd be off, Erin said she'd consider coming to Cape May. *Yes.*

He pulled out of the McClures' side street onto Shore Road, checking both ways. Not much traffic at one in the morning. When he saw a single pair of headlights in the distance, he accelerated down the open road.

Darrell couldn't believe he'd made this next

appointment for 1:30 at night. One he knew he dared not tell Erin about. That *would* blow any chance of getting her back.

While at the McClures, he was so focused on making up with Erin, he'd not let himself even think about his newest *visitor*. Now that he had a glimmer of hope to reclaim his job and get Erin back, his thoughts returned to his other problem, the spectral one. He only knew one person who might be able to help him. Yesterday, he'd called and set it all up.

He checked his watch again and pressed harder on the gas. As the shoreline whizzed by on the left, he could see the reflection of an elongated crescent moon in the rippling black water. Windows open, he inhaled the scents of the Bay—brackish water, kelp, and fish—smells he'd come to love this past year. As he rounded the bend, he slowed and noticed the new telephone pole, and memories of last fall's collision exploded in his head. The black SUV coming straight at them. Their Jeep sliding out of control. The telephone pole—the one now replaced—hurtling toward him. Eight months had passed, but in that instant, as he braked around the curve, tires singing on the pavement, the visions leaped painfully back.

Only one of the problems they'd encountered chasing the Wilshire ghost. He dreaded what havoc this new ghost might wreak. He had to get a handle on it. Once past the crash site, he sped up again.

A flashing light lit up his car from behind, the red streak striking his rearview mirror and blinding him. A second later, the siren followed. Darrell glanced at his speedometer, cursed, and pulled the Corolla over to the curb.

He stared at his side view mirror as the cruiser pulled off the road behind him, the blinking strobe turning the tan and gray patrol car into a black and white in the dark. The cop fiddled with something in his car, making Darrell wait, he guessed. His gaze went from the side view to his Pulsar watch and back. He was going to be late. Eying the mirror, he noticed it was smudged and he pulled out his handkerchief to polish the glass. When he finished, he could make out a tall, slim figure approaching, but the cruiser's brights washed out any details.

When the officer came even with his door, he barked, "License and registration."

Hearing the voice, Darrell relaxed a bit. "Sorry, Brad, I didn't realize I was going so fast. I just came from seeing Erin." Officer Brad Bishop had caught security detail at some football games last fall. About the same age as Darrell, they had talked sports a few times after the games. Darrell liked him. Maybe this wouldn't be horrible.

"It's Officer Bishop, *Yankee*. License and registration."

Confused, Darrell handed out both. "Sorry, uh, Officer Bishop."

Snatching the two, the cop slid them under the clasp of his clipboard. "Doing sixty in a forty-five, that's way too fast." Darrell heard a slight southern twang in the words he hadn't noticed before.

The cop filled in the citation.

Darrell tried to study Brad's face, but a broad Smokey hat shaded it, one exactly like Officer Brown had worn the night Darrell had… Only, atop this young man's small head, the huge hat looked ridiculous, like a child wearing grown up clothes.

"Look, I'm sorry," Darrell started, realizing it was his second—or third—apology of the night.

"You're *sorry*. That's a laugh. And way too late." He stopped scribbling on the pad and looked at Darrell. "You were a damn good coach. The football team had their first winnin' record in years. Why couldn't ya merely stay with the program?" He shook his head. "Naw, you had to stir up all this ghost nonsense and look where it led."

The cop stuck the license and registration through the open window. "The Board sent you packin' and I'd advise you stay away. While you're here, you can be sure we'll be watching you." He tore off the ticket and thrust it at Darrell, then took one step and turned back again. "Oh, and have a nice night."

Edging back onto Shore Road, Darrell stayed well below the speed limit, the cruiser following close behind. When he turned onto South Drive, he watched as the cop continued down Shore. He let out a long breath. Darrell rolled past Nick's and heard the raucous country western music flowing through the open doors. He drove by but couldn't help staring at the side street where Ruby had been hit and killed months before. The bloodstain had long since disappeared, the crimson bleached into the asphalt. He shivered and kept going away from Tavern Row and into what passed in Wilshire for a red light district.

He found an open parking space around the corner from his destination. Walking down the sidewalk, he glanced up at the sign which read "Westminster Alley." He scanned his surroundings. Yeah, what a joke. Even though he was a little more than a mile from the shore, you'd never know it. Dilapidated three-story apartment buildings fronted each side of the street, the stoops littered with empty booze bottles and discarded syringes. He started across the street.

A pair of blinding headlights lit him up from behind. Like a target. A large engine growled at him. Motor revving, it headed straight for him. Darrell dove between two parked cars and rolled. The vehicle sped by, raucous laughter spilling out. A hundred feet past, it screeched to a stop.

Darrell jumped up, crouching, watching, weighing his options. Not the same car as Ruby's hit and run, who was never caught. This one was a big black pickup.

The truck's wheels squealed. It shot backwards and halted. The window buzzed down. The driver yelled, "We don't need your kind around here. Stop poisonin' our kids. Go home, Yankee, and take your crazy ghosts with ya." Then he sped off, leaving behind the smell of burnt rubber.

Darrell brushed the gravel off his clothes, fingering the new cuts in his jeans. It took a few minutes—and he was late already—but he needed to make sure he cleaned all the road debris off. Satisfied, he walked on. He knew where he was headed—he had been there twice before—but he pulled the dog-eared business card from his wallet. He stared at the image of a purple hand with an eye in the center and read the script beside it again.

Natalia Pavlenco
Psychic Medium with other talents

Chapter Five

Darrell didn't know what he'd expected when he first encountered the medium months earlier, but it wasn't Natalia.

Last fall Al had introduced him to the former Marching Pirate and cheerleader as someone who might be able to decipher messages from the Wilshire ghost. Much to Darrell's surprise, Natalia might not have looked the part, but she turned out to be far more skilled than he expected.

As he opened the door to 169 Cambridge Lane, he took in the shabby surroundings once again. Not much had changed. Careful not to touch the wood, he ascended the same rickety stairs with the wobbly railing. He passed a grinning client—a john, Darrell corrected himself—heading down the steps on shaky legs and buttoning an open shirt.

The bulb on the second floor landing had been replaced, but its light only highlighted the brown-splotched walls, giving the place an ugly, squalid feel. The filth creeped him out again, his OCD invading. He could not let it take over. He didn't want to be here, but he needed Natalia's help.

A floor above, a door opened and the pungent odor of marijuana drifted down, mixing with the smells of decay and filth. The door he wanted on this landing, Apartment D, still had the two-inch wide hole about two feet from the floor. He raised his toe to the spot. Somebody must've been pretty mad. Did she keep it there as some kind of reminder? He raised his hand to knock, but the door opened before his knuckles made contact.

"Darrell Henshaw, you kept me waiting," Natalia said with a breathy voice. She reached across the threshold and dragged him in, kicking the door shut with one black stiletto heel. Her slim arms snaked around his waist. "It has been too long." Up close, her scent enveloped him—pheromones, a strong floral perfume, and jasmine shampoo. Her eyebrows rose and a leer tugged at the edges of a smallish mouth. "Oh, I see you came by yourself this time."

Natalia had a smooth, dark complexion and curves that reminded him of a shapely, exotic model. Conjuring up an image of Erin, leaning out her car window as he kissed her, Darrell used both hands to extricate himself from Natalia's grasp. Two fingers of each hand held her arms at bay. "Now, Natalia."

Her bright red lips did a small pout. She thrust out her chest, the bronze edges of large breasts spilling out of the fabric. "I heard from my clients you and Erin were on the outs. I was so hoping you had come to sample my *other talents*." For the final two words, Natalia adapted the low and sultry voice he remembered from his earlier visits.

Darrell knew what was coming. "I do appreciate you don't give up easily." Darrell released her and she strutted into the apartment, long brown hair swishing as she walked. She wore another wrap around skirt, this one black and white.

With probably little underneath.

26

A white silk blouse with three buttons undone topped the outfit and she'd cinched a gold scarf around her waist. She turned, hands on hips, and stared at him. He considered her and realized they were both about the same age. If he hadn't just made up with Erin...? It was hard not to um, *admire* what she had to offer, but picturing Erin's shining emerald eyes, he braced himself, remembering why he came.

"I need your help. As a medium." She didn't budge. "With another ghost. I think."

She dropped her arms. "Of course, but Darrell Henshaw, like school, you can be no fun." Full lips went back to the leer. "You don't know what you're missing."

He had a pretty good idea.

She stomped across the room, untying the scarf from her waist and fastening it around her forehead, gypsy-style. "You know the drill." She moved to extinguish the lights, starting with the lamp by the bed. "Come, sit at the table."

As Darrell covered the distance across the small apartment, he noticed something different from his previous visits. Quite different. The place looked...spotless. No crooked tower of dirty dishes stacked in the sink. Pink covers on the queen-sized bed tucked and neat, not disheveled. Still, underneath the sheet? He shivered. Taking a chair at the table, he watched Natalia light one candle after another, sending flickering images across the room like stealthy intruders. He noticed there were no items strewn anywhere—on the counter, on the bedside table, or even on the round table where he sat. Nothing, except simple wax candles.

Did she clean the place up just for him? She must have other neat freak clients.

Natalia used a Bic lighter to ignite the two tall green tapers on the tabletop. Dark shadows flickered across her face as she settled in opposite Darrell. The gold bandana held the stray hairs back, and deep brown eyes met his. "Give me your hands." Her voice was mellow, deep and dead serious.

Hesitating only a bit, Darrell extended his arms and she grabbed both hands, her smaller fingers encircling his palms. Like on his previous visits, his hands and arms heated up at her touch, as if her very skin was radiating warmth. He squirmed in her grasp.

"You have come about another ghost," she said in a deep, creamy tenor, adopting the Slavic accent she'd used before. "Tell me vhat you can about…her."

How did she know the ghost was a woman?

"She, uh…the ghost…she's not from around here. Does that matter?"

"Many ghosts are not bound by the limits of time and space. Vhere did you encounter her?" She squeezed again, sending another streak of heat up his arms.

Darrell stared at his hands. He swore the exploding warmth shot across his flesh, but he couldn't see anything. "I, uh, I'm working in Cape May right now. You know, only for this month."

She glanced up. "I have heard of your troubles, Darrell Henshaw. As my babushka used to say, bad mojo. But I see brighter days ahead." She stared into the candles. "But it is not surprising you have had another encounter with the spirit vorld there. Cape May has a powerful spiritual presence, a place of many roaming specters. Others have vitnessed apparitions

28

there. Tell me about your ghost."

While Darrell looked across the table in the near darkness, Natalia sat perfectly still and her eyes rolled up in her sockets. All he could see were the whites of her eyes. Jeez, he remembered this. He shivered again and started talking, jabbering really, the story of the shadow chasing him through the streets of Cape May tumbling out in short, quick sentences. Her dress and her changing, bloodied image.

When he finished, Natalia tugged on his hands, sending another bolt of electricity up his arms. Her brown pupils rolled back down, her eyes again fixed on him.

She said, "I sense…no, I hear many voices, all female, many very young, only children." She stopped and looked up at the ceiling. Darrell followed her gaze and noticed the brown scar of a water stain on the plaster. She jerked her glance down, eyes blazing at him. 'No, not children. Teens. Teenage girls."

"Teenagers?" Darrell shook his head. "No. The…the…the—"

"Spirit," Natalia supplied.

"Yeah, spirit. I don't know how old she was, but the spirit who asked for help wasn't, wasn't a teen, I don't think." He forced himself to recall the vision— small figure, full chest, mature face with the bruise on the side, sad eyes, one blackened. The bloody hands. "No, not a teen. Definitely twenty-something." He pulled his arms back. "Maybe you have your psychic wires crossed."

"I have no vires crossed, Darrell Henshaw," Natalia said, the Slavic accent heavier. She yanked both arms, pulling the elbows hard, making him wince. "And

I am no psychic. I am medium."

Darrell wrenched his hands out of her grasp and massaged them. "Okay, okay. I merely thought maybe you were getting vibrations from other spirits."

She took his hands again and the fire jumped once more from her skin to his. "No, the vail of your spirit is buried in the middle of the other girls' cries."

"Other girls' cries? You mean there are more ghosts?"

"I did not say all those veeping are ghosts. Some have passed and are now spirits, others have not. All have suffered, though."

"Suffer?" What the hell does that mean? He remembered the bloodied face of his stalker. "Suffer how?" He leaned back in his chair. "And who is this ghost who chased me? How am I supposed to help?"

"That is not clear yet. I sense your ghost, a young voman from Cape May." Natalia opened her eyes again and stared at him. "Did you say she vore a torn vhite dress?"

"Yes."

"I see a vedding." Natalia turned her head to the side, as if listening. "And I hear music. A song." She sang softly, her voice melting a bit. "Can you feel the love tonight?"

Darrell listened, mesmerized. A song?

Abruptly, Natalia stopped and released his hands. "I see a vedding and a death."

Darrell rubbed both palms. "Oh, that's great. A wedding and a death. I'm supposed to find a dead bride. In Cape May? Where I don't know anyone?" He watched Natalia rise from her seat. "Why me? I've only been there a little more than a week."

"I am surprised Darrell Henshaw that you vould ask. This ghost must realize you are a sensitive, just as I can. Be careful. A shroud of evil pursues this ghost as vell. No doubt, she is seeking your help vith some unfinished business, like our Vilshire ghost."

Natalia rose, moved toward the door and undid the scarf from her head, retying it around her waist as she walked. One hand out for payment, she turned the lock on the door with the other.

"And we all know how well that turned out." Darrell pulled out fifty dollars. "Four dead bodies."

Chapter Six

"Josh, you need to cut quicker, if you want to beat the defender," Darrell yelled down the sidelines to the lanky eighth grader. "If you don't, any decent linebacker will figure out what you're doing and beat you to the ball. Now, everyone, try that route without the ball. Damon, you lead them off."

Darrell studied teens of almost every size—from barely under five feet to well over six—and every shape—from tall, slim, and willowy to short, chunky, and solid. He watched them run, trot, and streak down the field. He glanced at the sidelines and saw Kurt Wagner. The head football coach at Lower Cape May High School stood on the chalk line, arms crossed, relaxed, watching Darrell work the students. Kurt was running the junior high football camp and had hired Darrell to assist. This week, he'd assigned Darrell responsibility for teaching receiving, and Darrell had worked out a schedule of lessons. Monday, it had been catching and tucking away the ball. Tuesday, they had practiced fighting off interceptions. Today was running routes, but Darrell was afraid some players didn't seem to be picking it up.

His gaze returned to the students and, seeing them busy, allowed himself a minute to think about the past weekend. With the McClures' help, he'd made progress on his road back to Erin. His run and breakfast date with her Sunday morning at Ben's-by-the-Water had gone pretty well. Not the old intimacy yet, but getting there. He'd even been able to get Erin to laugh at a few of his jokes. And most important, she agreed to come to Cape May and spend this coming weekend with him, away from the prying eyes of Wilshire. He needed to get this right.

And, as typical with Natalia, the medium had helped, but also raised more questions than she answered. *A haunted bride and other female ghosts in Cape May.* At least, he hadn't seen his personal ghost so far this week. Of course, he'd taken a different route back to his boardinghouse each day. Simply to play it safe.

So, to keep his fears at bay and his mind occupied, he'd decided to throw himself into the football camp. In the bright New Jersey sun, on the hard-packed field, he'd pushed his body and his psyche, right alongside the teens. With all the exertion and demands of the schedule, he'd been able to keep his anxieties at bay and his OCD under control. And each night he'd found refuge in the study of the football strategies buried in his coaching books. Perhaps his plan was working, because he wasn't a basket case. Not yet anyway.

Once the players had all run the assigned route and assembled themselves back in front of him, Darrell explained, "The whole point is to make the move so quickly, the defender doesn't have time to react. Now let's try the same thing with passes this time." As the boys lined up, Darrell had each teen run the ten-yard route and then threw the football as they made the cut. They seemed excited to have a chance to compete against each other, enjoying the challenge and celebrating with high fives after each acrobatic catch. In fact, this time every teen caught the pass, except Josh.

He turned to the high school student standing next to him. "Reggie, would you throw to them? Okay, guys, let's run the route again. A little more hustle this time." He tossed the football to the older teen and turned. "Josh, could you come over here a minute?"

The student, Josh Dawson, a tall, wiry kid with a bright shock of red hair and a face pockmarked with acne, was usually one of the best. Last week Josh had the surest set of hands, catching everything thrown at him. Today he dropped his seventh pass, and the last one had hit him in the numbers. Even though Josh and the rest of these kids weren't *his* students and Darrell was only with them for a few weeks, he couldn't help himself. He was concerned and decided to do his teacher thing.

The young man sidled over to the sidelines, pencil arms dangling at his side. "Yeah, Coach?"

"Josh, you feeling okay?"

"I'm okay," said the skinny young man, though his words held no conviction.

"Your hands not working right today, Josh?"

The teen looked at his hands, but wouldn't meet Darrell's eyes. "They're okay."

"Something bothering you, then?"

"Sorry for screwing up, Coach. I'm having trouble concentrating. It's not football. Nothing to do with football."

"Maybe I can help," Darrell offered. "What's wrong?"

The pimpled face looked up at Darrell, worry evident in the blue eyes. "I don't see how you can help.

No offense, You're a Shoobie, Coach."

"A what?" Darrell asked.

"No, it's nothin' bad." The kid gave a hard chuckle. "It's an expression we use for people from out of town."

"A Shoobie?" Darrell repeated.

"Yeah. I don't get it either, but my mom told me the nickname came from the visitors who used to arrive on the train with their lunch in a shoe box. Get it? Shoobie."

Darrell nodded. "Shoobie, that's pretty good. But, even a Shoobie can listen."

Josh sighed. "It's my sister, Josie. No one's seen her since Monday."

"How old is she?" asked Darrell.

"Josie's sixteen, a little crazy and a real pain sometimes. But it's been two days, and I'm worried."

"She ever run away before? You know, take off and not tell anyone?"

"Sure. Josie and mom, they'd fight and Josie would run off and hide out at her friends. Usually, she'd let me know, and she'd always come back after a few hours or the next day at least."

"Teenagers and their parents fight sometimes," Darrell said. "Good Lord, I fought enough battles with my mom and dad."

"Yeah, but she's never been away this long."

"Have your parents reported her missing? You know, to the police?"

"My mom said Josie is only pouting because she won't let her get her license yet. She said Josie will come home when she wants to. But I don't know, Coach. I got a bad feeling about this. Know what I

35

mean?"

Darrell knew exactly what Josh meant. The hairs on his neck began to prickle. He sensed something, a premonition. But for the teen, he faked it. "Maybe she came home while we've been practicing. Why don't you head on home and see if she's there?"

"Okay." Josh nodded a few times and trotted off the field. A few steps away, he turned back. "Thanks, Coach. Maybe, she's home right now. See you tomorrow."

"Bright and early tomorrow, Josh," Darrell called back, smiling at him, though he didn't feel like it. He turned and half-expected to see an apparition in a torn, white wedding dress floating across the field. All he saw was the other players scrambling down the sidelines.

The screams of other teenage girls? He shook his head, trying to clear it.

Scanning the entire field, his eyes landed on the woods across the way. He saw movement in the trees. Was that a flash of white? The hairs on his neck had not relaxed.

Chapter Seven

Hell, since Kurt was buying, Darrell was drinking. He saluted his host with his beer.

Coach Kurt Wagner announced, "To another day of making the world safe for football. Or at least making our corner of Cape May safe for football." He and Darrell clinked bottles and they both took long draws. Kurt finished first and set his bottle on the bar. "I know I told you this before, but I'm certainly glad you agreed to help me out with the camp."

Darrell really liked Kurt, and not simply because the guy had thrown him the lifeline of coaching at the football camp. Hardly the image of the typical football coach, Kurt wore his black hair long and a moustache like Darrell had last seen on reruns of *Magnum P.I.* At least two decades older, Kurt was short and carried a wide paunch with an even wider smile. But he was a great football coach. His Stallions were almost undefeated last year.

"Glad to be here," Darrell said, "and I can really use the money." He glanced around.

The place Kurt chose, Carny's, was a long-standing tavern on Beach Avenue, famous for a massive U-shaped bar and a historical mural covering one wall. The twenty-foot painting captured in great detail a scene from when Cape May was a thriving harbor. The fourth wall at the end of the bar held two huge mirrors, making the room look twice its size. Martina McBride's voice flowed out of hidden speakers. When they entered together, several guests around the bar and in the booths called out greetings and Kurt took time to introduce each one to Darrell. He also stopped to shake hands and talk with each person. Even the bartender gave Kurt a high five. Either Kurt was well known in the community, or a regular here. Or both.

They sat at the end of the bar on raised stools, the mirrors on their right. Darrell examined the glass, checking to make sure it was clean, spotless even. Using the mirror, he could see the whole room and he studied the dozen or so other patrons in the bar. Then, unable to help himself, he turned to make sure every figure in the room had a matching image in the mirror. When he counted the fourteen customers and an equal number of corresponding reflections, he released a long breath. Kurt interrupted his examination.

"I heard about your problems back at Wilshire." Kurt set down his second beer. "It's all a bunch of crap. They can't ask us to be babysitters as well as coaches. But what do you expect from a damn school board?" He took another drink.

"Well, I believe I hear Coach Walter," called a strong, bass voice across the room.

Kurt swiveled on his stool and grinned. Two men wearing sunglasses in the darkened room approached, both in matching tan suits that looked to be custom-tailored, crisp, white shirts and blue ties pulled in precise Windsor knots. The one older had close cut blond hair graying around the edges and an erect bearing with strong, squared shoulders. The second looked like a younger version of the first, without the gray hairs. Father and son, Darrell guessed. As both made their way across the room, the young man led and the older one followed, keeping a hand on the son's shoulder. It was slow going. Almost every patron rose to shake hands with the senior, who bestowed one benevolent smile after another. When they arrived at the bar, both men shook Kurt's hand.

"How's our favorite coach?" asked the father, life lines etched into a patrician face.

"Working hard grooming the next group of players," Kurt said. "We're in the middle of junior high football camp."

"Any promising prospects coming up?" asked the younger man.

"A few, but none to match you, Travis." Kurt turned to Darrell. "Travis here was one of the best running backs it's been my privilege to coach. League MVP in '88. Could make more defenders miss than anyone I've seen. If he hadn't gotten hurt at Princeton, might have made the NFL."

The young man shrugged and Darrell sized him up—large torso, broad shoulders, well over six feet, probably a muscled two hundred pounds. Might've been hard to bring down. Like his father, handsome, rugged features that no doubt must have driven the girls wild. He glanced at the young man's left hand. Probably still did.

"Excuse me. Where are my manners?" said Kurt. "This is my colleague, Darrell Henshaw, head coach at Wilshire High School. Darrell, James and Travis Armstrong."

Still leaning on his son, the older man stepped forward, found Darrell's hand and grasped it. "Wilshire, huh? That's the little team you were telling us about?" He directed the question at Kurt.

"The one and same. In one year, Darrell turned their program around. Read about him." said Kurt. "That's why I asked him to help out with our camp."

"Good to meet you, Darrell. Well, we don't mean to interrupt and we're here to meet some clients," the elder Armstrong said. "We merely wanted to stop and say hi. Travis, find us a booth and lead the way." Both men waved and walked away, James' hand again on his son's shoulder.

When they were out of earshot, Darrell said, "Bet there's an interesting story behind that family."

"The Armstrongs?" Kurt raised his hand to get the bartender's attention and swirled it to order another round. "Hell of a football player, that Travis. And the dad, James, never misses a game, even though he can't see much."

"He blind?"

"Legally blind. Not sure how much he can see. Army Ranger in Vietnam, I heard. Caught in an explosion in Da Nang. Eyes got the worst of it." Kurt watched the pair settle into a vacant booth. "Still, he's a big supporter of our program."

Darrell downed the last of his beer and set the empty bottle on the walnut counter. He noticed it left a wet ring on the wood and wiped it off with a napkin, trying to look inconspicuous. "What do they do? What kind of business?"

The server, a tall, gaunt young man with spiked black hair and a cobra tattooed on his neck, arrived with the next round. Kurt said, "They're into a lot. Mostly shipping and transport. You've probably seen their trucks up and down the coast." He drank from the new bottle and then wiped his arm across his mouth. "Anything new on your situation back in Wilshire?"

Darrell detected no intrigue in the question, only interest. "Not sure, but I think things *may* be getting sorted out."

"Well, if they don't work out there, I'd love to have you here at Cape May. We have an assistant coaching position open, and I happen to know the junior high is looking for a social studies teacher."

Darrell shifted on the tall stool. "Really? Thanks, Kurt. I'll think about it."

"Bu-u-ut?"

"I have this girl, Erin. At least, I think I still do. And she's a nurse in Wilshire, loves her job. Wants to stay there."

Kurt raised his bottle and took another swig. "Oh, I know how the fairer sex can be. I'm on marriage number two."

Darrell set his bottle on the bar, making sure it was centered on the napkin this time. "Hey, maybe you can help. Erin's coming for the weekend and I can't have her stay in that boardinghouse. Any suggestions?"

"What are you looking for? Romantic or historic?" Kurt asked.

"I don't know—both, I guess. Some place she'll love and I can romance her." Darrell drank some more.

"Cape May has a bunch of great options, but my first recommendation would be the Inn of Cape May. It's an old inn, really historic with lots of old stories to match. Can get rooms with an ocean view, and they have a great pool. Only a few steps from the beach. Is this gal hot?" He grinned. "I mean, will she rock a bikini?"

Darrell grinned. "Plenty hot. And she can certainly rock a bikini."

"Oh, it's not cheap, though." Kurt tilted his half-empty beer bottle back and forth. "You get what you pay for."

"She's worth it. I still have some money saved. And I can't think of a better use."

"Nothing like romancing your woman." Kurt winked and then polished off his drink. "I need to go. I promised Maureen I'd be home for dinner."

When Kurt turned to leave, Darrell put a hand on his arm. "I got a quick question for you. Do you know this kid in the camp, Josh? Josh Dawson?"

"Yeah, know the family. Had his sister, Josie, in my Geometry class this year. Why?"

Darrell shared what Josh had told him about his sister going missing. When he finished, Kurt said, "It's nice of Josh to worry, but I'm not too concerned. From what I remember, Josie is a real looker, but flighty. She wanted to be a model and get rich. You know how these kids can be. No time for bo-o-oring school stuff." Kurt threw a couple bills on the bar. "She's probably goofing off with her friends or shacking up with some guy. She'll show up soon enough." He pointed at Darrell. "Next time the beers are on you." He headed for the door.

"You got it, and I hope you're right."

Even as Darrell said those words, he thought...no, he *knew* somehow Kurt wasn't right about Josh's sister. As he watched the coach weave his way through the tables, the hairs on his neck stood on edge, his warning system going off again. He counted the patrons in the tavern again, and then, after he turned in his stool, their reflections, too.

The math didn't add up. A shudder rippled down his spine.

Chapter Eight

He counted again, just to be sure. Finished, he couldn't take his eyes off the strange woman.

"Hey, is there some kind of theatre doing a nineteenth century play, some Jane Austen story or something?" Darrell turned and asked the bartender who passed, delivering two beers to a couple down the bar. Darrell hoped his question sounded simply curious but was afraid it came out desperate.

After he dropped off the drinks, the guy stopped in front of Darrell and picked up Kurt's empty bottle, using a towel lodged in his apron string to wipe off the wood. "Oh, you mean Margaret?" The server grinned, showing a few missing teeth.

Darrell swerved in his seat to point out the woman sitting at the second booth down the row. But she was *gone*. "She was right there." He pointed to the now empty table in the center of the room. "She wore this gaudy makeup and this fancy, old-time, flowing red dress. I saw her there a few seconds ago."

The barkeep chuckled and pointed at the inked snake on his neck. "With black ruffles on the collar?"

Darrell nodded.

"Oh, that was Margaret. She…um, you might say, she floats in here from time to time." He tucked the towel back into its place. "She's one of the ladies of the evening from the House of Royals. And…she's pretty

44

much a regular round here."

"The House of Royals?" Darrell asked.

"Yeah, they tell me one of our hotels housed a famous bordello about a hundred years ago."

"A hundred years ago? You mean…?"

The server, whose badge read Rob, moved his bony shoulders up and down in one fluid motion. "Uh-huh, she saunters in here from time to time. People report seeing her. I've never seen her myself, but others say you can't miss her in that outfit. She comes in, sits down, then disappears."

"You mean she's a hundred-year-old *ghost*?" Darrell said.

"Welcome to Cape May, my friend. Haven't you read the promo, 'Cape May: the country's most haunted seaport.' " His hand went to his spiked hair, patting it.

Darrell couldn't tell if the guy was serious or simply repeating some advertising slogan. Or pulling his leg.

Rob continued, "Gotta admit, it takes a little getting used to. Believe it or not, we get a bunch of customers who heard the stories and come looking to catch a glimpse. You should count yourself lucky. Not many folks can see her."

Lucky, huh?

A high-pitched voice across the tavern interrupted them. "Well, as I live and breathe, it's Travis Armstrong!" Darrell watched as a young woman entered the bar and pranced over to the Armstrongs' booth. She stopped only inches away from the young man, who'd stood up. "You look fab-u-lous in that suit."

The young woman, like Travis, was in her

twenties, short and busty with blonde hair worn in a sculpted cut, the wisp of golden bangs floating across her forehead. An open-neck, sleeveless blue tee showed off well-tanned arms and plenty of cleavage. The top was matched with a tight pair of designer jeans that hugged her body. Something about her reminded Darrell of Carmen, his ex-fiancée from Ann Arbor. Not a happy memory. The woman practically bounced in close to hug Travis. The young man barely responded, and the senior Armstrong stiffened, even though he couldn't see what was going on. Travis and the woman started talking in low tones.

The bartender stood, eyeing Darrell taking in the scene. "Nice pair, huh?"

From his look, Darrell wasn't sure if the man meant Travis and the new arrival or the girl's boobs. Darrell said, "There must be a story there." His head nodded to the two, still conversing quietly. The young woman patted Travis' arm and laughed, tossing her hair in the process.

"You could say that." Rob leaned in close and spoke in a conspiratorial voice. "That would be Jennifer Thomas. She and Travis were quite *the item* in high school." He intertwined two bony index fingers. "You know, head cheerleader and football star. She even followed him to Princeton. It was no secret she wanted to marry him. She was devastated when he asked Amy Palmer instead. Was furious. Said she wanted to kill Amy. Looks like she still hasn't gotten over him." His eyes went to the couple, who were splitting apart now.

Darrell watched the two, something tugging at his brain, but he had trouble recalling it. Jennifer glanced across the space and waved. Rob wiggled a finger back.

Darrell noticed she had a pretty oval face, with a petite nose and pouty lips, all carefully made up. He looked from Travis to Jennifer, and then it hit him. He remembered seeing Travis' empty ring finger. "Did he marry this Amy?" He pointed to his own left hand.

"Well kinda," started the server. "The night—"

An older guy down the other end of the bar yelled, "Hey, Rob. How about a little service here? I'm parched?"

The barkeep straightened up and headed in the man's direction.

Darrell's focus returned to the Armstrong booth where father and son sat alone again, talking in hushed tones. He scanned the rest of the tavern but didn't see any sign of Jennifer.

The barkeep was back. "I saw you eyeing the girl. Can't blame you. She is easy on the eyes." The gaunt head did a quick swivel, making the snake flip around. "Since you're new in town, um…if you're looking for some *company*, I can help you out."

Images of Erin stretching after their run last Sunday, her hot, athletic body shimmering with perspiration, filled his head. "Thanks, but I'll pass."

"Simply offering." The server pointed at the half-empty bottle of Dogfish Head. "That's my favorite, too. You want another one?"

"Sure."

"How 'bout something to eat?" The bartender pulled a menu from under the bar and slid it to Darrell. "I'll give you a bit." He headed down to greet a young couple who grabbed two stools.

Darrell fingered the greasy menu, only by the edges, digesting what Rob had told him. "O-kay, then," he said under his breath. He searched the room again, looking for Margaret. No nineteenth century harlot. Studying the patrons, he remembered what Natalia had said. "Cape May has a powerful spiritual presence, a place of many roaming specters."

Roaming specters?

Darrell turned his attention back to the menu and, when the barkeep returned, ordered a burger and fries. To help relax the still stiff hairs on his neck, he downed another beer, feeling the buzz by the time he finished. He rose, a bit unsteady at first, and paid his check.

Darrell headed out, hoping the breeze off the beach would do him some good. Halfway across the bar, he stopped. The booth where he'd seen the ghost was still empty. Though new patrons had filed into the other tables and booths, no one chose to sit at the table where he'd seen Margaret. A ragged piece of paper, sitting on the clean red tabletop, caught his eye. He glanced at it and saw a few words scribbled in black ink on the faded sheet. His nose detected the strong aroma of some cheap perfume. He frowned, shook his foggy head, and started to step around the table. Then he caught sight of his name, glaring at him from across the top of the page. He stopped and picked up the note.

Darrell,

Please help her and rescue the others.

Chapter Nine

Darrell snatched the note off the table, folded the paper precisely in half, and slid it in his pocket. He strode toward the door, glancing around. The Armstrongs were now in deep conversation with two other business types. All the other patrons seemed preoccupied with their own affairs as well. He caught the barkeep watching and tried for a casual wave as he pushed the door open.

The stickiness hit him first. Even this late, after seven, the June heat had not let up, the temperature well in the eighties, the mugginess rampant. The odor of saltwater floated on the air, and he headed down Beach Avenue. When he arrived at the intersection of Ocean Street, he stopped, gazing across at the tide rolling up over the beach, the white waves stretching out and then disappearing into the sand or being called back to the ocean in a quiet murmur. For a moment, he stood, breathing in the saline aroma and letting the cool breeze off the water wash over him. He took one deep breath, then another.

He missed the Eastern Shore, but he had to admit Cape May had a lure all its own. Besides the stunning Victorians on almost every street—he passed three meticulously painted homes on Columbia—the town boasted this expansive white sand beach. His eyes feasted on the sight, pleased to find no sign of his spectral visitor, and took another deep breath. He couldn't wait the two days to show the town to Erin, certain she'd be fascinated. Which reminded him where he was going, and he headed farther up Beach Avenue.

Sitting across from the bay, with the high surf rolling in, the Inn of Cape May made quite the impression. The building's four floors of white clapboard siding formed a tall L surrounding a sparkling blue pool where kids splashed and young beauties in tiny bikinis lounged. When he climbed the wide steps to the entry—careful not to touch either railing—and entered the lobby, bouquets of brilliantly-colored flowers greeted him, decorating the white room and releasing a delightful floral scent. *Oh, Erin's really going to like this place.*

It took only a few minutes—and his almost-maxed-out credit card—for him to reserve an "ocean side suite with a breathtaking view and a spacious king bed" for the weekend. Darrell figured he might as well go all out and, when he confided his plans to the receptionist, she winked at him.

Feeling poorer but pleased, he headed back down the painted stairs. He found focusing his mind on romance and his body on lust a pretty effective way to keep ghostly fears at bay.

With no direction in mind, he ambled across the street and onto the Promenade. Feeling the concrete path beneath his feet reminded him of his first encounter with the ghost. His gaze followed the boardwalk down to the Convention Hall, where she'd huddled in the corner. When he caught no sight of a figure in a tattered white dress, he released the breath he didn't realize he was holding. He patted his shorts pocket, where he'd stashed the note from Margaret, and decided to keep it right there.

He stepped onto the sand. As he strolled down the slope toward the water, the ocean breeze grew stronger, the wind blowing steadily off the water, and he stood, letting it soothe him. As he neared, the splash of the waves upon the shore grew louder, cascading one on top of the other. His gaze searched the stretch of beach and caught sight of only a few kids and adults. His eyes swept left and right across the sand, left and right. No ghost. He took two long breaths.

He looked down at his feet and thought, what the hell.

Before coming to Cape May, he couldn't have appreciated the simple pleasure of his toes in the sand. The grating feel of the coarse grains against the bare skin of his feet was enough to make him wince. Though it was a challenge at first, he beat back his apprehension. The first time he'd made sure no one else was watching and had tested the process with only one foot. He'd found the sensation tolerable, and, once he got used to it, relaxing even. After a bit, the warm sand and cool water had become an almost daily ritual following the hot and sweaty days at the football camp.

Darrell took off his shoes and socks, letting his toes wiggle in the sand like a little kid, finding the granules warm, but no longer hot. He collapsed onto the beach, his bare legs below his shorts basking in the warm sand. Though he had to turn a bit, he stretched out his tired body almost parallel to the waves, his face toward the west. Leaning back on his elbows, he stared at the mesmerizing rhythm of the waves rolling onto the shore, one after another. The quiet sound of the surf splashing onto the beach, over and over, relaxed him, and he felt his breathing slow to match the cadence. Using one arm to block the glare, he stared across the watery expanse and watched the sun's reflection break onto twenty different marching waves.

He breathed deeply. Thinking about the job offer from Kurt, Sara's efforts to rescue his position back in Wilshire, and his chance to reconnect with Erin, he felt the best he had in a while. Oh, and maybe the three beers were helping too.

Others on the beach, three kids and their parents, continued their play, running into the oncoming waves and jumping into the water. Nearby, two teens tossed a Frisbee and an errant throw landed the disc near Darrell. He picked up the yellow circle and flipped it back to the pair, who waved like he was an old friend.

Darrell didn't know how long he stayed there, easing his body into the warm sand, and didn't care. He simply watched the waves making their endless march to the shore and the sun inch lower in the sky, all the while surrendering to the hypnotic gurgle of the ocean. When he came out of his trance, he glanced around and noticed he was now alone on the beach. Checking his watch, he was stunned that more than an hour had passed while he lay there, half asleep, half awake.

He decided he'd better get going. He still had to walk to his boardinghouse, grab a shower, and do some planning for tomorrow, before he called it a night. As he sat up, facing west, the sun hung barely above the water. Gathering up his shoes and socks, he trudged over to the faucet to rinse off his feet and stole one last glance back at the water.

He blinked. A figure appeared in the water farther

down the beach toward the sunset, apparently walking *out* of the waves. The image seemed to shimmer and then crystalize. He shook his head. A late swimmer or surfer? A silhouette in the center of the orange ball, the figure emerged as if directly from the sun. Darrell adjusted his arm to block the glare and squinted.

His gaze shot up and down the beach and he realized he was now alone, completely alone on the sand. Behind him, he heard a few cars on the asphalt of Beach Avenue. His focus returned to the waves. The figure was closer now.

And Darrell recognized her.

He shook his head again, hoping it was a mirage or a bad dream, or at least a hallucination from too much alcohol. As she emerged from the waves, the water ran down a torn, white dress and dripped off the tips of her blonde hair. Her wedding dress, Darrell figured, remembering Natalia's words. Then, as he stared at the figure, the streams pouring down one side of her face transformed from clear to an ugly red. Now blood flowed from her scalp to her eyes, her cheek, and onto her neck. The right side of the white dress was stained red down her body and legs. He shuddered. Now only twenty feet from him, she held out her hands, exactly as she'd done the first time he'd seen her.

You helped Hank Young get justice. You can help me.

Darrell stared. He hadn't seen her lips move, but he heard the words in his head, quiet and clear even over the sound of the rolling surf. He froze. How could she know about Hank? Did she also know what he'd had to do to *get* justice? Did she know that four people *died* to achieve that justice? Did she know it nearly cost him

53

his life?

He wouldn't go back there.

Darrell backed up, feet stumbling, and snatched up his shoes. The sand no longer felt soothing to his feet, the grains suddenly grating his skin. He had to get his shoes on. He shot another look at her. She kept coming, not hurrying, but moving across the sand as relentless as the waves.

Please help me.

The voice sounded pleading, a desperate urgency in the three syllables. Still, he couldn't do this, wouldn't do this. He jammed his feet into shoes. The hell with the socks. He tried to run, though it was hard going in the sand. He reached the concrete path of the Promenade. He looked back. She kept coming, moving, almost floating, a mere ten feet behind. Now her voice in his head was louder, insistent, drowning out the noise of the ocean. She was no longer pleading. This time her words sounded like a threat.

Help me or more girls will suffer and die.

Darrell turned around and fled, his untied Nikes slapping with every step.

Chapter Ten

Josh Dawson held the poster against the telephone pole and Darrell stapled it to the wood after making sure it was perfectly straight. The student said, "Thanks, Coach, for helping me."

"Glad to. Let's hope somebody sees this and can tell you something." Darrell's gaze went from the student beside him to the photo of the teen on the poster. Josh's red hair was matted from being crushed under the football helmet, and lines of sweat marked his narrow acned face. The girl in the color photo had the same eyes as Josh, brilliant, piercing blue, but that's where the resemblance ended. In the picture, her oval face looked near porcelain quality perfect, with a snub nose and full lips. She was smiling, as if she'd just gotten away with something. Below the image, the flyer gave the essential details, "Josie Dawson, age 16, missing since June 14. Have you seen her?"

Four days, Darrel thought. Her mom had finally called the police.

"The cops think she's just another runaway," Josh had said after practice. "They said they'd put out an APB. Big deal." He'd shown Darrell a copy of the four-color poster he'd put together and said he had fifty more in his backpack, which he planned to put up around town. They now had forty-five to go.

Josh wiped his nose with the sleeve of his jersey

and pulled another poster from his stack. Darrell accompanied him down Beach Avenue, where the teen had said he hoped the flyers would be noticed.

After Wednesday's unsettling apparition of his ghost—Jeez, Darrell was already thinking of her as *his* ghost—he had made it safely to his boardinghouse, though once inside the locked room, it took about thirty minutes for his heart to return to normal. When he finally stumbled into bed after a long, hot shower, his sleep had been troubled. Images of the white clad figure, blood streaming down her face, arms outstretched haunted him. Twice he awoke in a sweat, gasping for breath.

When Thursday morning hit and Darrell arose, groggy and with a killer headache, he'd made it to football camp where the suffocating demands of herding teenagers took over. After the day passed with no more stalking by his ghost, he relaxed a bit and slept better. Today had felt almost normal with a scrimmage game in full pads, which the teens loved. Even Josh had gotten into it. After the scrimmage, Josh had asked for his help.

They walked down the block and stopped at the next telephone pole. While Josh held it against the wood this time, Darrell shot the staples, securing it to the pole above a flyer for Elaine's Dinner Theatre and below an ad for the Cape May Carriage Company. Josh turned to gaze at the ocean across the street, tears in his eyes. "I remember when Josie and me were little and we'd run together on the sand and jump into the waves." The teen sniffed. "You think these are going to help?"

"Let's hope so."

Darrell glanced up, following where Josh was staring, and noticed they were almost opposite the spot where he had lounged on the beach Wednesday. At the corner of Ocean and Beach Avenue, where he'd last seen that ghost. The Inn of Cape May sat just beyond, with its swimming pool glistening in front. He glanced at his watch and thought of Erin.

Ninety minutes.

Darrell swiveled his head, checking the stretch of beach, looking for, almost expecting, the ghost to reappear. Though he didn't see her, he felt *something*. No hairs standing on end, but something, as if they were being watched. His gaze swept the area, but he didn't notice anyone in particular and saw nothing out of place. While they stood there, tourists flowed around them, carrying striped beach chairs and brightly colored umbrellas, no doubt heading back to their hotels. A few paused to take note of Josh's poster, but no one made a comment. Darrell shook off the sensation and tried to focus on helping Josh. Then getting ready to meet Erin.

Putting an arm around Josh's shoulder, he guided him a little farther down Beach Avenue. As they crossed at the next light, they heard a siren. A police cruiser slid down Jackson Street and turned onto Beach, pulling up alongside them. The siren gave one yelp and died, though the strobe atop the car continued, red light pulsing around and around. Josh edged close and Darrell could feel the boy's body stiffen. He placed a reassuring hand on the teen's shoulder. Together they watched a beefy uniform in his forties with salt and pepper hair slide out of the front seat, put on his cap, and saunter toward them.

"Afternoon," the man said, his eyes hidden behind

mirrored sunglasses.

"Afternoon, Officer—" Darrell started, squinting into the sun behind the cop. He used his arm to shield his eyes and read the name on the uniform. "Officer Barnaby, how can we help you?"

"Could I see one of those flyers, son?" the cop asked. Josh looked to Darrell, who nodded, and the boy peeled off a poster, handing it across. The officer took it and, raising the sunglasses, studied the paper. He lowered the glasses back on his nose and stared at the teen. "You're Josh Dawson. Lorain's boy, right?"

"Yeah," the boy squeaked. Darrell could feel his shoulder twitch. "Josie's my sister." He pointed to the poster the cop held.

"Yeah, I got the word about your sister when I came on duty." Then he shook his head. "I'm sorry about this, but you can't put these up here. We got a complaint."

Josh's eyes went wide. He stared at the officer, then at Darrell. "Why? I'm only asking people if they've seen Josie. I thought you guys were looking for her too." Darrell could hear the edge of panic in the kid's voice.

Barnaby held up the poster. "These are against city ordinance 127.25, regarding public notices and littering on public facilities."

"What does that mean?" Josh asked with a sharp tone.

Officer Barnaby returned the poster. "It means you can't attach these to the telephone poles here like you've been doing."

Darrell pointed to the pole next to them. "What about these notices?" His finger tapped the ad for the play at Elaine's Dinner Theater and a flyer for a bike rental. He quickly counted six flyers attached to this particular telephone pole. "How is Josh's any different than these."

The officer cleared his throat and looked away. "Those were all approved."

Darrell asked, "Okay, who should we see to get Josh's flyer approved?"

"You can't," the cop said flatly, no expression on his features. At least the ones they could see.

Josh's free hand balled into a fist and he peered at Darrell.

Darrell said, "Officer Barnaby, could I speak with you a minute? In private?" He gave Josh's shoulder a squeeze and, without waiting for the officer, stepped around the corner onto Jackson Street. He moved into the shade of the building, allowing a few tourists to maneuver around him. After a moment's hesitation, the cop joined Darrell. Standing close in the shadows, Barnaby tilted his head up and looked at Darrell through the silver sunglasses.

Darrell spoke in a quiet, calm voice. "Officer, that boy is really worried about his sister. I don't know if these posters are going to help find her, but they are allowing Josh to do something, to not feel so helpless. I'm sure you can understand that."

Barnaby nodded. "I do. Who are you, by the way?"

"My name's Darrell Henshaw. I'm one of the coaches at the Cape May Football Camp."

"You're not from around here, right?"

Darrell felt nervous about the tenuous situation in Wilshire but plunged ahead anyway. "I coach football at another high school." When that didn't seem to register, he added, "I'm from a small town in Maryland. Coach Wagner asked me to help out with football camp. I've been working with Josh and the rest of the kids for the past two weeks."

That seemed to satisfy the cop and Darrell went on, eyes focused on the uniform. "What's really going on here?"

Even with the sunglasses, Barnaby couldn't meet Darrell's gaze and stared at his feet. "Like I said, we got a complaint. We're a big tourist town and the merchants feel like Josh's poster conveys a message they don't want associated with Cape May. People may get the wrong idea, might think this kind of thing happens all the time."

"Because a teen disappeared? Where doesn't that happen?" Darrell shook his head. "Come on. There's got to be more than that."

"It's what they told me. They don't want these flyers out on the public poles, where all the tourists will see them." Barnaby paused and glanced around, lowering his voice and leaning closer to Darrell. "Have the kid take the flyers farther uptown, away from the beach. He can put them up on some poles there." He started to walk away and stopped. "But I didn't tell you that."

Darrell followed him back to where Josh stood waiting, his face expectant. Darrell said, "Thank you, Officer Barnaby."

Getting into his car, the cop waved. "Have a nice day now." Darrell, remembering the last time a cop gave him that salutation, thought Barnaby might actually mean it.

As soon as the black and white pulled away, Josh

asked, "Well?"

"Come with me," Darrell said in a comforting voice. "We've got more posters to put up." He guided him up Jackson Street away from the shore. Darrell decided he didn't want to burden the student with the whole story, so he simply said, "Officer Barnaby said it'd be fine if we put them here."

They stopped at the next telephone pole, a little more than a block from Beach Avenue. Josh seemed to rally as he extracted the next paper, and together they attached it, right below two other posters. Darrell scanned the flyers, reading the ads to see if he might catch something fun Erin would be interested in. His gaze traveled down the pole, quickly scanning the notices vertically. One near the bottom was partially hidden behind some tall weeds that had escaped trimming. He pulled the weeds aside to see the face of another pretty teen girl, this one with beautiful black hair, deep brown eyes, and dark features. His sense of premonition returned as he read. "Brooke Stanley, age 15. Missing since April 1. Have you seen her?"

Darrell recalled what Barnaby had said. "People may get the wrong idea, might think this kind of thing happens all the time."

Maybe it did.

Chapter Eleven

At least Josh looked a little less hopeless.

By the time they finished, Darrell wasn't sure what else they'd accomplished, but that was something. Josh stood a little straighter. As they worked, though, Darrell's concern only deepened when he discovered notices for two other missing girls—a cute, black fourteen-year-old named Latoya Brown and another blonde, cheerleader type, age fifteen, listed as Tiffany Sexton. Both flyers sat at the bottom of poles, partially hidden behind overgrown grass. Neither was from Cape May, but both girls lived in nearby towns and had gone missing within the last two years. Two years? Maybe they'd been found in that time, though he doubted it. He blocked them and tried to keep Josh from seeing them. The boy was carrying enough baggage.

Darrell checked his watch and noticed the time. He had to hustle, and he'd have to figure out what all this meant later. He'd intended to head directly from camp to his boardinghouse for a shower and change, and then meet Erin at the Inn. But Josh's plea altered those plans. Once again, he found himself putting his students' needs ahead of his own—even if they weren't "his" kids.

His mind returned to Erin. He really wanted everything to go well this weekend.

With Josh on his way, Darrell had only enough

time to move the car from Beach Avenue to the lot across from the inn. Thankfully, he'd had the foresight to throw a packed bag in the car, just in case. A few minutes before six, he stood at the foot of the steps in soiled and sweat-stained shorts and tee. Every fiber of his body screamed for a shower, but he promised he'd meet her here and didn't have time, so he waited. He'd tell Erin about Josh's sister and hoped she'd understand.

Before he had time to consider, a yellow Jeep Wrangler screeched to a halt at the curb. "Well, if it isn't my favorite coach," said a familiar coy voice. "Looks like you could use a ride." Her gaze scanned him up and down. "And a shower." He walked into the street, leaned through the open window, and kissed her.

After she pulled into the lot across the street, he reached into the rear and pulled out her slim case and then grabbed the bag from his car. Once inside the beautiful lobby, painted a pristine white and dotted with fragrant bouquets of colorful summer blooms, his filthy appearance made him self-conscious. He tried to hold the bags in front of him while he checked in and paid. A few minutes later, they took the antique elevator to the fourth floor and arrived at their suite. Darrell stood, a suitcase in each arm, and held the room door open for her. She went through, straight to the large windows. As she stared, he watched her taking in the sight and reminded himself. No ghosts. No missing girls. For now, only Erin and him. He followed her gaze, taking in the aquamarine waves slowly rolling onto the long sand beach—still dotted with tourists—the bright orange orb igniting the water, and directly below, the glistening blue of the large, oval swimming pool.

She said, "Gorgeous."

"You enjoy the view and I'll grab a quick shower. I've made dinner reservations at Aleathea's for 6:45."

Without another word, he headed into the bathroom, stripped, and stepped into the tub. He scrubbed, getting all the sweat and grime off. He'd just lathered up his hair when he heard a sound. With the streams of water running down his face, he turned to see the shower curtain pull back and Erin step into the tub. One thing led to another and now…He gazed at her next to him on the bed.

They missed their dinner reservation.

Her impulsive ardor *had* surprised him. Not that he was complaining. When he planned their weekend, he'd hoped for the best, but was not sure how it would go. Last week, when they parted, things between them were better, but not like earlier. Before he lost his job. Tonight, as they made their way, laughing, from the shower to the bed, he decided he wasn't going to question it. Afterwards, while they lay against the wonderfully disheveled sheets, catching their breath, Erin confessed. She admitted, after she had time to think about it, she was convinced he was framed and, more importantly, believed he was the same guy she fell in love with. She admitted she'd missed him as much as he missed her.

But as they talked, sometime in the last hour, he must've let something slip about the ghost. He didn't want the ghost to ruin their romantic weekend. Damn.

"You saw another ghost? When? Where?" Erin asked.

She leaned on her elbow, and the silky cover sheet slid down, revealing a peek. She stared at Darrell, her emerald eyes wide with excitement, but he didn't hold her gaze and didn't answer right away.

She saw him admiring and grinned, but she persisted. "Come on, tell me. Who is this new ghost? Where did you see him?"

He dragged his gaze away from her body and met hers. "You simply make it so hard to concentrate."

"But I want to hear about this new ghost. Tell me about him?"

"Her."

"Her? You mean the ghost is a *girl*? A female ghost?"

Darrell looked her in the eyes and smirked. "I'll make you a deal. I'll tell you all about her during dinner, after…"

Her eyes twinkling, she gave a slight nod.

****

Arm in arm, they walked into Aleathea's around eight thirty, the aroma of sizzling shrimp greeting them and the rays of the setting sun striking the expansive glass windows of the restaurant. This late into the evening, they weren't the only diners, but almost. While Darrell and Erin were escorted to a table on the porch, they passed two other parties deep into their meals. Lazy, Caribbean fans swirled above them as they drank in the incredible view of Cape May Beach, and beyond, the sun a shrinking orange disc hovering above the water. From unseen speakers, the silky tones of Santana's hit "Smooth" floated to them.

A uniformed waitress, short and slender, dressed in black slacks and a long-sleeve white shirt with a Windsor-knotted black tie, ambled over to their table. She mumbled a welcome and announced the drink of the day, some summer cocktail, which they both ordered. When she sulked off, Darrell and Erin shared a glance. They studied the menu and returned to exchanging lecherous grins.

When the girl returned a few minutes later with two Sunset Punches, Darrell read the name tag, "Cassie." She had short black hair, amber eyes, and a small nose with a silver piercing in one nostril. He noticed several more studs in each ear. Her eyes bore large, tired circles, her posture slouched, and she wore a scowl. She looked young to be a server, maybe fifteen or sixteen. Studying the girl, he figured there must be a story there. Darrell thought of some of his surly students back home and, without thinking, went into teacher mode. He smiled at her, made a point of calling her by name.

"Cassie, huh. That's a different name." Darrell said. "Is it short for something?"

"Cassandra," the server snapped. She chewed a wad of gum and asked, "Have you had enough time to study our menu of sumptuous offerings? Have you decided what you'd like?" Her words sounded rehearsed and stiff.

Darrell recited both orders, salads and entrees. When the waitress slouched away, Darrell whispered, "Life is short and we've already had dessert."

Erin grinned, her face a little red, and then patted his arm. "First, tell me about this kid, Josh and his missing sister. Then I want to hear about your latest ghostly visitor. About her."

Darrell glanced around. The restaurant was indeed empty, the other couples having finished and left. Shadows engulfed the interior in the dim light. Darrell started in, telling Erin what he knew about the missing teen girl on the poster, as well as the flyers for other girls he found. Then he explained about the appearances of the bloodied ghost in the tattered gown. He was just finishing the episode about the figure emerging from the waves earlier this week when he heard a quiet sound from behind.

"Uh-hum."

He jerked his head around to see their server behind him, holding two salads. She'd been so quiet he hadn't heard her approach. She set one bowl down in front of each and backed up.

"Your entrees will be up in a few minutes. Since you're our last guests for the evening, the chef is making quick work of your order."

Darrell again checked out the vacant restaurant. "Cassie, are we too late? Are we going to hold you up? We can take it to go."

"Um, no." The server let out a long breath. "I'm supposed to be off, but I can handle one last table." She rolled her eyes. "It'll be good not to have to run around like a crazy woman." She pointed to the salads. "Anything else I can get for you?" she asked, though she didn't sound like she meant it.

Darrell looked at Erin, who shook her head, and he said, "It looks fine. Thanks."

"Okay, then, I'll check on the rest of your meal." She started to go and then turned back. "Would it be okay if I asked you a question?"

In that moment, the server's demeanor shifted. The earlier pout disappeared, and her gaze darted to the server door, as if checking for eavesdroppers. She hesitated, looking for a moment like a student in one of his classes ready to raise an uncomfortable question. Darrell eyed Erin, sipping her pink drink, and said, "Sure. Ask away."

"Did you say you've actually *seen* the Haunted Bride?"

Chapter Twelve

Darrell stared at the waitress. "What did you say?"

Her face reddened. "I, uh…uh, I'm sorry." She backed away, muttering, "I'll go and check on your entrees." She scurried through the doorway into the darkened restaurant before Darrell could get out another word.

He stared across at Erin. "The haunted bride?"

"Well, you said the ghost wore a tattered white dress. Could've been a wedding dress." Erin took an idle nibble of her salad.

Without thinking, Darrell pondered aloud, "Um, that would fit what Natalia told me." He stopped. Oh, crap.

Mid bite, Erin stopped eating. She slammed her fork down. Her gaze came up to meet Darrell's and she sat up straight in her chair. "What Natalia told you? When?"

Damn. Watching Erin's eyes narrow, Darrell realized he had little choice, so he started explaining about his late night visit to the medium the previous weekend.

Erin interrupted him. "You went to see Natalia without me. Did she come on to you again?"

"She did, but I put her off." God, he hoped he hadn't blown it. Again. Darrell stared into her eyes, silently pleading. A bead of sweat rolled down his temple. "You and I had just started to patch things up and…and I didn't want to risk anything." He shook his head. "Anyway, yeah, Natalia did her thing, but I told her I was only there because I needed her help as a medium." He reached across the table and took Erin's hand in his. "I told her I had you and you were all I ever needed."

"You did." Erin let a small smile show. "Maybe I'll forgive you. Okay, tell me what she said about the ghost." She extricated her hand and finished her salad while he talked.

He was almost through when a short, older gentleman with a round paunch appeared at their table, carrying two plates. He was dressed in a similar fashion to Cassie, white shirt, black pants and tie, and had a small, groomed moustache, graying at the edges. "I believe the beautiful young miss ordered the shrimp linguini and the young man the sea scallops." He set the dishes down with the grace of a seasoned professional. "Does everything appear to be to your satisfaction?" When both Darrell and Erin nodded, the man said, "Pardon me. My name is Antonio, and I'm the owner of this fine establishment." He made a small sweep with his arm.

Darrell exchanged a handshake with the man, and Erin commented on the beautiful restaurant.

Antonio said, "I do not want to keep you from your meals. These are best served hot and aromatic. Enjoy. Let me know if you'd like anything else."

As Antonio turned to leave, Darrell asked, "Is Cassie still here?"

Antonio stopped and turned back. "I sent her home and told her I'd deliver your food. She's had a long day." He stared at the floor and folded his hands. "I apologize if she, uh…spoke out of turn."

Darrell didn't want to get the girl in any trouble. "No. She seemed a little…tired, that's all."

"Cassandra is not one of our regular servers. Usually, she buses tables and delivers food, but I try to give her a chance to wait when I can." Antonio fiddled with the perfect knot of his tie. "She is…uh, an acquired taste. I hope she did not offend you." He glanced toward the interior of the restaurant. "She's had a hard life and I'm giving her a chance here."

"She was fine," Darrell said. "I only wanted to ask her a question. If she's still around."

"She may not have left yet. I'll check." Antonio took off, disappearing through the same door Cassie had earlier.

While they waited, Darrell and Erin started in on their entrees. No sacrifice. As they savored their seafood, the tastes and smells filling their senses, they exchanged contented grins. Between bites, Darrell filled in a few more details about his newest ghost.

Erin stopped eating for a moment, twirling some of the sauced pasta around her fork, and glanced toward the interior of the restaurant. "I hope we didn't get her in any trouble."

"Me, too," Darrell mumbled through a bite of risotto.

A few minutes later, Cassie reappeared. Her tie was pulled almost all the way down and the first two buttons of her white dress shirt were open. Her posture still slouched. She didn't look at them. "I'm sorry for what I said. I didn't mean anything." She muttered. "I mean, it's none of my business. Antonio said I shouldn't ask customers questions like that."

She bore the look Darrell had seen before in his classroom, when one of his students had been caught passing a note or taking another student's paper. "It's okay. We're not upset. I'm not upset."

"You're not?" Cassie's posture straightened a bit. She placed a hand on a chair at their table, her fingers absently caressing the curved, wooden scrollwork. Darrell saw her nails, done in black, stark against the white wood of the chair back. He hadn't noticed them earlier...or she just re-did them.

He said, "No, we simply wanted to know what you meant? You know, by 'haunted bride'?"

Cassie's gaze went from Darrell to Erin. Then it jerked back toward the kitchen, like a kid in trouble. "It's just that...Be careful." She spoke in a stage whisper, though her voice carried easily across the empty porch. Another quick glance back. "I mean if you've actually seen the ghost—"

"Cassandra?" Suddenly, Antonio appeared at the door to the kitchen and beckoned.

Cassie's eyes grew large. "Sorry, I've got to go." She started toward the kitchen and called back in a whisper, "Maybe we can talk more another time." She hurried back toward the waiting owner.

Erin grinned at Darrell. "Well, Mr. Henshaw, you bring me on some of the most unusual dates. Wonder what you have planned this time?"

His gaze flicked from the empty doorway back to Erin. "I try not to be boring."

Chapter Thirteen

Cassie pounded down the white wooden steps into the near dusk. The sun sat just above the water. Its final rays struck her eyes, blinding her. Damn. She blinked and jerked up her arm to block the glare. The high tide rolled in, the waves sloshing across the sand, the sound echoing off the side of the Inn.

She glanced back at the porch and studied the silhouette of the couple as they rose from the table. Watched the guy wrap his arm around the girl's waist, lean in, and kiss her. Stared as they left the restaurant, Antonio waving to them.

God, Antonio pissed her off tonight. The boss could've let her talk with them, at least. She would've argued with him, tried to explain that she was only looking for someone like her, but what was the use? When he said "no" like that, there was no budging him. Besides, he'd be the last person she'd tell about her "gift."

She'd had another crazy dream last night. And maybe, this one wasn't so crazy. She'd dreamt about another person with her "gift." A guy. Someone else who could see ghosts.

She watched the couple disappear into the lobby. Could this Darrell be the one from her dream? Had he really seen the Haunted Bride? Or was he simply trying to impress his girl? She'd caught their room number on the check, a suite on the fourth floor. Shit, those rooms cost. Could that guy be…be like her?

She'd checked the couple out when they entered. She couldn't help herself. He was tall, not bad looking with blue eyes that didn't miss much—she could tell he was sizing her up—with strong arms and brown hair, a little tousled. The girl, Erin, was pretty, really pretty, like Cassie wished she was. With gorgeous red hair and sparkling green eyes and a beaming smile, looking a lot like the cheerleader types at her old school. The ones Cassie hated. Only, she didn't get that vibe from Erin, that "I'm better, prettier than you" vibe.

The two of them really seemed into each other. The girl, Erin, had hugged his arm and he'd given her a warm smile. Cassie could tell, from their flushed, grinning faces, they'd just had sex. She might be young, but that didn't mean she was dumb. She knew that look, seen it often.

Still, she wasn't sure whether she'd come clean to him. So far, the guys she'd run into only cared about themselves. And they all wanted the same thing from her.

At home, all her dad ever gave her was grief. Yelled at her. Grounded her. Beat her more than once. Blamed her for her mom leaving. Still, he was her dad. Scared and confused about her visions, with her mom gone, she came to him. She was only thirteen and there really wasn't anyone else. Then she didn't know what to think. Even thought she might be going crazy. So what did he do? Her own damn father tried to have her committed.

"Can't have a girl of mine seein' no damn hallucinations!"

So she ran. For that, and a hundred other shitty reasons. Only to end up here in Cape May. Yeah. Here, her "gift" unearthed *way* more visions.

Great decision, she chided for the umpteenth time.

She took one more glance back at the inn. The restaurant dark now, the glows from the hotel rooms were the only lights in the spreading gloom. She kept walking. If that couple was on some romantic weekend, why would the guy be jabbering on about ghosts? Maybe telling some ghost stories to scare the girl. That way she'd cower in his arms and he'd get back in her pants.

Still, he *could* be the one. From her vision. It'd be good not to feel so alone in this. She'd reached out a time or two before, but it came back to bite her. Maybe Darrell would be different.

In her time here, she'd learned pretty much every place in this town claimed its own particular ghost. Pretty much every B & B, every restaurant, every hotel had its own haunting tale. Even the Inn of Cape May had its own "Lady in Blue." She'd overheard other servers at the hotel talk about the resident female ghost. Back then, Cassie was interested, excited even, thinking others could see what she saw. She pressed them. Fuckin' idiots. Sure, they talked a good game, but no one else actually *saw* the ghost. No, the other servers were merely repeating stories good for tourists.

So, of course, she never admitted to any more paranormal visions. And God, she'd never mention her...her...what had that book she'd "borrowed" from the library call it? Her foresight.

But *she'd* seen ghosts. Including the Lady in Blue. And the Haunted Bride. Most of them were harmless.

Only spirits stuck between this world and the next. But the two times she'd seen the Haunted Bride, something felt off. Bad, maybe.

And she'd really like the chance to learn what someone else saw. Felt?

Man, was she tired. Nine hours on her feet, all while Antonio screamed at her. "Deliver these orders. Get those tables bussed. Go help the bartender." But she had to admit he was better than most guys. At least, he gave her a job. And didn't ask too many questions. And didn't expect "favors."

She frowned. Where was she headed? She was so exhausted, thinking hurt. Oh yeah, she was crashing at Troy's crib tonight. She pictured the guy—pale, skinny, with a scraggly beard he never shaved, way older than her, thirty-something, probably high. He'd most likely expect a little "rent." Guys didn't help for nothing. Maybe she could put him off. Claim she was wiped. If she had to, she'd give him a quick one—barf—and then crash.

Still, better than living on the street.

She straggled down Jackson. Darrell's words about the ghost came back to her. His description was so detailed and precise. He must've seen the Haunted Bride. How else could he know about the bloodied side of the ghost's face and body, the right side?

Cassie sped up. She needed to get to Troy's. Antonio put her on early tomorrow. And she had to do a split shift. "Report by six a.m. and stay through lunch. Then come back at four for the dinner shift." Shit. Probably close to twelve hours tomorrow. Her legs hurt merely thinking about it. At least tomorrow was Saturday. Maybe, if he let her wait some, she'd have a chance to pick up a few dead presidents.

And, maybe, catch up with the couple. The guy seemed decent enough. The way he treated the girl. Darrell and Erin. Room 421. If she worked all three meals, she'd have to run into them sometime, right? Didn't they have to come out of their room for a little…air? She'd figure out some way to talk with him. Ask him about the Haunted Bride.

Cassie gazed up at the cloudless sky. With no moon tonight, the stars twinkled like tiny diamonds in the inky black. Diamonds she'd never have. Not in this fuckin' universe. Kept walking.

It'd be good to be able to talk with someone else who actually saw what she saw. Maybe, tomorrow wouldn't be so shitty. She needed to get home, take *care* of Troy—she rolled her eyes—and get some sleep. She picked up her pace.

Chapter Fourteen

"Come on, let's hit the beach!" Erin stood at the foot of the bed in a stunning string bikini, hands on hips, swaying to Cher's song, "Believe," oozing from the radio. She wiggled her very shapely parts to the music.

After their late dinner last night, they had discussed the sightseeing possibilities Darrell had researched. But this morning Erin seemed focused only on frolicking in the ocean. Taking in the sight of her sleek body, her essentials barely covered by the sunny yellow two-piece, Darrell felt little need to focus on anything else.

They'd already slept in, after which he treated her to what he'd learned was a Jersey shore breakfast tradition, Uncle Bill's Pancake House. She wolfed down scrambled eggs and a stack of flapjacks, professing them "superb." He even purchased matching blue and white Uncle Bill's T-shirts for them. Now, they weren't back in the room ten minutes before she turned on the radio and changed into the swimsuit. She posed for him, twirling like a model.

"I love living on the Chesapeake, but there we can't play in the waves like we can here. Come on." She dragged him up off the bed.

Darrell had trouble sharing her enthusiasm.

When he thought about venturing back onto the beach, the terrifying vision of the bloodied ghost emerging from the surf returned. He was on a collision course with the Haunted Bride, exactly like with Hank's ghost in Wilshire. "I told you. I encountered the ghost twice already on that beach. Are you sure I can't talk you into something else? How about a carriage ride? Or let's go climb the Cape May Lighthouse."

Erin strutted two steps away and turned around, her arms out, hands in tight fists. "If the Haunted Bride comes back, I'll protect you."

Seeing her sleek body in a fighter's posture, Darrell said, "Very funny," but couldn't help laughing.

In the end he went, of course. After all, Erin had spent most of the last evening shredding his willpower. Which he hadn't minded. He was thrilled to be back in her arms. Darrell raised both hands in surrender, changed into swim trunks, and retrieved the sunscreen. As he smoothed the sunblock into the curve of her back, he thought how lucky he was. Ten days earlier, he wasn't sure he'd ever get the chance to see Erin again, and here they were, together. More than he'd expected. Better than he'd dared to hope. He would brave any ghosts for her.

The short walk along Ocean and across Beach Avenue took them only a few minutes. Cape May Beach lay before them, the tide out, the shining white sand extending for what seemed like miles, the waves' quiet gurgles onto the shore. It was closing in on eleven and the beach was crowding up, colorful umbrellas sprouting from the sand like vibrant flowers. Everywhere they looked, beach towels and beach chairs of different hues decorated the shore. Darrell paid for two tickets for the beach and Erin led, scurrying around bodies sprawled in the hot June sun. She found a suitable spot, turned a three-sixty, and proclaimed success. She claimed their space by laying out their towels, then grabbed his hand and tugged. They ran into the surf, both laughing like little kids.

The day bloomed exactly as Erin had promised and nothing like Darrell had feared. The sun was hot, the water cool, no creepy ghosts appeared. Talking and chuckling, they walked hand in hand along the beach, the waves lapping at their legs, the saltwater smell strong. They inspected sandcastle masterpieces crafted by kids, extolling the excellent designs. Farther on, they passed young moms, crouched under multi-colored umbrellas, dividing their time between their little ones and their beach romance novels. With one free hand, Erin snatched an errant Frisbee thrown by two teen guys. When they came to retrieve it and couldn't take their eyes off her bikini, Darrell was pretty sure their toss had been deliberate.

A couple walked by, arm in arm, a short, blonde-haired twenty-something and a squat, powerful young man with black hair cut short, displaying hard, bronzed pecs and powerful biceps. Her bikini consisted of three bright pink triangles connected by string so thin it looked like fishing line. His black swim brief wasn't much larger. Trying to watch without being obvious, Darrell realized he recognized her, though it took him a bit to remember. And Erin smacking his shoulder didn't help.

She planted her feet and yanked him to a stop. "Uh-hum," she announced, eyes blazing.

Darrell shook his head hard. "No." He pointed toward the couple. "It's just that I recognized her."

"You recognize her? Oh, really?"

Darrell put his arm around her. "No, it's not what you think. I saw her a few days ago, at a bar, when I was with Kurt. Only then she was fawning all over a different guy." He scrunched his forehead. "I think her name was Jennifer Thomas."

Erin wasn't placated. "You remembered her *name*?"

This wasn't coming out the way he wanted. "No…uh…it's not that." He scrambled to explain. "A couple days ago, I saw her flirting big time with this other guy, Travis Armstrong. At Carny's, Kurt introduced me to Travis, a former student who played for him about ten years ago. Now, look at her with him." His glance went from the departing couple back to Erin, not sure she was buying it. And he definitely didn't want to kill the mood. He tried, "And seeing her play off both guys reminded me of Carmen."

Erin's gaze followed the shapely young woman down the beach, the naked back of her body striped only by two thin strings. "Did your ex-fiancé look anything like that?"

Darrell fudged. "Pretty much."

Erin kissed him, long and hard, right there on the beach, making him forget about Jennifer. And Carmen.

When they'd decided they'd had enough sun, they headed back inside, showered and rested a while. Well, mostly rested. As wonderful as they found the surf and sand, they enjoyed the rest of their escape day almost as much. Later, they tackled the Cape May Lighthouse, climbing the long, winding staircase and passing two couples and a family with a little one on their way down. As they ascended, Darrell silently counted all one hundred ninety-nine steps. When they reached the final one, he caught himself. It was the first time he'd "slipped" into his condition all weekend. He glanced at Erin, mouth crinkling, red hair blowing in the breeze, and reminded himself to let go and enjoy the moment.

Once up in the lantern room, they found they were alone and took their time, reading the displays about the 150-year history of the lighthouse. Then, they moved to the glass, soaking in the incredible, panoramic view. Erin pointed out three sailboats cutting across the bay, all sloops, their single white sails full. Together, they peered out toward the watery expanse to the east. Ever the historian, Darrell said, "You know, the English explorer, Henry Hudson, was the first white man to discover this land."

"Oh, really." She smiled up at him, an eager student. Or maybe she merely loved the teacher.

"Yeah, he was actually searching for the Northwest Passage and decided to check out the Delaware Bay. Only trouble was his ship got stuck on a sand bar up there a bit." Darrell pointed northwest. "He had to wait till a storm blew in and freed his boat."

"Did he name it Cape May?"

"No. A Dutch captain, one Cornelius Jacobsen Mey, surveyed the area and named it for himself."

"And who else would you name it for?" Erin chuckled and kissed him. For a moment, they lingered in it, all alone atop the world.

The sound of steps echoing up the stairwell broke their reverie. More tourists would be joining them soon. They pulled their attention away from the water. Down below, the people and cars looked like tiny figures on a game board. Turning, they could even make out the buildings of Cape May in the north. One arm around her, Darrell use the other hand to point off in the distance. "If you squint, you can make out Beach Avenue and can almost see the Inn of Cape May."

She looked where he indicated and, for a few minutes, neither said a word.

Erin glanced back at him and asked, "Thinking about the Haunted Bride?"

"How'd you know?"

"Because I know you. You're going to have to figure this out, aren't you?"

Darrell grinned. "You do know me well. Yeah, but it can wait till later. We have one more adventure to cap off the day."

They finished the day with a romantic carriage ride, taking in the sights of the remarkable Victorian mansions around town, their painted colors and stained glass windows vibrant in the setting sun. Much like Darrell when he first arrived, Erin marveled at the surprising number of intricately decorated houses.

Darrell indicated the row of five Victorians they were passing, each house in a bolder color than the last. "You know Cape May owes all this to a fire."

Erin grinned. "Do tell."

"In 1878, a major fire hit, destroying almost thirty blocks of the town. They rebuilt and most of the new residences went up in the modern style of the day, which we call Victorian. Cape May has worked hard to preserve them since."

"Remind me to always bring a history teacher on my trips," she whispered. "I find they can come in quite handy."

As they passed another mansion called "Angel of the Sea," Erin proclaimed it her favorite. Her eyes wide, she stared at the intricate gingerbread trim, towering turrets, and the three floors of porches, each outlined in white latticed fencing.

Darrell explained, "That inn was originally some wealthy guy's summer cottage that was later separated into two separate buildings connected by a long porch. Now it's operated as a sprawling bed and breakfast." He grinned. "And it's rumored to have its own ghost."

"Of course," Erin said. "but I think our Haunted Bride is enough for now."

For the last part of the ride, they relaxed to the clip-clop of the horse's hooves, Darrell's arm snuggling Erin to him. After a bit, he asked her about dinner.

"Aleathea's. Maybe we can get our favorite waitress." She added, "You know, the one who knows about the Haunted Bride."

Chapter Fifteen

They were late to dinner again. Back at the room, both had succumbed to a much needed nap. When they arrived at Aleathea's, already packed with the Saturday night dinner crowd, Antonio welcomed them by name, but apologized a table would not be available for a while. The wait turned out to be a little longer when Darrell asked the owner if Cassie could be their server.

Antonio raised his eyebrows. "Cassie? You sure? She's not serving tonight." He paused and added, "For such a lovely couple, I'll see what I can do."

As the owner ushered them to the bar, Darrell unfolded a flyer from his pocket and showed it to him. "One of the boys in the football camp is putting these up around town." He indicated the picture on the poster. "His sister went missing this week, and he made these up to see if anyone has seen her. Could I post one here?"

Antonio stared down at the paper, one finger touching his moustache, and slowly shook his head. "I am sorry, sir, but the Inn of Cape May has a no posting policy." He raised both hands. "Not mine, you see, but I must observe it. I apologize." With that, he waddled back to the front desk.

After they ordered drinks, Darrell and Erin leaned against each other on the high stools, their backs to the bar. They observed the restaurant. In the middle of all the server activity, Darrell spotted Cassie. Though her face still bore the partial pout he'd seen yesterday, she moved among the tables in a quick and easy manner. He glanced over and noticed Erin eying her as well.

"You watching Cassie?"

"Yeah, a little different than last night," Erin said. "She's all over the room."

Cassie hurried from one area to another—bussing tables, delivering drinks and plates of food, getting refills. In fact, she looked to be doing more than any other wait person. Studying her, he hoped they had a chance to grab a few minutes to talk about the Haunted Bride. With the way she was hustling tonight, Cassie certainly wouldn't have any time to linger at their table, even if Antonio let her serve.

As he was scanning the restaurant, Darrell noticed someone else he recognized. "See the guy in sunglasses at the table by the window?" He gestured. "That's James Armstrong, the big trucking magnate Kurt introduced me to this week."

"Okay?"

"He lives on this big place up the coast but sent his kids to Cape May Schools." Erin still looked puzzled, and he continued, "I met him and his son, Travis, who played football for Kurt."

"The same son you said that tramp on the beach was flirting with."

"One and the same." Darrell nodded toward the window. "We don't have anything else to do. Let's go say hello. I love showing you off."

Before Erin could answer, Antonio came up beside them, one hand upturned. "I have a table ready for you. And Cassie will be your server. If you'll follow me."

Leading them across the front of the restaurant, the owner took them past the table Darrell had just pointed out. He tapped Antonio on the arm and stopped, addressing the table. "James Armstrong, you probably don't remember me, but we met a few days ago at Carny's. Darrell Henshaw."

The face with the sunglasses turned toward Darrell. "Of course. You're that great coach from Maryland Kurt imported to help with the football camp."

"Very good memory, sir. Though I wouldn't claim to be great," Darrell said.

"Nonsense. I'm not very good with faces, but I never forget a voice." He chuckled. "And son, I've learned in this world we receive far too few compliments. We need to be gracious enough to accept those we get."

Darrell felt his face redden a bit and was glad Armstrong couldn't see it. He grinned. "Thanks, sir, I'll try to remember that."

Armstrong indicated the woman on his left. "And may I introduce Andrea, my better half."

The woman maintained a tight, taciturn face, the taut skin making Darrell think of plastic surgery. Her face bore an upturned nose, a stiff smile, but her blue-gray eyes looked hard as two marbles. "Pleased to meet you," she said, her voice clipped.

Armstrong cleared his throat. "And Darrell, I smell a delightful perfume, different than Andrea's, I believe. Allure, perhaps? I hardly think it belongs to you."

Erin gave a brief chuckle.

Darrell said, "John and Andrea, I'd like to introduce my girl, Erin Caveny, also from the Eastern Shore." He indicated Erin, even though the blind man couldn't see her. Still, it was Armstrong who extended his hand.

Erin took the offered hand. "So nice to meet some locals. We're really enjoying your town."

Andrea raised a hand to her shoulder. "Oh, we're not from Cape May. We have an estate on the water up the coast, in Venice."

James Armstrong added, "But we love coming to Aleathea's for dinner." He turned toward Erin. "I hope Darrell here is treating you to some of our enjoyable spots."

"Yes, we love your beach, of course. Back home, we have plenty of beautiful shoreline, but nothing like your beach," she said. Armstrong asked Erin about home and her parents and Erin gushed on.

All the while, Darrell studied the local couple. When he'd met James earlier this week, the man had been friendly enough, but was all business. Tonight, he seemed to greet Darrell and Erin like long lost friends. Like he was glad they had stopped by. Darrell watched him smiling at Erin. More likely, it was Erin. The beauty she radiated could capture even a blind man's heart.

But Darrell wasn't sure what to make of Andrea Armstrong. The way she acted, Darrell had seen it before. As "merely a teacher" at some social functions, he'd experienced similar treatment. From Mrs. Armstrong's bearing, he recognized she was mentally putting them in their place. He tried to puzzle out if she had a problem with Darrell and Erin, or if she simply had a problem. He noticed a look pass from Andrea to Antonio.

The owner interrupted Erin's response to another

question James had raised. "Sir, I trust everything was to your satisfaction."

Darrell thought he saw a look of irritation on James' face, but it was Andrea who answered. "Oh, thanks, Antonio," she said, all sweetness and light, "the sea bass was excellent. Give my compliments to Chef Pierre."

Darrell decided Andrea had a problem with them.

Antonio turned toward Darrell. "Your table, sir." His eyes roamed across the restaurant.

Darrell got the message. They were being dismissed. "We simply wanted to say hello."

James Armstrong waved. "Good to see you again. Get it, see you?"

Erin chuckled as they were seated at a table and accepted menus. "Interesting guy." She cast a conspiratorial glance at Darrell. "Not so sure about *Mrs.* Armstrong."

When Cassie first approached their table, looking harried, her greeting was quick. "Welcome back to Aleathea's."

"You know we asked for you specifically," Darrell said.

"Antonio told me. Thanks." The tiniest of smiles crossed her face. She shot a quick glance around the restaurant. "I don't know how we'll have time to talk. I'm—"

"Don't you worry about that," Erin said in a soft voice, placing a hand on the server's arm. "Just do your job. We'll figure something out later."

Cassie returned to their table three times— appetizers, a second round of drinks, and entrées—but each time had only been able to stay a moment. Much as last night, Darrell and Erin took their time savoring another incredible meal and sharing quiet confidences.

Later, Cassie bustled over to their table. "Could I interest you in one of our award-winning desserts?" Her eyes took in the table and she removed the empty plates to a nearby serving stand. "Or maybe another glass of wine?"

Erin looked toward Darrell and said, "Thanks. I think we've had enough."

The server shot a look around the space and lowered her voice, as she produced the bill. "I'm sorry. I wanted to talk with you about the Haunted Bride, but I haven't had a moment to even breathe tonight."

Darrell signed the check. "I've noticed how you hustle. You're quite the worker."

"When they give me a chance."

Erin said, "What time do you get off?"

Cassie cast a look at the clock on the back wall. "About twenty minutes."

Erin asked, "Is there someplace we could talk? About the Haunted Bride." When Cassie didn't immediately respond, she added, "Then you and Darrell could compare ghost stories. Maybe down here in the lobby?"

Cassie shook her head. "No. They frown on staff, you know, hanging out with guests. And Antonio." She shook her head harder.

It was dark and late, almost ten, and the only places open now were bars. Darrell glanced again at Cassie. Despite what she had said, the teacher in him was pretty sure Cassie was too young. He didn't want to take her to any bar. Still, he'd really hoped to talk with her about the ghost.

"Do you live close to here?" he asked. "Maybe we could head there after you're off to talk a—"

"No," Cassie blurted out. She bit her lip and her gaze wandered around the restaurant, he figured looking for Antonio. She lowered her voice. "You guys have a suite. How about we talk there?"

"Okay, um, sure," Darrell said, casting a quick glance at Erin.

Erin lifted on eyebrow. "Room—" she started.

Cassie glanced down at the check in her hand and finished. "421."

Chapter Sixteen

So tired, Cassie could hardly stand. She dragged open the door to the small metal locker. Squinted in the tiny mirror. She pulled the other studs from the shelf and inserted them, one after the other. Stared at her face, twisting her head side to side. Yeah, that was better. The tiny steel pieces sparkled even in the low light. She shed her uniform and stepped into street clothes. Grabbing the gel, she worked it into her hair.

She sighed. She could simply bug out. Forget the whole thing and head to Troy's.

Don't think so.

Using the mirror, she applied her favorite lipstick and puckered.

Was she really going to meet this couple in their suite? Why had she come up with that? If Darrell was, you know, like her, it'd be okay.

She wasn't concerned. She could handle herself.

Besides, they seemed all right. He said he noticed how hard she worked in the restaurant, even complimented her on her taking good care of them. Most people never cared. Shit, she didn't receive many compliments. She pulled the bills out of her jeans pocket and counted the take. Antonio made her work all day and only let her serve a few tables. She'd done okay, thanks to *their* tip. Her fingers thumbed Darrell's twenty dollars. Two wrinkled tens left on the table. He hadn't added it to the check. If he had, she'd have to share it with the rest of the staff. This way she could fudge. That had about doubled her take.

She'd almost given up seeing them. Put in ten hours busting her ass before they showed up. Then they asked to have *her* as a server. They had to wait an extra twenty minutes, Antonio said. Darrell probably only wanted to talk with her about the Haunted Bride, but still. It felt nice to be requested. She fingered her tip. Really nice.

Did Darrell expect something extra?

Most of the guys she'd known *always* expected something. Something in return for their "investment." That's what one guy called it. Some hip banker type from New York she met in a bar. Just one more fuckin' jerk. Cassie shook her head.

She decided she liked Erin. She seemed nice enough. She'd made a point to thank Cassie herself. For taking care of them. Then Erin had touched Cassie's arm. Cassie didn't let many people touch her, but with Erin, it seemed okay. But still, Erin's touch had felt comforting, reassuring. Almost like an older sister. Which Cassie never had.

Did Darrell really see the Haunted Bride? Was that why they wanted to talk with her? Why he left a twenty-dollar tip? To talk about the ghost?

Or did they want something else?

She shrugged. It wouldn't be the first time she'd been invited to a guy's room. But a couple's room? The ugly cynic in her warned, "You've been burned before." Maybe Darrell was simply one more guy out for what he wanted. And maybe this Erin wasn't as harmless as she seemed. Their flushed faces made it clear what they'd been doing in the suite. Maybe they were bored. Looking for a threesome?

She slammed the locker door.

Maybe she shouldn't go. She needed to think this through.

This guy was rich, right? Why would he care about the Haunted Bride if he wasn't the one she'd seen in her dream last night?

No, dammit. Her cynic side was wrong. Everyone else in the world wasn't necessarily an asshole. Maybe Darrell *was* another, uh…you know. Someone else who really saw ghosts. Someone she could share this secret with. And wouldn't laugh at her. Or try to have her fuckin' committed.

Darrell looked harmless enough. Handsome and somewhere between jock and geek. Nice hair, eyes almost the color of the ocean. Of course, Cassie knew looks couldn't be trusted. She remembered that guy— what was his name? Rod. With his buffed physique, perfect hair, and a face that could play in Hollywood, she knew most girls found him drop-dead gorgeous. Admit it, so had she. Until she got to his place. She remembered what he tried to make her do. And how she kicked him in the nuts.

Cassie learned the hard way there was no way she could trust guys based on their looks.

But somehow, she sensed this Darrell was different. He couldn't be too bad. Cassie had seen the flyer on the table. The one about the missing girl. She hadn't said anything. Just overheard Darrell talk about helping some kid in the football camp find his missing sister. Would some rich, selfish jerk even care?

She walked out of the locker room into the lobby.

Turned the corner and another thought struck her. She'd gotten a good look at the girl on the poster. Pretty in a cheerleader, perky kind of way. A little like Brooke Stanley, the girl she ran into on the street. Who she hadn't seen for a while. She heard something 'bout what happened to Brooke.

Should she tell Darrell about Brooke? She exhaled, too exhausted to puzzle it out. She pushed the call button for the elevator.

She slid the black, old-fashioned gate open and stepped inside. "I'll see what the hell they want," she said aloud. "Then, I'll figure out the rest."

Chapter Seventeen

As soon as they returned to their suite, Darrell scurried around the room, retrieving discarded undergarments and swimwear. They lay strewn everywhere. As he grabbed a stray white sock, it hit him. The mess hadn't bothered him earlier. Maybe his libido was stronger than his compulsion. Maybe his OCD wasn't completely beyond his control.

But knowing a teen would be knocking at their door any minute flipped a switch. For a moment, Erin watched him hustling around the room, grabbing up clothes, and chuckled. "Well, Mr. Henshaw, I do believe you might be a bit embarrassed."

Darrell glanced up at her grinning and felt his face get hot. "Well, she's only a teenager. I keep thinking about the kids in my classes."

Erin joined in, snatching up her bikini, which hung over the edge of a chair and stashing it out of sight. "I'm pretty sure Cassie is no innocent. I have a feeling she's seen a lot worse than our hotel room." She moved to the side of the bed.

"You're probably right, but still," Darrell said, when he spotted one last item. He reached for the purple flowered bra at the same time Erin grabbed it. Holding each end of the garment, both stared first at the bra and then at each other, chuckling.

A quiet knock interrupted them. Erin snatched up

the last piece of evidence and tossed it onto the closet floor, sliding the door shut. She surveyed the room and, satisfied, nodded to Darrell.

"Coming," he called as he too scanned the room and yanked the door open. "Glad you could make it—" he started and stopped. He blinked. The young woman in the doorway wore a black T-shirt and jeans, her black hair in angry spikes erupting from her scalp like some ebony tiara worn front to back. A small pout tugged at black lips. Multiple studs in her nose and face gleamed in the overhead hall lights. A black eyeliner pencil had darkened her eyes to match. He stared at the visitor, wide-eyed. But her appearance alone hadn't stopped him. Beyond the cosmetic transformation—studs, clothes, and makeup—Darrell sensed something else different about the girl, but couldn't put a finger on it. "Hey, Cassie," he said, having trouble getting the name out.

Erin came up behind and nudged him out of the way. Placing a hand on the young girl's shoulder, she guided her inside the room. "Don't mind him. He's probably never seen an enchanting Goth like you." She gestured at the visitor's outfit. "*This* looks good on you."

Escorting Cassie across the room, Erin cast a glance at Darrell that he read as *Let me handle this*. He did, still perplexed by the different vibe he was receiving.

Cassie settled into one of the overstuffed chairs in the sitting area. "You really think so?" She sat cross-legged, easing her back into the upholstery, and glanced around the room. Like she owned the place.

"No doubt," Erin said, as she perched on the edge

of the sofa, eying the girl. "That outfit and those studs are truly dope."

Cassie fingered the two metal piercings in her nose, as if she wasn't quite comfortable with them. "Antonio makes me take most of these out while I work, but I feel better with them in. Feel more like...me."

Cassie's glance went to Darrell, who still couldn't help staring. He cut his eyes to Erin, who grinned and rescued him. "Don't mind him. He teaches high school, and I don't think our school allows students to dress like that. He's probably never seen a full-fledged Goth before."

"I- I-I didn't recognize you at first, Cassie," Darrell recovered. "And I've seen my share of Goths. You're right, though—Wilshire has some rules on piercings." His eyes met Cassie's. "Doesn't your school here have regulations like that?"

"I don't go to school," Cassie said, her eyes going to the floor.

"Really. How old are you?" he asked.

"Eighteen."

"Huh. I would've guessed fifteen or sixteen," Darrell said, then realized his tone was coming off as interrogating.

Erin saved him again. "Cassie, can we get you something? A soda, maybe."

When the teen nodded, Darrell retrieved a can from the little fridge. Grabbing a paper towel from the roll, he wiped off the top and cylinder surface of the can. Then he handed it to their guest. She pulled the top, the snap and fizz sounding loud in the quiet room.

He studied her, the vibe coming off her stronger now as she eased back into the chair. The sensation was so strong, he wondered why he hadn't picked up on it before, in the restaurant. Tonight or last night. Then he realized earlier he'd probably been so overwhelmed by Erin, he might not've caught the warning signs of a tornado.

Cassie sipped. "Thanks. Oh, and thanks for the great tip. One of the few I got today. And definitely the best." She stopped and glanced around the space and then at her hosts. "I hope you don't expect anything, uh…you know." Rather than continue, she took another drink, but her eyes stayed glued on Darrell.

For the moment, the comment squelched the vibe he'd sensed, and he flashed a look at Erin, feeling his face redden. Again, she recovered first. "No. Uh, no." Erin laughed nervously. "The tip was for your great service."

He blurted, "You earned it. The way you bustled around tonight. Nice job."

No one spoke for a moment and in the silence, Cassie glanced around, craning her neck to take in the sleeping area of the suite. "Pretty nice digs." Drink in hand, she rose, ambled past the bed to the sliding doors and stared beyond at the brightly lit pool and the darkened shoreline. Without turning around, she said, "I've never been in one of these suites."

Erin asked, "How long have you worked at Aleathea's?"

"Almost a year. It's okay, though Antonio can be a prick sometimes. He makes me do the shit jobs. You know, bringing out the food, bussing the tables, delivering drinks. Most days, he doesn't let me serve, so I don't make that much." Cassie turned around. "But I get to meet some interesting people. Like you two.

What's your deal?"

Darrell and Erin exchanged a look, but before either could answer, Cassie asked, "Did you really see the Haunted Bride?"

"The Haunted Bride?" Darrell echoed, feeling Cassie's gaze on him, scrutinizing him.

"Yeah, the ghost in the torn wedding dress with blood running down her side. I overheard you describing her. That's what I call the ghost. Have you really seen her, or are you simply repeating a rumor?"

"What rumor?" Darrell asked.

"You first." The teen girl returned to the chair and rearranged her legs under her, but her gaze never left him.

The sensation Darrell had picked up earlier returned. He felt as if Cassie could peer right through him. He squirmed. He didn't know this girl, wasn't certain how much to reveal. With Cassie's bizarre looks and that strange vibe, he wasn't sure how much he could trust her. While he was trying to decide, Erin jumped in.

She said, "Darrell told me about this ghost. You've seen her too? This figure in the wedding dress?"

Cassie nodded, taking another sip from the can.

Erin shot a quick glance at Darrell and kept her voice quiet. "Are you a…sensitive?"

"A what?" Cassie's eyes went wide and her hand tightened on the aluminum.

Erin didn't seem to notice any change in the space, but the vibe Darrell had picked up on earlier grew intense. He could feel it coming across the room in waves.

Erin said, "You know, someone who can see

ghosts. A sensitive. You can sense things others can't."

Oh hell, Darrell decided to chance it. After all, that's why they wanted to talk with Cassie. Maybe she knew something, could reveal some secret about this ghost. Help him prepare for the upcoming collision. "It's okay. I see ghosts too. Even when I don't want to." He shrugged. "Especially when I don't want to."

At first, Cassie simply sat there. Then she unfolded her legs, stood, and walked over to Darrell. She extended her hand. "It's good to meet another, what did you call it…a sensitive?"

When Darrell took her hand, the heat exploded onto his palm and up his arm.

Chapter Eighteen

Cassie felt like a sparkler had exploded in her hand. Darrell's touch eliminated any doubt about him. His hand felt like it was on fire. Electricity ran up her arm. She and Darrell stared at each other for a moment and then both let go. She rubbed her hand on her pants and, when she looked up, Darrell was doing the same.

Had she and Darrell touched before now? In the restaurant, she'd brought the check and Darrell jotted down the room number. Left cash on the silver tray. They'd never made contact there. Now, damn.

She had no instruction book for this whole crazy ghost thing. Wished to hell she did. But she was pretty damn sure about this. Her gaze went to Darrell's hand. It looked perfectly normal. So did hers. Her dream last night had been right. He *had* to be the one.

She returned to her chair. Settled back in. Tucked both legs under. Rubbing her palm, she said nothing.

The silence must have made Erin uncomfortable. "So, Cassie, um, how long you been seeing ghosts? Darrell told me his visions started when he was thirteen."

"About the same." She didn't want to talk about her Goddamn past. She looked at Darrell. "Is that why you came to Cape May? Because of its ghosts?"

Darrell shook his head. "Oh no. I only came for a summer job. I needed the money. I'm working the Cape

May football camp." He rubbed his right hand. "I might not've come if I'd known about any ghosts."

So, he wasn't some wealthy dude?

He added, "The last one almost got us killed."

Killed? Cassie sat up straighter. "What happened?"

She watched him glance at Erin, who nodded. Without saying a word, he moved to the other side of the room. He examined the bed and knelt next to it. After straightening one pillow, he tugged at the puffy comforter and smoothed it with one hand, like he was readying the bed for inspection.

Cassie shot a glance at Erin, who held up one hand in a "wait" gesture. Just when she was ready to ask what the hell was he doing, Darrell started speaking.

Without moving from beside the bed, he gave a halting rundown of his encounters with a ghost named Hank Young. From some place in Maryland. While he talked, his attention never left the bed, hands fidgeting with the cover, fingers smoothing the border. He didn't once look at Cassie. He seemed to finish his work with the bed and his tale at the same time. And when he stopped, he looked pale, like he ran out of steam. He returned to the couch and sat next to Erin again.

After taking his hand, Erin filled in a few details about their investigation to find Hank's killers. Which they almost didn't survive.

Cassie eased back and studied the couple. Something was off about this guy. What was the thing with the bed? He was not like anyone she'd ever run into in Cape May. Or anywhere else. She'd never felt that heat with anyone else. She wasn't sure she wanted to trust him. To trust anyone. But still…

"What can you tell us about this Haunted Bride?"

Erin asked, her voice tight.

"What rumor were you talking about?" Darrell cut in.

"Rumor?" Cassie echoed, confused for the moment.

"When we asked about the ghost before," Darrell said, "you asked if I'd really seen the ghost or was only repeating some rumor. What rumor?"

Cassie fingered the second stud in her nose. "Since I've been here, I've found some locals think it's really wick-ed to repeat these ghost rumors. Something they heard or read about one of our resident ghosts. Even though they've never actually seen any."

"*One* of our resident ghosts?" Erin repeated. "How many ghosts are there in Cape May?"

Cassie smirked. "Who knows? Welcome to Cape May." Her hands mocked a billboard. "You haven't heard their marketing slogan, America's oldest and most haunted seaport?"

"I have," Darrell said, deadpan. "What's the rumor about this Haunted Bride?"

Cassie said, "The ghosts I've…" she searched for the right word. "Most of the ghosts I've sensed are pretty harmless. No big deal. But this Haunted Bride is supposed to be different."

"Different how?" both Darrell and Erin asked in unison.

Cassie glanced from one to the other. Rolled her eyes. How much did she want to tell these two? "If you see this haunted bride, some evil is supposed to befall you. Blah, blah, blah. More nonsense."

Darrell glanced at Erin. "I'm not so sure. Natalia told me about the same thing."

"Who's Natalia?" Cassie asked.

Erin answered, "Natalia's this weird medium back in Wilshire, who has *other* talents." She made cupping motions in front of her chest. "Her advice has been helpful before."

Cassie stared at Darrell. "You know a *real* medium?"

Cassie caught a look from Erin to him. A look she'd seen before. The tone of Erin's next words confirmed it. "That slutty medium shared some revelation you forgot to tell me about?"

His face a little red, Darrell hurried on. "Sorry. I-I-I didn't want to spook you. What she said was, 'A shroud of evil *pursues* this ghost.' "

Eyes wide, Erin repeated, "A shroud of evil?" She turned toward Cassie. "Do you know anything, anything at all about this Haunted Bride?"

Cassie said, "Not much. From what I've heard, she's supposed to be some young bride who was set to marry this rich guy in a big wedding here on the beach at Cape May. Something happened on their wedding night. She died."

Erin asked, "What do you mean? What happened?"

"It's all rumor." Cassie shrugged. "Supposed to have committed suicide. Walked right into the water. Now likes to haunt the shoreline." She stopped and no one said anything. The silence bothered even her. "Probably only a myth."

"Maybe not. That's where I saw her," Darrell said, glancing at Erin. "Twice." He stopped as if thinking and then asked, "Have you heard anything about why she roams the beach?"

Maybe these two aren't so sharp. "'Cause she

committed suicide there. Duh."

Darrell added, "There's got to be more. Because she wants something. She asked me to help her."

Cassie wasn't sure she heard right. "She *asked* you?"

Darrell reached both arms out. "She said, quiet like, 'Please help me.' "

This guy had to be putting her on. Cassie heard about some guys who claimed to talk with ghosts. Figured they were fakes. She'd seen what, four or five ghosts. None ever said a word to her. Besides, the stories never said anything about the Haunted Bride speaking.

"The ghost spoke to you?" Cassie asked.

Darrell nodded. "Yeah. That's what she said the first time."

"The first time?" Cassie asked. "She spoke to you more than once?"

Erin jumped in, "Yeah, and the second time was even stranger."

Darrell said, "The second time I saw her, she came out of the water and said she knew I had helped Hank. The ghost in Maryland. She said she knew I could help her."

"Holy shit." Cassie's gaze went from Darrell to Erin. "Wait. Did you say she came *out* of the water?"

Darrell's head went up and down. "Yeah, like a surfer or swimmer. That's what I thought she was. At first. Then I saw the white dress dripping with water. Then the blood started at her face and ran down her body."

Cassie felt her breathing pick up. That's exactly what she'd seen. Though not at the water. First, bride in wedding gown and no blood. Then, the next minute, red oozing down her side. She asked, "What'd you do?"

Darrell's glance went to floor. "I got out of there. Off the beach."

Erin said, "Then the ghost threatened him."

He looked uncomfortable. "Well, I think it was a threat. She said, 'Help me or more girls will suffer.' "

Cassie sat forward in the chair, her whole body leaning toward them. Couldn't believe she heard right. "What girls? How will they suffer?"

"I don't have the faintest idea," Darrell said. "But it wasn't the first message about the girls. At least, I don't think so."

"What do you mean?" Cassie asked.

Erin spoke up. "A few days ago, Darrell got this message from another ghost, Margaret." She reached down into her purse. A few seconds later she handed Cassie a scrap of paper. "Darrell found this on a table at Carny's."

Cassie's glance went from Darrell to the sheet. She caught a slight vibration from the paper. She thought. Looked at Darrell again. "Who?"

He said, "The nineteenth century ghost from the House of Royals? Margaret, that's what the bartender, Rob, said her name was."

This was a little much to believe. She studied the paper and noticed Darrell's name at the top.

Darrell,

Please help her and rescue the others

"And this ghost, Margaret, gave this to you?" Cassie asked.

"No, she left it on the table and then disappeared. After she, like, vanished, I checked out the booth where

I saw her and found it."

Cassie had never heard of a ghost calling a human by name. No rumor ever mentioned that. And the paper? What did they call that in that book she got from the library? An artifact?

Shit, she didn't know. Maybe Darrell had faked it. She studied him. Remembered the electricity of his touch. Hard to fake that. And the paper still quivered in her hand.

She handed the sheet back, glad to be rid of it. "What are you planning to do?"

"Do?" he said.

"Yeah, about the Haunted Bride?"

"I didn't *want* to do anything. Both times I saw her, I didn't even stick around to find out. She creeped me out. The way she looked or maybe I was picking up this evil vibe we were talking about. I don't know."

"And now?" Cassie asked.

Darrell exhaled. "I doubt I'll have much choice. I've been here before. I have a feeling she won't leave me alone." His glance went out the French doors, into the darkening night. "Is there anything else you can tell me about the Haunted Bride?" When she didn't answer, he added, "Do you have any idea when she was supposed to die? If I'm going to somehow help her, I need to find out more about her."

Cassie bit her lower lips, chewing on a stud. "I dunno. Not that long ago. Five or ten years ago? Nobody's willing to say much. Or don't know. Maybe because of the curse. Who knows?" She checked out Darrell's face. Maybe this guy knew something she didn't. "What can you do?"

Erin glanced at Darrell and said, "Let me guess.

Another history field trip coming up?"

Chapter Nineteen

Darrell watched the confused look bloom on Cassie's face.

Earlier, Erin had pre-empted his decision. But, with the young girl's question, now he needed to decide how much to confide in her. For all he knew, Cassie might well be propelling him toward a collision with the Haunted Bride. Hell, she could be driving the car at eighty miles an hour heading straight into a hairpin curve. With him in the passenger seat. He wanted her information, but did he trust her?

Erin rested her hand on his shoulder, interrupting his indecision. "Darrell's a history expert. Actually, he's a history teacher and researcher. With our last ghost, he was able to track down a few answers for the investigation with some historical research."

"What could history have to do with the Haunted Bride?" Cassie asked.

Darrell recognized the look of bewilderment. He'd seen it often enough on the faces of his students. Staring at Cassie made him think again of his kids back at Wilshire. Okay, he had no true Goths in his classes with their black outfits, spiked hair, and belligerent cynicism, but he'd seen that same skeptical look more than once on his students' faces. He would have pegged Cassie as a sophomore or junior and, without thinking, went into teacher mode. "Erin's not talking about history like you're thinking. Like 1492 or the battles of the Civil War. She's means recent history of the area. Local history."

"Local history?" Cassie looked puzzled. "Still don't get it."

He exchanged a glance with Erin. He'd heard the same thing from his students a hundred times. "It's like this. Before I can help this *Haunted Bride*, I need to see what I can learn about her. Maybe, find out something about her death. Maybe why she committed suicide. And just maybe, that will give me some inkling of how to help her."

"Okay." Cassie nodded. "I guess that makes sense. Never thought of history like that. Not how they taught it in school."

"I know." He sighed. "I have the same discussion with my students all the time. They think history is something that happened to somebody else. It's a notion I try to get them to change."

Erin asked, "Is there anything else you can remember hearing about the Haunted Bride? A name? A place? The name of the family?"

Cassie pulled her legs out from under her and stood. "Not that I can think of. But I can ask around. See if I can learn any more." She wandered over to the counter and set her empty can next to a pile of flyers about Josie.

Darrell got off the sofa and came up next to her. On reflex, he picked the stack and, holding them together, hit them against the Formica top, first on one side then the other. Satisfied they were straight now, he returned them to the counter and pointed to the one on top. "That's a sister of one of the kids in the football camp. His name is Josh. He's fourteen and he's worried sick about her." He indicated the photo. "She's only sixteen." He searched Cassie's face and thought he saw something register.

Cassie started to shake her head.

"Cassie, do you know anything about Josie?" The question came from Erin, and Cassie glanced over at her.

"No. Um…Gotta go." Cassie started toward the door.

Darrell stepped in front of her. "Cassie, if you know something, you've got to tell us." The entreaty came out more demand than plea, and the urgency in his voice surprised him. If he was going to deal with the "Haunted Bride," he was going to need Cassie. The last thing he wanted to do was alienate her. But he couldn't help it. He was worried about Josh and Josie. He always cared about "his kids." Worried about them. Anguished for them. Sweated for them. And this was about two teens he hardly knew, had known for only two weeks.

Cassie's glance jumped from Darrell to Erin and then back to Darrell. "I don't," she blurted out. "I mean, I don't know anything…about Josie."

Erin jumped off the sofa and moved next to the teen. "Cassie, if you know anything, anything at all, please tell us." She laid a hand on the girl's arm. "It might help."

"I don't, but I know some people who *might* know something." She held a hand up before either Darrell or Erin could say anymore. "Look. Been on my own for a couple of years and have hung out on the street a lot. Met some people who run with a different crowd. Maybe they heard something. I'll let you know if I learn anything."

"Thanks. We'd appreciate that." Erin wrapped her in a hug. Cassie stood stock still, as if she wasn't sure how to react.

Or hadn't been hugged much.

"I need to go," Cassie said. She still hadn't moved a muscle. "It's been a long day and I'm whipped."

Erin released her and stepped back. "Thanks for sharing what you know about the Haunted Bride."

"Wasn't that much." Cassie took another step toward the door.

"It's more than we had before," Erin said, her voice bright.

Darrell moved and got to the door before Cassie. His hand held one of the posters and he offered it to her. At first, Cassie simply stood there, then slowly raised her hand and accepted the paper.

Darrell's voice was still anxious. "Please let me know if you learn anything that could help us find Josie." He pulled the door open.

"I will." Cassie walked through.

Darrell added, "And I'll let you know if my research turns up anything on the Haunted Bride. Where do you live?"

She sighed and muttered, "With this guy."

"I mean, can I have an address? Or phone number?" Darrell asked. Cassie didn't answer right away, as if she was trying to decide what to tell them. She stepped into the corridor. "Where can I find you? You know, if I learn something."

Cassie kept moving down the hall. Without looking back, she called, "Downstairs. Duh."

Chapter Twenty

Another real—what had Erin called her? A "sensitive," yeah. Darrell was another real, live sensitive. One a whole lot more plugged in than her. One ghosts talked to. Damn.

Made her feel *almost* normal.

The couple turned out to be…okay. Erin even liked her Goth outfit.

Maybe Cassie *would* help. With the missing girl. She stopped under a streetlight and stared at the poster in her hand. Realized the girl—Josie—was the same age as her. Her real age. Like her, Josie probably just ran away from a shithole of a home.

She stashed the flyer back in her pocket and dragged her beat-up Walkman out of her bag. Pulling the headphones around her head, she punched the play button, sending the cassette spinning and Green Day railing. Satisfied, she started walking again.

She could ask some of the gang. See if they knew anything about this Josie. She glanced up at an antique clock at the corner. Eleven thirty. They'd be hanging out under the bridge by now. She'd told Darrell she was tired, but she lied. Meeting and talking with him—and that electricity in his touch—had kicked her adrenalin into high gear.

Besides, she was glad to be outside. Not cooped up in the restaurant anymore. Inhaling, she caught a hint of the salt in the air from the ocean. The heat had fled and the temp wasn't bad. She might enjoy hanging out under the stars. For a while. And she was in no hurry to get to Troy's place. Maybe, since it was Saturday, if she came in late enough, he'd be completely fried and out of it. He usually was.

What she really wanted was a hit. When she got to the overpass, Vince would be there. He'd have some for her.

Head swaying to Green Day's "Nice Guys Finish Last," she headed up Ocean Avenue past the showy B & Bs and the ritzy homes. Most of the places looked quiet, slumbering almost. A few dim lights in upstairs windows looking like soulless eyes. Up ahead, one front yard sprouted spotlights that lit the garish purple and pink trim. These places practically screamed, "Look at me. I'm rich." Could the owners be any more in your face?

A few blocks down, she turned onto Washington, cutting through the business district. Hurried past shops and stores, all shuttered and silent, hawking items she couldn't buy. The few things she spied in the display windows—beach towels, calendars, garish T-shirts— were all for the tourists anyway. Nothing she'd want.

As she neared a bar, a whiff of cigarette smoke drifted her way. Outside the entrance, a cluster of smokers talked and puffed, the haze of smoke thick under the sign's neon glow. She caught a hoot of laughter and crossed the street. Pulled the thin black hoodie over her head and turned up the music.

Shit on them. The laugh reminded her of the first time she'd ever seen a Goth. For real. Back in her school, what, three years ago? She could still hear the teacher snort and call the Goth a "witch" and thought, maybe that should be her. With her special gift. When she tried it all on—the piercings, the dark makeup, the black clothes, the hair—she found it suited her. No, it *was* her. Kept most people at a distance too.

Which was the way she liked it.

Once beyond the lights of the business district, she picked up her pace. Made this trip plenty before. The ground smooth, the path familiar. She knew she had another twenty minutes ahead and wished she'd bummed a ride. What the hell, she kept going.

When she strode past the Physick Estate, tall red turrets looming in the darkness, she thought of the ghosts…and her special talent. After all, this grotesque building was the most famous haunted site in Cape May. *Big* tourist draw. Though she'd never picked up on any ghosts on the grounds. She wondered if Darrell had noticed any vibes at the site. If he'd done the tourist thing and taken Erin there.

Once past the estate, she used Sidney to cut over to Lafayette. Just had to follow it all the way to the overpass. Her only company along the road now was the occasional passing car, heading back into town to their hotel or B & B for the night. Or maybe barhopping. The headlights of each car struck her, their beams igniting her silhouette for a second before crawling down the street. The large mansions and Victorian monstrosities gave way to normal houses—one story places and bungalows. Where normal people might live.

Hell, like she'd know.

While she moved along the white sidewalk, huge trees, massive oaks and maples and sycamores, towered over her, shrouding her in their shadows. The limbs of the trees stretched out wide as if they were reaching to grab the black sky. She kept her head down and kept moving. In a black hoodie and jeans, she was almost invisible in the darkness. Or at least felt like it.

****

By the time she completed the two-mile jaunt, most of her adrenalin was wiped out. She was relieved when the concrete structure of the overpass came into view, streetlights bleaching the cement structure bone white in the night. She cut in front of the huge "Lobster House" sign and headed alongside of the sloping concrete structure. She knew better than to draw attention to herself, even though only two cars passed her as she disappeared into the darkness of the gravel parking lot. She took off the headphones and stashed the Walkman into her backpack. Away from the lights and in the shadows, she stooped and scrunched inside her hoodie. Almost invisible in the night again.

When she got to the edge, pebbles skittered out from under her shoes and bounced into the flowing water. Inside the darkness ahead beneath the structure, she heard movement. She stepped into the gloom.

"Chill," a raspy, male voice called. "It's only Cassie."

She took another step into the space, her eyes scanning the steep hillside.

"Great to see you, Cassie. Been a while," the voice continued.

"Hey, Vince," Cassie called, head swiveling, taking in the few other figures and then settling back on the speaker.

Vince lay sprawled on a ratty, red-checked blanket,

head propped on one arm, crooked teeth barely visible in the dark. He hadn't changed. His hair was unkempt, black unruly tufts sticking out of an old stocking cap. Even in the limited light, his face bore the shadow of a beard he could never seem to grow. He eased back against the cloth again, his stomach straining the buttons of the old shirt. His right hand held something thin, and she saw the faint glow at the end.

Her head made the smallest nod toward him. "Got any for me?"

"For you, girl, anytime." Vince patted the space next to him on the faded blanket.

Cassie walked over and settled onto the blanket. He took a long toke, exhaled, and passed her the joint. She accepted it and did the same. She saw four bodies huddled around the space and thought "Vince's Posse," at least, that's what he called them. She chuckled and caught several more glows in the darkness. She could even make out a couple doing it maybe twenty feet away, their laughter drifting in the air.

Vince saw where she was looking and said, "Don't mind them. That's Max and Slick. They're doing their own thing." He smirked. "They won't bother us."

Satisfied, she took two slow draws into her lungs and felt the familiar hit. Relaxed a bit and passed the joint back. She lay on the blanket, the dirt and rocks against the concrete wall rough against her back. Her breathing slowed. Water gurgled by. She inhaled deeply, the sweet scent of weed intermixed with the fish smells from the water. Overhead, cars and trucks rolled across the concrete surface, the steel girders rumbling with the impact. Sounds became rhythmic, comforting even.

Vince gave her the joint again, smaller now, and she took another drag, inhaling slowly. Passed it back. He took it with his right hand, while his left flicked a small lighter. On and off. On and off. In her mellow state, she followed his movements and watched the small flame brighten his chubby face with plump cheeks and green eyes. Then another flick and darkness again. Next, she heard him take another deep inhale and felt one hand drift over onto her boobs. She let him. It felt good. Funny, how much nicer it was when Vince felt her up than when Troy's hands were all over her.

Or maybe it was the weed.

This was chill. She'd almost forgotten how chill. She let her thoughts drift as if they were traveling with the lazy string of smoke from the burning joint. There was no Antonio barking orders at her. No ghosts or even a Haunted Bride. No Darrell and Erin. Then she remembered why she came. Well, one reason she came. She put her hand on Vince's. "Hey, hold on a minute."

"Why?" Vince managed to squeeze both protest and pout in the one word but stopped groping.

Cassie sat up and turned toward him. "Need your help with something. Look at this." She pulled the poster from her back jeans pocket, unfolded it, and held it out to him. "Seen this girl?"

In his stupor, Vince peered at the flyer. Cassie reached across him and picked up the Bic lighter. He took one last draw on what was left of the joint and then ground it out. He grabbed the lighter and held it up to the paper, the halo of light encircling the photo of Josie. Then he lowered the flame so he could read the print.

"Josie hangs out with us sometimes. Mostly at the Mad Batter. Yeah, I remember seeing her there with that guy." He flicked the light off and settled against the slope.

"What guy?" Cassie leaned over him.

Vince spoke without opening his eyes. "Some slick dude. Said he worked for a New York modeling agency. Brad or something." He took a deep breath as if still inhaling the weed. "Good shit, isn't it?"

"Yeah, great." Even in her brain haze, she sensed something was off with Vince's comment. And she felt her mellow mood evaporating. "He works for a modeling agency? Like looking for models?"

He laughed. "Easy there, tiger. I don't think they're looking for too many bitches on the runway that look like you."

She punched him on the shoulder.

"Ouch, that hurt. Shit, you can hit." He sat up and rubbed his shoulder. "Hey, it's just a damn pick up line. You know, so he can get laid. We guys are like that."

"When? Do you remember? The girl's gone missing."

"I dunno." Vince yawned. "Last weekend? Maybe she's shacking up with him."

Cassie said, "Need a favor."

"What do I get for this *favor*?"

She could see the smirk even in the dim light. Guys. Shit. They were *all* looking for something.

"Oh, we'll think of something." She slid her hand to his upper thigh. "I'd want you to ask around and see if anyone's seen Josie since. Can you do that?"

"For you Babe, sure." His hand covered hers and he groaned.

Chapter Twenty-One

The next morning, Sunday, Darrell awoke with a groggy head and massive dragon breath. Disoriented, for a moment he couldn't remember where he was. Sunbeams, streaming through the French doors, danced across his face, clearing a few cobwebs. After a bit, he recalled he was in their suite at the Inn of Cape May. His and Erin's *suite. Sweet.*

After Cassie left last night, he and Erin had enjoyed another drink or two, discussed the Haunted Bride a bit more, and indulged in a few…pleasant distractions. Smiling, he extended his arm across the bed. Not there. He glanced around but didn't see her. Not in the room. Where was she? A momentary panic seized him.

He took a breath. Erin was a big girl. She could take care of herself. At least, most of the time. He didn't need to panic. He forced himself to think—not easy with this headache. Scrunching one eye shut and one eye open, he recalled doing the same thing earlier, catching Erin slip out of bed. Dressed in a bright blue top and matching running shorts, she murmured something about going for a jog along the beach. With a wink and a wiggle of her butt, she'd tried to tempt him to join her. He'd rolled over and fallen back to sleep.

How long ago had that been? He had no idea.

He staggered into the bathroom to do his business and took a quick look at his face in the mirror. Man, he looked ragged. A shower might help. Hopefully, the pulsing water from the large shower head would wake him up. And—if he was really lucky—Erin would be back soon. After all, she'd need a shower after a hard run on the beach.

Pulling the curtain back, he turned the faucet on high and gave it time to warm up. He reached for his toothbrush and brushed hard to chase the dragon breath away. After he spit into the sink, he looked in the mirror and noticed the small bathroom was filling up with steam, the glass already misted over.

He climbed into the tub and pulled the heavy plastic curtain around the inside. For a while, he stood there, head under the pounding jets, hot water cascading through his hair. It canceled out all other sounds. The rushing water felt like warm liquid BBs against his skin, waking him. After he sudsed up his body, he worked the shampoo into his hair, inhaling the herbal fragrance and reminding him of Erin. Smiling, he broke out into song, a falsetto version of Cher's "Believe," using the handheld showerhead as a microphone. The same song Erin had shimmied to in her yellow bikini yesterday.

How could one guy get so lucky?

When he reset the shower head in its holder, a wave of cold air swept into the room, as if the bathroom door had opened. Hey, his luck was holding. Erin was back. Head still under the water, he turned and stared through the translucent curtain and saw an outline of a blue figure in the bathroom. He broke into a wide grin.

He said, "Erin," and then added with a little

innuendo, "right in the nick of time."

No answer.

"Erin?"

Darrell pulled his head out from under the spray. Staring through the plastic, he couldn't make out much, but thought he saw movement. Flashes of blue that seemed to…shift.

He tried again, "Erin?" a slight quiver in his voice. The only response was movement of the blue toward the sink. In spite of the hot running water, goosebumps ran down both arms.

Then, the shower water turned shockingly cold, the jets like frozen needles on his skin. He yelped and stepped out of the spray. How in the hell could someone divert all the hot water? Wait a minute. He hadn't heard the sink faucet turn on. He shivered. His heart thudded against his chest. Standing there naked, cold and dripping, freezing water splashing into the tub at his feet, he felt exposed and vulnerable.

His mind raced to latch onto some rational explanation. Would Erin want to trick him like this? He shook his head. No, she enjoyed teasing him, but she wouldn't do this.

Maybe it was the room maid. Did they have blue uniforms? Would she simply come into the bathroom? Didn't he put the "Do not disturb" sign on the door last night? Maybe Erin had taken it off when she went for a run.

He turned the shower off and peered through the plastic. The blue figure stood still but seemed to shimmer in the steam.

"Hey! Who are you? What are you doing here?"

No answer.

He yanked back the top of the curtain, stuck his head through, and stared into the bathroom. His adrenalin spiked. He gulped. The steam was so thick all he could make out was a streak of blue moving toward the open door.

Wrapping the curtain around his body, he yelled, "What do you want'?"

Darrell heard the key in the room lock and the heavy door to the suite open.

Oh, thank God.

"Erin, in here," he called and jerked his attention back to the bathroom. The blue figure was…gone. His glance darted around the small room. The whole place was so steamy, it looked like a scene out of a gothic novel. He saw no one. His heart felt like it was going to jump out of his chest.

"Erin, can you come in here? Now!" He didn't let go of the curtain and his gaze searched the bathroom.

Erin laughed. "Easy, big boy. Let me get these sweaty clothes off first."

Darrell finally released the shower curtain, which fell back against the tub. He wrenched it, the links clinking on the metal rail, stepped out, and sat, dripping, on the edge of the tub.

A few seconds later, Erin appeared in the doorway, all smiles. At the sight of her, her very real body shimmering with perspiration, relief swept over him. His heart started to return to normal. He shook his head, feeling stupid for letting his imagination go wild. Rising, he met her at the doorway.

"You have no idea how glad I am to see you," he said, wrapping his arms around her.

"Well, me too." She gave him a long kiss.

Glancing into the room, she continued, "But first I need to take a shower. Looks like you already took—" She froze and stared at the mirror, her eyes wide.

Darrell turned his head and what he saw made his heart rate thunder again. "What the hell?"

Written on the mirror, letters now streaking with long drips, were six words.

SHE
IS
ALMOST
OUT
OF
TIME

Chapter Twenty-Two

Darrell and Erin both grabbed white towels, and she sat down on the lip of the tub next to him.

"I was doing a little impromptu karaoke in the shower and when I turned around, she was there." Darrell tugged at the terrycloth, trying to adjust it and even out the folds.

"Who was it? What did she look like?" Erin asked.

"I couldn't see much in the steam. Long blue outfit. I think." His gaze went to the door and then back to the mirror. "Didn't you see someone? She had to go right past you." His fingers kept fiddling with the towel. "I mean, after she left the bathroom."

"I didn't see anybody—"

"You had to. Maybe she was the maid. You know, room service." His words tumbled out, like he couldn't control them. He didn't look at Erin, his focus on his towel. "I didn't call room service or anything, but maybe this is some special service with this suite. Special Sunday toiletries or something." His eyes darted around the room in search of exclusive soap or shampoo.

Erin put a hand on his and he stopped fidgeting. "Take a breath."

Staring into her kind face, he took two deep breaths. He felt his heart slowing, getting closer to normal again.

"A little better?" She waited until he gave a quick nod and then went on. "Now, I don't think it's the maid." She shook her head.

"How do you know?" His words were desperate, and his eyes again fixed on the mirror.

She grabbed his chin and turned it toward her. She held his gaze. "Because I saw two of the maids on my way back up to our room. After my run. One is working right down the hall. Their uniforms are red. Well, red with some gold trim. Definitely not blue."

He broke out of her grip and stared again at the words wiped on the glass, each letter sliding down, as if the words were weeping. His shoulders slumped. "It must've been the Inn ghost then," he mumbled.

"What?"

He pointed to the smearing words, recognition in his face now. "Remember last night, when you were asking Cassie about Cape May resident ghosts?"

"Yeah?"

"Cassie mentioned the Inn has its very own ghost. I remember she called her the 'Lady in Blue.' Something about a gal who worked here a long time ago and wears some kind of blue uniform."

"Oh yeah. I remember her talking about some ghost here."

"It had to be her. Damn." Darrell couldn't take his eyes off the words, now only long smears on the glass.

"Another plea from beyond?"

"Looks like it. Man, Cape May is something else." He shook his head and took another breath. "So, the Haunted Bride is running out of time. Why?" Darrell checked out the mirror again and looked at her.

Erin met his gaze and then studied the mirror. "I

got nothing."

"Damn, like I said, they're not going to leave me alone. I need to do something, to see what I can learn about the Haunted Bride. How I can help her."

"Want to head over to the library today? I could help." She smiled, a few drops of perspiration still clinging to her cheeks. "I was pretty good at finding the info on Hank."

"You are pretty good at almost everything, but no can do." His fingers brushed off both cheeks. "The library's not open on Sunday. I'll have to head over there after football camp this week. But thanks for asking." He kissed her and they lingered in the kiss. "Besides, like I said, this weekend is supposed to be for us. I have some more fun planned and don't want any ghost to interrupt that."

"Well, before we go anywhere, I need a shower." She rose from the tub, her towel loosening. "It's too bad you already had yours."

He stood up and tugged on her towel. "I guess I didn't explain. My shower karaoke was rudely interrupted, and I wasn't able to finish. I think I may still have shampoo in my hair." He pointed to his scalp and gave a little pout. "I think we should shower together. You know, to save water and all."

"To save water, huh?" She pulled on the edge of his towel and it came free. Turning, she stepped into the tub, her own towel dropping to the tile floor. Over one naked shoulder, she grinned. "Only if I get a repeat karaoke performance."

"I'll give you a performance you'll never forget." He stepped into the tub behind her, the ghost visitor forgotten.

Erin turned the water on, the faucet gushing at their feet, and after a few seconds, flipped the switch for the showerhead, drenching them both. "Promises, promises."

Chapter Twenty-Three

"So that's the Emlen Physick house," Erin said, standing on the crushed stone pathway and taking in the entire three-story structure.

"Supposed to be the most famous haunted site in Cape May." Darrell studied the large house of white siding with gray edging. What he was most impressed with was the huge wrap around porch with the stick-like brackets. Others valued the mansion more for its traditional Victorian characteristics like the upside-down chimneys, hooded dormers, and huge turrets. And the fact that it was haunted.

Erin asked, "Did you catch any ghost whisperings in there?"

He looked at her and then turned his glance back toward the famous house. "Not a one. I guess Isabel and Emile were taking the day off."

She grinned at him. "Or their ghosts didn't want to speak to you with all the other tour guests around." She tickled him in the side. "Maybe they'll wait 'til you're alone."

"Maybe." He shrugged. "Still an interesting old place."

"That. And dark and dreary. Especially coming from the beach."

After they'd finally gotten out of the shower and dressed, they checked out of their room and grabbed a quick breakfast sandwich. Then, one last time, they walked the beach, enjoying the sunshine and the mist off the ocean and watching the kids playing in the water. Of all Cape May offered, the beach was Erin's favorite, after all. Well, after him, he hoped.

Afterward, he'd talked her into visiting the famous estate and they got there in time for the noon tour. Kurt had said no trip to Cape May was complete without it. Still, after this morning's unsettling encounter, Darrell was thrilled not to receive any more ghostly messages on these grounds.

Erin smiled. "I don't know what it is about the beach and haunted houses, but they always make me hungry. Are you planning to feed a starving girl?"

"I was thinking about Carny's. They have some nice lunch salads and sandwiches. It's on Beach right across from the water."

"Isn't that where you saw that, that—"

"Yeah. That Victorian lady of the evening," Darrell said. "Thought you might like to see the place. And the food was pretty good."

Lunch at the vintage bar turned out to be normal, not paranormal at all. No ghost of a 19th century call girl. No missing images in the mirror at the end of the bar. No mysterious notes. And a couple of great burgers. Darrell was happy to show Erin where the ghost appeared, but even happier to not have a repeat performance. Not today.

Erin glanced at her watch and reached across the booth. "I'll have to be heading back in a little while. How about a stroll down some of these historic streets, so I can soak up some more of this ambiance before I go?"

Darrell didn't release her hand at first. If he had his way, he wouldn't let her go. They'd stay and enjoy much more of what the resort town had to offer. Maybe get a couples' massage. Take a sail aboard a Yankee schooner. Catch a play at Elaine's Dinner Theatre. Not to mention take full advantage of the bed *and* shower of their wonderful suite at the inn. And perhaps, most important, she could be by his side when he tracked down what…whatever came next with the Haunted Bride. Her presence beside him gave him courage. Made him braver.

Of course, he was about at the end of his funds, though he didn't want to admit it to her. He couldn't afford another day, much less a week, at the inn's prices. And somehow, his tiny room at the boarding house, with its shared bathroom down the hall, did not evoke such romantic possibilities. The last thing he wanted was for Erin to leave, but it was mid-afternoon already, and he knew well how long the trip back would take.

He said, "Okay, let's appraise a few more beautiful Victorians."

After he re-fed the meter, they headed down Beach Avenue and then cut up Decatur. A half block north, Darrell led her and they strolled onto Columbia, holding hands and admiring one old house after the other. The street was busy with visitors, sometimes congested with couples and families coming down the steps of the residences, hustling past them on the sidewalk. With Erin beside him, Darrell was at ease, relaxed and the crowds didn't even faze him. Her love seemed to trump his OCD. The two of them were content to amble down the road and take in the sights.

She was particularly taken with one called the John F. Craig House, a large, striking Victorian with its distinctive siding decked out in mauve with teal accents. Even Darrell had to admit the result was enchanting, certainly different. A few steps farther down the road, Erin stopped them in front of a charming two-story period house. It was done in a more traditional blue and orange and, of course, boasted a full front porch with inviting rocking chairs.

She indicated the sign hanging in the small front yard, which read "Mason Cottage" and glanced up at Darrell. "I think it'd be romantic to stay in one of these next time."

"Can't argue with that, though many don't come with private baths. You have to share with other couples.".

Erin raised her eyebrows at him and grinned. "Well, you'll simply have to find one with a private shower."

She slid her arm through his and they continued their stroll, turning onto Ocean Street. The Victorians gave way to businesses, small shops selling saltwater taffy, swim wear, and other tourist must-haves. Since Darrell's wallet was light, he kept them walking and Erin didn't protest. She did pull them up at another striking Victorian at the corner of Hughes, this one the siding a brilliant teal and the trim a shiny white.

"I don't think I've ever seen any place quite like this town," Erin admitted. "It was everything you promised. Thanks so much for inviting me for the weekend."

"Believe me, it was my pleasure." He pulled her to him and kissed her, long and hard, there on the sidewalk in front of the B & B. He didn't care who saw. When they came out of it, both faces a little red, they noticed an older couple in the porch swing watching them. They waved to them and the older couple smiled and waved back. Erin merely chuckled.

They turned and kept walking, hand in hand. Like perfect lovers, Darrell thought. He led them away from the beach. He knew she had to go back to Wilshire soon, but at the same time wanted to put off her departure as long as possible.

They stopped, admiring another splendid old house. After a bit, he said with all seriousness, "I really miss being able to talk with you. I've decided to break down and get one of the cellular phones. Even though our schedules are still out of kilter, we could at least talk some of the time."

She stopped and faced him. "Can you afford that? I mean, I know they're pretty pricey."

"Actually, no," he said. "but I'll find a way. Load up the plastic a little more. I like working the football camp here but being away all week—and not being able to talk with you—is killing me."

"Been working a lot while you've been gone. Picked up extra shifts. But it's no picnic for me as well." She stood on her toes and kissed him again. "Be great to be able to call and talk during the week. How much longer do you have to work here?"

"At least another week. Then it depends on what happens. With my job back in Wilshire."

"You know Sara's working her sources," Erin said. "May have something by then."

"God, I hope so." He held her close. "We'll figure it out."

This part of town seemed a little less crowded. Small knots of people shuffled around them, but neither Darrell nor Erin seemed to notice. He felt they were incognito, almost like being alone on the sailboat on the Chesapeake last month. There on the sidewalk, he wrapped his arms around her and kissed her again. She didn't resist.

Darrell looked around to get his bearings. He found a street sign at the corner. Franklin and Hughes Streets. The street name gave him an inspiration.

"Hey. That's one of the corners where Josh and I tacked up a poster. Here, let me show you." He pulled her to the telephone pole at the corner and pointed about waist high at the wood surface. But it wasn't there. A little higher up on the pole a flyer about "The Gingerbread House," another historic inn, stood affixed to the pole. Confused, Darrell said, "I could've sworn we stapled one here."

He glanced around and, after a moment's hesitation, dragged Erin down Franklin to Page Street. There he halted at another wooden pole. "It should be right there." He gestured to eye level on the pole, but there was no Josie poster. Instead, a flyer for the Cape May Carriage Company hung in the space. Darrell edged close to the pole. "I don't get it." His finger examined the rough surface and, a little above the ad for a carriage ride, he found two staples with triangles of purple paper trapped beneath them. The same purple paper Josh had used to print the flyers about his sister. It was her favorite color.

"What the hell?" Darrell asked. He glanced around, checking to see if anyone was watching them, but didn't catch anything suspicious.

"You think someone took Josh's poster down? To put up this ad?" Erin sounded incredulous. "Why would they do that? There's plenty of other room on the pole." She indicated the still naked wood of the telephone pole. This one held only one other flyer, a crude notice about a local band at a bar.

"I don't know. Let's go see." Darrell led and they followed the path he'd taken with Josh two days before. Together, they checked five more telephone poles before quitting. Each time they found no Josie flyer. Twice, another flyer hung in the place where he remembered stapling the notice. Three other times, only the staples remained, with the telltale tiny triangles of purple paper. And, the farther they checked, the more certain Darrell became they'd tacked up papers on each pole.

Erin asked, "Why would anyone want to take them off? Go to all that trouble?"

"I don't know, but I don't like it." Darrell explained that Officer Barnaby had said they should post the flyers farther away from the shore. "That's why we put them on these poles."

Then Erin voiced the question he was thinking. "You think someone still doesn't want them up here? Like they're give the wrong image for the town?"

Darrell shook his head. "Maybe. But I'm starting to wonder if the motive might not be that innocent."

Chapter Twenty-Four

For the next two days, work at football camp almost wiped him out. When he arrived early Monday morning, Darrell was hoping to talk with Kurt. Instead, as soon as Darrell walked through the locker room door, the head coach took him aside. He announced that some college scouts were arriving any minute to check out a few of his seniors, so he had to meet with the reps.

"I need to leave these kids in your capable hands," he'd said, right before he ran out to greet a new rental that pulled up next to the practice field. "You know these kids and, by now, they know you. You got this."

So, for the last two days, Darrell had to be everywhere—running drills, giving instructions, providing encouragement, and even breaking up fights. It hadn't left much in the tank.

He'd wanted to ask Kurt—since he was the local and might have some idea of what was going on—about Josie's posters being pulled down. But, with the head coach schmoozing the scouts, in two days he never got even five minutes to broach the subject with him.

Darrell glanced up at the wall clock in the Local Resource and Genealogy Room of the Cape May County Library. 6:45. He'd already put in over ninety minutes and had turned up nothing. His exasperation escalating, he sighed.

He'd shown up yesterday at 5:10 to find the library locked and dark. Then, next to the door, he noted the posted hours, Monday and Saturday 10 to 5 and 10 to 7:30 Tuesday through Friday. Today, as soon he'd showered and changed—he couldn't show up caked in sweat and filth—he made a beeline for the library. He hadn't even taken time to eat. Now, it looked like he'd wasted almost two hours.

Was this some wild goose chase? Maybe this wasn't going to yield any info about the Haunted Bride.

Darrell raised his gaze and tried to focus on the microfilm reader, again. When he arrived, he'd asked for the librarian's help in getting past issues of the *Cape May Citizen Courier* on film. It took him a few tries to get the first spool of film loaded onto the reel and threaded through the machine. Cranking the two handles, he watched as the photos of the old newspapers scrolled across the small screen. Satisfied, he settled in. Then, using the little information Cassie had given them, he started scanning the old editions.

He had no idea where to start, so he began his search ten years earlier, 1989. He concentrated with what passed for "society pages," hoping to find something in the engagement and wedding announcements. What he found overwhelmed him. There seemed to be an endless supply of "happy couples" featured and, week after week, the pages held major splashes about "important nuptials" in town. But, as he worked his way through five spools of film, nothing caught his eye. He didn't recognize any faces.

In a burst of inspiration, he decided to concentrate on the summer issues, since Cassie had mentioned a wedding on the beach. He went back through each reel, looking for photos of sand and sun and white wedding dresses, but found nothing about a wedding on the beach. Eyes close to the screen, he examined the picture of each newlywed couple, but none of the young ladies looked like the face of the Haunted Bride. At least, what he remembered as the face of the ghost.

He pondered, not for the first time, whether Cassie's information was reliable. He knew almost nothing about her. Not where she was from. Or even how old she was, despite what she claimed. Could he trust her? Did she lie to them about the ghost?

What reason would she have to lie?

His head spun with unanswered questions, and he yearned not to be here alone. He shot a glance at the empty carrel next to him. God, did he miss Erin. Reaching into his back pocket, he pulled out a clean handkerchief and polished the screen again. For the nth time. He realized that last year it was Erin, not he, who'd made the first big discovery in the U of M archives. If she were here, she'd think of something. He needed her to bounce ideas off.

After this past weekend, he realized how much he wanted her to be a part of his life. His arms ached to hold her. He even pondered the four letter word.

Then, just like that, an inspiration struck him.

Maybe thinking about her, conjuring up an image of Erin's beautiful face next to him was enough. Why not simply check the front pages of the papers? Wouldn't a bride at a big wedding who'd gone "missing" or walked into the ocean be major headlines in a small town? It certainly would've made the front page of the *Wilshire Gazette*. He rewound the reel starting with the summer months of 1989 again and searched every front page. He went through all five reels of microfilm. His concentration focused, he scrolled through each summer, scanning, stopping, and searching for a story about a society bride gone missing. Nothing. At least, he didn't find anything about any missing bride.

His butt hurt from the hard wooden chairs, his head pounded, and his stomach started growling. He had to get up and stretch.

Seeing a sign for restrooms, he trudged that direction. Once inside, he headed straight to the sink, turned the star-shaped chrome handles, and waited for the water to get to the right temperature. Where could he check next? He splashed water on his face, then he started the ritual of washing his hands. Using soap, he lathered them both up, rinsed, and then repeated the process. Satisfied—at least he didn't *have* to wash them three times now—he yanked down paper towels and dried off each hand and then wiped off his face. He grabbed another piece to turn the door handle. On his way back to his carrel, he located a trash can, sitting next to a water fountain. He curled up the used paper and took time to make a perfect swish and then stared at the fountain. His throat ached, parched from the hours of scanning, and the water'd be cold, but when he thought of all the mouths which had been on there…

His stomach growled again, reminding him to get to some food, and soon. His gut rumbled so loudly, Darrell glanced around to make sure he didn't disturb anyone and read the clock on the wall. 7:20. He didn't have much time. As he headed back into the resource room, the lights inside the room flickered. Twice. He figured it must be the librarian's not so subtle way to tell him they were closing soon. After all, she still had to return the microfilm reels to storage.

"Okay, I got it," he said aloud. "I need to wrap it up."

He hurried across to the readers. The more he came up dry, the more he questioned himself. Maybe Cassie had the details wrong. Or had speculated the years wrong. Or more likely he'd missed it, passed right over it as he was turning the levers. His stomach rumbled again, and he decided to call it a night.

Tomorrow he'd rethink everything and try again. Since he'd gotten a cellular phone yesterday, at least he could call Erin tonight when she got off. Maybe she'd have an idea. Whether or not, it'd be great to hear her voice and share his misery.

Distracted, his mind on Erin, he approached the carrel and heard something that drew his gaze. The spools on the microfilm reader were spinning. On their own. His eyes jumped from the monitor to the two handles, gyrating fiercely. The pages whirled by on the screen and stopped. The print zipped through the viewer, creating irregular streaks of black across the screen, stopped—the printed words in focus for only a second—and then the levers resumed spinning. He shot a look around. No one. He was the only person in this room. He glanced at the row of carrels. The other microfilm readers sat silent. His machine was the only one moving, the reel almost empty now. He lurched for the spool before it ran out and bounced onto the desktop. Right before his hand touched the knob, the reels stopped. On their own. His gaze darted around the room again.

His neck hairs prickled.

He sat and stared at the screen. Some full-page ad from the local hardware store? He caught the date, July 21, 1994, and started scrolling, slowly. Two days later, a front-page headline caught his eye. HAPPY OCCASION ENDS IN TRAGEDY. He read the accompanying article, holding his breath. He took his time, studying the report about the mysterious disappearance of the bride-to-be and the speculation about her walking into the ocean to drown. The second page held the wedding photo of the young bride. His first vision of the ghost on the promenade—before the face was bloodied—leaped into his head. It was *her*.

"Sorry, sir. It's time for us to close up." Darrell jumped at the sound of the librarian's voice.

"Oh. Yeah. I'll be done in a minute." He held one finger up, his eyes glued to the screen. The name of the groom jumped out at him. ARMSTRONG. TRAVIS ARMSTRONG. He hit the print button.

Chapter Twenty-Five

Cassie hated country music.

As soon as she climbed the three steps into the screen-in front porch and moved past the empty booths, she heard it. Some raucous song spilled out from the bar area, fiddle and banjo notes quick and jumpy. Obviously, from the boisterous clapping and foot stomping inside, others did not share her disgust.

She liked the Mad Batter. Normally. She picked this place to meet because she hung out here with the gang sometimes, Vince and his posse. When they weren't down under the overpass. Most times, the owner didn't mind them hanging around.

But she hadn't thought about this. The place had live music most nights, usually a rock group or some heavy metal band. Not *this*. She rolled her eyes.

Standing at the entrance to the bar area, she searched the individuals around the bar, the boots, cowboy hats, and enormous belt buckles hard to miss. No Darrell. He'd shown up a few hours ago at Aleathea's and wanted to meet. Excited, he said he had info about the Haunted Bride. But when she asked, Antonio demanded that she finish her shift, so she'd put Darrell off and suggested meeting here. Now.

Damn. With all this noise, maybe not a great place to meet after all.

Since Darrell had dropped by, she hadn't been able

to stop thinking about the Haunted Bride. Did he really find out something about the ghost? Like who she was? Or how she died? She hoped that the information she'd given Darrell helped him. At least some.

Then, in the next breath, she wondered why she even cared.

The band stopped and she had time to take in the small space, noticing a series of vintage guitars hanging on the one wall. When the next song started, two girls shrieked and jumped up to do some kind of line dancing, the fringe on their leather vests swinging in their jerky movements.

Cassie shot a glance at her own outfit, all black and studs. Sweating under her leather, she shoved her way through the cluster of bodies, the odors of spilled beer and sweat hitting her. She got a few scowls and catcalls from the "cowboys." Ignoring them, she pushed her way past the white-topped bar and then the tiny stage, with a fiddler, a guitarist, and a banjo player going crazy.

Once through the bar, she went down the three steps and pulled the door shut behind her, lowering the obnoxious twanging. She took a long breath and checked out the nearly empty room, her gaze finding the large, empty fireplace and landing on a wall of nature photos with obscene prices. Who would pay $150 for a snapshot of the damn beach?

Oh well, she was only here to see Darrell about the Haunted Bride.

Where was he? Didn't he understand she said to meet here? Maybe he didn't know about the Mad Batter? At Aleathea's, she hadn't bothered to ask.

She kept going and pushed through the next

doorway that led out onto the patio and spotted him, almost out of sight in the far right corner. Alone at the table next to the trellis. She headed over.

Darrell was fidgeting with the flatware at his place. He lifted and then replaced the knife, fork and spoon on the glass-topped table, arranging each piece so it sat precisely parallel to the one next to it. Standing still, Cassie watched him for a bit. What was it with this guy? She had her own issues, but this guy?

Sliding into a chair across from him, she could see why he'd picked this place in the restaurant. The music was only a quiet rumble out here and, this late in the evening, he was alone on the humid patio. Not far away, a gentle fountain gurgled in the near dark, the water splashing onto uneven rocks.

She pointed to a small, gray cellular phone sitting parallel to the knife. "See you got one of those. Wow."

"More than I could afford, but I wanted to be able to talk with Erin." He moved the spoon a half inch to the left. "It's hard being apart so much. Being able to talk helps a little. It's not the same, but it helps."

She stared at the small plastic phone on the glass tabletop. Heard what those cost. Would she ever find someone like Darrell? Someone who'd spend money on a cellular phone—money he didn't have—just because he wanted to hear her voice?

Huh, not in a million years.

"Cassie, you okay?" Darrell asked, and she could hear concern in his voice, even though he hadn't taken his gaze off the place setting.

She didn't want to encourage that. "Could've used a regular phone. Or even a phone booth."

"A phone booth? No way." His shoulders shaking,

he shot a horrified glance at her. "Anyway, thanks for meeting me."

"Yeah, whatever," Cassie said. "You said you found something?"

That seemed to bring him out of his...distraction. "Yeah, I think." He touched the flat knife blade once the with his index finger and eased back. "Could I ask you something first?"

She squirmed in her seat. "What?" She heard the bite in her word but didn't care.

His face flushed, but he said, "When we talked Saturday, you mentioned something about a ghost at the Inn. I think you called her the Lady in Blue."

Cassie let out a breath. This wasn't about her. Still, she didn't soften her tone. "Yeah?"

"Well, what can you tell me about her?" Darrell asked.

Puzzled, Cassie said, "Ah, I don't know. She's supposed to be someone who worked at the hotel. Years ago. Nobody's said what happened to her, only that she likes to roam the hallways and sometimes appears inside rooms."

"Yeah, but...I mean, do you know what she looks like?"

She leaned her head to one side and released a sigh. "I've never seen her, but according to the stories I heard, she's supposed to wear some sort of blue uniform? Like maybe a maid's uniform?" She noticed Darrell's eyes go wide and added, "Probably just another haunted tale for the tourists."

Darrell shook his head. Hard. "It's not just a tale."

"Really? You saw her?"

Darrell laid both hands on the table and told her

146

about the Lady in Blue showing up in his bathroom. While he was in the shower. And the message left on the mirror. All this, the morning after they'd talked.

Cassie edged back a little, pulling her hands in. She wasn't ready for another electric jolt. Like Saturday. "Did Erin see her?"

"No. She was out jogging on the beach. All she saw was the message on the mirror…"

"Okay, then." Cassie didn't know what else to say. Damn, this guy brought out ghosts like nobody. Never heard of anyone like him. "Is that why you wanted to meet? To ask about the Inn ghost? You said you had news about the Haunted Bride."

"No. Yes." He shook his head. Then nodded. "Yeah, I wanted to ask about the Lady in Blue, but that's not what I came to tell you. My research at the library turned up something." He reached into a leather bag on the floor and pulled out two sheets of paper, both with black smears of a copier. "I found out a few things about our Haunted Bride." He pointed to a photo on the top page.

Cassie took the first sheet and examined a photo. Small, pretty young woman in a white dress. Smiling. That *could* be the Haunted Bride. She brought the paper closer and studied it, squinting at the picture. Yeah, it looked a helluva lot like the face she'd seen. Minus the blood. She read the name under the photo, Amy Palmer. That didn't ring any bells. Not that it would.

"And this is what I found about her, uh…disappearance," Darrell said.

Cassie took her time and read. Then read the whole article again. She wasn't the fastest reader, but Darrell waited, not saying anything. When she finished, she said, "Well, it fits. It says she walked into the water." She slid the page across the table.

He pointed to the paper. "No, it says they *guessed* she walked into the ocean. No one actually saw her."

"Okay, but I don't get it. What's the diff?"

"I don't know." He shook his head again. "But there's gotta be more. Why else would she be asking me to help? And what does it all have to do with more girls suffering?"

"Hell if I know."

"See who she was marrying?" He pointed to a name in the article. "Travis Armstrong. Know him?"

"Know the name. Another Armstrong—James, older guy, wears sunglasses, blind I think but I never asked—comes into the restaurant with his wife. The boss always makes a big fuss over them." Then she thought of something else. "Acourse, I see their trucks on the roads all the time, Armstrong Trucking. Pretty hard to miss 'em."

"Erin and I saw him at Aleathea's Saturday night. James, not Travis. And his wife Andrea." Then Darrell pointed to the picture. "Actually, I met James and his son, Travis, at Carny's last week."

Cassie picked up the copy of the newspaper article and studied it again. "This happened August 21, 1994. Five years ago. Before I came to Cape May." She dropped the paper. "Okay, we got a name for this person who may be our ghost. Who was a bride. What can we do now?"

"Hold that thought." Darrell reached into the brown case and pulled out a metal clipboard. He flipped up several pages with some diagrams of x's and o's. He folded three sheets back and slid the clipboard over to her. She stared at a list of names. She didn't recognize any, except a few more Armstrongs.

His fingers stabbed the clipboard. "I went back to the library tonight and did some more digging. The family had this big wedding shindig on someplace called Poverty Beach."

"Yeah, it's at the end of Beach Avenue."

"Well, the article said they had this big party right there on the beach. Brought in tents and bars and food and even a dance floor and set it all up on the sand. Never heard of such a thing. Anyway, here's a list of the guests at the wedding. At least, the ones named in the article."

Cassie glanced again at the names and then back at him, shrugging.

Darrell blew out a sigh. "Don't you get it? These people were there when the Haunted Bride, when Amy…disappeared. Maybe they know something about how she died."

"So? If this was some rich guy's wedding, they would've had hundreds of guests." She pointed to the clipboard. "A helluva lot more than these. And it was five years ago."

"I know, but it's a place to start. Better than nothing." He sounded desperate.

"Okay, but I wasn't even in town when all this went down." Duh. "What d' ya expect me to do?"

"I don't know. Couldn't you ask around? Maybe some of your local…um, friends might know something about some of these people." He stabbed the clipboard. "Or they might've heard something."

Cassie hesitated. She still wasn't sure how deep she wanted in. She studied Darrell, who looked wretched, and relented. "I can ask around. Vince may know somebody."

Darrell pulled out the sheet with the list of names and handed it to her. "I made a copy. You can have this one." He smiled. "Erin was right."

"Right? About what?"

"She said you'd help. She had a good feeling about you."

She did? That was new. And nice.

He pointed to a series of numbers in blue scribbled at the top of the sheet. "That's my new number, for the cellular phone. In case you need to reach me." He started to get up.

Cassie took the paper, careful not to touch his hand, and said, "I found out something else."

"About the Haunted Bride?" He sat back down.

"No." She caught the expectant look in his eyes. She wasn't used to someone counting on her. Not sure how she felt about that. "I asked around about the kid's sister—"

"Josie?"

"Yeah, Josie." She nodded, then shared what Vince had told her.

"Your friend thought she took off with some guy from a modeling agency? For real?"

"Well, Vince says he's not sure how much *modeling* she'll be doing. He figured it was a line so he can shack up with her. Or something else. He wasn't sure."

"Okay. Thanks," Darrell said, but didn't seem grateful. "'Something else?'" he repeated to himself.

Chapter Twenty-Six

"Okay, guys, break it up!" Darrell yelled.

Two players in full pads, minus only their helmets, wrestled on the grass, one on top of the other, arms swinging and legs kicking. The rest of the teens spread out around them in a semi-circle, ogling and cheering like an excited audience at a Roman coliseum.

Stepping between two battling adolescents was a tricky proposition anytime, and this time both were wearing football equipment. Darrell made a quick assessment. He couldn't make out who was on the bottom, but the kid on top, Kevin, look to be taller and had fifty pounds on his opponent. Kevin swung a knee and hollered, "It's not my fault your sister is a dirty ho." He hauled an arm back to take another swing at the boy on the ground.

Before Kevin could throw the punch, Darrell stepped in, grabbed his arm and yanked hard. The kid stumbled, tripping over his own feet, and fell back behind Darrell. In two seconds, the teen on the ground sprang up. He ran toward Kevin, trying to sidestep Darrell. With both arms raised, he screamed, "You're a fucking liar."

Darrell grabbed the second fighter before the kid could get past him, jerking him to a stop. Then he recognized him. "Josh? What's going on here?"

Both kids had bloodied lips and Josh sported a

nasty black eye, which was going to morph into one hell of a shiner. Josh spit onto the ground, blood and saliva mixed together on the brown dirt. "As' him. His mous started it." He rubbed the one side of his jaw and, from the boy's slurred words, Kevin must've have landed a hard punch there.

Darrell turned and faced Kevin, who'd gotten to his feet. The taller teen only smirked. "Simply tellin' the truth."

Darrell felt Josh squirm in his grasp, trying to free himself and get at Kevin. Darrell held fast. "Okay, you two are done. For today. Hard to believe you guys would pull this crap on our second to last day. You might not make the last day." He jerked his head toward the taller combatant. "Kevin, you hit the showers." The teen stood still, unmoving. "Now."

Kevin sauntered over, snatched up his helmet, and started across the field. Darrell called after him. "I'll let Coach Wagner decide if you can come back for awards tomorrow." Then Darrell turned toward Josh, still in his grasp. "You head over to the bench till I come to talk with you. Got it?"

Josh hung his head. "Yeah, Coach." He moved to scoop his helmet up and trudged over to the wooden bench, rubbing his jaw with his free hand.

Darrell turned to the rest of the teens. "I don't suppose you guys want to tell me what's going on here?"

Every kid stared at the ground, feet shuffling in the grass. No one said a word.

"Okay, then, since we don't seem to be in a talkative mood, everybody gets to do four more laps."

"What?"

"That's not fair."

"Give us a break, Coach."

"Anyone want to clue me in on what's going on here?" Darrell pointed at Josh across the field. The players stayed silent. "Okay, then, four laps. All the way around." A few of the boys started to remove their helmets and Darrell said, "In full gear. With helmets. Now, move."

The teens managed some quiet grumbling and bad language he chose to ignore.

Darrell had had it.

For the third day, with two more college scouts in town, Kurt had left him alone to handle the "campers." He promised today would be the last time. Darrell appreciated that the head coach placed such confidence in him—especially since Darrell hadn't known any of these kids before a few weeks ago—but it had taken all his coaching skills to keep the group on target. Now, this. Of course, it hadn't helped tempers that the temperature had hovered in the 90's pretty much all day. He kept sending the kids for water but knew there was only so much hydration could do.

Standing there, watching the teens make the circuit, Darrell pulled the already drenched towel from his back pocket and wiped his forehead again. With the heat and humidity, he'd sweated so much he'd soaked his shirt. He knew he reeked. Their young bodies, bursting with adolescent fervor, released a nasty, fragrant wave as they passed.

Once they jogged by, he glanced at Josh, slumped over on the bench, his small body shaking. Was he crying? Maybe he was hurt worse than Darrell thought. He trotted over to the boy, even while keeping one eye on the other players circling the field. When he got close enough, he could hear Josh cussing through clenched teeth.

"That lying sack of shit. Damn him anyway." Josh looked up and, seeing Darrell approach, went silent again. The boy's face betrayed a miasma of emotions— anger, embarrassment, worry, fear —and the kid struggled to keep the tears at bay. He lost that battle, as twin streams poured down his cheeks.

Darrell sat beside him on the bench and placed his hand on the teen's shoulder. "Okay, Josh, you want to tell me what's going on?" He tried to keep his voice quiet.

The teen raised his head and met Darrell's gaze. The boy's one eye looked uglier, the orb bloated and the bluing spreading. It must hurt like hell. Josh didn't say anything at first, his gaze moving to the left. Darrell heard the pounding of forty feet as the players rumbled past. When they were out of earshot, the kid said, "Kevin called Josie a whore."

"What? Why would he do that?"

Josh sniffed hard and made a small hiccup. "Then I called him a fuckin' liar and he hit me. So I punched him back." He blushed then. "Oh, sorry, Coach."

"What started all this?" Darrell asked.

"I dunno." Josh spit again onto the grass, and Darrell was glad to see no more blood in the phlegm, at least. "After he caught a pass from Troy, I tackled Kevin and he went down hard and I celebrated a little. Then he jumped up and said, 'If you were really any good, you'd stop moping about your stupid sister.' So I got in his face and asked 'what do you know about Josie' and he said that crap about her being a whore. He said his brother was hitting some clubs last weekend in New York and saw Josie in Greenwich Village, all made up in this tight dress that showed off her…her…you know. Said she was hanging out with these two other sluts, doing tricks. That's what he said." Josh was near tears again.

Darrell nodded. "Maybe Kevin was just running his mouth. Let me check into this. I'll see how much of this is real and how much he's simply making up to get under your skin." He moved his hand to the teen's arm. "Look, I know how much you want to find your sister, but you can't let these guys get to you."

The rest of the students made another lap and Josh waited till they passed again, a few stragglers bringing up the rear. He used the sleeve of his jersey to wipe his eyes and sniffed, on the verge of losing it again. Josh said, "I'm *really* worried about her. It's been ten days and now Kevin's saying—"

"Let's don't go there yet."

"Okay, but that'th not all. Yesterday I went to check out thome of the telephone poles where we tacked up the flyers about Josie and—" Josh broke down and started crying again, quiet sobs through his words. "—they're all gone. At least, I couldn't find a thingle one we put up."

Darrell didn't know what to say. Should he tell Josh he noticed the same thing Sunday? But then, he'd have to admit he'd been so busy between football camp and his research on the Haunted Bride, he hadn't done anything about the missing flyers. Instead, he said, "I'll tell you what. I'll go talk with Officer Barnaby. See if he knows anything about it."

As the players came jogging by again, Darrell

stood and put up a hand. "Okay, that's enough. Everybody, hit the showers." The players turned, en masse, and headed for the locker room. Darrell turned back to Josh. "You too, get in there." The kid got up and took a step. "You'll have to answer to Coach Walter about the fight today. You *and* Kevin."

"I know." Josh trotted toward the school, head low.

Darrell stood, watching the teen trudge across the grass.

Kevin's brother saw Josie dolled up, doing tricks at some club in New York City? Not long after Cassie's friend saw Josie take off with some modeling agency guy. From New York?

Darrell got a bad feeling about this. A really bad feeling.

The Haunted Bride's warning leaped back. "Help me or more girls will suffer and die."

A question tugged at the edge of his consciousness: could Josie's plight be connected to the Haunted Bride? He had no idea how, but he felt the hairs on his neck prickle again.

Chapter Twenty-Seven

"For the most improved player this year, the award goes to…" announced Coach Kurt Wagner, "Josh Dawson. Come on up here, Josh."

With a stunned look, the teen ambled up to the front. When he raised his head and shook the hands of Darrell and Coach Wagner, Josh flashed a rare smile. Darrell handed him a shiny blue ribbon with the words "Most Improved" embossed in white.

Kurt continued, "With everything you've dealt with the past two weeks, with your sister going missing and everything, you still worked harder than pretty much everybody. Including me." All the teens laughed. "Keep up the effort. You're going to be a solid defensive lineman."

The rest of the students clapped as Josh loped back to his spot on the metal bleachers.

Coach Wagner concluded, "I've enjoyed working with all of you the past couple weeks, both as football players and as young men." Kurt's gaze swept over the group. "I look forward to coaching you on the high school team soon. Now, I know you have other places to be, so get the heck out of here." He gave a quick wave.

The boys shouted back and hustled off.

Darrell watched the teens as they trotted over to their parents and a fleet of waiting cars, trucks, and

SUV's. When he looked back, only one kid remained sitting. Josh.

Darrell walked over. "Hey, Josh, got a ride home today?"

Josh stared at the ribbon in his hand. "Later. Mom's gotta work and can't get here for another hour. It's okay. I don't mind the wait."

Darrell said, "Look, I'm heading out and I'll be happy to drop you off."

"Sure. Okay."

As they walked together, Darrell said, "I talked with Coach Wagner yesterday about the fight you and Kevin had."

Josh looked up and nodded. "I know. Coach told me you said Kevin started the fight. That's why he let me come back today." He held up his award. "And I know I wouldn't have gotten this without your say. Thanks."

"Yeah, but Coach Wagner was right. You earned that. We're proud of how hard you worked." Darrell took a deep breath. "Look, I also talked with Coach about what Kevin said. About Josie. He said don't believe *anything* Kevin says. And his brother is worse. Coach had Turk—Kevin's brother—in class. He said Turk is always running his mouth. So, for now at least, let's don't pay attention to what he said. Okay?"

Josh mumbled, "Yeah."

For Josh's sake, Darrell acted far more optimistic about Kevin's claim than he felt. As they walked across the grass, he studied the kid whose shoulders slumped and feet shuffled. Unless he knew for sure, he wouldn't add to the kid's burden.

Neither said any more until they climbed into the

car and were heading into town. Darrell turned down the radio. "Hey, Josh, do you mind if I make a stop first? When I went by the police station yesterday to talk with Officer Barnaby, they told me he was off, but would be back on duty today. I was planning to stop there before I leave town today. To ask him about the missing posters. You want to go with me?"

"Yeah. Thanks, Coach. I'd like that."

Five minutes later, they pulled up outside the Cape May Police Station on Washington Street. As they exited the car, Darrell saw a middle-aged man in a blue uniform descend the three steps. When the man slid the mirrored sunglasses from atop his head to cover his eyes, Darrell recognized him. "Officer Barnaby?"

The cop turned and Darrell, making sure Josh was with him, scurried across the street. Barnaby stopped at the foot of the steps and waited. When Darrell got within earshot, he said, "It's Coach Henshaw…from the football camp."

The officer crossed his thick arms in front of him, stretching the blue fabric tight across his broad shoulders. "Vivian said you left a message yesterday. I was going to look you up but hadn't got around to it. What's up?"

"I came by to ask about—" Darrell started and then stopped. "You remember Josh Dawson? He's still looking for his sister."

"Hey, Josh," the cop said in a soft tone.

"Anyway," Darrell continued, "Josh and I noticed the posters that we put up last week have been taken down. Do you know anything about that?"

Before the officer could answer, the teen blurted out, "And we put them where you said. On the poles away from town. And they're all gone. Every one of them. Torn off."

"They are?" Barnaby appeared genuinely surprised. He raised the sunglasses back atop his short salt and pepper hair. Looking down at Josh, he said, "Sorry, son. I didn't know that."

"Did the department get a complaint or something?" Darrell asked.

"Not that I'm aware of. Certainly not anything official." He glanced at the teen again. "I can check on that for you and let you know."

"Can I put some more up? I ran off more copies," Josh asked, his voice expectant.

"You shouldn't do that, until I can check into it," said the officer, his voice kind. "We're still searching for your sister, you know. Don't give up, eh?"

"Never," Josh said.

"I'll let you know what I learn out about your posters." The cop looked from Darrell to the teen. "How can I get a hold of you?"

Darrell said, "I just got a cellular phone. You can call me on that no matter what." He retrieved the phone to look up the number he hadn't yet memorized. He read it off.

"Got it." Barnaby scribbled into a small notebook and stuffed it in a pocket. "I'll see ya. I've gotta head out."

Darrell placed a hand on the officer's arm. "Could I talk with you for a minute? About something else?" He turned. "Josh, give me a minute with Officer Barnaby, would you? I'll meet you at the car."

Josh nodded and shuffled across the street.

The cop slid the mirrored sunglasses back over his

eyes, arms relaxed at his side. "Okay, but make it quick. Like I said, I'm due on patrol." Then he grinned and added, "Got some tickets to write. You know, make my quota."

Darrell had been in town long enough to recognize the half joke and chuckled. "Good. But make it be somebody else please. Anyway, do you remember a few years back when a new bride ran out on her big wedding and was supposed to have walked into the ocean? Her name was Amy Palmer." Darrell stopped and waited, looking for any reaction from Barnaby, but all he could see was his twin reflections in the mirrored lenses. It was unnerving, but he held his breath.

After a bit, the cop said, "Name doesn't ring a bell. It's sad, but suicides are not exactly rare here in Cape May. We've had more drownings than we'd—"

"She was marrying Travis Armstrong."

"O-o-o-h, that suicide." Barnaby shook his head and studied the sidewalk. "I remember. Really sad, that one. It hit Travis hard. The whole family was really shaken up." He looked up again. "What about it?" He paused a bit. "Why do you want to know?"

Darrell pretended he hadn't heard the second question. "The newspaper articles I read said the family thought she walked into the ocean and drowned. Do you know if they ever found the body? I mean, were the police ever able to confirm it was a suicide?"

Barnaby stared at him through the sunglasses. "I don't remember for sure, but I don't think they ever found the body. But that doesn't mean anything. Depending on where the victim went into the water, the tide might carry the body out and we'd never see any sign of it. Or the fish can take care it." He shifted on his feet and crossed his arms in front. "Why are you asking?"

Darrell figured the cop would ask and thought he had a plausible answer ready. "Well, I don't know if you know, but when I'm not coaching, I'm teaching history. In Wilshire. Over in Maryland." He waved one hand in the general direction, west. "Anyway, I'm kinda an amateur historian and like to check out local history. I was reading some of your local history here and this story seemed interesting."

Darrell tried to sound nonchalant but wasn't sure he'd managed. Inside, his heart was pounding against his chest, but he kept a crooked smile on his face. A bead of sweat slid down the side of his head.

Barnaby didn't answer right away, his eyes focused on Darrell. At least, Darrell thought the officer was staring at him, but couldn't be sure because of the sunglasses. After a bit, Barnaby said, "I'll tell you what. When I get a chance, I'll call in and have the Sarge pull the file on her death." He pulled the pad back out. "What was her name again?"

Relieved, Darrell said, "Amy Palmer," and watched the cop jot down a few words.

Barnaby stuffed it back into his pocket. "Check with the desk sergeant. You can look it over there."

"Thanks."

The officer turned and headed toward the lot of police cruisers. "Gotta head out. You know, protect and serve." He gave a small wave.

The farewell sent a shiver through Darrell. He recalled the last time a cop had uttered those words to him. Back in Wilshire. A cop who later tried to kill him.

Chapter Twenty-Eight

"Well, I'm glad to see you don't discriminate against ghosts." Al held the glass of amber liquid and tilted it toward Darrell, careful not to spill a drop. "Here's to an equal opportunity ghost hunter."

"What are you talking about?" Darrell asked, even though his tired brain urged him not to.

"Well, last year, here in Wilshire, you found Hank, definitely a guy ghost." Al paused and took another sip. "Now, in Cape May, you're chasing down three female ghosts. Impressive and equal opportunity."

"Very funny. And it's more like they're chasing me."

Darrell sat on the sofa in the McClure family room, a much-needed Dogfish Head beer in his hand. He'd spent the three-hour trip back to Wilshire reviewing everything he'd discovered in Cape May and was glad to have the willing ears of Al and Sara. After all, who else would believe him? Except Erin, of course, and he'd already told her most of what he'd learned. But he should've realized Al would find some way to needle him.

"You want funny?" Al asked. "Well how about this? Do you know why ghosts like elevators?"

Darrell glanced over to Sara, who rolled her eyes. He couldn't help grinning as he replied, "No, I don't know why ghosts like elevators, but I bet you're going to tell me."

"Because they lift their spirits." Al slapped one hand on the chair arm. "Lift their spirits. Going up." With the other, he raised his almost empty glass in the air. "Going down." He drained the drink.

Sara said, "That's your last one tonight, Al. I'm cutting you off."

Darrell was glad he was back here, in Wilshire, with his friends and soon, with Erin. As if to welcome him, it was a cool night on the Bay, unusual for June, a slight breeze wafting in through the open windows. He caught the familiar hint of brackish water and inhaled. That scent made him feel at home.

Sara reached down and stroked the back of the pug, whose sleeping body was wrapped around Darrell's leg. "But it sounds like you're making progress. With the mystery of the Haunted Bride anyway."

"I'm not sure I'd call it progress," Darrell said. "I've put a name with that…" Darrell closed his eyes, picturing the ephemeral figure, bloodied on one side. "That tragic face. And I've got a date when she disappeared, but not much else. I've got absolutely no idea why she's haunting me. Or what she wants me to do. Or how I'm supposed to *save* any girls?"

Al said, "You said she committed suicide. Walked into the ocean, right?"

Darrell's head shake was emphatic. "No, I said that's the official version." He picked up the notes he'd made from the police report. A gruff Sergeant Harris at the station in Cape May had let him look at the file, but the entire report didn't even cover one page. Darrell didn't have many notes. "No one actually saw her walk into the water. Several witnesses reported she seemed upset, and one guest said he watched her run out of the house. And that's the last anyone saw of her."

"Maybe that's what she did." Al's voice was quiet, no tease this time. "Maybe she simply walked out there and let the waves take her. She wouldn't be the first."

Darrell lowered his eyes and gave his head a slow shake. "It doesn't feel right. I can't explain it, but it doesn't." His eyes came up and he pointed with one finger. "Besides, how would that explain the bloodied side of her face and body? From some final stroll into the ocean?"

Darrell's question hung in the air and, for a while, no one spoke. The noise of a throaty muffler passing by drifted in from the road. Darrell took another swig of his beer.

Sara asked, "And you think this ghost bride may have something to do with this girl who's gone missing?"

"I don't know." Darrell shook his head again, one hand holding the beer, the other petting Pogo's head. "The messages mention helping the Haunted Bride and saving girls, but I haven't found any way to put the two together. Regardless, I'm worried about Josie. Her younger brother, Josh, is such a great kid. If she's anything like him, I can't believe she'd jump into that life. Not willingly anyway."

Al levered his footrest down and set his glass on the end table. "You think this sixteen-year-old girl disappears from this small town in Jersey, maybe runs away with this talent agent—" He made air quotes. "—and a few days later is part of some stable of working girls in New York?"

"I hope not." Darrell shook his head again. "But

from what I've read, that would follow a pattern other girls have reported."

Al flashed him a look. "How'd you become an expert on big city whor—" He saw the look from his wife and stopped. "Let's say, ladies of the evening? Darrell Henshaw, do you have a devious side you've hidden from us?"

At the sound of his master's name, Pogo's head shot up.

"Hardly." Darrell chuckled, rubbing the pug's fur. "I simply did a little research, isn't that right, boy?" The dog licked his hand and Darrell let him, not even feeling the compulsion to whip his handkerchief out to wipe off his fingers. *Maybe he was getting a little better.* "After I discovered the details about Amy Palmer, the haunted bride, I had a little time and wanted to do something about Josie. I checked some more recent editions for stories about missing girls in the area. One of the pieces led me to an article on sex trafficking in the US."

Sara said, "I thought sex trafficking here mainly involved immigrants. You know, kids from other countries."

"Most of the time it does," Darrell began. "They lure young girls—and sometimes boys—from South and Central America or Eastern Europe with the promise of a job. Instead, they end up putting them into sex slavery for years, often getting them hooked on drugs in the process."

"Well, none of that would apply to your Josie," Al offered.

"True, but what I found out," Darrell said, "was the same traffickers are baiting pretty young girls,

American girls, with the promise of a modeling or acting career. Only first, the girls have to do a little other work. On their backs." He glanced over at his hostess, not wanting to offend any more than necessary. "Of course, the modeling and acting career never quite materializes. According to one report, the experts believe more than five hundred *American* girls have been trafficked this way in the last five years. Primarily in big 'modeling' cities like LA and New York."

"That's a lot of teen girls," Sara said. "Why haven't we heard more about this?"

"According to what I read, it's because the girls are mostly runaways. They come from all over the country and from scores of different cities and towns, all with different police forces. Too many times, this isn't a high priority for local law enforcement."

"Whew," Al said.

"Of course, these numbers are only estimates, based on reported runaways and missing girls. They say it could be much higher."

"God, I hope that's not what happened to Josie," Sara said, setting a hand to her chest.

"So do I, but I don't know. I forgot to tell you. I tracked down the older brother of the kid who'd run his mouth and started the fight at football camp. This guy, Turk, was pretty specific about the club where he saw Josie in New York City. And, what she was doing there. Before I break the bad news to Josh, I think I'm going to head to New York and check it out myself."

"Our big boy on the prowl in the Big Apple. I'm going to tell Erin," Al said, managing to sound like one of the whiny girls in his junior high band.

Sara threw a coaster at him and he ducked.

Darrell said, "I think I better let her know myself. I know she won't like it. But I feel it's what I've got to do."

For a moment, no one spoke and then Sara piped up, "Sounds like you could use some good news."

Darrell said, "You got that right."

She asked, "Have you told your coach friend in Cape May whether you're going to take the job they offered?"

"Not yet." Darrell shook his head. "I went to the district office and picked up an application, but haven't turned it in. I like Kurt and wouldn't mind working with him but can't stand the idea of being away from Erin. This long-distance romance stuff is tough." He blew out a breath. "But I've checked out about every school close by and so far, nothing. There's still time, but Cape May is the only option I've found, and I have to have a job. A guy's gotta eat."

"Well, you might want to—" Sara started, but the sound of the front door opening stopped her.

"Hey, honey, I'm home," sang a lilting voice from the entry.

Darrell would recognize that voice anywhere and jumped up to meet Erin before she got through the family room door. He grabbed her up, inhaling the familiar scents of her—faint perfume, flowers and herbal shampoo, and a trace of hospital disinfectant. She wrapped her arms around his neck, her purse thudding onto the wood floor. Ignoring Al and Sara ten feet away, they kissed, long and hard, lingering in the sweetness of the moment.

After a bit, Al said, "Okay, okay. We get it. You're in love. Get a room already."

They stopped kissing and laughed self-consciously, like two high schoolers caught making out behind the bleachers. Darrell felt the best he had all week. He held onto Erin's hand and brought her over to the couch with him. As soon as she settled against the sofa back, she stretched out her long legs and flipped off her shoes.

Erin said, "What a shift. Man, my feet are killing me."

"Sounds like you could use a foot massage," Darrell said, suddenly forgetting about his own weariness. He knelt down and kneaded her soles.

"Aw, that feels great. Thanks." Erin glanced from Darrell to Sara. "Have you told him yet?"

"No. He's been filling us in on Cape May. I was just about to."

"Great. Then I can be the one to give him the big news."

From his perch on the carpet, Darrell's gaze went from Erin to Sara. Both wore wide smiles, neither speaking for a few seconds. "Okay, I'm dying here. What news?"

Erin chuckled. "I wouldn't take that job in Cape May yet."

Chapter Twenty-Nine

"Well, I believe our friend Sara has done it." Erin pointed at the older nurse. "I believed in you from the start. Well...pretty much from the start and figured you were set up. I wanted to do something about it, but I didn't know what to do. Who to talk to. Sara has the network."

"Done what?" Darrell glanced from Erin to Sara. "What network?"

"Got your job back," Erin said, triumph in her voice, then added, "We're pretty sure."

"What? How?" Darrell's heart leaped in his chest. His old job? Here with Erin. "What do I need to do? Who do I talk to?"

Erin said, "Sara tapped her medical network and learned one of the nurses in Remington's practice, Tammi Botkins, was really upset about what happened with you and the boys and the steroids."

"Do I know this nurse? The name doesn't ring a bell."

Sara jumped in. "No, she wasn't concerned about you. I don't think she knows *you*. She was upset about Jason Thompson. You see, Tammi's best friend is Francine Thompson, Jason's mom."

"Who?" Darrell was getting lost.

"Your quarterback. His mom."

"Oh, Mrs. Thompson. Yeah, I know her. Of

course."

Sara continued, "Anyway, when all this came out and Jason almost lost his scholarship, Francine, Mrs. Thompson, was frantic and came to her friend. She told her Jason would never take steroids."

"That's what I said all along," Darrell complained.

Sara went on. "Tammi started digging, you know, trying to find some way to help her friend, but before she got very far, you did the noble thing and fell on your sword. When Jason's mom found out he could keep his scholarship, she was so relieved, she and Tammi had a good cry about it at a booth at Nick's. Part way though their second drink, Tammi told Francine she thought she'd found something. In case the Board went back on their word."

Darrell said, "Okay. I think I have the players straight. What did Remington's nurse find?"

"Tammi remembered she'd sent a copy of Jason's file at the end of the season to the orthopedic specialist in Annapolis. That was in November. For the work to clean up the bone spurs on his shoulder. The file had everything—blood tests, everything. *If* Remington had doctored the files, Tammi thought this one would prove Jason was clean."

"Why didn't she speak up then?" Darrell looked up from his place on the floor. "Maybe she could have saved my job?"

Erin leaned forward and took his hand. "Because she was afraid *she'd* be out of a job. If Remington goes down, so does his practice. She's a single mother of three kids. So she never brought it up." She stared into Darrell's eyes. "You can understand, can't you?"

"Yeah, I guess I can. I wouldn't want any more

people to get hurt in this mess." Then he looked at Sara. "But you got her to confide in you? How?"

"It's what I do." Sara had a twinkle in her eyes. "I've known Tammi for almost twenty years. We went to the same nursing school, though I was a year ahead of her. I talked to her and told her about you. About you and Erin. Told her Remington had no right to destroy your reputation. I appealed to her better nature." Then she smiled. "And I promised I'd help get her a job at the hospital."

Erin clapped her hands. "So, while you were hunting ghosts this week, Sara went with Francine to the surgeon's office in Annapolis and requested a copy of Jason's record."

Pogo got to his feet and snuggled over to Sara, as if he sensed she was the hero of the day. She reached down and petted him. "I made some excuse about needing a copy for a file at the hospital. That we'd misplaced ours. And the office manager was kind enough to make a copy and hand it over."

"So you have it? Did it prove Jason didn't take steroids?"

"It certainly does." Sara rose, went over to the desk at the front of the family room, and pulled a manila file out of a drawer. She walked back and handed it to Darrell.

He flipped through the pages, scanning abbreviations, notations, and a series of numbers. Little of it made sense to him. He turned to Erin. "A little help here?"

Erin took the file from him and set it on top of the coffee table. Skipping past the first three sheets, she stopped at a page with a column of numbers listed. "If there were any steroids in his blood, the markers would have shown up here." She pointed halfway down the column.

Sara added, "In fact, when I showed it to Tammi, she said it was identical to the file that Remington put out, *except* for the listing of steroids in Jason's blood."

Darrell stared at the line where Erin pointed. Of course, he couldn't read medical jargon, but he believed his two nurse friends. Not many doctors were smarter than these two combined. Certainly not Remington. Still?

Erin's voice rose a bit. "When we show the Board this, they *have* to believe you. They'll know you were set up."

"I'm not so sure." Darrell shook his head.

"What?" both women exclaimed at the same time.

"Wouldn't Remington simply claim *we* doctored the records?" Darrell glanced from one woman to the other. "I'm thrilled with what you found. It confirms what I've said all along, but Remington's got clout in this town."

Erin's voice grew shrill. "But the ortho surgeon in Annapolis still has the original records. He'd back us up."

Al stirred in his recliner. "Knowing Remington, he'll make a call to Annapolis and the record will get lost." He slipped one palm over the other. "Poof. He'll say he needs the surgeon to help protect him from a couple of nosy nurses. That how the doctor network works."

Silence returned as both women seemed to acknowledge Al's point.

"But—" Erin said, her voice desperate. "We've got

to do something." Her gaze searched Sara's and then Darrell's.

Darrell got up off the floor and joined Erin and Sara on the couch. He laid a hand on Erin's back and ran it through her red hair. "As usual, you're right." He stared at the medical file on the coffee table and came to a decision. "What we need is a confession. From Remington."

Al said, "How many beers have you had, kid? Remington's not going to confess."

"He just might, if we give him a nudge." Darrell picked up the file. "And this may do it."

"What? You're going to show *him* the file?" Sara asked.

Pogo's head came up. Darrell watched him and said, "Come here, boy." The pug trotted back to his owner and Darrell scratched him behind his head. "I'm going to need your help with this."

Then, he laid out his plan and Al, Sara and Erin all broke out in broad grins.

Chapter Thirty

Darrell glanced around the small park, struggling to look nonchalant in his fresh navy shorts and white Polo shirt. This afternoon, getting ready for this "meet," his adrenal glands had worked overtime and he sweated through his first outfit. With the day hot and humid, he wasn't concerned about the clothes—not much anyway—but he was worried about appearing too nervous.

He didn't see Remington yet.

Last night he'd tried to come off as confident, even certain, as he laid out his plan. Now, in a harsh afternoon sun that glared like an all-knowing yellow eye, he was anything but certain. What if Remington decided not to show? What if he suspected something was up?

Earlier, he'd phoned the doctor and asked to meet. Darrell said he was leaving town, that he'd taken another coaching job for more money, and wanted to clear the air before he left. Remington, all arrogance and bluster, replied he had more important things to do.

That's when Darrell dropped the line on him.

"Doc, it doesn't matter now, since I'm going on to greener pastures, but I thought you'd want to know I came across some evidence that would've exonerated me *and* the students. It's too late now since I've accepted this other job, but I...uh, thought *you* might have some interest in what I came across."

He let it hang in the air, allowing the silence to drag on. He could almost hear the doctor thinking, calculating.

Finally, Remington said, "Son, I'm sure I don't know what you're talking about. I've no idea what *evidence* you could mean. You and I both know you gave your players those steroids."

Darrell had to bite his tongue. He wanted to reach through the phone and punch the man, but he'd held himself in check. Inside his head, he said, "Grin and reel him in."

Remington made a show of clearing his throat. "I want you to know. I took no pleasure in turning you in, but for the kids and our community, I had to do it. I feel sorry for you, son, I truly do. I hope you can use this new job as a chance to start over."

Darrell wanted so much to call the man on his obvious deception, but instead he mumbled, "I'm sure." Now, Darrell made a deliberately loud show of clearing his own throat. "Well, if you don't want to see what I...um, uncovered, that's okay." He waited a beat and added, "I'm sure I can find someone else who will see its...um, its value."

When the doctor didn't respond, Darrell called his bluff, all the while sweating and swearing to himself. "Thank you for your time, sir."

He thought he lost him, but right before Darrell was going to hang up, Remington said, "Maybe I could give you a few minutes."

Darrell rattled off the meeting details and got off the phone, his hands wet.

That had been three hours ago.

Now, Darrell was here, at Bayside Park, and his anxieties flooded his system. He tried to shake them off and climbed the two steps into the gazebo, Pogo at his heels. This late in the afternoon, the summer sun was still bright, looking like it hung high over the opposite shoreline. There was little activity in the park. A sideways glance took in a dad with two toddlers on the jungle gym, their shouts evidence of their glee. On the beach behind, he spied a teen girl splashing alone in the surf. Good, he didn't want too many visitors. Remington wouldn't want eavesdroppers.

He and the pug had roamed the park, and he let Pogo do his business (and he cleaned up). He needed the dog settled and calm for this to work. Slipping a brown canvas backpack off his shoulders, Darrell pulled out the cassette recorder he'd brought. It was a small one, about the size of a paperback, with five buttons at the end that looked like truncated silver piano keys and a built-in microphone. He pushed the button marked EJECT and the cartridge popped out. Turning it over in his hand, he examined the tape and, satisfied, slid it back into its compartment. He pushed PLAY, checking that the recorder was working. When he saw the light come on and the cassette wheels start to rotate, and he hit STOP. He settled it beneath the bench, next to his legs.

"Come here, boy," he called, and the pug obediently trotted over, though the treat Darrell pulled out may have had something to do with it. Pogo scrunched down and settled next to his master's legs. Darrell checked, bending over, and looking underneath the bench, confirmed it. As Pogo gnawed on the bone, his little body completely blocked the recorder.

Darrell settled against the bench back and took a slow, deep breath. The waters lapping a few feet away, he smelled the fragrance of the Bay, that familiar combination of fish, brackish water, and algae he'd come to associate with his new home. With Erin. With his students at Wilshire High. Cape May had an enchantment and beauty all its own and he'd enjoyed his time there—well, mostly—but he'd missed Wilshire and the Bay. He prayed what he was about to do would win back his job and his home.

He glanced at his watch, 3:55, and scanned the environs of the park. Still, no Remington.

His gaze landed on the other side of the gazebo, where the bench wrapped around. It wasn't lost on him that this was the place of his first date with Erin. Well, where the date started, their jog through town. When she pretty much whipped his butt. Recalling the experience, he grinned. He pictured her, that first time, doing her stretching exercises in the neon-colored jogging outfit that had his heart racing. Right now, if he squinted, he could still see her there. Those bright emerald eyes teasing him, while her flowing red hair cascaded down her beautiful shoulders.

He shook his head and looked around. No Remington. He stared as the numbers on his watch flipped to 4:00.

Of course, Erin wanted to be here, to be with him, but Darrell had vetoed the idea. He felt certain more bodies would make Remington more suspicious, but he ached to have her here, close to him. He was merely better with her next to him. And she made him braver.

But he couldn't take that chance.

A noise at the end of the gravel path jerked his

attention back. A short figure approached, taut body dressed in blond khakis and a teal golf shirt, underarms darkened. Darrell gave a small wave but didn't rise—he couldn't afford to disturb Pogo—and the dark-haired head gave a brief nod, as if he were royalty deigning to recognize a commoner.

When Remington got to the gazebo, Darrell, instead of extending his hand, reached down as if to pet the Pug, but actually depressed the "record" button. Then, to be sure, he slid Pogo another treat and heard the dog give a contented whimper. "Dr. Remington."

"I see you still have the mutt." Remington's eyes examined the entire gazebo. He took a step, first right and then left, his gaze checking beneath the bench, before scanning the rest of the small park. Without asking, he grabbed up the backpack and examined it, pulling out the manila folder and then returning it inside. Darrell realized the doc was probably looking for a recorder. Or maybe a second person who could overhear their conversation.

A bead of sweat rolled down the side of Darrell's face. He forced himself not to glance at Pogo and willed Remington to ignore the dog. Finally, the doctor dropped his fireplug of a body onto the other end of the bench with a thud. Darrell hoped the recorder could still pick up the man's voice.

"Well, let's see it. This *evidence* you mentioned." Remington fingered his thick goatee, thumb and index finger stroking the black hairs. "I don't have time for this nonsense."

"Oh, sure." Darrell feigned deference as he retrieved the manila folder from the canvas bag.

The physician's sausage-like fingers snatched the

folder out of Darrell's hand. He let the doctor read through the report as pudgy fingers flipped pages.

After a bit, Darrell said, "I don't know medicine, but those who do tell me you'll find the *evidence* about halfway down page three." He mimicked the same inflection on the word Remington had used.

The doctor turned to the third page and his eyes scanned it. "So?"

For a moment, Darrell's heart stopped. Could Sara and Erin have been wrong? They said the evidence was there, plain as day.

He cleared his throat and plunged on. "Well, like I said, I don't know that much about medical reports, but those who know a whole lot more than me explained, *if* Jason had been using any steroids, it would have shown up in the blood test results right there." He reached over and indicated the numbers Erin had pointed out last night.

"This is a patient record from my office. This is privileged information. You're not allowed to have this."

Darrell ignored him. "If you read the date in the upper right hand corner, you'll notice this report is from November. No steroids. Right about the same time you said you found evidence of some. This record—from your office—would completely contradict the accusation you made against the boys. And me."

Remington didn't lose his bluster. "You know it's against the law for you to have a patient's records. If you broke into my office and got this, I could have you arrested. Hell, I can have you prosecuted just for having this."

Darrell ignored him. "Some would argue this file—

with that stamp from your office, by the way—proves you doctored the records you showed the Board."

"That's preposterous. I demand you tell me where you got this." He waved the manila folder in the air.

"Right now, I think that hardly matters," Darrell said. "Besides, Jason and Seth got their scholarships and will be off to college in the fall. And like I told you, I have a new job, with more money."

Remington looked confused. "Then why am I here? Why even show this to me?"

"I thought you could see the...um, value of this report."

"I have no idea what you mean." Remington cast a glance behind the gazebo toward the water.

Darrell dropped the pretense. "Okay, Trevor. If you're not interested in this report, I'm sure I can find someone else who is. Like maybe the *Wilshire Gazette*. I think they might find it *quite* interesting." Darrell reached over to take back the report.

Remington yanked the folder back and, in a quick motion, yanked out the third page. He dropped the rest on the ground. As Darrell reached to pick up the folder, the doctor used both hands to tear the single sheet over and over again. When nothing was left but tiny white pieces, he dropped them, and they cascaded down like confetti onto the concrete surface.

"Now, Mr. Henshaw, it's garbage," he said with a triumphant smirk, white teeth bright inside the triangle of the black goatee.

Chapter Thirty-One

Remington eased back against the bench and crossed his arms. "Now, as I was saying, I wish you the best in your new job. Away from here."

His face a mask of feigned shock, Darrell's gaze went from the scattered white pieces to Remington's grin. "Tearing that up doesn't change the facts." He pointed to the ground. "We both know the truth."

The doctor made no response and simply shook his head, grinning.

This wasn't going the way he expected, and Darrell knew he needed to push him. "I don't get it. Why did you almost ruin two boys' chances at a college education?"

Remington laughed. "Hell. I knew you'd do the *noble* thing and resign. In fact, I was counting on it. You and that high and mighty sense of ethics. I got nothin' against those two boys. Well, maybe Seth."

"What did I ever do to you?"

"What did you do to me?" Remington echoed. "We bought new uniforms for your whole team. Hell, Bud and I offered to buy you anything you needed. Anything! Other coaches would have been thrilled." One fat finger pointed toward Darrell as if it were puncturing a balloon. "But how did you repay such generosity? Hell, you took everything we did for you for granted. And then you turned on us!" He eased against the wooden back again and crossed one leg over the other. He glanced around, casting a look at the waves.

Darrell needed more, so he stayed silent. Which was damn hard. Another bead of sweat trickled into his eyes and he used his finger to brush it.

When Remington's glance returned to Darrell, the doctor shook his head. "Come on. You can't really be that dense. I'll give you two words. Williams and Brown."

Darrell wanted to respond, but he held his tongue.

Remington went on, "And it was an *accident*, a misunderstanding some thirty-five years ago. When they were teens, for God's sake. And, worst of all, the whole thing was over some stupid black kid!"

Darrell couldn't help himself. "Yeah, who they *accidentally* lynched."

"*It* was a Goddamn accident!" Remington jumped up and stood over Darrell, his face flushed, his cheeks beside the goatee brightening. "Bud was my friend for more than thirty years and he never lied to me and he said it was an accident."

For a minute, Remington looked like he'd come after him, so Darrell sized him up. Broad shoulders, flat abs, and strong arms. Darrell could tell the guy tried to stay in shape, but the doc was smaller and some thirty years older. Darrell decided he could take him.

God, he hated to sit here and do nothing. He wanted to get up in the man's face and confront him, but he couldn't risk it. If he moved, he was afraid Pogo would move with him. Besides, he had to keep Remington talking. So he held himself in check and tried to look chastened.

The doctor seemed to collect himself, glancing around, and sat back down. "And you had to dredge it all up and drag Wilshire's good name through the mud." He waved both hands around, as if indicating the town. "I know you don't care, but Wilshire is a great place, with great people. We have two hundred years of proud history and heritage. Our own culture. And families like the Williams and the Remingtons have built this town. Given everything to this town." Small specks of spittle flew off his lips as he talked.

Darrell thought about the cassette rolling but fought the urge to glance down. He realized he hadn't gotten enough on tape yet. At least not anything that would exonerate him, so he waited and held his tongue.

Remington raised one finger and pointed at Darrell. "Not to mention these idiotic stories about some ghost." He chuckled. "You know, a helluva lot of people in this town are going to be only too happy to see your ass hit the road. For good. Now that you're disgraced and gone, maybe the town can forget about this ugly chapter. Maybe, just maybe, people won't have to hang their heads in shame the way you want them to."

The doctor's gaze roamed the small park again and he straightened as if to rise and leave. Darrell figured he needed to say something. "You know, I-I-I," he stumbled and finished, "I wasn't trying to make Wilshire out as some bad place. I've learned most towns have good sides *and* ugly secrets. You might find it hard to believe, but I've come to love Wilshire."

Remington smirked. "The only thing you love is that piece of tail. Who only happens to live in Wilshire. Can't blame you for that." He chuckled again. "A course, I couldn't blame the string of guys who had that tail before you either."

Darrell felt his self-control evaporate. He clenched his fists but didn't move. Through gritted teeth, he managed, "You can't ignore history. Sooner or later, the truth will come out."

"Maybe in that ivory tower of yours, but not in the real world, kid." Remington rose. "Well, as they say, my work here is done."

The doctor moved down the two steps. Darrell realized he was going to lose him. Was going to blow his one chance. He called out, "Hey, Trevor, one more thing?"

Remington turned, a little off balance, and shuffled his feet. "What?"

Darrell pointed to the torn paper on the floor of the gazebo. "You don't think that was the only copy?"

Remington grinned. "Doesn't matter. In a few minutes I'll call my doctor buddy in Annapolis." He shook his head. "I figured out where you got that record. Anyway, I'll give Ken a call and by tomorrow that file won't exist anymore." He gave a little wave.

Darrell glanced from the doctor to the dog. Or rather, the recorder behind the pug. He prayed Remington hadn't moved out of range of the microphone. He figured this was his last chance. He blurted out, "So that's why you doctored those records and framed me?"

Remington stopped at the foot of the gazebo and looked around, no doubt checking to make sure no one else could hear. Darrell followed his gaze and noticed everyone else had left the park.

The doctor said, "It worked pretty damn well, didn't it?" Whistling, he started walking away and turned as if he'd forgotten something. "Coach, good luck wherever you're going. Now, get the hell out of my town."

Darrell wanted to yell back at him, to tell him the asshole he hadn't won, but he waited, watching the older man go. He wanted to make sure Remington was far enough away. After the doctor climbed into his black Porsche and roared down the street, Darrell stood up. "Okay, Pogo, it's time."

The Pug got up, revealing the tape player, and Darrell saw the cassette still rolling. *Oh, please, catch what Remington said. Please.* Darrell picked up the recorder and hit the stop button.

He rewound the tape a bit and hit stop again. Realizing he was holding his breath, he let it out in a loud whoosh. "Come on. Be there," he whispered.

He depressed the play button and closed his eyes. The doctor's voice came through, faint but unmistakable. "Well, it worked pretty damn well, didn't it?"

Darrell grinned. "It sure did."

Chapter Thirty-Two

Erin stood with both hands on her hips, glaring at Darrell. "Let me get this straight. You're going alone to some *gentlemen's club* in New York City?"

"It's not like that. You know I'd rather have you with me, but you have to work. Now, thanks to you and Sara, it looks like I'm going to get my job back, and I won't be making the trip to Cape May much longer. Before I leave there, I want to see if I can do anything to help Josh."

They were standing outside Ben's By-the-Water in Wilshire, after a great Sunday morning brunch. At least, it had been going great, before he mentioned his plan to hit the Big Apple.

Over omelets and Ben's delicious croissants, Erin and he had again marveled at Remington's confession. Last night, after both nurses completed their shifts, he returned to the McClures with the recorder and they all listened to the tape together. In a rare moment of admiration, Al had declared it a "coup de grace." Now, with Jason's actual medical records and the good doctor's admission on tape, Sara was confident she'd be able to persuade Board members not only to re-employ Darrell, but give him back pay. If only to stave off a potential lawsuit. As Darrell and Erin recounted the triumph, the spirit during the brunch had been downright euphoric. They'd even celebrated with mimosas.

Until Darrell mentioned New York City. And a gentlemen's club.

Darrell's argument didn't faze Erin. "Still. A gentlemen's club? With a bunch of girls wearing almost nothing."

"I promise I won't look," he said, grinning.

"Your nose is growing, Pinocchio."

"I figure, even on Sunday, the trip will take more than three hours, and you have to head to work. When does your shift start?" Darrell asked, trying to be rational, even though he knew Erin's objection had little to do with reason.

She glanced at her watch and mumbled, "In about an hour."

"And you won't get off until 7:30. That'd be too late, and I don't think I should wait any longer. I'm only going there to check on Josie. To see if she's there. Maybe see how much trouble she's gotten herself into." Darrell reached a hand out to Erin's shoulder. "Maybe I'll even have a chance to bring her home."

She crossed her arms and shook off his hand. "What if you do find her and she doesn't *want* to come home? Or can't come home? How is that going to help Josh?" She shook her head. "You might make things worse."

"If I can find her, Josh and his mom will at least know she's alive."

In the end, Erin acquiesced, but Darrell could tell by her tepid goodbye kiss that she still wasn't okay. Even his promise to call tonight and report hadn't softened her attitude.

He couldn't explain it to Erin, but he *sensed* he

needed to go, needed to try to find Josie. His heart broke for Josh and he wanted to help him, but he also sensed Josie's situation was connected to the Haunted Bride. Somehow. Hell, he didn't understand it himself, how could he expect Erin to? He hated upsetting her, but he didn't know what else to do.

So, he'd gone to his apartment and enjoyed rambling around in the familiar surroundings for a while. He even took time to work a little on his computer. He longed to get back home, to his own place. To Erin. Glancing at the clock, he realized he had to go and closed the door behind him. He'd decided he wanted Pogo with him in Cape May—even if pets weren't allowed at the boardinghouse. He'd figure out a way. So he swung past the McClures, picked up the pug, and headed north.

That had been almost three hours ago. He felt like he'd been driving on I-79 forever.

"Look, Pogo," Darrell said, reaching across the front seat to pet the pug. "Here comes the Holland Tunnel. We're almost there."

Without Erin, the whole trip seemed to take forever. The longer he spent in Cape May, the more he missed her. It was becoming hard to think about life without her around. And he was pretty sure Erin felt the same way.

He prayed he hadn't frayed that connection today.

On the trip, the radio was only so much company. He listened to the Baltimore Orioles lose, again, and then flipped around trying to find music he liked. For a while, he tuned in to a news station, the journalist reporting on the signing of the Kosovo Peace Treaty. He realized the settlement was important and would save lives, but he found it hard to focus on problems so far away.

Eventually, he turned the radio off, spoke out loud, and the Pug listened. He went over each kernel of information he'd discovered thus far about the Haunted Bride— —Amy, he corrected himself out loud.

"Her name was Amy Palmer. A pretty young bride who disappeared," he said. He remembered that when he was searching for the Wilshire ghost, it helped when he thought about him, not as some ethereal being, but as a person, a real flesh and blood victim. He was going to do the same thing with Amy. Then, as the miles stretched on, he'd told the Pug about Josie going missing. And the message the ghost—er, rather Amy— had left about helping some other girls.

Pogo sat listening, and each time Darrell glanced over at the dog, he was staring back, those big black eyes focused on his master. Darrell really missed Erin sitting next to him but was glad to have his canine companion back.

Following the flow of traffic, Darrell moved from the highway onto 12th Street and took exit 3. He'd taken time to print out a map and directions from Mapquest or would've been lost by now. Holding the map in one hand, he used the other to steer the car through the crowded streets. Speaking aloud, as if he were explaining to the dog, he called out the streets. "Let's see, left onto Broadway, now left onto 6th Ave and—" He turned the wheel hard. "—and finally a right onto 14th Street. See, Pogo, I told you we could do this."

As he drove past 5th Avenue, he spotted the gaudy neon sign, "Less is More." A terrible pun on the latest corporate maxim, Darrell thought, when the kid had told him the name last week. As he passed, Darrell slowed and studied the sign. To eliminate any confusion, right beside the three words, the owners had painted a female with "less" on. Much less.

It still took Darrell another twenty minutes to find a place to park and then, when he pulled into the garage entrance, he almost choked at the cost. "Twenty-five dollars for the first hour and twenty for each hour after," the attendant said.

"What?" Darrell mouthed, even as he reached for his wallet, and the man repeated the numbers. Two cars behind Darrell laid on their horns hard and he handed over his credit card, trying not to think about his mounting debt. He drove the car up the steep sloping ramp and found a space, pulling in.

The sun had dropped lower, and the canyons of the city created a false dusk, lowering the temperature. Inside the dark, dank garage, it was even cooler. He gave Pogo a treat, kept windows on both sides of the car cracked open, and promised he'd be back soon. Satisfied with a bone to gnaw on and the extra treat, the pug settled down.

When Darrell stepped out of his car, the heavy odors struck him—oil and urine, in equal parts. Holding his breath, he worked his way down the ramp and out onto the sidewalk. As he crossed the busy blocks, the sounds of the city surrounded him—cars and trucks honking, people on fire escapes above yelling, televisions playing loud enough to be heard through open apartment windows. A siren blasted and Darrell halted, watching a police car screech by and careen around the corner ahead. Everyone else seemed to ignore it and kept on walking. Darrell had to keep moving or be roughly jostled, so he resumed his pace.

As he waited at a light, he spotted the sign ahead at the end of the next block, blazing in the fading light, the letters flashing pink and red. He crossed the street and headed down the sidewalk, eyes focused on the sign and the neon-painted door beneath. About fifty feet before he got there, a hand grabbed his arm and pulled him to a stop. The fingers were soft, but the grip firm. Glancing across, he saw a young woman, tall, with almond skin, long, straight black hair, and eyes and lips wildly made up, vicious black mascara and bright red lipstick.

"Where are going in such a hurry, cowboy?" The girl—she didn't look more than sixteen—leered at him. Her voice was low and husky, like a lifetime smoker, and the aroma of cheap perfume flowed off her.

Darrell's stare went from her face to her hand on his arm. The girl released her grip. "You don't need to go in there." Her head made a side nod toward the club. "I've got everything you need right here." Her hand drifted down to her blouse, the top two buttons open, revealing plenty of cleavage.

Darrell shook his head once. "Thanks, no." He brushed past her and resumed his pace to the bright pink door of the club.

A large, muscle-bound man stood at the entrance, thick arms crossed in front of a massive chest. The guy was so tall, Darrell, at six-foot-three, had to look up into a scowling face that sat directly atop broad shoulders. With no neck.

"Thirty dollars." The voice growled, low and guttural. "Includes one drink."

Yanking out his wallet, Darrell checked his cash,

noting the compartment getting thin. He pulled out the bills, waving them, and the bouncer stepped aside. Darrell hesitated a beat. Now that he was here, he wasn't sure he wanted to see what was behind this door. He took a deep, slow breath, turned the gold, heart-shaped handle, and stepped through the opening.

Chapter Thirty-Three

Cassie paced the dingy hospital waiting room, tense, unnerved. No, angry. Why hadn't anybody told her anything?

She hated hospitals.

She quickened her marching down the partially darkened hall, but it didn't help. Glancing up, she noticed two fluorescent tubes struggling to stay lit, flickering and casting weird shadows across the floor. She shot another glance at the wall clock. Damn, how long had she been here? And Vince was brought in how much before that? She wasn't sure.

She didn't even know how the hospital knew to contact her at Aleathea's.

When Antonio had pulled her aside in the middle of her shift, she thought she was in trouble. He scowled at her, his black moustache drooping, and said, "Someone called from Burdette and said a guy you know was just brought in. Said his name was Vince. Something about him being hit on the overpass." He'd eyed her up and down. "A friend of yours?"

Cassie had trouble speaking and gave a short nod.

"Then, you better get over there." When she didn't move, he gestured around the half-empty dining room. "It's slow for a Sunday night anyway. Get going."

Shock rooted her to the spot.

Antonio stared at her for a moment. "Oh, stupid of

me. You don't have a car." He grabbed a bus boy going past. "Steve, will you take Cassie up to Burdette? On the clock. Her friend was in an accident."

She didn't remember much else. Not talking with Steve while he drove the ten miles or so to the hospital. Not how she navigated her way through the nearly deserted hallways to the information desk and then to the Emergency Room. But no matter where she went or who she asked, no one would give her any information about Vince.

Why was she even here?

In fact, when she thought about it, she guessed Vince had given her name to the EMT's, but she didn't know why. Were she and Vince that close? Vince had other friends. He had his "posse," as he liked to call them. The gang who hung out with him and smoked weed together under the overpass. Why call her? Oh, maybe he didn't have any way to reach the others. What were the EMT's going to do? Call the Mad Batter? Send a cop car out to the overpass? Not hardly.

To distract herself, she inspected the depressing ER waiting room. Dog-eared magazines lay scattered across two small end tables. The blue plastic cushions on the chairs sagged from the weight of exhausted souls carrying too many heavy fears. On a silent TV mounted up high, baseball players scurried around some ball diamond.

Like she cared.

She walked over and collapsed onto one of the dilapidated cushions. Heard the air squeak out from her weight. Tapped her foot. God, she hadn't had time to grab her Walkman. At least, the screaming music might distract her for a bit.

Glancing around, she took in the row of tall windows across the front. In the daytime, she figured they brought in sunshine…and hope, maybe. But tonight, the encroaching dark seemed to creep in through the glass and only layer gloom atop her worry.

Her gaze drifted down to her clothes and she noticed the stupid white apron, wrinkled and stained with tomato sauce. She jumped up and went over to the trash can in the corner. Yanking off the smock, she threw it into the can. She barked a dark laugh. Only that left her in this even dumber white shirt and little black bow tie. God, she wished she had her own clothes on. And her studs.

She wrapped her arms snug around her body, shut her eyes tight. And just like that, it hit her. The last time she was in a hospital, in an emergency room, was when her mom… She shook her head hard, dislodging the memory. No, she wasn't going there. She was not.

The loudspeaker above blasted, jolting her. "Dr. Houston, Emergency Department, stat."

The entrance doors to the ER swooshed open and two EMT's rushed in, pushing a gurney with a small form partially covered by a white sheet, already stained with splotches of red. A few feet away from where Cassie stood frozen, they stopped and met a doctor bursting through the door.

The first paramedic rattled off the details. "Four-year-old hit by a car. Fractured skull, broke both legs, looks like. Parents on their way."

The doctor took one quick look at the boy on the stretcher. "Let's go, bay number four."

As the group passed, Cassie saw the dark look the doctor exchanged with the lead paramedic. Her breath caught. Even before the group disappeared behind one of the curtains, the tears started. Twin streams rolled down over her cheeks and into her mouth, and she tasted their salt.

What the hell, she didn't even know this kid.

She couldn't do this. When she arrived at Cape May two years ago, she'd decided she didn't want to get close to anyone. She needed to stay on her own. Depend on herself. Miss Independent.

She needed to get out of here.

"He a friend of yours?" Antonio's question echoed in her head. When she recalled his words, she realized Antonio had been nice to her. Well, nice for Antonio. And that shook her.

She and Vince, exactly what were they? Friends? Friends…with benefits? She certainly didn't love him. He was…convenient, that was all. They usually had fun together and he always seemed to have good stuff…when she needed some. And besides Vince had contacts, knew people, could get things. He had gotten her a fake ID. A good one. And he always knew where to get the best weed.

No, they were only friends.

Her thoughts roamed back to last night. Some might argue they were more than friends. Last night, they had…fun together. When she got off work, he'd been waiting for her in that old, beat up Beetle, and they drove out to the overpass. She'd been tired, exhausted even, but he'd helped her relax and feel better. After, she returned the favor and from the sounds he made, Vince certainly enjoyed it. As they lay together on his thin, ratty comforter, she heard the smile in his voice when he told her what he'd discovered. She wasn't sure though if the smile was from the sex or his pride at digging up some info for her. Maybe both.

Now that he'd given her some leads on the Haunted Bride, Cassie wanted to share them, was even excited about telling Darrell. Then a thought struck her. What if Vince didn't come through? What if he couldn't talk, you know, had one of those tubes in his mouth? Last night they never got around to the list of wedding guests Vince had worked on.

She pulled the grubby backpack off and rummaged through the contents. She had to make sure she still had that list with his notes. The sheet was there, with Vince's scribbled words beside a few names. Good thing she'd met up with him last night and he told her all he did. Otherwise, she wouldn't know what he learned about the night the bride disappeared.

Then, just as quickly, another thought struck her. She felt her face flush as her hand covered her mouth, the moisture from her tears soaking her fingers. What if Vince's accident wasn't an accident?

She couldn't think that. It was only an accident. A streak of fear shot down her back, feeling like when her dad had dragged a hot poker there.

Vince's accident couldn't have something to do with him snooping around about the Haunted Bride.

Could it?

Chapter Thirty-Four

Once he stepped through the doorway of the Less is More Club, Darrell glanced around, but had trouble peering through the smoke. The music blaring from huge amplifiers didn't make it any easier. What he could make out were paneled walls, red velvet settees and a small, wooden dance floor in the center. The place looked crowded, even on a Sunday night. As he strolled through the club, the thudding bass pounding out of massive black speakers made his ears ache. Slowly, his eyes adjusted and he could make out clusters of different guys—designer suits with silk ties pulled down, police and fire uniforms, city workers in NY Metropolitan outfits, guys wearing dark green New York Jets jerseys. They congregated in knots of three to four in the red booths, laughing, drinking, and smoking. Interspersed in each group was a similar number of girls with outfits that emphasized the "Less." All the females strutted around topless and most wore skimpy miniskirts, each in one of the brilliant neon colors of the outside sign.

The smells assaulted his nostrils, reminding Darrell of the innumerable contagions here. Odors of spilled alcohol, smoke of cigarette and potent weed hit him. The smell of sweat and other bodily fluids overwhelmed him and sent off warning bells to not touch anything.

At one booth, a girl raised one leg up onto the padded bench, nestling it in the crotch of an eager young man, who pawed the offered limb. From his vantage point, Darrell could tell that the girl was wearing nothing beneath—he figured that was probably the point— and she turned, saw him watching, and blew him a kiss.

Darrell had been in a few "gentlemen's clubs" before. The others were mostly like this—loud music, banquettes in red or some other dark velvet, and girls of every skin tone and hair color, always with "less" clothing. He noticed here the assembled breasts looked especially perky, nubile even. In fact, studying each girl working here, he realized what was different about this club. As he wandered around the crowded space, what struck him was that *all* the girls looked young. Really young, like the teenagers in his classes. Like Josie. Like the hooker outside, all these girls wore way too much makeup, big pouty lips, and long, thick eyelashes. He realized it might not be that easy to pick out Josie, if she was even here.

Stepping under one of the few overhead lights, he pulled the flyer out of a jeans pocket and unfolded it. Concentrating, he tried to memorize Josie's face, especially her eyes, so he he'd have a better chance of recognizing her. Between the dim lighting and the girls' elaborate makeup, he wasn't sure his luck would hold.

He kept moving, trying to look like he had a destination in mind, his eyes scanning each space, as he worked around the room. All the while he was careful not to touch anything. The kid in Cape May, Turk, seemed pretty certain Josie had been here. He'd given the impression that he and his buddies knew this place, came here plenty. Saw Josie a few times. But Darrell didn't see her. At least, he couldn't find any girl he thought was Josie. She could be anywhere now. Another club? New York City was beyond huge.

What was he doing here?

Darrell decided he better hit the bathroom. He shuddered to think of what was spilled on the tables and the couches. Seeing a sign for MEN in the corner, he headed that direction, reminding himself to wash his hands more than three times tonight. That was not OCD, simply plain sanitary caution.

He never made it to the bathroom.

Near the corner, he caught a glimpse of a face at a table he was passing and looked twice to be sure. It was Josie, sitting in a small booth with this one guy. Darrell's heart started racing. Without thinking and with no plan, he hustled over.

"Josie? Josie Dawson?" he said loud enough to be heard above the booming music.

The girl's head jerked up.

The guy with her turned toward Darrell and said, "Hey, big guy. Her name iz Lacey, not Jozie. She's with me. Go get your own girl."

Darrell stepped up to the booth, and the guy took a wild swing. Darrell ducked. The man caught only air and fell to the floor in a clumsy, drunken heap.

"I only want to talk with the young lady for a minute," Darrell said.

From the floor, the guy grunted, "Young lady?"

Josie's eyes grew large, and Darrell didn't want to startle her, so he placed a hand on the table. "I'm a friend of your brother. He and your mom are worried about you."

She stared at him "Josh? Who are you? I know Josh's friends, and I don't know you."

"Fair enough. I'm one of the coaches at the football camp Josh was in. I've gotten to know Josh pretty well. He's really concerned about you."

"I'm okay." Josie shot a look around and Darrell saw a ripple of fear cross her heavily made-up, azure eyes. "I'm fine. Tell them both I'm doing great in the Big Apple. Tell them to stop looking for me." She mustered up an obviously fake smile. "Only paying my dues to become a famous model."

Darrell heard what she said but saw something else in her face—desperation and dread. Terror, even.

She reached across and touched Darrell's arm. "I got to go. Tell Josh I love him and to leave it alone."

Then her gaze shifted, her eyes going wide. Darrell followed her glance and saw another large dude, who could've been a twin of the bruiser out front, but with a badly broken nose. He gave some signal with one large hand, which Josie got. Without another word, she turned and headed toward the back.

Unsure, Darrell hesitated a moment and, when he made to follow her, the enforcer with the deformed face blocked his way. Darrell tried to look around the guy, but he could see little beyond the wide body. Darrell took a step to the side but couldn't locate Josie. He turned, eyes scanning the club, but couldn't find her anywhere. She'd vanished.

Darrell hoped he hadn't gotten her in trouble. Or more trouble. Any fool could see she was terrified.

He held his position a bit longer, staring down the ugly bouncer. He felt he could hold his own, but he knew he was out of his element, definitely outsized and outnumbered. More important, he couldn't think of anything more he could do here. He'd learned what he came for. At least Josie was alive. He found his way back to the front door.

Once outside, Darrell stepped onto the sidewalk, letting the sounds of the city rush over him again. Sweat ran down from both armpits and he wondered if it was from the warmer temps outside or his tension. The bouncer Darrell saw when he entered hadn't moved and eyed him, the big man's gaze examining him as if he were some specimen at a zoo. Darrell took a few steps and glanced back over his shoulder. The guy was still watching him. Then it occurred to Darrell. No, not like a specimen. The bouncer was studying Darrell to memorize what he looked like.

Darrell gave a little wave as the bouncer took out a phone and, still staring at Darrell, started talking to someone.

Chapter Thirty-Five

Darrell made his way back to the garage, noting another hooker, this one a short, voluptuous blonde, had replaced the girl who propositioned him earlier. He hurried past and when he hit the crosswalk, a muted jangling inside his pocket surprised him. Then he remembered his new cellphone and, hustling across the street, stepped inside a doorway. He pulled it out. "Darrell."

"It's Cassie."

"Cassie? Hey."

"Can we meet? I-I, uh—I need to talk to you." She sounded scared.

The outside noises of the city crowded in on him and he put a finger in his other ear. "I'm in New York right now, getting ready to head back to Cape May," he yelled into the phone. "It'll take me more than two hours. Want to meet tomorrow morning?"

"No. Tonight," she snapped. "I don't think it can wait till tomorrow."

Darrell glanced at his watch, calculating when he'd make it into town. "Okay. Where do you want to meet?"

"Burdette Tomlin." When he hesitated, she added, "The hospital. On the Garden State Parkway, north of town."

"Are you okay?"

"Yeah. It's not me. It's my…uh, friend, Vince."

"Vince. Your buddy that has all the contacts?"

"Yeah." He heard her clear her throat. "Somebody ran him down, tried to kill him."

"What? What happened?"

"Don't know the whole story yet. Tell you when I see you."

Darrell checked his watch again. "That'll be after eleven, at least."

"Okay. See you then." She hung up.

He stared at the now silent phone. Stashing it in his pocket, he hurried the rest of the way, but stopped when he got to the entrance to the garage. He decided he might as well call Erin, while he knew he had a connection and before he got back on the road. Moving inside the doorway, he pulled out the phone and punched in her number. Huddled against the wall, he took a few minutes to fill her in on his night, ending up with his failure to resolve anything about Josie's situation.

She didn't chide him. Instead, she said, "You okay?" He heard the concern in the question, grateful for it.

"I'm all right." Then he told her about the surprise call from Cassie.

Through the phone speaker, Erin's voice came through tight. "An accident? How did Cassie sound?"

"Rattled. She asked me to meet her. At the hospital. She's keeping vigil for Vince and said she needed to talk to me *tonight*. Even though I won't get there till almost midnight."

Erin didn't answer at first and then said, "This must've really shook her up. I'm glad you can be there for her. And Darrell?"

"Ye-e-s?" He held his breath.

"We think we have your job back here. I don't want anything in Cape May to screw that up. Don't take too many chances."

"Got it."

"And be careful on the drive."

A few minutes later, he'd gotten his Corolla out of the garage and navigated his way through the congested city streets, once again glad for the printed Mapquest directions. Back on the highway, he released a big sigh and glanced over at Pogo.

"What do you say we find a rest area, so you can get out and stretch those little legs?"

The pug slurped once and, a few miles later, Darrell spotted the exit and pulled into the parking lot. After doing his business, he let Pogo do the same, cleaning up after him and giving him the run of the place. Darrell found where he packed the water dish, filled it up, and gave it to the pug. When the little dog finished drinking and went on to sniff and explore, Darrell's thoughts wandered back to their place in Wilshire. And to Erin, of course. He and Erin on the couch with Pogo at their feet.

He realized Erin had let him off easy about Josie and the gentlemen's club, and he appreciated it. But it also made him feel guilty. Had Erin been right? He certainly wasn't bringing Josh any good news. Was it possible he'd made things worse for Josie? The look he saw cross the teen's eyes made him worry. The frozen smile never left the teen's mouth, but those deep blue eyes told a different tale. And the twin bouncers conveyed true menace. He was pretty sure those behind the "Less is More" club were running a high-end brothel, with teen girls. He was convinced all the girls were underage.

But what could *he* do about it? He'd seen a few cops still in uniform at the club. He'd report what he learned to Officer Barnaby back in Cape May, but he was pretty sure what the cop would tell him.

"Sorry, that's out of our jurisdiction. It's in New York City, in another state even. We'll pass along your complaint to the NYPD." And then nothing would happen.

Darrell felt useless.

And what was he going to tell Josh and his mom?

Seeing Pogo had finished his roaming, he hustled the dog into the car and got back on the road. Inside the restroom area, he'd used the posted highway map to confirm his route back to Cape May and to the hospital. The directions he'd printed up last night took him on some back roads—so he'd avoid some tolls—and he wanted to double check. It turned out to be good advice as the traffic thinned on his route, making the traveling easier. The miles passed quickly and, as dusk surrendered to dark, he made his way around Philly and through a series of state highways. When NJ 347 gave way to NJ 47, he saw the first sign for the hospital and Cassie's words echoed in his head.

"Somebody ran him down. Almost killed him."

A prickle in the back of his head slithered down his neck. How could what happened to Vince have anything to do with him? Or the Haunted Bride? That was plain paranoia.

He'd gotten the impression from Cassie that Vince was into a lot of questionable things—drugs, probably a little theft, living on the edge. It could've been anything. Or maybe an accident.

The traffic light ahead of him turned red and he stopped. The crossroad was labelled NJ 646 and under the number he read another sign for Burdette Tomlin. Out of habit, he flipped on his blinker—even though he saw no other car on the deserted road—the light changed, and he turned left. The road ahead rolled on, an unlit, two-lane road bordered on both sides by long stands of towering trees, broken only by an occasional driveway. Closing in on midnight Sunday night with no moon and no streetlights, the road looked incredibly dark. As he drove on, getting closer to the shore, a heavy fog rolled in, blanketing the road and making Darrell strain to peer ahead. He lowered his speed. Worried about crossing deer or other wildlife emerging out of the fog, his gaze darted from side to side and then returned to the road ahead.

During one of these quick distractions, when he took his eyes off the road, it happened in a split second. When he yanked his attention back to the center, he spotted someone. Right in the middle of the asphalt. She seemed to emerge out of the swirling fog. His headlights lit up the figure, revealing a short woman in white. She must've stepped right onto the highway.

Someone was crossing the road, out here?

He had no time to react. Before he could even slide his foot to the brake, the car was on top of her. A half second before, she turned her head and stared at him. His headlights ignited two bright blue eyes, draped in a curl of fog. Then she turned back, and he was on her. Darrell braced for it. His body stiffened, braced for the sick certainty.

Only the thud never came.

He stared, stunned, as the car sped right *through* the figure. He slammed on the brakes. The Corolla fishtailed, halting sideways on the road, half in his lane and half on the shoulder. He threw it into park. Shooting a quick look up and down the highway, he saw the rest of the road was empty and dark.

He jumped out, Pogo only a second behind, and started to run back to...to whatever, and stopped. There, not fifty feet up the road, the Haunted Bride stood in shimmering luminescence, her figure brilliant in the blackness. She didn't say a word. He gaped at her, his body trembling, and the Pug gave a quick yelp. Blood now flowed down the right side of her face and oozed onto her dress, staining the white with rivulets of crimson. Her wedding dress. Then her image, bleeding there in the southbound lane, shimmered and disappeared.

Darrell froze, unable to drag his eyes from the place where she'd been. It was *her*. It had to be her. Why had she appeared? And why here? He shook his head, trying to make sense of what he saw, and when he peered back at the spot he saw...a small deer? He shook his head and squinted. The doe, a golden tan with a white patch on its rear, looked back at Darrell, its black eyes huge. Was that what he saw? He took a step toward the creature and it leaped. Its legs made two quick bounds and it disappeared into the woods, the patch of white the last to be swallowed by the trees. Darrell stood, immobilized in the center of the dark, empty road, trying to process what he'd seen.

The Haunted Bride? A hallucination? A deer?

A blast jerked him out of his trance. A dark pickup

whizzed by him in the other lane, heading north, horn still echoing off the rows of pines. He watched the truck barrel up the highway, its lights igniting the spreading fog, and then caught another pair of headlights streaming over the rise toward him. He hurried back to his car.

After he jumped through the still open door, right behind the quick Pug, he turned the Corolla back onto the road, accelerating and kicking up gravel. Back on the road, a mile later, it dawned on him.

He knew how the Haunted Bride, Amy Palmer, had been killed.

Chapter Thirty-Six

Cassie glanced up at the clock again. The longer she stayed here, at this hospital, the more this place creeped her out. While she paced, the two overhead lights that had been flickering finally gave up the ghost and quit.

Did she just think that? Ghost? All this might be that damn ghost's fault.

She kept up her pacing. Now, only murky shadows bathed the hallway, casting an ugly pall of gloom over the space. How long till Darrell got here? She needed to talk with him. No, she corrected herself, she needed to talk with *someone*. Had to sort this all out. She wanted someone else to convince her Vince's *accident* wasn't her fault. To tell her Vince wasn't lying in that hospital bed because of her.

Huh, some Miss Independent.

After the hospital shift changed, a little past eleven, she'd checked in with the nurse—a new one, who didn't know her—and went through the lie she'd rehearsed. Only then would the RN tell her anything.

"Oh, I'm Vince's younger sister, Cassie. Our parents are camping in the Maine wilderness. I'm trying to get a hold of them."

Good thing the woman hadn't asked for any ID. Still, Cassie hadn't learned much. Vince's official condition, guarded. They'd set his broken bones—one leg, his left arm, and a hip. He was in excellent hands. Still unconscious and couldn't have visitors. They would know more in the next few hours.

That news unleashed another torrent of tears. Her body shook, and streams erupted from her eyes, spread like tiny floods down her cheeks, dripping onto her collar. Shit, why was she crying? Maybe Vince *was* more than simply a...a friend. She yanked the stupid black tie all the way open and flung it to the floor.

She shot a glance back at the nurse. The sobbing worked for her lie, but still.

Cassie took three deep breaths and sniffled. She brushed both cheeks with the starched sleeves of her white work shirt, the fabric feeling like cardboard against her skin. God, she wished she was in her own clothes. One hand straying to each ear, she fingered the holes where she'd removed her studs for work.

She eyed the wall clock again. Thirty minutes. Darrell said he'd get here in about thirty minutes. She didn't know why she'd even reached out to him. Hell, who else was she going to call? Maybe, he could make some sense of the whole thing. She doubted it but didn't know what else to do.

Unable to stand still, Cassie drifted aimlessly through one hallway after another, the slap of her soles echoing behind her like some wary predator. Turning a corner, she almost ran into an orderly with an acned face edged by a scraggly growth of beard. Flattening herself against the wall, she stopped, her back against the cracked, peeling wallpaper. The med tech shot a furtive glance at her and muttered "sorry," but kept pushing a gurney around the bend, his steps slow and heavy. As the stretcher passed, she stood transfixed. It held a still body, now covered with a long white sheet. She gulped. He was heading to the…the morgue.

Would Vince be next?

One evening a few weeks back, as she cleared a table at Aleathea's, she remembered overhearing a couple discussing a friend who'd suffered a heart attack, was taken to the hospital, and died there an hour later. In angry whispers, the pair repeated the local nickname for this place. "Bur-death."

Oh, hell.

She moved on, increasing her pace, on her way to nowhere. Lowering her gaze, she now noticed the stained linoleum, with dark, jagged streaks running down the hallway. Worn, ugly flooring, faded, peeling wallpaper, collapsed and cracked chairs. The whole place carried the feeling of some dying beast. Bur-death was almost as depressing as the rural hospital they took her mom when…

No, she wasn't going there.

She raised her head and kept going until she found her way back to where she started, the ER waiting room.

The long room sat empty, looking desolate and deserted. She guessed the couple who'd rushed in a few minutes behind the ambulance had been ushered somewhere to be with their son. At least the kid had someone who cared about him. The lighting in the room had dimmed—strange for a "24-hour emergency department"—but what did she know? Darkness now blanketed the windows that fronted the room. Haunting shadows stretched from the darkened panes onto the worn furniture. Even the high, mounted television was black and silent.

As she stood at the entry, the eeriness she'd encountered before returned, this time much stronger. The hairs on her neck stood on end. The temperature in the room seem to drop, and Cassie shivered. She glanced around, certain she'd sensed something, sure someone was watching.

Standing there, eyes adjusting to the dimness of the room, Cassie noticed something. Something she'd missed. A few seconds ago, she would've sworn the waiting room was empty. Now, she wasn't alone. In the far right corner, next to one darkened window, sat a figure, head bent, peering at something on the end table. Cassie couldn't tell much about the person, since he—she?—was hunched over, facing away from her.

The prickle crawled down her back.

The figure sobbed quietly, and, Cassie, in spite of her anxiety and unease, felt herself drawn. When she crossed the half-lit space, she saw the person was dressed in white, though the clothes were stained black in places. Two more tentative steps brought Cassie close enough to make out a small woman, head bent toward the table, weeping and shoulders shaking.

Cassie edged closer—five feet away now.

In a slow tentative movement, the woman raised her head and turned. The right side of the figure's face was matted in blood, one eye misshapen and blackened.

Cassie recoiled and sucked in a breath. Stunned, she stared at the woman, realizing now the stains on the dress weren't black. They were *red*.

Blood.

She'd seen the woman before. On the beach and in the shadows by the Convention Hall. But not like this. Not close, like this. Intimate almost.

"You!" Cassie hissed. Her glance darted around the room, looking for help. Where was Darrell?

She saw no one else, of course. When she looked back at the chair, she expected the apparition to have vanished, but the figure still huddled there. Cassie squinted. The ghost looked less substantial now, as if the image were wavering.

Cassie's tired brain fought to recall the bride's name in the newspaper article and then it popped into her head. "Amy?"

The Haunted Bride nodded and her one clear, blue eye stared back. Cassie felt the eerie sensation spread all the way down her spine. She cringed. She wanted to scream at this…this…this ghost. Blame her for Vince's accident. Instead, she felt the young woman's own pain and anguish. Waves of desperation flowed off the shimmering figure.

Amy pointed to the table, then looked back up. Cassie never saw her move—the specter seemed frozen in place, hovering now—but Cassie *felt* Amy touch her right hand. An electric current zapped through it, much like when she touched Darrell's palm, only hotter and more searing. On reflex, Cassie's eyes went to her hand, and her left reached to rub it. The sensation faded in a second, almost as quickly as it came. Maybe, she imagined it.

When Cassie looked back up, the figure was gone, the room empty. She jerked her head around. Scanned the room and the corridor. No one. Cassie stood frozen in place for a bit, and then shook herself.

She was exhausted, maybe further wiped than she thought. Her gaze examined the space, the chair. Was she hallucinating? Then, Cassie remembered the streak of heat across her hand. It still tingled. She rubbed it again. That was one hell of a hallucination.

She closed the few feet to the chair where the ghost had appeared. Sliding into the same seat, she studied the entire area, her gaze scrutinizing the space, searching for...something, some evidence of the ghost. Something that would tell Cassie she wasn't going crazy. The same dog-eared magazines she'd seen earlier lay strewn across the table—*Parents*, *Good Housekeeping*, *Health*. She couldn't find anything out of the ordinary.

Then, off to the side, Cassie noticed a brightly colored magazine with a photo of a bride on the cover, looking like it had just come out of the protective plastic wrap. She picked it up. Another bolt of electricity shot up her arm. She dropped the magazine. It struck the table and lay flattened, a single sheet of paper sticking out from between the pages. Gingerly, Cassie pulled the paper free with two fingers, but found only a blank white page.

Jesus. Now, she *was* imagining things.

In disgust, she threw the paper back down and, as she did, it flipped over. Four words in large caps stared back at her.

BE CAREFUL

THEY KNOW

She shot a glance around the room, over her shoulder. Searched the dimness. She picked the paper up again and studied it, thinking maybe the words would shimmer and disappear like the image. But they stayed, black and stark.

Who knows?

Chapter Thirty-Seven

"Oh, there you are," a voice called from the doorway. Cassie jumped at the sound and dropped the sheet. Then she snatched the paper back.

"Hey, Darrell." A hard breath rushed out of her.

The sliding doors swished, and he entered the ER, striding over to where she sat. For a minute, he looked like he was going to hug her and then must've thought better of it. She collapsed back into the chair the ghost had occupied, and Darrell took the armchair across.

"Are you okay?" Darrell's eyes searched her face.

Why does he always ask that?

Darrell added, "You look as tired as I feel. How's Vince doing?"

Cassie told him what she knew about Vince's condition. What little she knew.

"Did you find out what happened? I mean in the accident?"

"A couple of his posse came by earlier," Cassie started, saw the look on Darrell's face, and explained, "that's what Vince calls the guys who hang out with him. One of them, Eggy, said he saw Vince get hit on the overpass. Well, almost saw it. He saw a white eighteen-wheeler speeding up the bridge. Driving away from where Vince lay bleeding on the road."

"I'm truly sorry, Cassie."

She looked down at the paper in her hand and tried

to keep her mind on Vince. "Eggy flagged down the first car that came by and got the driver to take Vince straight to the hospital."

"The truck never even stopped? That's horrible." He shook his head, frowning. "I don't know what to say."

Darrell looked really uncomfortable, but Cassie pushed anyway. She wanted to know if he'd been thinking the same thing she had. "Do you think this could've happened because…" She paused and looked across at him. "Could Vince have been run down because he was asking questions about that wedding? You know, the one with the Haunted Bride?"

"Why would you say that?" Darrell shook his head again. A little too hard, she thought. "Didn't you tell me Vince knew some shady characters? Maybe he got in trouble with one of the them."

"Not likely. Everybody loved Vince. If this is my fault—" she started and stopped, feeling the tears trying to squeeze out again. Damn. She didn't want to cry. Not in front of him.

Darrell reached to take her hand and stopped. He yanked his arm back and wouldn't meet her gaze. "Maybe," he mumbled. "I didn't know anything would happen. *You* couldn't have known."

"What is it about this ghost? How could asking a few questions about the wedding make Vince a target?"

"We don't know that," Darrell said.

"Maybe not. We know this girl, Amy—?"

"Amy Palmer."

"We know Amy disappeared the night of the wedding, but we don't even know if she's dead. Hell, maybe she took off somewhere. Or maybe she did commit suicide. Did walk right into the ocean." Cassie recalled seeing the ghost a few minutes ago and stood up. She took two paces and returned. "Okay, we know she probably died, but we've no idea how."

"I think now I know how she was killed."

"You do, how?"

"The Ghost Bride, Amy, showed me tonight." He leaned forward. "I think. And it wasn't from suicide. She didn't walk into the ocean." He recounted the details about the "collision" on NJ 646. "Remember we both noticed she was bloodied on the one side and didn't know why?"

"Yeah, her right side," Cassie said, picturing the image she saw a few minutes earlier.

Darrell started talking faster. More animated. "I think she was struck by a car. Same as I did tonight. Well, almost did. Well, I did, but it didn't hurt the ghost."

Cassie nodded. "That would explain the injuries. Say she was hit by a car. She was crossing the street and didn't even have time to turn, and the car hit her on the right side." She turned in the chair like the ghost had done earlier. And pointed to the right side of her face. "That would've messed up the whole side."

"Same as our ghost."

Cassie sat back, sensing a few things clicking, and noticed the paper in her hand. "Our ghost has been busy tonight." She showed Darrell the paper and explained about the ghost appearing here earlier.

Darrell studied the page. "Who's they?"

"Damned if I know." After Darrell laid the sheet on the table, she pointed to it. "Isn't much help. If the ghost is trying to warn us, why wouldn't she give us more?"

Darrell's gaze stayed on the message. "I don't know."

"The message is a little late for Vince."

"You're right," Darrell said and then, as if he thought of something important, he asked, "Remember that medium I told you about?"

"Natalia?"

"Yeah, Natalia. Last year I had the same problem with messages left by the Wilshire ghost. They were cryptic and I had trouble figuring out what they meant, so I asked her about it. Natalia said it takes tremendous psychic energy for a spirit to send a message from beyond, even a few words. She claimed it was all the ghost could manage."

"Oh good. I found you guys," called a voice from across the room, near the corridor.

Cassie and Darrell both jumped.

Erin called, "I've been all over looking for you."

Darrell got to his feet, sprinted across the space, and wrapped both arms around the visitor. "What are you doing here?"

Erin offered a tired smile. "After you called me tonight, I decided you might need my help. Since I have the next three days off, after you told me about Cassie's call, I ran home, threw a few things into a bag, and drove straight here. Though those back roads are not much fun in the dark."

Erin broke from Darrell and walked over to Cassie. "How are you holding up?"

Cassie had trouble getting any words out and Erin closed the gap, giving the younger girl a huge hug. In a quiet voice, Erin asked, "What's the latest on your friend?'

Cassie's lips trembled. "It doesn't look good," was all she managed before she collapsed into Erin and the tears came flooding again. Cassie sobbed and shook while Erin held her, talking quietly into her ear. After a few minutes, Cassie was able to stop and the two girls sat down, side by side, holding hands. Darrell took a chair opposite again.

He explained what Cassie had told him about the accident. Probably giving her time to breathe.

"Well, we're here for you," Erin said and patted Cassie's hand.

Darrell explained about his encounter with the ghost on the highway and Erin's eyes grew wide. Cassie started to tell Erin about the ghost appearing and the warning on the paper when another person came through a door. A young man, dressed in wrinkled blue scrubs with ugly splashes of red, walked over to them and glanced at a clipboard in his hand. "Miss Rawlins?"

The three of them exchanged glances and then it hit Cassie. That was Vince's last name. It's supposed to be her last name. His sister. She rose from the chair. "I'm Miss Rawlins," she said, shooting a quick glance at Darrell and Erin. She hoped they got the message.

The young man's face came up and he stared at Cassie. He had sad brown eyes. Cassie felt her stomach clinch. "I'm sorry, Miss Rawlins. Your brother had internal bleeding we didn't catch. His heart stopped. We did all we could…"

Cassie didn't hear the rest. She fell back into the chair. "Oh, God."

Chapter Thirty-Eight

Darrell was so tired, his eyelids hurt. All he wanted was to curl up somewhere and sleep. It'd been one hell of a day. But it was another two hours before they managed to leave the hospital.

Cassie had insisted on seeing the body, even though Erin had advised against it. "I owe it to him," Cassie said through more tears. "After...after everything."

While Darrell followed a pace behind, Erin kept her arm around the teen's shoulder. When the attendant drew back the sheet to reveal Vince's face—or rather what had been his face—Cassie covered her mouth and uttered a small shriek. Vince's features were no longer recognizable, the skin blackened, nose badly broken, eyes swollen shut, long slashes stitched together in some horrible Frankenstein parody.

"Oh, God." Cassie collapsed into Erin, burying her face and weeping again. Silent and solemn, the orderly brought the white sheet back up. Then he escorted the group into the hall, the metal doors swishing shut behind him.

He lingered beside the trio and said nothing for a minute or two, allowing Cassie to slow her sobbing. When Erin asked what they needed to do next, the attendant, keeping his eyes somewhat downcast, asked what she wanted to do with the body. At this, Cassie started crying again, so Erin pulled her in tight, patting the teen on the back.

Darrell interrupted in a harsh voice, "Can't this wait?"

Unsure, the orderly left to find a supervisor, while Darrell, Erin, and Cassie waited, all three drooping with exhaustion. Thirty minutes later, the white-clad aide returned to ask for a contact and told them someone would call tomorrow. Darrell gave him the number for his cellular and led the two girls outside.

As he exited the building, the night air struck him, warm and humid, and Darrell caught a scent of saltwater in the breeze. It just felt great to be out of the disinfected air of the hospital. He held the door and, when Cassie climbed into the front seat, Pogo jumped up on her lap.

"Oh, hi there," Cassie said, petting the pug's head.

"His name is Pogo. He's my bud," Darrell said, putting the car in gear. As the dog snuggled down onto the girl's lap, she ran her fingers over his short hairs.

A few minutes later, he made it back into town and through the nearly deserted streets of Cape May, Erin following in her yellow Jeep. Outside a shabby apartment complex, he dropped Cassie off at Troy's place, promising to meet back up tomorrow. Then, as arranged, he led the way to his boardinghouse, a few streets away. His room wasn't much, and the double bed would be tight, but right then he was glad he kept up the rental on the room for the week. At least, they had a place to sleep.

Both cars pulled up in front of the long, dark building and they grabbed their bags, Pogo springing off the seat. Watching the dog follow Erin up the three steps to the entrance, it dawned on him that he wasn't supposed to have any pets. Oh hell, it was late, and he was too drained to be concerned. Anyway, the pug was quiet, at least most of the time.

He glanced over at the window at the end of the long wooden porch, the one to his room, which he usually kept open at night. Even this close to the water, most nights were warm and humid, and the old place had no AC. He could always lower the pug out that window, if it came to that.

Once in the room, Darrell threw open the sash and they all settled into their places. Not even bothering to undress, they fell into bed, Erin in front, Darrell spooning behind her. Pogo huddled in a heap at his master's feet. In less than a minute, Darrell heard Erin's quiet snore and he relaxed and surrendered to blessed slumber.

"Ar-r-g-g!"

The sound of Pogo growling startled him awake. His unconsciousness tugged at him, pulling him back, not wanting to let go. Now? What was the matter with that dog? He dragged his eyes open and saw the pug. The dog was perched on the edge of the bed in the small space in front of Erin's middle. His legs stood rigid, head thrust forward, big black eyes focused on something on the floor.

"AR-R-R-G-G!"

"Pogo, hush. You're going to wake Erin." Even as he said that, Erin squirmed beside him. For only a moment, the dog shifted its gaze to Darrell and then glared right back at the floor. "It's probably a mouse or something," he whispered. He'd seen a small gray creature scurry across his floor once before. The perils of being on the first floor. With an open window.

"AR-R-R-G-G!"

Hoping not to disturb Erin, Darrell raised up on his elbow to peer over her. Trying to get his eyes to adjust, he peered around in the gloom, searching the area where Pogo was facing and thought he saw movement. What was that? His fatigued brain was too confused to make sense of what he was seeing. He heard a small rustling sound near the floor, then something that sounded like scratching against the wood. What was that sound? He couldn't even tell where it was coming from.

He fought to concentrate, trying to rouse his drowsy senses. He stared at the floor and saw some shape move in the darkness. No, not move. Slither. Shit, a snake. Then the scratching on wood came again. What was that?

He stared into the shadows. It was probably only a garter snake. He'd seen one or two in the shrubs around the building. They were harmless. Ate bugs and mice. He looked again. The muted light from the streetlamp streaming through the window turned everything black and white. But, even in the dim light, the markings on the snake looked off for a garter. Garter snakes wore thin bright stripes along their long body. This one had a stripe but with a series of black splotches on its back.

He sat bolt upright, bumping Erin hard.

"Hey, Darrell," she said, without opening her eyes. "Not tonight, I'm way too tired. Maybe in the morning."

Darrell gaped as the creature slid along the ground, covering the short distance from the window to the bed. "Hurry. Get behind me."

The urgency in his words must have nudged her. Her eyes struggled open, gazing at Darrell on his knees, over the top of her.

"Quick. Behind me. Now." He used a little gymnastics to get his legs over her, so that his body shielded hers, but he made no quick movements.

Erin complained, "What's the matter?" Still lying, she turned, and her eyes followed Darrell's gaze to the floor. "Is that what I think it is?"

In the dim light, the head of a snake rose up, its long body sliding along the floor. The evil tongue jutted in and out of a triangular head. Timber rattler! It made only the smallest sound, a slight rustling along the wooden floor. Then the scratching noise again, which now Darrell realized wasn't scratching. It was rattling. But they'd been so far asleep, they'd probably would never have even heard it, if it hadn't been for Pogo.

"AR-R-RG-G!" the pug growled again, as if challenging the intruder.

Darrell searched frantically for something to defend themselves, a weapon, anything. He had to protect Erin, at least. He wasn't sure what to do. The creature slithered farther into the small space. It raised the ugly head higher, the forked tongue flitting in and out. It was huge. Based on the part of the snake's body Darrell could make out, he guessed it to be almost five feet long.

Darrell saw the pillow, a flattened, thin thing, but better than nothing. He snatched it up and held it in front, working to keep it between the snake's head and them. As the snake slithered along the floor, Darrell had to crawl on his knees along the edge of the bed to keep the pillow between the snake and them.

Then the rattling intensified, the movement of the creature's tail a blur.

Out of the corner of his eye, Darrell caught something else, a long handle. The maid must've left an old broom in the corner next to his bed. Without taking his eyes off the snake, he still held the pillow in one hand and reached out slowly with his other arm, feeling for the smooth wood handle. He grasped it. Yanking it, he swept the straw end toward the rattlesnake and the creature slithered back a foot or so, away from the bed.

He jumped onto the floor. He used the broom to scoot the snake farther back, away from Erin and Pogo. Then he heard Pogo's paws scrabble off the bed onto the floor beside him. The dog growled again. Hearing the snarl, the creature turned, raised its head, the rattle shaking furiously. Its tongue flicked in and out, as if tasting the fear in the air.

Darrell's gaze went from the pug to the snake. It was going to strike. He dropped the broom, the handle smacking the wooden planks. The slam startled the snake, which withdrew a few inches and turned, ready to attack again. Then, in one swift motion, Darrell wrapped the pillow just below the snake's head and grabbed it. He stumbled a bit but managed to right himself and keep his arms out stiff. The creature writhed fiercely in his hands, its tail lashing at Darrell's legs.

Pogo growled louder now and Darrell called, "Stay back, boy."

He gripped the snake's head and held his arm stiff out in front of him. Darrell inched out the door. He'd read that he shouldn't make any quick moves. In the silence, his slow footfalls echoed in the wooden corridor. The pug stayed at his heels, panting. The hallway seemed impossibly long. Twice in the trip, the snake whipped its long body back and forth. It struck Darrell with such force, he yelped and almost dropped the creature twice. Chest heaving, he reached the front door, bounced the push bar open with his hip, and tiptoed down the steps. His eyes scanned the surroundings, desperate, looking for an option. He couldn't just let the snake go. He was standing there barefoot. He'd make a perfect target. Not to mention Pogo.

He spied what he needed chained to a post, a metal garbage can. With a metal lid. In a slow, easy move, he pulled the lid off and dropped the snake, pillow and all, inside the metal can. He slammed the lid down and held it in place. The snake thrashed inside, its body striking the metal sides again and again. Though muted through the metal, the rattle grew louder, angrier. Pogo scurried over to the can and growled again. Panting, Darrell drooped over like an old man, his adrenalin expended, his mind rushing to catch up.

How did the snake get in? Darrell glanced over at the open window of his room. Could it have crawled through there? Timber rattlers lived in the area. Kurt had told him the players had seen one out by the practice field. But here, away from the woods and close to the water?

The snake thrashed some more, trying to slither up the side, followed by another series of furious rattles. Taking the two steps back to the can, Darrell double checked that the lid was set tight. He couldn't leave it there. Someone could come by in the morning, lift the lid to toss a Styrofoam coffee cup and…damn. He had to tell someone, notify somebody. It was dark, and he glanced at his watch, which he'd been too tired to take off. 3:47. No one moved on the street, as far as he could see. He decided it would be safe enough, if he was quick. Then, as he headed back inside, he stopped. Who was he going to call?

He remembered Officer Barnaby and his attitude toward Josh. But would the cop be on duty now? In the middle of the night? He doubted it but didn't have a better idea. He climbed the steps, trying to decide what he was going to tell 911.

His body drained, his brain exhausted, he crossed the area to the stairs, the gravel rough against the bare soles of his feet. He only wanted to go back to sleep. When he landed on the top step, it hit him.

First, Vince starts asking questions for Darrell about the wedding and someone ran him over. Now, someone had just tried to kill him. And Erin.

Chapter Thirty-Nine

Buzzz. Buzzz. Buzzzz.

What the hell was that? Darrell wrenched his eyes open and dragged himself from the luxurious tendrils of sleep. The damn cellular phone. He yanked his legs around, jostling Erin in the process. Stumbling out of bed, he collapsed onto the floor. As he reached for the knapsack, he glanced at his watch. 9:15.

They'd only been asleep for three hours.

"Darrell Henshaw," he growled into the phone.

A crisp, authoritative voice of an older woman said, "This is Miriam Sinclair. I'm the office manager at the morgue, here at Burdette Tomlin. I was told to contact you concerning a deceased. A Mr. Vince Rawlings."

"Uh, ma'am, we've had a pretty rough night after a killer day. This isn't a good—"

"Mr. Henshaw, there is no time to dawdle. It's important we make arrangements for Mr. Rawlins. We don't have space to keep remains here at Burdette. Besides, it's not considerate to ignore the deceased."

Darrell struggled to get his brain to function, but it wouldn't cooperate. He tried to evade, to postpone, to reschedule, but Mrs. Sinclair would brook no delay. Seeing he had little choice, he finally agreed to meet her at eleven. He crawled back to bed and hugged Erin's smooth body to him, inhaling the herbal fragrance of her soft red hair, craving only a few more minutes of delightful slumber.

"How much time do we have?" Erin mumbled, without opening her eyes.

"Um, time for a quick one," he squeezed her, "or a shower."

She sniffed the arm that encircled her body. "I vote for a shower."

The episode with the snake and the officer responding—not Barnaby—as well as the animal control people took over two hours. Darrell felt like he hadn't slept at all. Erin, after an eight-hour shift on her feet and then time with Cassie, and finally with the snake episode, was probably suffering more. He would never have known it.

Sliding out of bed, she hauled up her tote and headed toward the shower. "First, we're going to pick up Cassie and then I'm going to eat the entire Uncle Bill's Special," she hollered back, already halfway down the hallway.

After they'd showered and dressed, they roused Cassie, and all three had enjoyed the Uncle Bill's Special, supplemented by strong coffee. By the time they finished, they all looked a little less fried. Fortified with the protein and carbs laced with the sweet scent of syrup, Darrell found his brain working once again.

After the server cleared their plates and refilled their coffees, Darrell led the uncomfortable discussion about taking care of Vince's body. Though he never voiced it yesterday, the weight of his possible guilt for Vince's death gnawed at him. He couldn't yet connect the dots, but he knew—like with Ruby last year, when he watched her bleed out on the pavement after a different hit and run—he knew, somehow, he bore responsibility for this young man's death. A man he'd not even known.

"Is this going to cost something?" Cassie asked, her voice sharp. "If we take care of him, are they expecting *me* to pay for some funeral costs?" She held the cup barely below her mouth, so it looked like the two studs in her upper lip rested on the rim. The wisp of smoke that rose from the hot java curled around the silver piercing adorning one nostril. Her black hair lay calmly on her head, no spikes erupting from her scalp today. Her amber eyes looked hollow, the whites streaked with red. Darrell guessed she'd not finished crying yet. Helpless and angry, he gripped the spoon tighter.

"Don't worry about that," Erin said, reaching her hand to the teen's across the table and exchanging a quick glance with Darrell.

"I'll see what I can do when we get there. You've been through enough," he said, even though inside he shuddered at the thought of his mounting credit card debt.

By the time they arrived at the morgue in the basement of Burdette Tomlin, they'd decided. Cassie said Vince would've wanted to be cremated and they all agreed. Cassie continued her charade as Vince's sister, and it took only a few minutes for her to complete the paperwork. A surprisingly comforting Mrs. Sinclair held the teen's hand, offered her tissues, and whispered quiet assurances. Darrell studied the two women, huddled together, looking like grandmother and granddaughter sharing grief. Where was the shrew who interrupted his sleep this morning?

Papers signed, the office manager made a call, spoke for a few minutes, and then turned to the group. "I've authorized the Jefferson Funeral Home to collect the remains, as they have their own facility onsite. They know your wish is to have Mr. Rawlins' body cremated immediately, and I've requested them to do so as quickly as possible. They said they'll send someone right over and you should be able to pick up the cremated remains in a few hours."

In less than thirty minutes—Mrs. Sinclair was certainly efficient—they found themselves standing outside the entrance of the Medical Center, the high sun steaming up the concrete walk.

"So that's it? That's what a whole life comes down to? A pile of ashes?" Cassie snorted, a hand shielding her eyes against the bright sunlight. "How can the sun be shining right now?"

Darrell had no idea how to respond.

As usual, Erin came through. She wrapped a protective arm around the younger girl's shuddering shoulders. "At least, you're not alone. Darrell and I are right here with you. We didn't know Vince, but you did, and that's enough for us. He was important to you, so he's important to us."

Cassie sniffled.

Darrell offered, "How about we drive you to Aleathea's? They probably know about Vince. I'm sure they'll want to see you."

Cassie glared at him. "Oh shit, I'm supposed to work today."

Erin said, "I'm sure they won't expect you to work, but let's head over there to make sure and take care of things."

Once inside the restaurant, Darrell was glad to see Cassie mobbed by the other servers, who came over, one after another, as they could pull away from their stations. There were nods, quiet words of condolences, gentle gestures, and a few uncomfortable hugs. Even Antonio dropped his imperious attitude and tried to comfort his server, his top lip and thin, black moustache quivering a bit.

Watching Cassie standing there, stunned, as the older workers patted her arm and tried to console her, Darrell realized how young she looked. Young and fragile. Struggling with Vince's death and now confronted with such unaccustomed kindness, her hard shell was cracking. Darrell could see that, in the tears running down her cheeks and the trembling in her bottom lip. Once that shield was gone, what would be left?

Was all this *his* fault?

After Cassie finished and Antonio assured her she could have off whatever time she needed, they headed over to Jefferson Funeral Home, the inside of the car bathed in anguished silence. He pulled into the empty, circular driveway, parking the car in the shade of a huge oak tree. He shut off the engine and sat there, his gaze searching Erin's face. She shrugged, so he turned to the back seat. "Cassie, would you like me to go in and take care of this?"

Sniffling, she gave him a nod, a tear clinging to the edge of one eyelash. Darrell climbed out and went through the front door. Sixty minutes later, he exited the same way, carrying a white cardboard container about the size of a cigar box. Opening the back car door, he lowered the box into Cassie's shuddering fingers. By the time he let go, his hands shook as well.

He slid into his seat and started up the Corolla, rolling it quietly around the rest of the driveway. He didn't know what else to say and Erin stayed quiet, the silence in the car by now almost strangling. Then, as he weaved his way through the busy streets toward the beach, Cassie's bitter words erupted from the back seat. "This is all that's left of him. He deserved better than this."

The silence broken, Erin spoke up. "Cassie, are you sure you want to do this now? Don't you want to reach out to Vince's friends? See if they want to be here?"

"Eggy and the guys stopped by Troy's place before you picked me up. They heard about Vince and came by to say how sorry they were." Cassie shook her head. "Eggy said they don't do death." She gave a dry chuckle. "If I wait, this will only get harder. Let's do this now."

Darrell found a parking space on the street about halfway down the beachfront. Along the shoreline, groups of swimmers, young and old, still splashed and screamed in the white crashing waves. But today, the brilliant sunshine, the frolicking beachgoers, the unchanged ebb and flow of the waves seemed grossly out of place, as if cruelly mocking Vince's death. Harsh reminders of the world's indifference.

Holding the sterile white box in both hands, Cassie led their way across the promenade and onto the fishing wharf. They passed two diehard anglers, who, this deep into the afternoon, still sat on their benches, with long, lazy rods extended into the water, the poles' only movement with the wash of the waves. The smell of decayed fish and bait floated into the air. Ignoring everything else, Cassie kept up her grim march, only stopping when she reached the very end of the gray wooden pier.

She looked into the bright sun and yelled into the wind that had picked up, "Well, Vince, you loved to be near the water. This way you'll always be catching the waves."

She opened the lid and shook the box out toward the ocean, the dirty gray ashes fluttering in the breeze. As she did, a gust of wind picked up the powdery remains and twirled them around, lifted them in a mini tornado, and carried them farther out onto the water.

Still staring out into the watery deep, Cassie choked, "The world won't be as much fun without you, Vince. You knew where to find the best weed and how to party." Her body shook as if she were suddenly cold in the bright sunshine and Erin stepped up, wrapping her in a hug. Cassie turned from the water and buried her head in Erin's chest, the box dangling from one hand.

Darrell's own chest heaved. He stared at the water, certain he could still see some white and gray ashes floating along the top of the whitecaps. Watching the fleeting evidence of death, he remembered how his effort to find justice for Hank back in Wilshire cost others their lives. The picture of those he'd lost flashed back. Darrell's anger flared, finding himself back in the same place again, this time with a friend of Cassie's. Without realizing it, he'd dragged her and her friends into this quagmire. Now, one was dead. Darrell feared Vince wasn't going to be the last victim.

Damn. He couldn't let this stand. Someone would have to answer for this.

Chapter Forty

Darrell, Erin, and Cassie stood alone at the end of the short pier, wrapped in the wind coming off the water. And their grief. No one spoke. Darrell searched the faces of the two young women, both with red eyes and wet cheeks. He swallowed hard and turned away, glancing up. A lone seagull flew lazy circles above them, its silhouette passing in front of the orange ball to the west, and then coasted onto a piling a few feet away.

The bird's descent onto the post seemed to awaken the world again, and the laughter and shouts of those playing in the waves down the shore echoed up. A car horn sounded, loud and angry, from Beach Avenue. Down the pier, a fisherman swore and yanked up his fishing pole, cranking hard. Once he had the line in, he brought the tackle box up onto the bench and slammed it down on the wood.

Erin said, "Am I the only one hungry or could anyone else eat?"

Thrilled with the break, Darrell said, "You're always hungry, but yeah, I could use something." He turned toward Cassie. "Where'd you like to go?"

Cassie didn't hesitate. "The Mad Batter. It was Vince's favorite."

On their way down the pier, Cassie held the empty white cardboard box, still clasped in both hands. Darrell watched as they exited the wharf and Cassie, eyeing the large trash cans, came to a decision and tossed the box inside one. Erin placed a protective arm around Cassie and whispered, "Come on."

Ten minutes later, they were seated at the end of a long table in the back room of the restaurant, which was really a screened-in porch. Darrell had asked, and when the manager saw Cassie, she came over and patted her arm, saying she'd heard about Vince. She escorted them to the table and then scurried off to get their drinks. Darrell desperately wanted a Dogfish Head beer but didn't see it on the menu. Instead, he settled for a soda like Erin and Cassie, deciding he might need his head clear.

The waitress came and, on Cassie's recommendation, they all ordered the crab cake sandwich. "Vince's favorite," she said with a catch in her voice, "when he had money to buy it."

After the server left, a group of four youths—Darrell would've guessed late teens and early twenties—came over to their table and took the chairs next to Cassie. He started to object when Cassie intervened.

"Darrell and Erin, these are a few friends of Vince." She indicated the visitors. "This is Eggy, who found him."

Across the table, a short, round-bellied guy with a broad face gave a small wave. With his flat nose, stretched green eyes, and ears that looked like two parallel protrusions, he reminded Darrell of some cartoon image of Humpty Dumpty.

"And that's Eggy's girl, Myra."

The girl, clearly still a teen, had the opposite

physique from her beau, a willowy thin, waif-like figure. Beneath dirty blonde hair, she offered a nod, with sad gray eyes that seemed too wide for her narrow head.

Cassie pointed to her left. "And these two are Slick and Maxine."

The guy looked like a kid's idea of a Jersey "made man," tall with slicked back, black hair and gaudy rings on three fingers. The girl, who was older—Darrell thought maybe closer to thirty—was all gloss and curly brown hair. Her green eyes looked wet, the black mascara running in streaks.

Without smiling, the girl muttered, "I go by Max. Just Max."

Cassie said, "These are the guys Vince called his posse."

Erin said, "Nice to meet you. Sorry it's under these circumstances."

The waitress returned and took orders from the four newcomers, who only asked for drinks. When the server left, an uncomfortable silence settled around the table, everyone studying their placemats. Darrell's silverware wasn't aligned right, the fork slightly crooked and not parallel to the knife and spoon. Glancing from one newcomer to the other, he fought a compulsion to correct the arrangement. Creased brows, red rimmed eyes, downturned mouths—they all wore the heavy mantle of grief. Instead, he searched for something to say, some way to let them know how sorry he was. That he realized how senseless Vince's death was.

And maybe his fault.

The kid called Eggy said in a squeaky voice, "I'm

sorry we couldn't come to say goodbye to Vince. We just couldn't. We wanted to remember him the way he was."

Cassie said, "I get it. I really didn't want to be there either."

Then Eggy asked, "Have you heard anything about the guy who ran over Vince?"

Cassie squirmed in her seat, her face flushing red. "An officer came to the hospital and took my statement, but he said without a license plate or any identifying marks, they didn't have much to go on. Unless somebody comes forward." She stared back at Eggy. "Did you talk to them?"

Eggy whined, "Shit, no. You know how I feel about cops. Besides you told them everything and they're not going to do anything."

Standing her fork up, Max asked, "If it wasn't a damn accident, do we have any idea why anyone would do that to Vince?"

Her question brought another strangled silence around the table and Cassie kept her head down. Darrell sighed and said, "We don't know for sure, but we're afraid it might have to do with him asking questions about the Armstrong wedding."

A confused look on his face, Slick said, "You mean the one where the bride disappeared?"

Darrell glanced at Cassie, who nodded.

Slick turned to Cassie. "Hell, we all know about that. Vince talked to us about it."

Eggy asked, "Have you showed them that sheet Vince worked on? The one with the wedding guests?"

Cassie slid the worn backpack off her chair and took out the paper, sliding it between Darrell and Erin.

Max and Slick got up and stood behind to peer over their shoulders.

Slick said, "Yeah, that's what I was talking about. We all worked on it together." He leaned over and pointed to the second name on the list. "Jeremy Tucker, the best man, he's quite a keeper." He leaned closer to read the scribbled words. "Yeah, he used to go with Amy. Before she dumped him and hooked up with Travis. He was none too happy about it."

Darrell turned and asked Slick behind him, "Bars? You know what Vince meant by that?"

Slick said, "Oh, yeah, I remember. This guy, Jeremy. owned this string of bars up the Delaware shore, a bunch of dives and biker joints. Rough joints, if you get my drift."

Erin read the next name aloud. "Jennifer Thomas. Where have I heard that name before?"

"That's the girl I told you about," Darrell said and then, seeing the question in her eyes, added, "The one on the beach who was wearing almost nothing and hanging all over that guy. After I saw her flirting with Travis the day before."

Eggy said, "That's because she used to be Travis's girl through high school and college. Until he met Amy and dumped her. She did *not* take it well."

Erin asked, "And she was invited to the wedding?"

Eggy said, "The Thomases and the Armstrongs go back a long way. Fuckin' major family bonds."

Erin said, "We've got plenty here for a lovers' triangle. Or maybe two."

"Damn yeah," Eggy said. "Vince thought you guys might want to do a little more digging." He glanced at Cassie and Darrell. "He had me get you hired on as temps for Houston's Catering."

"Temps? What, as waiters?" Darrell asked.

Eggy said, "Yeah. Cassie's the only one with a steady gig. At Aleathea's. The rest of us pick up what we can. Shit, we don't want to work too much. Anyway, we're all working for Houston's Wednesday." There were nods around the table. "It's a pretty damn good gig. Deep pockets. And if we get lucky, some really nice tips."

"Why us?" Darrell asked, though he realized, with the bills he'd piled up lately, he could use the extra money.

Eggy settled his bulk back into his chair. "Oh, sorry, I left a few details out. Wednesday night is this fuckin' huge bash the Armstrongs throw every year for their clients and friends. It's this crazy ass party on Poverty Beach."

"Poverty Beach?" Darrell said.

"Yeah, Poverty Beach, at the end of Beach Avenue. You been there?" Eggy asked.

Darrell shook his head, turning to look at Cassie and Erin. "That's the same beach where they had the wedding reception. The one for Travis and Amy. The one we were talking about."

Eggy looked from Darrell to the others, probably figuring he was missing something, but went on. "Any who, the waitress Vince talked to will be there, Shelley. She's a regular, and Vince thought you might want to talk to her."

"What waitress?"

Cassie started, "That's my fault. I was all set to tell you yesterday when…" Cassie put down her drink. "Vince told me this waitress, Shelley Dominic,

242

overheard part of the argument between Travis and the bride—?"

"Amy," Darrell supplied.

Cassie said, "Yeah, Amy. She said Travis and Amy had this big fight, something about the business, and then she stormed out."

Erin leaned forward. "They were arguing about Armstrong Trucking? On their wedding night. I wonder why."

Cassie said, "That's all Vince told me, but he thought you'd like talk to her."

Eggy added, "Oh and that bartender, Andy Hauck, he's supposed to be working also."

"Bartender?" Darrell asked.

Cassie shot a look at Eggy, who shrank in his chair. "I'm sorry. Like I said, I was planning to tell you all this yesterday." She took another gulp of her soda. "Anyway, this bartender claims he saw the bride, Amy, leaving the reception walking down the road. Down Beach Avenue."

"Not into the water?" Erin asked.

"No, he told Vince she was headed for the road, alone," Cassie added.

Cassie's eyes met Darrell's, and he thought he could read the same revelation strike her. He got a flash of the image of his car striking the Haunted Bride last night. Was that only last night? Amy was walking away from the party. On Beach Avenue. A few pieces clicked into place. He needed to talk to this guy.

"When are you scheduled to work?" Darrell asked Erin, hoping, praying she could stay with him. It was just better when she was beside him.

"Right now, I work second shift Thursday. But I

might get that covered. I'll see." Erin placed her hand on Darrell's.

Cassie's eyes looked determined. "And I'll tell Antonio I need a few more days. He said I could take as much time as I want."

Eggy said, "I'll talk to my guy at Houston's and get badges for all three of you."

A waitress came to deliver their orders, the crab cake sandwiches and fries smelling delicious. As they dug in, he glanced around the table and realized they were all involved. They all knew things about the wedding and maybe had asked the wrong questions. They could all be in danger. Unless he could get to the bottom of this. And fast.

Chapter Forty-One

Sitting together on the edge of his cramped double bed on Tuesday morning, Darrell reviewed with Erin what they needed to do next. "I'm not looking forward to it, but I have to tell Josh what I learned in New York."

"Going to be a difficult conversation." Erin took his hand. "I can be there with you."

"I'd appreciate it." It felt great to have her with him, but Darrell hoped her presence wouldn't make a tough situation even harder. Josh was bound to be embarrassed. And angry. "First, I need to tell Barnaby about finding Josie and the club."

"You think there's anything he can do? I mean about Josie."

"I doubt it, but I've gotta try," Darrell said. "Then, we'll stop and talk with Josh. After that, if we have time, I'd like to pay a visit to Frank Armstrong, the bride's father, and Coco Patterson, the maid of honor. See if they can shed any new light on Amy's death."

"They in town? Here in Cape May?"

"No." He pulled out his clipboard and checked the list he'd gotten from Cassie. "Vince made a note they're from someplace called—" He stopped and checked Vince's writing and then finished. "—Medford Lakes. Last night I asked the manager at the Mad Batter and he said it's about a ninety-minute drive."

"Doable," Erin said.

He stuffed the clipboard back into the bag, leaned across, and kissed her. "I'm thrilled to have you here. Thanks for making the trip. It's been really hard being apart these last few weeks."

"No picnic for me either." She held Darrell's face in both hands. "Having to put up with Al's terrible puns without you. I mean, torture."

Darrell chuckled, realizing one more thing he liked about Erin. She could make him laugh, even during tough times. Sunday night they were attacked by a poisonous snake, yesterday they had to spread some poor kid's ashes, and this morning she was cracking jokes. One amazing woman. He kissed her again.

They headed out and he held the door for her and Pogo, then locked it. He'd already made sure the window was bolted shut. He didn't want any more uninvited visitors.

As they crossed to his car, he asked, "How about we skip breakfast and pick up a couple of bagels this morning, so we can track down Barnaby?"

"Okay, but if we're going to see Officer Barnaby, shouldn't we pick up doughnuts instead?"

"Fun-ny." Darrell grinned, holding open her door as she slid in.

Next to the car, Pogo stared at the door, legs straight. He gave a low growl.

"What's with you, boy?" Darrell stared at the Pug and, opening the back door, lifted him onto the seat. He hustled around the car and got in. Throwing the car in reverse, he turned to check behind when Erin placed a hand on his arm.

"Hey, look at this."

Something in her voice froze him. He put the car in park again and glanced across. In her hand, she held one of the Josie flyers. She passed it to him.

Confused, he took it. "What about it?"

She pointed a finger. "Turn it over."

He did and felt a streak of heat race up his hand and arm. He let go, the paper fluttering to the seat, landing upside down. Stunned, he stared at the words in dark black capitals.

IF YOU HELP ME

YOU RESCUE HER

"Where...where'd you find this?" His gaze darted from the paper to Erin.

"Right here. On the seat." Erin seemed as confused as he was. "You unlocked the car to let me in, and when I got ready to slide in, I noticed the flyer on the seat and picked it up. When I went to buckle my belt, I dropped it and it flipped."

"If you help me, you rescue her," Darrell repeated, his voice dreamlike.

"The Haunted Bride, Amy. She's telling us her death has something to do with Josie's—" She stopped as if she didn't know how to name it. "—Josie's situation."

Darrell couldn't tear his eyes away from the paper. "But Amy's death was five years ago. And Josie disappeared, what, two weeks ago? How could they be connected?"

"I don't know, but Amy does." She pointed to the flyer. "I think we better go see Barnaby now."

He handed it back. "Agreed. We can't say anything about this, but yeah."

She retrieved the backpack from the rear and

stuffed the flyer inside. He put the car in gear, skipped the bagel store, and drove the five blocks to the police station. The morning was still cool, and the breeze through the Corolla's open windows carried the pleasant trace of saltwater. Paws on the window frame, Pogo kept his head in the breeze, his tongue panting. On Washington, as they neared the station, the perfect parking spot appeared and Darrell grabbed it, turning onto Franklin and pulling the car in. He didn't even have to parallel park. It was a sign.

Erin got out first and, after he cracked the windows, he followed, grabbing the backpack and petting the pug. "Okay, boy, you oughta be fine. See, I even found a cool, shaded spot for you to hang out. We won't be long."

After they checked with Sergeant Harris at the front desk—the same cop who'd given Darrell the skimpy missing person report on Josie—they found their luck was holding. Barnaby was here. The brusque sergeant led them into an interrogation room, where Erin sat in one of the rickety chairs and Darrell stood and paced. He glanced around at the grimy room, noticing the long mirror along one wall. One-way mirror, he corrected himself. A few minutes later, Barnaby joined them.

"Sorry for the accommodations." The officer waved a hand in the air. "The captain's using the conference room. Rank has its privileges." Arms crossed in front, he leaned back against the mirror. "I've only got a few minutes. Sergeant Harris said you had some information about a missing persons case. Is this about Josie Dawson?"

"Yeah." Darrell noticed this time the cop wasn't

wearing his sunglasses. Maybe he could get a read from the man's hard blue eyes. Darrell moved beside Erin and then detailed what he'd discovered at the club in New York. About finding Josie. About her and the rest of the girls. And what he suspected. He spoke quickly, the words spinning out like an unraveling reel of film.

While Darrell talked, the cop said nothing, only nodding from time to time. When he did respond, his answer was almost verbatim what Darrell had predicted. Barnaby would file a report and attach it to Josie's missing person's case but doubted much would come of it. Too much "jurisdictional squabbling," he said. "Besides, from what you're telling me, it doesn't look like Josie was being held against her will."

"No, but she's underage and I could tell, from the look in her eyes—"

"No offense, but your gut doesn't count." The officer ran one hand over his short blond hair. "I'm sorry about Josie and I'll pass on the info to NYPD, but I'm not sure how much more I can do from here. Now, I'm due out on the streets." He straightened up.

Erin spoke up for the first time. "So there's nothing we can do to help Josie? We're out of options?"

For a moment, Barnaby looked taken aback by her question and glanced at Darrell.

Darrell blurted, "Officer Barnaby, this is Erin Caveny, my girlfriend."

The cop turned to face her, and Darrell thought he'd give her the brush off, but Erin forestalled that. She buried the smallest smile in the earnest look she gave the cop. Barnaby shifted his position. "I didn't say that. Where did you say this club was?"

Darrell said, "Greenwich Village. In New York."

"Hmm. It's a long shot, but you said you're a researcher, right?"

"Yeah, why?" Darrell felt his heart race.

"It's a long shot. Sometimes, businesses in New York like to incorporate in New Jersey. We got less red tape in our state. If they did, we could follow up, have a little more clout. Anyway, why don't you go see Hilda over in county records? If there's a connection between that club and New Jersey, maybe there'll be something on file. Maybe an LLC or something. It's not much, but it's something." He pulled his sunglasses out of a side pocket and put them on, signaling he was finished. "Tell her I sent you."

Barnaby looked uncertain, as if he couldn't decide to say something or not. Darrell watched him and waited him out. After a bit, the cop said, "I've got a buddy from high school, played ball with him, Eddie Michael. He's NYPD now. Last I heard, he was stationed at Precinct 6—that's the precinct that patrols the area of New York you're talking about. I'll give him a call. See if he knows anything."

Thrilled, Darrell started to respond, but Barnaby cut him off. "Don't get your hopes up. It's a big place, NYC. Not like here."

"Still, thanks." Darrell stuck out his hand and they shook.

Chapter Forty-Two

Darrell and Erin headed out the front door and went to check on Pogo. They found him snuggled down on the floor of the backseat, slumbering in the shade. Not wanting to disturb him, they walked around the corner to the Cape May County records building.

Then their luck faltered. They spent the next hour at the records building, first waiting for Hilda, then explaining what they were looking for. When she appeared, Hilda Wainwright turned out to be a short, sixty-something woman with a full head of white hair, shining blue-gray eyes, and a welcoming smile. Her smile immediately reminded Darrell of Harriet Sinclair, the Wilshire High School secretary who'd helped him. He hoped that was a good omen. When they mentioned Officer Barnaby had sent them, Hilda's features lit up, both small cheeks dimpling.

"You know, I used to babysit little Stewart. When he was a wee one." She chuckled. "He was a holy terror. And now, he's one of Cape May's finest. Never can tell."

Darrell and Erin glanced at each other and he mouthed, "Stewart?" He explained about Josie going missing and how he'd been trying to help one of the football players search for her.

"I heard about Josie Dawson. My heart goes out to Lorain." Hilda shook her head sadly.

Then, he filled her in on the rumor he'd heard about some guy propositioning Josie with a fake modeling agency job. Finally, he told her how he learned of the club and discovered Josie there.

"Oh, that poor child." Hilda's hand went to her mouth, covering a pronounced O. "Does Lorain know yet?"

Erin piped up, "We're headed there next. We were hoping we might find something here that could help."

Hilda straightened up, her five-foot-four frame looking taller. "What can I do?"

Darrell shared the idea Barnaby had given them.

"Stewart always was a smart kid." She pointed to the chairs where Darrell and Erin had spent the first half hour waiting. "You two have a seat and let me go see what I can find. It may take a little time, so make yourselves comfortable."

They tried.

Erin was able to sit most of the time, but Darrell was up, pacing back and forth, then making a trip to the bathroom—never a bad idea to wash his hands when he was in a public building, though he was careful not to touch any fixtures. Then he hit the vending machine for a day old jelly roll, which he shared with Erin.

Bored, Erin picked up a copy of a newspaper someone had left and sat reading it, while Darrell returned to his pacing. When he was making his third pass, she stopped him. Holding up the paper, she asked, "Remember, you told me Josie seemed to get really scared when you said Josh was worried about her and that's why you were looking for her?"

"Yeah. She freaked and told me to tell him to stop looking for her."

"Ever since you told me that, it's been bothering me. Why would she be scared because her brother was worried about her?"

"Well, those bouncers were definitely scary," Darrell said.

"Yeah, but I think it was more than that." She pointed to an article on the front page. "I was just reading the interview about that girl they rescued in Tennessee, I think. Kelly something." She looked down at the paper. "Yeah, it was outside Knoxville."

Darrell glanced toward the office where Hilda had disappeared. "Okay, but what's that got to do with Josie?"

"Well, this guy held her captive for almost nine months and according to the article, when they asked her why she didn't escape earlier, she said if she tried to leave, he told her he'd hunt down and kill her younger brother."

"So you think—"

"Maybe the reason Josie never called or contacted her mom and told Josh not to come looking for her, was because the people who have her threatened her family."

"That would explain a lot," Darrell said, thinking. "It would also explain the look of terror I saw in her eyes when I mentioned her brother. Can I see the article?"

Erin handed him the newspaper. He was halfway through the passage when Hilda emerged with a frown. "What did you say the name of the business was?"

"Less is More," Darrell and Erin answered at the same time, coming out of their chairs and standing on the other side of the counter.

Hilda shook her head. "I couldn't find any business with that title registered in the New Jersey records. I even tried a couple variations of the name. No luck. I'm sorry."

Darrell was too stunned to speak. After getting the message from the Haunted Bride this morning and the help from Barnaby, he felt certain they were on the right track.

Erin interrupted his thoughts. "Well, we appreciate your help, Mrs. Wainwright."

The older woman reached a blue-veined hand across the counter and placed it on Erin's arm. "It's Hilda. And I'm sorry I couldn't be of more help."

Darrell murmured, "Thanks," and turned to go. Disgusted, he thought they better go get something to eat. Half of that jelly roll only went so far.

"I wonder," Hilda mumbled aloud, and something in her voice stopped him. He turned back. She had a finger on her lips and looked up at the ceiling. "It might not be any help, but then again, it might. After all, Stewart sent you."

She came to a decision. "You know, New York City recently put their building records online. We're planning on doing that next year, I think. Anyway, they have their records available online." She shook a finger at Darrell. "Now these records are not available to the general public yet. They say that's coming, but records offices like ours can access them. Kinda like a trial basis."

She went over and flipped open the counter divider, motioning them through. "Come on. You know, I have to take some records over to the municipal court." She glanced at both of them and grinned, as she led them to her workstation. "I *might* have left my computer on, and maybe, I was checking out some files in the New York business records database. I mean, I'm old and sometimes I forget things."

She entered her password, hit a few keys, and opened a file. Then she squeezed Erin's arm and left, whispering, "I'd say, this trip will probably take me about an hour."

Erin mouthed, "Thank you."

Losing no time, Darrell slid into the chair. He caught the faint scent of some floral perfume and wintergreen. Breath mint, he guessed. He started striking keys, tentative at first, then faster. Erin hovered over his shoulder, studying the small gray screen punctuated with tiny green letters. He had trouble finding his way through the program, so Erin grabbed the instruction manual off the metal shelf above the monitor. Flipping through the pages, it took them a bit to find the section on how the search function worked. A few times, Erin had read from the manual, helping him navigate the DOS commands.

Darrell checked his watch. Hilda had been gone twenty minutes already and they hadn't found anything helpful. Nervous, he glanced around the office, certain that any moment they would be discovered and thrown out. A bead of sweat rolled down from his hair line. Seeing no one around—yet—he returned his attention to the ancient workstation. With Erin's help, he found the directory of building files. It took three wrong steps, but he eventually stumbled upon the permit for "Less Is More," issued to an LLC entitled "Great Horizons." Peering over his shoulder, Erin moved her face closer to the small screen to read the recorded officers of the

LLC in a quiet voice. Neither recognized a single name on the Board of Directors.

"I don't think that helps us, but we should take down those names." Erin pointed to the screen.

"First, I have one more idea. Let's see if there are any other companies tied to this Great Horizons LLC," Darrell said, his fingers back on the keyboard. Now that they were in the right folder, the going was easier. When he put "Great Horizons" in the search bar, a list of some twenty entities scrolled down the screen. After checking some dates, he figured out the list was in reverse chronological order, the most recent business ventures first. "Less is More" was the fourth item on the list, preceded by what Darrell guessed from the names were other gentlemen's clubs. He pointed to three quarters of the way down the list and Erin let out a quiet squeal.

Darrell whispered, "Armstrong Trucking." He glanced around and spotted an old dot-matrix printer in the corner of the office. Frantic, he searched the screen for a print command and came up empty. "Let me see the manual again."

Erin started to hand it over and stopped. 'I've got a better idea. Get up a sec."

Darrell rose and Erin slid into the chair. "I had to use a program at the hospital a little like this," she explained as she hit keys. "If I remember, the print function is hidden in here." She finished typing and shot a glance at the old printer. For a few agonizing seconds, nothing happened. Darrell and Erin both held their breath. Then the old machine started up, shooting the print head across the paper one line at a time. They stood next to the old printer, watching. It took an eternity to print the three pages. When it finished, Darrell reached forward and tore the pages off at the perforation.

One last time, Darrell checked the office, and seeing no one, they headed down the hall, tentative at first, glancing back over their shoulders. When they went through the office door into the hallway, they took off in a full run, their footfalls echoing off the marble floor.

Chapter Forty-Three

"Thanks, Pogo, you did great." Darrell tossed the pug a treat from his bag, as he and Erin got back into the car.

During their time inside, the morning had warmed a bit, the New Jersey sun rising over the city, but since he stowed the car in the shade, the interior was still cool. Pogo had been fine, dozing. Leaving the windows down, Darrell pulled out of the space and turned back onto Washington Street. Stopped at a traffic light, he watched as waves of tourists crossed in front of his car, talking and laughing, heading to their destinations.

He turned onto Jackson and, right before he got to the intersection, the signal changed and he had to hit his brakes. He glanced to his left, noticing the Mini Golf he'd seen before on the corner. He'd even considered taking Erin there for a little quiet diversion. On a hole near the road, he watched a young couple, about the same age as Erin and him. The guy leaned over the girl, guiding her arms as she putted, and she beamed up at him. The guy stole a quick kiss and the girl laughed. Darrell pined for what they had—a normal, carefree holiday in beautiful Cape May, playing a simple game right at the beach. No ghosts. No murders. No missing teens.

He was about to say as much to Erin, when she disrupted his reverie. "Armstrong Trucking and this

Less is More club are owned by the same company." Nose still stuck in the printed pages from the records office, her words conveyed her disbelief. "But Armstrong Trucking is one of the largest shipping and transportation companies on the East Coast. I mean, they own their own fleet of trucks and even their own shipping line." Darrell glanced over and noticed she kept her eyes on the papers. "Why would they want to get in bed with a sleazy place like Less is More? And you said you thought some of the other companies listed were probably *gentlemen's clubs*? Doesn't that seem off to you?"

"I was only guessing from their names, but yeah, I think they're gentlemen's clubs." The light changed and Darrell turned his attention back to the road, working his way around the slow traffic and making the turns to get them out of town and onto the Parkway.

But, when he thought about it, what they had in those pages wasn't that much. Admittedly, he was no expert on business. What he knew was history, and football, and kids. But he'd heard a lot of LLC's had very diverse interests. It wasn't that unusual the same LLC would have a reputable, well-established transportation company like Armstrong Trucking and a not-so-reputable gentlemen's club in their portfolio.

Still, it was a hell of a coincidence. And he found, where a ghost led him, there was no such thing as a coincidence.

"You know where you're going, or do you need my help navigating?" Erin looked up from the copies, glancing at the traffic.

"No, I'm fine. I took Josh home a couple of times after football camp. I know where we're headed." Up ahead, he spied their favorite fast food place. "How about we pick up a couple of burgers?"

"As long as we get fries and sodas with them."

Darrell made the detour and, five minutes later, they had burgers on their laps and he was trying to drive and not get sauce all over his shirt.

"Are you going to tell Josh about this?" Taking a large bite, Erin pointed to the printed pages, now on the floor.

One hand holding a fry, he shook his head. "No. not yet. It's going to be hard enough just learning about Josie being at that club."

The pug jumped up on the back seat. Darrell tossed him the fry. "I'm hoping you can help out with Josh."

"What'd you have in mind?" Erin asked.

"I thought I'd ask Josh if Pogo here could hang out with him, while we go talk to Frank Palmer and the maid of honor." He accelerated into the left lane. "We're going to be gone a good part of the day and I didn't want Pogo stuck inside the car the whole time." He shot a quick glance over at Erin before moving around a car and settling back in the slower lane. "I've been thinking about it and I thought it might be good. Pogo can get Josh's mind off his sister. At least, for a while."

"Not a bad idea. Have I ever told you you're pretty smart? For a coach anyway."

He raised his eyebrows at her and hit the blinker. Three quick turns took them into the driveway of a small bungalow with blue-gray siding that was so washed out, it looked almost bleached. The structure struggled to hold up a sagging charcoal roof with several missing shingles. Surrounding the house, a good-sized yard spread out—though most of it had gone to dirt—with a rutted, gravel driveway running along the side. Erin climbed out and Darrell followed, freeing the pug, who shot to a nearby stand of trees. The dog lifted one leg and did his business.

The front door banged open and Josh tromped down the steps. "Hey, Coach Henshaw."

"Hey, Josh." Darrell grabbed the teen and wrapped him in a bear hug. When he released him, he turned to Erin. "I'd like you to meet my girl, Erin Caveny."

She took a step forward, extending a hand and a small version of her incredible smile. At first, Josh looked uncertain what to do, then shook her hand limply. The boy shoved both hands in his pockets and stared at the ground. "Have any news for me? About Josie?" His voice caught in his throat, the words swollen with anticipation *and* fear.

So, standing there in the dusty yard, Darrell told Josh about finding Josie at the club, like Marcus and his brother had claimed. Though he left out most of the salient details.

"Was this club…I mean, was she doing…?" Josh couldn't finish. Then suddenly, his head jerked up. "Why didn't you simply grab her and bring her back?"

Darrell stepped forward and placed a hand on the boy's arm. "I tried. I talked with her, but before I could say too much, this goon came up and took her in the back."

The kid dropped his gaze again.

"I'm not sure what all she was doing there," Darrell said, knowing the words were a lie, as soon as they left his mouth. A good lie. Josh was hurting enough. "She said she's doing okay, paying her dues.

261

And she told me to tell you she loves you. And not to worry about her."

Josh teared up and brought both fists to his eyes. "Maybe you could take me up there and I could talk to her. And maybe talk her into coming back."

Darrell recalled the fear in Josie's eyes and what Erin suspected. He also remembered the look on the bouncer's face, and the snake in his room. He didn't want to endanger anyone else, if he could help it, especially not this kid. "I don't think that's a good idea." Darrell glanced over at Erin. "I'm working on something that may get your sister out. Erin here is helping me. Give us a couple days."

Josh nodded, tears leaking out of both green eyes.

In a quiet, gentle voice, Erin asked, "What are you going to tell your mom?"

The boy's face flushed. "Not much yet." His gaze went from Erin to Darrell. "Unless you think I need to—"

Darrell interrupted him. "I'd hold off, at least for a day or two."

Pogo trotted over to the trio and curled around Darrell's leg. Josh's eyes grew large at the sight of the dog.

"And this is my bud, Pogo," Darrell said. The pug went over to Josh's foot and sniffed. "He's been hanging with a friend in Wilshire, where I live. I'm not supposed to have him in the boardinghouse I've been staying at here." The dog returned to Darrell, who rubbed his fur. "But I missed the guy, so I'm trying to have him around."

Darrell pointed at Josh. "Hey, could I ask you a favor?" The pug scampered back to the teen, almost as if he understood his master's proposition, and Josh bent to pet him. "Erin and I have to do a little driving. To go see someone. Would you mind keeping Pogo until tonight?"

One knee on the ground, Josh glanced from Darrell to the dog.

Darrell said, "I've got food and treats in the car. All you have to do is let him run around. And when he needs to, he'll do his business in the trees over there."

"Sure, Coach. I can watch him for you," Josh said, and Darrell thought he saw the tiniest smile in the boy's eyes.

It wasn't much, but it was enough for now.

Chapter Forty-Four

"They killed her. They killed my baby," Frank Palmer said, as soon as Darrell and Erin introduced themselves and mentioned they wanted to ask about his daughter, Amy. At the older man's words, they exchanged a quick glance, but didn't interrupt him.

"I know they did. That kid, Travis, she gave him everything and he broke her heart. It was more than she could take, so she killed herself. I blame him. And that family." Tears welled up in his gray eyes, but he didn't wipe them, as if he were proud of his grief. Resolute.

Of course, when Frank Palmer had railed, Darrell thought the man meant something else, thought he might know something. Now, he didn't pry because he didn't want to intrude on the older man's grief.

In a quiet voice, Erin asked, "Could you tell us a little about your daughter?"

While the man recalled his daughter in a reverent tone, Darrell and Erin sat perched on the overstuffed beige sofa in the center of the family room—quiet, listening, respectful. Frank Palmer rested calloused hands on the arms of a matching recliner, leaning forward, his grizzled face etched with lines beyond what Darrell would've guessed his age—fifty-something. With receding graying hair, he looked closer to seventy. He was a large, sturdy man with a bowed bearing, much like a hoary oak that had been battered by one too many storms. He wore a plain navy T-shirt over blue jeans and boots, his outfit an apt reflection of his surroundings.

The home was actually a large log cabin, with huge brown and tan logs stacked tight to form the outside walls, lines of bleached caulking between each log. The far wall sprouted two sets of antlers, as if the animals had been captured trying to vault through the space. In fact, the Palmer house was a log cabin home sitting on a small inland lake.

Getting to the Medford Lakes turned out to be easy, a quick drive up the Parkway and the Garden State Turnpike. But once there, he and Erin had a devil of a time locating the Palmer house amid roads that snaked around the lakes. They had to consult the map he'd printed out more than once. But, once he got his bearings, Darrell was struck by the incongruity between their destination and where they'd come from. Cape May captured the quaint, picturesque seaport, complete with remarkable Victorians, almost frozen in the nineteenth century, all bordered by a long, white sandy beach. Medford Lakes, nestled among towering pines and hardwoods and stuck fifty miles inland, turned out to be a warren of roads meandering around several small man-made lakes, with houses of all different sizes sporting small docks that backed up to one of the lakes. He wondered how a girl from here met a Jersey shore guy like Travis Armstrong.

Palmer pointed to a row of pictures displayed on the mantel above a white stone fireplace. "I was planning to put her wedding picture there but can't bring myself to. You know they had the photo taken and everything and offered me a copy. I said no."

Erin rose from the couch to take a closer look at one of the framed photos, one of father and daughter. "I don't see a picture of your wife. Amy's mother." She spoke in a quiet, plaintive tone.

The man shook his head. "Naw. I lost Cherise when Amy was three. The cancer. I had to raise her alone. It's been just me and Amy." His eyes teared up again. "Now, it's just me."

Erin said, "I know we said this at the start, but we're so sorry for your loss."

Darrell noticed she always seemed to know the right thing to say and the right way to express it. At least, way before he did. He was so glad to have her along.

"Talking about her is about all I have," Frank Palmer said, "and I'm always glad to tell people about my Amy. And I'm glad to have someone ask. After all this time." His eyes got hard and he stared at Darrell first and then cast his gaze to Erin. "But I need to ask you a question. Why are you doing this?" When neither answered right away, he added, "Why come around here and ask questions about my daughter? I mean, she's been gone for almost five years. Are you some kind of nosy reporters or something?"

In the drive over, Darrell had told Erin he expected something like this and decided he'd tell the truth, or at least part of it. "No, we're not reporters. Erin here is a nurse, an OB nurse. And I'm a teacher, a high school history teacher."

Palmer's expression didn't change. If anything, his frown lines deepened. "That's nice, but that don't answer me. Why you'd come around asking about my girl?"

"Sorry, no, it doesn't. You see, I'm also an amateur historian, especially local history. I find it very intriguing. Anyway, I've been in Cape May for a few weeks helping out with their junior high football camp—I'm also a football coach—and in my spare time I was doing some research and came across Amy's story. It intrigued me and I thought, well, we thought we'd want to see where Amy grew up."

"Hmm." Palmer didn't look wholly convinced. "You ain't from around here, are you?"

"No," Darrell said, "we're both from Wilshire. A little town on the Eastern Shore. In Maryland."

"Pretty place. Took Amy sailing there when she was little. A place called St. Michaels."

Erin said, "We know it well. Just up the road, er, rather as we say, up the Bay." She waited a beat and then asked, "What else can you tell us about Amy?"

"She was going to be a great scientist. Said she was going to find a cure for cancer. The one that killed her mom. Did you know that?" Palmer asked, but didn't give them a chance to answer. "Had a degree in microbiology from Villanova. All her life, she thought like a scientist, all black and white. She knew what was right and what was wrong." He shook his head, smiling. "Amy was the strongest willed person I ever knew. And I'm not just saying that. If she had her sights set on something, she was going to get it, by God. And you better not stand in her way. She had an unbreakable will. She could be damn exasperating sometimes."

He paused and then added, "That's why it didn't make any sense she would commit suicide."

No one spoke, the man's heavy words hanging in the air. Finally, Erin said, "And you never heard from her after the wedding night?"

Palmer shook his head. "You know, I was there at the reception when she went *missing.*" He said the last word like he was spitting out something foul. "I had a few too many drinks and the next thing I know they tell me she's gone. I was too sloshed to pay attention to what was happening with my own daughter."

Erin started to say something, but he waved her off. "Oh, I know, they said she might've left or run away. But I don't believe it. She would've told me. She's gone. I feel it in my bones. I don't know how, and I don't know all the why's, but I know that."

Erin let a little time pass and then asked, "Would it be okay if we had a look at her room?"

Instead of answering, Frank rose from the chair as if it pained him and led them down the hallway. At the end of the corridor, he opened a door, stepping aside. Darrell and Erin peered through the doorway and saw a small bedroom, with exterior walls of log like the rest of the house, but the rest very much feminine. A four-poster double bed sat in the middle of the room covered in a pink and white comforter with red pillow shams. The room looked untouched, as if Amy might come home anytime.

Palmer said, "Sometimes I feel like she's right here, trying to tell me something, after all this time." His gaze searched them. "Do you know what I mean? I know that sounds strange, as if she could talk to me or something, but sometimes I think I can feel her presence. And even her pain."

"That doesn't sound strange at all to us," Darrell said.

The older man choked up again. "I wanted to keep

her room exactly the way she left it, but I can only stay in here so long. It hurts too much."

Erin placed a hand on the older man's arm. "Do you mind if we have a look around?"

"Sure. Please leave everything the way it is." He left, and they heard his heavy footsteps down the hallway.

Darrell paced around the space, taking in the posters hanging on one wall, not of some teen heartthrob, but of the Franklin Institute and the Museum of Science in Boston. He stopped and examined a few candids pinned to a corkboard, Amy mugging for the camera with some girls he didn't recognize. But he didn't pick up any particular vibes.

While he wandered around, nervous, he watched as Erin sat at a white Queen Anne desk, with a few framed photos and a quaint white jewelry box sitting atop. Opening the box, she picked up a pair of ruby earrings, examining them in the light, while a quiet tune tinkled from the box. She replaced the earrings, closing the box, and the music died. She picked up a picture, a photo of a couple in a fancy, white wooden frame.

"This is Travis?" she asked, pointing to the handsome guy in the picture.

Darrell stepped over to the desk, peering over her shoulder. "Yeah, that looks like the guy I met with his dad at Carny's. A little younger."

Erin tilted her head, staring at the photo. "It could be us, you know?"

"What?"

"Well, look at them. I mean they don't look like us—"

"Oh, I'm much better looking," Darrell said.

"If you say so." She chuckled. "That's not what I meant. I mean, they look to be about our age, at least in the photo. And they look happy."

"Well, something happened. She's dead," Darrell announced. "And he's on to greener pastures."

Erin set the photo back on the desk and continued her searching, while Darrell resumed his nervous pacing.

"You don't see a diary or anything, do you?" Darrell asked.

"No, nothing like that." She opened the center drawer and pulled out two dogged-eared magazines. "Only a few odds and end and these Brides magazines. January and February, 1994." Idly, she flipped through the glossy pages and a paper fell out. She picked it up. "Hey, Darrell, look at this."

He stopped his restless roaming and came over to her, while she held up a faded flyer. He read over her shoulder. " 'Have you seen her? Missy Champlain, age 15. Last seen in Atlantic City, December 2, 1993.' An awful lot like Josh's sister."

"Coincidence?"

"I doubt it," he said.

She turned over the paper and scrutinized something on the back, near a ripped corner. "Look at this. I think she wrote 'Ask Trav—' The rest is torn."

After he had a chance to study the flyer, she slid it back inside the pages and replaced the magazines in the drawer. A few minutes later, they finished, leaving everything as they found it, and Palmer led them to the front door. As he got to the entrance, the older man turned around and faced his two guests. "You said you've been checking into…what really happened to my girl?" He scowled as if he wasn't sure he wanted to ask, but said, "Do you know for sure what happened to her?"

Darrell shook his head. "No, I don't. But I promise, if I do, when I do, I'll come back and tell you what I learn."

Chapter Forty-Five

The Maid of Honor was not at all what they expected. Not with a name like Coco.

Frank Palmer had been kind enough to direct them, as they were climbing into their car. "Oh, that's easy. See that house, the one with the green awning, three doors down. That's where Coco lives. Actually, it was her parents' place. When the Williams retired and moved to Florida, they sold it to her and her husband." He pointed around the ring of log cabins. "Coco and Amy about wore out the path between our houses when they were young. Thick as thieves." He glanced at his watch. "You might be in luck. She usually picks up Jeremy and gets home about now."

They found the house easily and followed a red minivan into the driveway. Darrell got out, Erin a few steps behind. As they approached the van, a petite young woman with short, sculpted brunette hair climbed out of the front seat. Balancing two plastic grocery bags on one arm, she unlatched a squirming toddler with the other.

"We're sorry to intrude on you like this," Darrell said. "I'm Darrell Henshaw and this is my friend, Erin Caveny. We just had a nice talk with Frank Palmer about his daughter and wanted to know if we could ask you a few questions about Amy."

Before the mother could respond, the little boy

squealed, "Down. Down. Down, mommy."

She released him, and he trotted toward the front door, his long tawny hair swishing as he walked. His mother gave chase behind, hollering over her shoulder, "Come on in. I'll get you a glass of lemonade and we can talk." She unlocked the front door, letting in the tyke, and followed, leaving the door ajar.

Watching Coco cross the driveway, Darrell felt like he was observing some kid. She was pretty with almond-shaped blue eyes. But she stood under five feet tall and had such a baby face with petite features, he would have thought her a teen, had he seen her on the sidewalk. Accepting the invitation, they followed her inside, Darrell holding the door for Erin.

"Make yourselves comfortable," Coco called from somewhere inside the house. "This little guy is way overdue for his nap. I'll put him down and join you in a few."

Darrell and Erin found seats, both settling onto a comfortable leather couch. The inside looked much like the Palmer home—exterior walls formed by tightly stacked logs sealed with stripes of neat white caulk. A simple fieldstone fireplace stood at the end of a polished hardwood floor. Darrell half expected more hanging animal trophies but found instead a few tasteful art prints and a large photo of a young family, all framed in dark wood.

In a surprisingly short time, Coco returned with a round yellow tray holding a shimmering pitcher of lemonade and three glass tumblers. She set everything down on a long glass-topped coffee table in front of the couch. "May I?" she asked.

"Please," Erin said, smiling. "You made quick

work of the little guy."

"Danny? He was bushed. Didn't take much coaxing." She shook her head. "He's nothing. During the school year I have to wrestle a whole class of five-year-olds."

Darrell accepted the glass. "So you're a teacher?"

"Yep. Kindergarten. Next year will be year number five." She handed a glass to Erin.

Darrell said, "So am I. High school. Social studies. American history mostly, but only three years under my belt."

"Around here?" Coco asked.

Darrell was in the middle of a sip, so Erin answered first. "No, we're from a small town in Maryland, a place called Wilshire. Darrell teaches there, and I'm a nurse at a hospital nearby."

"What brings you to our sleepy little burg of Medford Lakes? Oh, yeah, you said you wanted to talk about Amy." She dropped her gaze. "Poor Amy."

Darrell gave her an abbreviated version of the one he shared with Frank Palmer, and Coco didn't press. Instead she said, "I don't know what I can tell you, after all this time."

Erin set her drink on the table. "This is delicious." She pointed to the half empty glass. "Can you tell us how Amy and Travis met?"

Coco laughed. "That's easy. I introduced them, kinda. I was going with some guy from Atlantic City, Rick. Amy and I were on a girls' night at Harrah's, I think. That doesn't matter." She shook her head. "We ran into Rick and he had this guy with him, Travis. We weren't planning on it, but we kinda paired up, and Amy ended up with Travis. And that was it." She laughed. "Rick and I didn't last a month, but it was off to the races for Amy and Travis."

"A whirlwind romance?" Erin asked.

"You could say that. Amy fell hard for him. I could almost see the stars in her eyes when she talked of him."

"You think Travis felt the same way?" Darrell asked.

"Yeah, I think so. You know, he'd gone with this other girl all through high school and college, Jennifer something. Right after he and Amy met, Travis dropped Jennifer, just like that. No, I think he fell for Amy almost as bad as she fell for him."

Darrell thought he heard something in her voice. "Do I hear a but there?"

Two bright red lips puckered into an O. "I don't know. It was mostly a feeling. Something…in his eyes. I always thought Travis was keeping something from Amy. And I knew my friend. For her, it was all or nothing."

"Did you ever share your concern with Amy?" Erin asked.

"Not easy, with a girl in love, even if Amy and I were best friends," Coco said. She took a sip and set the glass back on the tray. "But once, not very long before the wedding, I had one too many margaritas at one of our planning sessions." She made air quotes. "Anyway, I let it slip and she said something to the effect that she and Travis promised to have complete honesty, to tell it all. Never to keep anything from each other. She said they still had things to talk about, to work out, but they agreed everything would be on the table by the time they were married."

"We heard Amy and Travis had a big fight the night of their reception, not long before she went missing." Darrell offered the sentence to see if Coco had any reaction, but he didn't pick up on anything. "Did you know anything about it? Did she say anything to you?"

Coco shook her head. "I don't think so. I'm embarrassed to admit it, but that evening I was wasted. I remember the Armstrongs kept the booze flowing, the good stuff too. I think pretty much everybody was drunk." Her small round face turned red. "Then, we were just having fun, celebrating a wonderful wedding. But now, after Amy disappeared, I feel pretty shitty about it."

"So you don't have any idea what happened to her? You've not heard from her? After?" Darrell asked.

"I don't remember most of what happened that night." Coco's eyes misted over. "You're going to think I'm crazy, but I've got to tell you." She looked away, casting her eyes through the front bay window. "I've never told anyone this. I could've sworn, a few times after she disappeared, I saw her. I'd come into my kitchen and see her sitting at the table, like we used to do, a wine glass in one hand, the other pointing a finger at me. I thought maybe she was trying to tell me something."

"What did you do?" Erin asked, her voice almost breathless.

"I shook my head and closed my eyes, you know like you do, and when I opened them again, she…or the vision was gone. Then, I collapsed in the same exact same chair and had my own glass of wine. Or three." Coco met their gazes again. "You must think I'm crazy."

"Not at all," Darrell said, without hesitating. "What do you think happened to Amy?"

Coco's eyes grew wet. "I don't know. I guess she could've walked into the ocean, like they said." She shook her head again. "It doesn't sound like Amy. I've never known her to surrender to *anything*, much less the frickin' ocean. No matter how upset she was."

They all heard crying coming from down the hall. Slow and plaintive at first, then growing. Coco stood. "Well, he didn't last long. Never can tell when I get him down this late."

Darrell and Erin both stood, setting their tumblers back on the tray. Erin asked, "Can I get these for you?"

"No, please leave them. I'll get them in a bit. After I tend to the prince." She extended her hand and they shook, first Erin, then Darrell. "Thanks for coming and asking about Amy. It felt good to talk about her, after all this time." Coco took a step toward the hall and turned. "Thanks for caring. It's nice to know what happened to Amy matters to somebody."

Chapter Forty-Six

The next morning, Darrell and Erin stayed in bed, huddled together in the steamy air flowing in through the window. They listened as the other boarders around them clambered out of their bunks, footfalls heavy on the wooden planks, and headed to their destinations, until the building settled into a heavy, creaking stillness. After the exhausting last two days, all Darrell wanted to do was put off the world and postpone fate a while, so he snuggled next to Erin a little longer.

Lying at the foot of the cramped bed, Pogo glanced up at the entwined pair and satisfied, rolled over. His reaction set Erin into a fit of giggles and, in a few seconds, they both convulsed into laughter. Afterwards, they rehashed what they'd learned.

"You really think Vince was killed because of…the Haunted Bride?" Erin asked, leaning on one elbow.

"Well, he started asking questions about the wedding, where she *disappeared,* and he gets run over." Darrell turned toward his partner. "And we're asking around and get a visit from a poisonous tourist."

"Don't remind me." Erin's gaze checked the open window and swept the room. "Then Coco tells us there was some secret Travis was keeping from Amy and that's why they were fighting that night. She thinks."

"And don't forget the poster Amy had for the missing teen. The one from Atlantic City." Darrell shook his head. "Too many questions, not enough answers."

"What time are we due for serving the Armstrong party?" she asked.

"Dressed and ready to go at 6:30."

Erin grabbed a nearby towel and wiped some of the sweat off her bare chest. "Oh, it's one sweltering morning."

"Only because you are so hot." Darrell's finger tried to trace the same path, but she used the towel to swat his hand.

She said, "Anyway, I vote we head to the water. One more dip in the waves. With how things are going, it might be our last chance."

So that's what they did.

When they'd had enough surf fun, they collapsed onto the towels, staring up as wisps of cumulus clouds sailed across a perfect azure sky. They lay there, not talking but holding hands, taking it all in. Darrell shot a glance at his partner next to him, Erin's sleek, tanned body set off by her dazzling yellow bikini.

A twenty-something couple pranced past, bronze bodies in tight, tiny swimsuits, blocking his view for a second and interrupting his musing. The guy reached across and tickled the young woman. She giggled and playfully escaped his grasp, but only long enough for him to catch up. As Darrell watched, the guy pulled her to him. They kissed and moved on, out of sight.

When they left, Darrell glanced back at Erin who'd been watching him. She asked, "Looking for other options?"

He turned to face her. "Just the opposite. I was wishing we could be like them."

"You like her better than me?"

"No." He shook his head. "I wish we could be here, you know, just for fun, goofing off. Not hunting ghosts and tracking down murderers."

"But if you weren't still chasing ghosts and bad guys, I wouldn't have come back and had more time on the beach with my favorite ghost hunter."

"No complaints on that account." Darrell released her hand and sat up on the towel, glancing back toward the town. "I have a proposition for you."

Her eyebrows arched. "I thought you *propositioned* me quite well this morning."

Darrell chuckled. "Not that kind of proposition. How about, for old times' sake, when we finish here, we make a trip to the library? I thought we might do a little more research on the Armstrongs. Check out some of the people we might run into tonight."

"Sounds like a great date." Erin leaned across and kissed him. "How about once more into the water and then we'll head back?"

Ninety minutes later, they sat at two carrels in the research room of the Cape May County Library, dressed in shorts, tees, and sandals. Darrell slid a microfiche reel of the *Atlantic City Post* onto the machine and started scrolling through the issues. Erin did the same with the *Newark Clarion*, both looking for any mention of the Armstrong family or the company.

Like before, Erin came upon something first. "Hey, look at this." She adjusted the focus as Darrell got up and peered over her shoulder, lingering in the delightful fragrance of her recently shampooed hair. She pointed to a grainy photograph on the screen. "Isn't that James Armstrong?"

He looked closer. The photo captured a group of men seated around a table with President Bill Clinton at the head. Next to the president was a compact man with short, salt-and-pepper hair, wearing sunglasses. Darrell read the caption. "Clinton meets with members of his Business Round Table." Then he read the names aloud and paused when he got to James Armstrong of Armstrong Trucking. "I'd say that would count as a little clout. Let's print a copy."

Darrell returned to his space and they both continued searching. In a 1997 Sunday edition of *The Post*, Darrell found an interview with the senior Armstrong, discussing plans for Armstrong Trucking. Halfway through the article, he read a passage to Erin, keeping his voice barely above a whisper. " 'Armstrong Trucking has never been more financially sound. We have great expectations for the company and are looking to expand into other markets and diversify our holdings.' " He pulled his eyes away from the screen. "Yeah, I think I saw one of those *diversified* holdings. A place called 'Less is More.' "

A few minutes later, Erin stumbled upon another photo in the *Clarion*, this one of James Armstrong and Rudy Giuliani, and pointed it out to Darrell. Her eyes scanned the text. "It says Armstrong was meeting with the New York mayor to ask to get some regulations waived for his company."

"Can I see?"

"Sure." She slid aside and he leaned in.

He read the article through, having to adjust the dial to move to the next page. "No details about which regulations, though. Let's print this as well."

Heading over to pick up their copies, he glanced at

his watch. 4:45. When he returned to the carrels, he said, "We've seen enough. I think we get the picture."

Erin shook her head, looking grim. "Darrell, these are some heavy hitters. We need to be careful tonight."

"I agree. Speaking of which, we still have to change into those uniforms and get to Poverty Beach. I say we head out."

Chapter Forty-Seven

God, this outfit was the pits, Cassie thought, as she tried to adjust the black bowtie again. No matter what she did, the wraparound strap was too friggin' tight. First of all, she had to ditch every one of her studs—at least ones they could see—and then put on this monkey suit.

She sat in the rear of Darrell's car and eased back against the seat, headphones on, listening to Nirvana's "Serve the Servants." She checked out her "uniform." Starched white shirt even stiffer than the one she wore for Aleathea's. Bowtie strangling her neck. Hard creased dress pants the same color as the tie. The catering company even supplied a shiny pair of patent leather shoes—black of course. "It's all part of Houston Look," Eggy had explained when he dropped off the uniforms. "All the servers exactly the same."

Cassie glanced over at the dog perched on the seat next to her. "What do you think, Pogo?" The pug gazed at her with those huge eyes and then turned to look out the window. See, even the dog hated the outfit.

To work this gig, she had to do a little finagling with Antonio. When the boss agreed, he issued a warning. "Miss Cassie, you must be on your best behavior. Do not embarrass us in front of all those important clients." She could still see Antonio's stern face as it broke into a wide, false smile. "And it would not hurt you to smile a little."

Pretty damn hard to smile with this tie choking her.

Where Beach Ave made the sharp bend, Darrell pulled onto the shoulder, next to a stand of straggly pines, and parked behind several older cars. She slipped off her headphones and stashed the Walkman into her backpack, stuffing it on the floor, out of sight. Most everything she owned was in that old bag. The three of them got out—looking like matching penguins—followed by the dog, which Darrell escorted into the nearby trees. This close to the evergreens, the scent of pine floated on the breeze.

"Pogo, this is the best I could do tonight," Darrell said, carrying two dishes, a long leash looped through one hand. "I know you would like to hang with Josh again, but when I called, he was out with a couple friends." Weaving his way through the gnarled tree trunks, he led the dog into the trees, where they both disappeared from sight. Metal pans hit the ground. "I've brought you some food and water," he said. "And you can poke around and investigate. The dead needles will provide a nice bed to do what you like most, sleep. I'll be back later."

A few seconds later, Darrell emerged from the trees, took one look behind him, and clicked the locks shut on the car. Checked his watch. "Ladies, if you're ready, we're due in ten minutes."

They needed all that time. First, they had to walk down the length of the short street to the house sitting on the bend of the cul-de-sac. As they worked their way around the few cars already parked in the circular driveway and approached the house, Cassie counted garages for ten cars. Ten garages? Then they had to walk through a tall metal detector erected inside a carport. Cassie stepped through the electronic arch and held her breath. The few piercings she hadn't removed better not set the damn thing off. When the machine didn't emit its loud shriek, she exhaled. Set high enough. The guard stared at her, so she called up Antonio's false smile. It worked.

Once registered, each server moved to the back yard and received a glistening silver platter of appetizers. They were told to follow the wooden walkway and spread out. Earlier, in the car, the three of them had discussed their "assignments" for the evening's inquiries. Darrell just had to be the teacher. No one said anything as the three of them were processed along with a few other waiters.

Cassie knew who she was supposed to find.

She balanced the tray with one hand. No problem. Followed the walkway through the opening in the shrubbery and tall sea grass. Took a few steps onto the beach. When she turned to glance back, she almost dropped the platter. Facing the blue water sat one of the largest houses she'd ever seen. No, not a house. Mansion. It was only two stories high—she counted two rows of windows, but their windowpanes had to be ten feet tall. They'd come around the back of the house to get signed in, but she'd hadn't noticed. Across the back of the huge house stretched the longest porch she'd even seen. In the center of the porch, James and Andrea Armstrong sat on a massive couch, watching their guests enter. Like royalty.

Below all this, where the sea grass ended and the sand began, stood a small string orchestra, a few violins, a cello, a double bass, and even a damn harp.

Sending that stupid classical music all over the beach. Cassie stood for a moment, trying to endure the music and studying the house. Then she noticed something. The house didn't sit parallel to the beach. Instead, it was slanted, one end closer to the water. She realized why. The fiery sun, now starting to set, lit up the end windows on the right.

Mesmerized, she stood there, staring, as a few servers stepped around her. Erin came up alongside, struggling to balance her own full platter. "You okay?" she whispered. Cassie gave two slow nods. "Good luck."

Cassie followed, moving toward a group of guests and glancing at the next house in the row. She stopped again, agape. It looked even more immense than its neighbor, though with a more modern look, all glass, gleaming metal, and crazy angles.

This was Poverty Beach?

She walked out onto the sand and glanced down. Something felt different. Though now on the beach, her feet rested on some kind of plush carpet. The Armstrongs had laid a line of friggin' Persian rugs over top the sand. The designs even created an undulating path between the booths. So their guests wouldn't get any damn grains in their expensive sandals? Shit.

The carpeted paths led to three, no four tents with the flaps up, scattered along the shoreline. Each housed a bar with more food stations. Tiny white lights traced the outlines of each tent and were strung across the beach from one tent to the other.

Cassie hoisted her tray and moved among the guests, offering her mushroom caps. She searched for her target. Darrell'd given her a pretty good description.

Besides, she still had a good memory of what he looked like in the newspaper photo. She checked out the guests, one after the other. Most were dressed casually, lots of tight tops and even skimpier skirts for the women. For the guys, bright Polo shirts and shorts. But casual didn't apply to the bling. A helluva lot of gold and diamonds, sparkling in the late day sun.

Going to refill her tray, Cassie passed a guy she thought she recognized, fairly tall in a tailored black suit. The suit alone made him stand out. Handsome enough and in his fifties, maybe. But his hair. Something was off about it. The girl on his arm was also dressed in black, a short, tight dress, which showed off as much as it covered. She looked younger, twenties, maybe, with the figure of a model. Had long blonde hair almost to her breasts, which lay half-exposed.

When Eggy passed her, carrying an empty platter, Cassie stopped him. She nodded toward the couple in black. "Who are they?"

Eggy lifted his eyebrows. "Some millionaire bigwig. Big real estate tycoon. Got this resort out in Atlantic City."

Cassie kept her eyes on the couple. "He important?"

"He's supposed to have more money than God," Eggy said, chuckling and making his belly shake.

"And the girl?"

"Don't know her, but like to." His smirk spread. "He's a big womanizer. I think he just dumped wife number two." He inched his eyebrows up and down once. "And she looks like some porn star."

Cassie rolled her eyes and kept moving. She had to

locate her assignment, Jeremy Tucker.

A few minutes later, she found him. By the fourth booze tent, the one closest to water. The guy sported a sky-blue tank top, stretched tight across his abs, over navy shorts. That was him. What had Darrell called him? A strutting peacock. Some raven-haired bimbo leaned in close, her fingers caressing one of his oversized biceps. Tucker held a half-empty glass of champagne—Don Perignon. She'd seen the bottles in one tent. From Aleathea's, she knew what that cost. Damn, the Armstrongs must be bleeding money. Tucker tossed back the glass, emptying it in one large gulp. He stepped over to the tent and grabbed up another from the bartender.

Before he could re-attach himself to his date, Cassie intervened. "A gourmet mushroom cap to go with the champagne?"

He stepped close and snatched two. She whispered, "I'd like to talk with you about Spikes."

Tucker stood up, appetizers in one hand, eyes narrowed and angry. He glanced around. "Don't know what you're talking about." He started to walk away.

"I'm sure your new fancy friend would love to know about your biker bars." Cassie shot a glance back at the girl.

The young woman, heavily made up and dripping with jewels—Cassie counted six jeweled rings alone—finger waved. She rose off the stool. She started over to Tucker, stumbling. "Hey, Jeremy," she said, though the words were a bit slurred.

When she got within a few feet, Tucker barked, "Go on back. I'll be over in a bit."

"But?" She wiggled her own empty glass.

"Shit, okay already. I'll bring you another damn refill," he growled.

She must've have missed his tone, because she blew him a kiss. The dumb broad hobbled back to her place.

Another server passing by overheard the exchange and offered, "Sir, I could fetch her a glass, if you'd like."

Tucker turned on the waiter. "No, I don't like." She backed away. Tucker took a few steps aside, away from the other guests. At first, Cassie didn't budge, holding a tray and eyeing him.

To Cassie, he said, "I could have you fired, you know that. I'm good friends with the Armstrongs."

Cassie trotted out the fake smile again. "Okay, let's go and I can tell them about your string of low life dives in Delaware. And maybe what all you deal out of them."

"If you think you can intimidate me…I'll make sure you never work again." He glanced around and added, real menace in his voice, "Or never be able to work."

"Oh, I don't think you get it." Cassie worked to keep her voice light, but she heard it crack a little. She tried to keep the fake grin plastered. "I only came over because I want a job." When he didn't say anything, she said, "Hire me for one of your…um, okay, let's say, inns."

He turned his head, obviously surprised, and looked her over. His cruel gaze scanned her up and down. "How old are you? I don't think you got the stuff."

"Oh, this?" she gestured with her one free hand.

"This isn't me. Here, hold this." She handed him the silver platter.

Tucker must've been too surprised to object, because he accepted it. Set his appetizers back on it. Cassie yanked the shirt tail out and started unbuttoning her shirt from the bottom, uncovering some skin.

Lust flared in his eyes. "Don't get any ideas." She lifted the stiff shirt to expose three studs across her midriff and the metal ring through her belly button. "Usually, I have about thirty more. All over. They made me take them out for tonight." Her hand brushed one pant leg. "I do black, but like leather."

Tucker stared at her exposed flesh, his eyes looking like they would undress the rest of her. "You're some tough broad, huh? Do you ride?"

Cassie didn't answer right away, buttoning her shirt again and tucking it into her pants. Her eyes checked out the other partygoers. Dumb broad was still clueless. No one seemed to take notice of them.

A lewd grin spread across his face and his eyebrows danced. "Maybe I should ride you?"

Cassie reacted swiftly. Her leg slammed up between his and stopped an inch below his crotch. His eyes bulged with fear. Tucker went to defend himself and saw both his hands were full, glass in one and tray in the other. His features exploded in rage. He gritted his teeth

She took her time to lower her foot to the ground and leaned in close. She grabbed the tray back from him. "You're lucky I'm feeling kind today." Her fake smile never faltered. "Otherwise, you wouldn't be walking. For about a week."

Tucker threw back some of the champagne and

tried to smirk, though he couldn't quite pull it off. "You got nerve. I'll give you that."

Cassie sauntered two steps away and turned back. "I got no idea why Amy dated you."

He choked on the drink. "What?"

"Amy Palmer. Can't believe what she saw in you?"

"That bitch. Why ya asking?"

Cassie kept walking, but Tucker's next words chilled her. "Did ya know that druggie who was asking around about the night she died?"

Chapter Forty-Eight

Darrell poured the expensive champagne as fast as he could, filling the line of crystal flutes. As quickly as he poured, Andy Hauck, the guy tending the bar, set the glasses up and patrons snatched them off the mahogany counter. Darrell knew the cost of Dom Perignon and figured he'd emptied a thousand dollars' worth of champagne in the last quarter hour.

After a few minutes of frantic activity, a lull settled in the booth and the bartender turned to Darrell. "Thanks for the help. For a bit there, I felt like General Custer getting overrun by the natives." He extended a hand. "Andy."

Darrell accepted it and shook. "Darrell. Glad to help. I was carrying my tray by and saw the crowd and thought you could use a hand."

Darrell had recognized the guy easily from Eggy's description—tall, handsome, with black hair, blue eyes, and a nose a little big for his face. Like a young Frank Sinatra, he'd said. Yeah, eyeing the barkeep, Darrell could almost see the resemblance.

Darrell picked up his tray of canapes. "The guests sure seemed more interested in free drink than free food."

Hauck raised his eyebrows. "When this stuff goes for forty dollars a glass, even the rich like free booze." He resumed pouring. "I haven't seen you around. You new in town?"

"I'm not from around here." Darrell set the tray back down atop the bar. "I'm from Maryland, only in town for a while."

"You're in Cape May for a while and you're working this gig. Must need the money."

Darrell laughed. "I do. I'm a high school coach. That's why I'm in Cape May, doing this football camp."

"With Coach Wagner?" Hauck asked. "Good man. Played a little ball for him in high school."

Another throng of guests stormed the tent, grabbing flutes of the bubbly. Darrell, seeing the bartender getting behind again, set down his tray and helped. This group congregated around a handsome, fifty-something woman with short, styled brown hair and a broad smile that ended in a pair of huge dimples. Darrell noticed she was flanked by two Secret Service agents.

When the rush passed, he looked at Hauck. "Okay, who was that?"

Hauck laughed. "You do need to get out more. That's Christine Todd Whitman," he said with a clipped voice. "The governor of our fine state."

Darrell stared, saw the woman walking among the crowd, shaking hands, and for the first time, he noticed some uniformed officers among the guests. Cape May cops. "Man, some heavy hitters at this party."

Hauck raised both eyebrows. "That's the Armstrongs. If you're important, politically connected or have big money, the Armstrongs will have you on speed dial."

The throngs had moved on, leaving their bar quiet,

at least for the moment. Darrell wasn't sure he'd get another chance. "I heard you do pretty much all the Armstrongs' functions?"

"Pretty much. It's good money," Hauck said. "And it's good people-watching."

Darrell glanced around to see if anyone was listening and noticed no one seemed to be paying them any attention. "Could I ask you a question? About another Armstrong function. Travis' wedding?"

Andy Hauck stopped pouring and looked up. His eyes got wide and Darrell could read the concern on his face. "That's a blast from the past. Why you asking about that?" He went back to filling more flutes.

Darrell lied. "I'm a friend of the bride, well, the bride's family, and just saw Amy's dad." He looked up to see if he was selling it. He thought Hauck was buying. Darrell swallowed and kept going. "Like I said, I saw Frank Palmer, Amy's dad, and he talked about her. I told Frank I'd check on it. Then I heard you worked the wedding party, the night she disappeared."

Darrell studied Andy Hauck, who uncorked another bottle. Darrell wasn't sure this was working and added, "You know, they never recovered Amy's body. Her dad's hoping for some closure."

At first, Hauck didn't respond, instead emptying the bottle, head bent over the glasses. Darrell was afraid he'd blown it but held his tongue. He'd learned sometimes silence was the best strategy. Often, in his classroom, he'd get his students to answer, if he merely waited. This was harder, and he felt twin streams of sweat on the sides of his face.

Hauck looked up. "I get it. A father would want to know what happened." He set down the bottle. "What did you want to know about that night?"

Darrell released a breath, a little louder than he wanted. "The cops told Frank that his daughter committed suicide. That she walked into the ocean and took her own life. Did you see her do that?"

Hauck said, "I didn't see that, but I read it in the paper."

"What *did* you see?"

The bartender stared down at his feet but didn't speak.

Darrell tried, "I know it's been five years, but do you remember her leaving the party?"

"How could I forget that? I mean, with her disappearing and everything," said Hauck, glancing around.

"You told the cops you didn't see her walk into the ocean, right?'

"Well, she might have taken a plunge that night. She wouldn't have been the only one to end up in the water. Man, the booze was flowing big time that night. Even more than tonight. I had to help two ladies after they 'fell' into the waves." His fingers made quotation marks in the air. "Got their expensive outfits all wet and see through, if you know what I mean."

"Is that what you saw Amy do?"

"No." Hauck shook his head, emphatic. "She was one of the only ones not sloshed that night. Well, she and Mrs. Armstrong. Ye old Battle Ax." The bartender glanced up toward the second-floor porch of the mansion and then back. "No, I saw Amy storm off right through that path there." He pointed to the walkway that threaded through the shrubbery and sea grass. "I can still picture her stomping down those wooden planks, that long white dress swishing back and forth. That was last I saw of her."

"Did anyone go after her? You know, follow her?"

Hauck shook his head. "Not that I saw."

"Okay. Thanks," Darrell said. "I'll pass it on to Frank. At least it's something." He leaned and offered a hand across the booth. They shook again. "Good to meet you. I better get some fresh appetizers. With the way this group is drinking, they definitely need something in their stomachs." He picked up his tray. "Thanks. I'm sure I'll catch you later."

Darrell threaded his way back to the food stations, accepting another tray of hors d'oeuvres, the aroma heavy by the burners. Platter in hand, he strode across the beach, searching for his second target, Travis Armstrong. Darrell studied the guests, congregating in small groups, some huddled in intense conversation, others laughing and giggling together. Trying not to look obvious, he scanned the entire crowd, maybe two hundred guests milling about on the beach. Except for the Secret Service agents who maintained their normal black suit attire and one couple in black formal outfits, most of the rest of the partygoers dressed in casual beachwear, vibrant colors still evident as sunlight gave way to the twinkling light strands.

Across the beach, at the other end of the crowd, he caught a flash of white, the contrast obvious against the background of colorful beach attire. He squinted. Someone in white moved among the brilliant beachwear, weaving between individuals and couples. The figure stepped between two groups and, though she stood almost a hundred feet away, he saw her clearly. It was…Amy, right here in the middle of the Armstrong party. He jerked his gaze around and saw no one else paid her any attention—as if they couldn't see her. But Darrell saw her and stood, transfixed, as she gazed back, tears flowing down her face. Then she turned and walked past the throngs, onto the path that led back to the mansion. *Exactly like Andy had described.* Darrell hustled to where she was, edging around guests, but before he got there, she turned and disappeared around a tall sand dune. He moved to the boardwalk, but he saw no sign of her.

For a while he stood there, frozen, puzzling out what it meant. He didn't know how long, but one of the waiters in charge came up behind and jostled him. It took Darrell a second to recover. He apologized and started walking back across the sand, carrying the tray and searching for Travis again. He spotted him on the outskirts of another crowd a few feet away, with a voluptuous young woman on his arm. When he drew closer, he could see—er, rather couldn't help but see— from the way her boobs practically fell out of her skimpy top, the girl was Jennifer Thomas. In fact, he thought she might be wearing the same tiny bikini top she'd strutted in on the beach. With Jeremy Tucker. Even without hearing the conversation he could tell Jennifer was putting on her best flirt for Travis. She seemed to have latched onto him, and Darrell wondered how he could get Travis alone for a few minutes.

As he approached, Erin cut in front of him, holding a tray with only three crystal flutes left. As Erin walked by, she angled past Jennifer, as if she was trying to step around her. His partner "stumbled" and tilted the tray expertly, spilling champagne onto the other woman's chest. Erin tripped and landed on the ground.

"What the hell?" screamed Jennifer in a high-pitched voice. "What's wrong with you, bitch?" The blonde-haired young woman looked around, waving her hands away from her soaked chest. "I'll have you fired!"

"Calm down, Jen. It was an accident," said Travis in a calm voice. He turned toward Erin and offered her his hand. "Are you okay?"

Erin took the hand and rose. "I'm fine. Just clumsy and embarrassed." Once on her feet, she turned toward Jennifer. "I'm so sorry. Can I help you? Maybe get something for you?"

"Hell, no," Jennifer said. "Thank God I have another top in the car." She turned toward Travis. "I'll be back in a few." She trounced toward the house.

Erin picked up the empty glasses off the sand, none of which had broken. "I better get these back and report. Or I *will* get fired." She headed out, winked at Darrell, and left him and Travis alone.

Darrell led with his tray. "A gourmet chicken wing or two?" Travis took a pair and accepted the accompanying napkin. With Travis' mouth full, Darrell started talking. "I'm Darrell Henshaw. I don't expect to remember, but we met a few weeks ago at Carny's."

Recognition seemed to bloom in Travis's face. "You're that coach Wagner brought in. The word is you did quite the job at the football camp," he managed between bites. "Did you enjoy it here in Cape May?" He licked the tip of two fingers.

"I did, very much. This is a truly unique town. I fell in love with the Victorians." Darrell exchanged Travis' dirty napkin for a clean one. When Travis helped himself to another pair of wings, Darrell said,

"By the way, Kurt told me about your company. How's the company doing?"

"The company?" Travis seemed thrown by the question. Either that or he was distracted by the chicken wings. Darrell had had a few earlier. They were quite good, and addictive.

"Oh, sorry for the shop talk. I can't help it," Darrell said. "It's an occupational hazard. You see, besides coaching, I teach history and am kind of an amateur historian. I'm fascinated by local history."

"Naw, that's all right." Travis waved away any concern with a half-eaten chicken wing. "The Armstrong Trucking Company is coming up on its fortieth year and has never been stronger. We're more diversified than ever before, with more profit centers. We expect to be one of the largest shipping companies in the US in the next five years. That's straight from our brochure."

"That's quite a goal. Good for you." Darrell stretched out the platter, as if he had to leave. "You want any more? Before I..." Darrell nodded toward the closest groups of guests milling around a nearby tent.

"Maybe one more," Travis said as he reached for the tray.

Darrell accepted his bones and soiled napkin and gave him a third fresh one. "Could I ask you another question?"

"Sure. Shoot," Travis said between bites again.

"In my research, I read about your wedding and your wife. Tough, I know. I lost one at the altar too."

"You did?"

"Yeah, but that's a story for another day." Darrell leaned in a little bit. "I know it had to be hard, but I'm sure you want closure. I was just wondering if Amy, if her body ever showed up?"

He thought he saw something in Travis's eyes—regret, anguish, guilt—but he couldn't be sure. Before he had a chance to ask another question, he felt a hard tug on his arm. Darrell staggered, almost dropping the tray in the process. When he looked up, he saw one of the Cape May cops, Sergeant Harris, had a firm grip on his arm. The cop dragged him away.

"I need a word with you, sir." The cop's tone was polite, but Darrell could see the fury in the officer's eyes. Harris said, "The incident was a very rough time for the family. It's taken young Mr. Armstrong several years to get over it. We'd rather you not ask him about that time. You're tearing off old scars for the family."

Darrell looked down at the hand squeezing his arm. Like an iron grip. "Sorry. Travis and I were only making conversation and—"

Harris kept his voice quiet, but steely. "I've been asked to see you out."

Chapter Forty-Nine

Darrell felt he'd been close. To something. Between the appearance of the ghost and the look on Travis' face, he sensed the almost groom was getting ready to tell him something. But that didn't happen. Officer Harris made sure of it. The same Sergeant who'd given Darrell all of ten minutes in the police station to review the file on Amy's death.

A firm hand on Darrell's arm, the cop hustled him through the crowd, not even letting him stop to talk with Erin or Cassie. But Darrell caught Erin's eye—she was serving guests near a tent they passed—and he was certain she got the gist of what was going on.

Darrell wasn't sure what he expected when the three of them descended on the party to ask a few questions, but it wasn't a police escort out.

While he waited for Erin and Cassie, Darrell checked on his dog, who seemed to have collected a small bone, gray and white and only a few inches long. Darrell tried to take it away and throw it back, but Pogo resisted, giving him a rare growl. He let the pug keep it. "Okay. Okay. Looks like everyone else is telling me what to do tonight."

About an hour later, Erin and Cassie found him pacing beside the car, Pogo at his heels. As they neared, Erin called, "Sorry it took us so long. The first chance we got, I grabbed Cassie and we bolted. I'm not sure the guy in charge is going to be too happy." She glanced over her shoulder. "He may come looking for us. Let's get out of here."

The three jumped in the car, hustling the dog in with them, and Darrell did a quick U-turn. Twenty minutes later, they settled into a booth at a dive in Wildwood, one of the few places still open this late. Besides, Darrell had decided they might need a little anonymity for their discussion and this place didn't mind his dog, who gnawed on his new treasure.

He started off recapping what he learned from the bartender and then mentioned about seeing the ghost.

Cassie's eyes got wide. "No kidding. So I didn't imagine it."

"You saw her too?" Darrell asked.

"Well, I saw, er, thought I saw, a figure in white on the other side of the beach, closest to where we came in and caught the white among all the colored outfits. When I tried to work my way around the guests to where I'd seen her, she'd disappeared."

"Yeah, I tried to follow her too, but when I got to the edge of the walk, she was gone," Darrell said.

"Well, I didn't see her," Erin said, a little disappointed.

"Don't worry. Neither did anyone else," Darrell said. "I watched her walk right between people and no one even looked up."

When no one spoke for a bit, he then explained what he'd gotten from Travis. "When I mentioned Amy's name to him, he looked…I don't know, tormented. As if he were still grief stricken or wracked with guilt. But my gut tells me he wasn't responsible for her death."

"No, but maybe he knows who is, or at least suspects." Erin took a drink of her beer.

"Maybe. I don't know." Darrell drank his too. Cassie took a sip of her soda.

"My money is on the guy who dated her first, Tucker," Cassie said. "From my take on him tonight, I'm sure he didn't like being dropped."

"Yeah, Coco said Tucker never got over her," Erin said. "Maybe he decided if he couldn't have her, no one could."

Cassie added, "He's got a short temper and he came off mean enough to do about anything."

Darrell didn't look convinced. "But the bartender said he saw her walk away and leave the party. On the same sidewalk through the sea grass we used tonight. The same path the ghost took tonight. And he didn't see Tucker or anyone else go after her."

Erin said, "And I talked with Shelley Dominick, the server that overheard the fight right before—" she stopped, shook her head. "Anyway, she confirmed that Amy and Travis had this big fight right before Amy took off. Shelley didn't hear much of the argument, but she still remembers it was about Armstrong Trucking. She remembers hearing Amy yell the company name out loud before she stormed out."

Cassie said, "And when I mentioned Amy's name to Tucker, he got ugly and even threatened me. Kinda. He asked me if I knew the *druggie* who'd been asking questions about the wedding. The one who got run over."

They were all quiet around the table, sipping and thinking. Then Cassie said, her voice small, "I get it. If I'd worked that night, I woulda kept my mouth shut too."

"What?" Erin asked.

"Well, I didn't get it, the way Antonio fusses over Armstrong when he comes in, but now I do. Did you guys see who was at that party tonight?" She shook her head. "If I was one of those working the wedding party, I'd be afraid to say anything to contradict the Armstrongs. The Armstrongs told the police Amy was upset and walked into the ocean, and all the *little people* went along. I mean, how are they supposed to take on that much money?" She glanced at Darrell and Erin. "If it comes to it, how are we going to take on the Armstrongs?"

Darrell reached a hand across the table to pat Cassie on the arm and stopped short. "I see what you mean."

Erin said, "A lot of heavy hitters at this party. I can see what Cassie's getting at."

Darrell said, "I know, but let's don't get ahead of ourselves. One step at a time."

Erin said, "Well, you confirmed that Amy left the reception on her own, heading *away* from the water."

"Hey, maybe that's what Amy was trying to tell us tonight," Darrell said.

Cassie added, "Yeah, that'd make sense. And, from your vision the other night, and how the ghost looks, we're pretty sure Amy was hit by a car and killed."

Darrell went on, "Since no one else saw Amy after she left the reception, we can be pretty sure she was hit on the road. While she was walking after she left the party."

Frowning, Cassie stared first at Darrell and then Erin. "If the ghost is trying to help us, why doesn't she just tell us who hit her?"

"Remember, I told you that the medium said it's very hard for the ghosts to communicate with us," Darrell said. "Maybe, she's told us all she—"

Erin put a hand on his arm. "No!" She looked at both of them. "She doesn't know. It was getting late, right? I mean when she left the party?"

Darrell nodded. "Yeah, it was an evening reception. Pretty much like tonight. It would've been dark. Or getting dark."

Erin picked up that thought. "And the car that came at her would've had its lights on. She's crying, stumbling around on the road in her heels, and she turns and sees a pair of headlights."

Cassie's eyes lit up. "She doesn't know. That's what all this is about. She wants *us* to find out who killed her."

Another brief silence settled over the table and then, after a bit, Erin raised, "Okay then, who hit her?"

Cassie offered, "Couldn't it have been anybody at the party? Maybe another guest who'd had too much to drink and run her down on the road. Maybe they were too drunk to even realize what they did."

Erin asked, "Okay, then what happened to the body?"

Darrell studied both women before answering. "I don't know. It could've been anyone. Travis or Tucker. Or Jennifer who was mad because Amy took Travis away from her. Or maybe even another drunk guest." He shook his head, arguing with himself. "But that would mean James Armstrong—or more likely someone who worked for him—would've had to get rid of the body. And then he had to make up the story about Amy walking into the ocean? I don't know."

He looked from Erin to Cassie, but neither one offered anything. He continued. "But we're missing something." He turned toward Erin. "Remember what Amy left on Josie's flyer. About saving her *and* the other girls. And the message I got from Margaret's ghost. I think it has something to do with Armstrong Trucking. And maybe Less is More. But I don't see how it all ties into Amy's murder."

"I dunno," said Cassie.

"Neither do I." Erin put an index finger on her upper lip. "But I think we need to see if we can find the car."

"What car?" Darrell asked.

"Well, if we're saying she was hit by a car, it would've done some real damage to the front end, right?"

"If they hit Amy along the side—" Darrell pointed to his right side. "—it would've left some damage to the grill, the fender, and maybe even the hood."

Erin said, "And we suspect it was someone at the wedding party."

Cassie objected, "But that was five years ago, how would we find out what car? We can't exactly ask the Armstrongs."

Darrell continued, "No, but if they hit Amy and damaged a car, they would've had it repaired or replaced. If we could find out which car was repaired or replaced shortly after the wedding, maybe we'd have a suspect."

Erin asked, "Wouldn't it have been suspicious? Wouldn't the driver worry about it being reported back then?"

Darrell said, "Remember, everyone believed the story that Amy walked into the ocean and committed suicide. Whoever hit her could simply report they'd hit a deer or something. No one would've questioned them. Remember we're talking about the Armstrongs here and their friends."

Cassie shook her head. "But all this was five years ago. How are you going to find out about some repair to a damaged car, five years ago?"

Darrell stared straight at both women. "I don't think *we* can find out that information. But I think I know someone who can. If I can talk him into it."

Chapter Fifty

"You're telling me a witness told *you* they saw someone run down Amy Parker and kill her five years ago?" Officer Stewart Barnaby took off his mirrored sunglasses and set them on the table.

The cop, Darrell, and Erin sat in a booth on the screen-in porch of the Mad Batter, cups of steaming coffee in front of each. The morning rush had passed, and only a few patrons lingered at nearby tables. Darrell had called Barnaby and asked to meet, saying he had some more info about Josie. Earlier, he'd confided to Erin his idea about a "witness" to the hit and run and his plan to get the cop on their side. She'd been skeptical, but agreed to follow Darrell's lead. He'd told the cop he had new information about Josie but had something else for him first.

"Why didn't they report this when it happened? Five years ago?" The officer's glare went from Darrell to Erin and back. "Who is this mysterious witness anyway?"

Darrell feared Erin had been right. He kept his voice even and glanced at her. "Look, we promised he, er, she, we'd keep it confidential. They wouldn't agree to talk to us otherwise."

"Why would they tell you this? An outsider?" Barnaby challenged.

"Because we're not the cops and because we're

from the outside," Darrell said. "They thought we might believe them. And not rat them out."

"Okay, why'd they wait five years?" The officer's pale blue eyes were hard, like agate marbles.

Darrell decided to take a chance and used his first name. "Look, Stewart, I asked around. I know you're a good cop. You try to do what's right. That's why we're coming to you." He let out a breath. "Also, you've been around long enough you'd know why anyone hasn't come forward before."

Barnaby picked up the cup and eased back in the booth. "Enlighten me." He took a sip.

Darrell said, "I read the police report, and the Armstrongs were pretty insistent Amy walked into the ocean. Even though no one else actually saw her do that."

"So?" Barnaby returned the cup to the saucer.

Erin spoke for the first time, her voice quiet and calm. "If you were a mere waiter, would you speak up and contradict the Armstrongs?"

"So you're saying it was a waiter who witnessed it?" Barnaby shot back.

"We're not saying who the witness is." Darrell fought the urge to flinch. "You get the point. Hardly anyone would be willing to challenge the Armstrong story."

The server approached and the three got quiet. The waitress said, "The gentleman ordered the short stack and his lady the omelet." She set both steaming plates in front of Darrell and Erin and turned to Barnaby, smiling. "And my favorite man in blue ordered his usual, three eggs sunny side up with bacon and hash browns." She set a third plate down in front of the officer. From a voluminous pocket in her checkered green and white apron, she pulled out a bottle of ketchup and a small pitcher of syrup. "Is there anything else I can get you?"

The cop held up his cup.

"Refills coming right up." The server stepped to a nearby warming station and returned with a steaming pot of coffee. In thirty seconds, she filled the cups and left.

For a few minutes, all three dug into their food, the booth quiet. Darrell checked the other tables and was pretty sure the few other customers took little notice. He was glad Barnaby was a regular here, so his presence didn't raise any eyebrows.

His anxiety eating him up, Darrell wanted to press his case, but held back. They'd just dropped a bombshell on Barnaby. Darrell figured he needed to let the officer mull over what they'd told him. So he dug into the pancakes, soaking each bite in syrup, which wasn't all that hard. They were delicious. Still, as he ate, he watched Barnaby, but couldn't read his eyes, even with the sunglasses off.

The cop polished off two of the eggs and one slice of bacon before he spoke. "I'll admit you have a point," he grumbled and grabbed the second piece of bacon, which he pointed at Darrell. "Okay. I'll bite. Did they say who struck the victim?"

"No." Darrell stopped eating and then added, "I asked, but they didn't say. I don't think they know who it was."

"How about a description of the car? A license plate?" Barnaby crunched on the rest of the bacon.

"I've told you everything we were able to get out

of them. Even after five years, they're still terrified," Darrell said.

The officer shook his head. "Okay, why are you telling me about the witness then?" He glanced around the restaurant and lowered his voice to a whisper. "We're talking about the Armstrongs here. What do you expect me to do? You don't have a suspect or a description of the vehicle. You want me to march up to the Armstrongs and ask about some hit and run." He looked the most uncomfortable Darrell'd ever seen him. "That would be career suicide. I'm not *that* good of a cop."

Darrell and Erin exchanged glances and she said, "Nothing like that. Besides, it may have nothing to do with the Armstrongs. There were a lot of other people at the reception."

She looked at Darrell, who continued. "We thought maybe you could check out the local auto body shops. Ask them to check their records? See if anyone brought in a vehicle with front end damage shortly after the wedding night."

Barnaby didn't look convinced, shaking his head slowly and not speaking. After a moment, he said, "Okay, I'm confused. What's all this have to do with Josie Dawson going missing?"

"In a bit." When Darrell saw the cop's eyes get hard again, he added. "Give me a minute and I'll get there."

"I don't know. This is all pretty thin. Sounds like a wild goose chase," Barnaby said.

Erin put down her fork and reached a hand across the table, resting it on the cop's arm. "Officer Barnaby, one kid already was killed merely for asking questions about the wedding."

"You mean Vince Rawlings. I thought that was ruled an accident."

Darrell said, "It was no accident. And Jeremy Tucker pretty much confirmed it at the party last night."

Pulling her hand back, Erin explained about them serving as waiters at Armstrong's big bash and Cassie's encounter with Tucker.

Barnaby said, "Trouble always follows Jeremy Tucker."

Erin spoke up, "And don't forget about our nocturnal venomous visitor." Barnaby tilted his head.

Darrell said, "Yeah, and last night when I asked Travis a few questions about Amy, your Sergeant Harris 'asked' me to leave. Said the Armstrongs didn't need me tearing open old wounds."

"Sergeant Harris?"

Darrell said, "Yeah, he was working security for the party."

"And how is all this connected to Josie's disappearance?"

Darrell reminded him about his visit to the Less Is More Club and talking with Josie, and then how he had discovered the club is owned by the same LLC that owns Armstrong Trucking.

"Really? A strip joint in New York?"

"From the records, looks like multiple strip joints." Then Darrell asked, "Did you get anything from your buddy in Precinct 6? About the Less Is More Club?"

Barnaby looked uncomfortable and didn't meet Darrell's gaze. "Off the record, Eddie told me he's pretty sure there's something hinky about the club, using underage girls like you said. But there's some major players protecting the place. He's not sure how far he can go." He shook his head. "Still, I don't see the connection between Amy Palmer's disappearance and Josie doing tricks in New York. Not to mention, I got no jurisdiction outside of Cape May."

"I don't yet know the connection, but there's something there," Darrell said. As Barnaby finished his breakfast, he studied the man, trying to read his features. Darrell thought he might be losing the cop. He shot a glance at Erin, who got the message.

She said, "Look, we're not naïve. Even if we're not natives, we get who the Armstrongs are. At last night's party, we got a close up look at the circles they run in. We get that you have to tread lightly." She reached across, setting her hand on his arm again. "But what if we're right and Amy didn't commit suicide five years ago? What if our witness is right and she was run over and killed? I know you'd want to catch her killer."

Erin let go, and Barnaby slid out of the booth. "Thanks for the late breakfast. I didn't get to eat before I walked out the door this morning." He stood and put his sunglasses on, his blue eyes hidden again behind the mirrored lenses. "I'll take it under advisement."

Chapter Fifty-One

Darrell worried they'd pushed Barnaby too hard. Or maybe, even a good cop in this town wouldn't be willing to stand up to the Armstrongs. They'd trusted a cop in Wilshire and that hadn't gone the way they planned. While they drank the last of the coffee, he shared his fears with Erin.

She set her cup down. "Let's not get ahead of ourselves. We've done what we could. We planted a seed, and now we'll have to see if it takes root. Even though we don't know Officer Barnaby that well, I have a good feeling about him. I think we need to be a little patient."

Darrell knew she was right, but he wasn't good at being patient. Doing nothing. Even though doing something often got him in trouble. He glanced at his watch. They had about an hour before they were supposed to meet Cassie, after she got off her breakfast shift. He needed to get his mind off this. "What do you say to a little stroll on the beach with your favorite guy?"

"Sounds like a great idea." Taking a final sip, Erin slid out of the booth ahead of him. When he'd slid to the end of the bench, she leaned down and whispered, "Because, if this all blows up and the Armstrongs raise holy hell with the locals, we might never be allowed on Cape May Beach again."

She was grinning, but Darrell could see from the look on her face, she was only half kidding. He dropped enough bills to leave a decent tip and cover the check. As they exited the restaurant, he did a quick sweep of the patrons, but didn't notice anyone paying them any particular attention. But still?

Out in the brilliant June sunshine, they both had to squint, and it took Darrell a moment to get himself re-oriented to where he was. He was amazed at how bright the Jersey sun was, even though the temps were still in the low seventies. He led Erin to his car, parked in the shade with the windows down a bit. Opening the back door, he called, "Hey, Pogo. Erin and I are going walking on the beach. You want to join us, or you want to stay here sleeping?"

The pug opened his eyes at the mention of his name, but didn't move from his perch on the floor beside his now favorite bone.

Erin said, "After the walk, we're going to meet Cassie."

The dog stood up and jumped out of the car. Darrell was unsure whether it was Erin's voice or Cassie's name that made the pooch move. Oh, well. He tried not to take offense. He attached the leash to the pug's collar, and they strode together down Beach Avenue. As they passed the Inn of Cape May, he glanced at the restaurant extension, searching the long glass panes for any sign of Cassie. When he found none, he was disappointed, but not surprised, as she moved in and out of the dining room. He noticed Erin checking out the same windows, probably with similar concerns. He hoped Cassie was doing all right. Right then, he almost headed up Ocean to go talk to her, but she said Antonio got upset when she was bothered during her shift.

Darrell checked his watch again. They could head over there in fifty minutes. It would be soon enough, wouldn't it? Just then, the hairs on the back of his neck prickled. He stopped, glancing around, his gaze doing a 360 sweep, but caught nothing out of the ordinary. Tourists loaded down with beach chairs and umbrellas heading for the sand. A few vacationers going in and out of shops. Cars rolling down Ocean and across Beach Avenue. No specters. No bloodied figures in the white.

"What? What is it?" Erin stopped beside him, the pug pulling up short. Her eyes followed his. "Do you sense something?"

The prickle receded—if it were ever there in the first place—and Darrell did a slow shake of his head. "No. When I was checking out Aleathea's, looking for Cassie, I thought I felt something. But I don't see anything. Anything out of place." He lowered his voice, so the couple passing them, hurrying to the beach, wouldn't hear. "No spirits."

Erin took his free hand. "We'll see Cassie in a little bit, and you can compare…um, notes. See if she felt something. Besides, someone promised me a walk on the beach."

They crossed at the light, and Darrell took in the sight ahead of them—a near perfect, expansive sandy beach edged by crystal blue water that seemed to stretch on forever, merging with a perfect azure sky. Smudges of white dotted the heavenly canvas, and small curls of white-topped breakers were sprinkled along the waters farther out. Quiet waves gurgled up upon the sand, before leaking back into the watery expanse. Even with everything they were dealing with, this image never failed to impress him. He inhaled, taking in the salty scent coming off the gentle sprays.

He could see why Cape May had been such a favored escape for more than 150 years. You throw in the meticulous architecture of all those Victorian mansions and B & B's, and you have a resort few places could match. If you didn't mind the ghosts.

He glanced at his two companions and realized he only felt this great because he got to share it all with Erin. And having Pogo along was a bonus. Taking their time, they sauntered across the top of the beach, his sandals sinking into the soft, white sand. They had to dodge excited tourists already staking claim to a patch of beach at ten in the morning. While they ambled, the pug running back and forth on the leash, Darrell pointed out the Convention Hall farther down the beach, where he'd first encountered the ghost.

They did a slow circle and returned to where they entered. After using the shower to wash the sand off their sandals and the dog's paws, they stepped onto the Promenade. Darrell checked his watch again and noticed Cassie still had another twenty minutes on her shift. "I don't know why, but I feel anxious about Cassie. She's awfully young, and we had her out pretty late. I only want to make sure she's okay."

"Well, then, let's head over," Erin said. "We can get another cup of coffee."

Darrell wiped a bead of sweat off his forehead. "Or maybe a glass of iced tea."

"An even better idea."

They crossed Beach Ave again and cut up the

sidewalk on Ocean to the Inn entrance. Darrell led Pogo around the corner of the flower bed to a shady area and tied the leash to a post. "You hang out here for a while. We won't be very long."

When they came through the door, Antonio greeted them with a broad smile, two hands in the air. "My favorite couple. You come for a late breakfast?"

Erin reached out and placed her hand on the owner's arm. "Thank you, Antonio, no. We're saving Aleathea's for a glorious dinner tonight." She winked at him. "Now, we're here to see Cassie after she gets off her shift. But we'd love a couple of iced teas while we wait."

The maître de never dropped his smile. "Of course. Follow me." He led them through the nearly empty restaurant to a table by the window. "Cassie, she's been a little tired this morning. She had a late night last night? At the Armstrong party?"

Darrell said, "You can say that. We're a little bushed this morning and we didn't have to go to work."

Antonio said, "Cassie is in the back." He glanced around the room. "As you can see, we are slow this morning. How about I let her go early?"

Darrell said, "That'd be great."

"I'll get her and tell her you're here." The small man waddled off toward the swinging doors.

Darrell and Erin glanced at each other, surprised. Maybe Antonio had a heart after all. They'd have to tell Cassie.

Thirty seconds later, he reappeared at their table, wrenching his hands. "Miss Erin, you are a nurse, no?"

"Yeah, I'm an RN. Does someone need medical help?"

He leaned over and whispered, "Uh, could you come with me?" His gaze darted around the restaurant.

Darrell asked, "Is something wrong?"

The owner's eyes did another quick sweep of the room. "It's Miss Cassie. She told another server she didn't feel so good. I went back to the break room and she has her head on the table. I can't wake her."

Darrell felt the prickle on his neck again, but before he had a chance to signal Erin, she was up and hustling toward the kitchen doors, Antonio at her heels. He jumped up and followed, hurrying to catch up. When they pushed through the swinging aluminum doors, Antonio indicated a table over in the corner. They went over and found Cassie slumped, head down on the red tabletop.

Erin stepped next to the slumped figure, placed a hand on her arm and said gently, "Cassie?" When the girl made no movement, Erin leaned down. "Cassie," she said louder. When that drew no response, she reached down, touched the girl's forehead, then moved her fingers to Cassie's neck.

Beside Cassie sat a basket of muffins in multi-colored cups, the plastic wrap opened at the top. Darrell lifted a decorative basket, examining it. A gift tag with a message hung from a fancy ribbon and he read it aloud. "Thank you, Cassie, for taking care of the funeral arrangements for our son, Vince. Your kindness did not go unnoticed. The Rawlins."

Darrell spotted a half-eaten muffin on a white plate next to Cassie. His first thought was the girl must've been so tired, she fell asleep eating. He set the basket back on the table, puzzling. The Rawlins? How would Vince's family even know Cassie handled the arrangements? The prickle shot down his back.

He glanced at Erin and saw the fear her eyes. He moved in closer to the girl. Cassie's complexion was pale, even for her. A white residue clung around her mouth. And her lips had turned an ugly shade of blue, and not from that crazy makeup she liked. Leaning over the teen, he sniffed and caught a weird smell, but couldn't identify it. He turned to meet Erin's gaze and ask her, but she cut him off.

"Antonio, call 911."

"What?" the owner seemed perplexed.

"Call 911 *now*," Erin snapped, a full on command.

Antonio shuffled out to the lobby, presumably where the phone was, Darrell hoped.

911? Oh God, not Cassie. She was only a kid.

"What is it? What's wrong?" he asked.

Erin didn't take her eyes off the teen. "I'm not sure." She used one finger to open each eyelid. "Cassie, can you hear me?" When that drew no response, Erin turned back to Darrell. "Her breathing is labored."

Antonio's anxious voice carried through the nearly empty restaurant, yelling into the phone, "Aleathea's. At the Inn of Cape May. Hurry."

This could not be happening again. "What?" Darrell asked.

"She's having trouble breathing." Erin gestured toward Cassie. "Here, help me get her on the floor."

The urgency in Erin's voice galvanized him into action. Working together, they got Cassie's limp body out of the chair and onto the dirty linoleum floor. Erin leaned in close to Cassie. She tapped on the girl's cheeks, one after the other, and called, "Cassie, it's Erin. Can you hear me?"

The girl's body lay still.

Darrell asked, "What is it? Do you know what wrong with her?"

"It's been a while since my toxicology class in nursing school and my turn in the ER," she said, "but if I remember correctly, Cassie is exhibiting symptoms of some toxin?"

"What?"

When Erin turned toward him, he could see terror ignite in her eyes. "I think she's been poisoned."

Chapter Fifty-Two

"We didn't have any choice. She stopped breathing in the ambulance."

Cassie heard the voice but couldn't see who was speaking. Everything was...dark. She tried to open her eyes, but she...couldn't. She had no idea where she was. Or what happened. Who had stopped breathing?

What *did* she remember?

She *really* hadn't wanted to come into work today. After their crazy night last night at the Armstrongs' party, she'd woken up exhausted and hungry. So starved, when she finally got a break at Aleathea's, she'd devoured one of those muffins from the gift basket Vince's family sent. Vince's family? The thing didn't taste that good, and she didn't particularly like muffins. She was so hungry, she didn't care.

Funny, she couldn't recall Vince ever mentioning his family. She didn't know anything about his family and was surprised they knew she helped out with the funeral arrangements. Maybe the funeral home got word to his family somehow.

Her stomach had cramped like hell and pain shot through her arms. Her head throbbed. She felt incredibly tired. She needed to lay her head on the table for a while, its surface cool on her cheek. Then she couldn't catch her breath.

Oh, God, she was the one who stopped breathing!

"Keep a close watch on her," a male voice said. "We had to put her in a coma to give her body a little time."

A coma? She was in a friggin' coma?

That couldn't be right. She needed to tell them she was awake, was right here. She could hear them. She tried to say something, to yell. When she went to open her mouth, there was a damn tube down her throat. She couldn't get any words to come out. Couldn't even get her lips to move. She had to do something. She struggled to raise her arms, to signal the doctor—she guessed he was a doctor—but found she couldn't move them. They felt…leaden.

Time for her body to do what?

"If her body doesn't respond soon, we'll have to move her to Philly Presbyterian," the doctor said. "We'll know soon."

The voices got quieter, farther away. They were leaving her. She wanted to scream, "Come back. I'm right here," but couldn't get anything to come out. When the voices died away, something beeped over and over again.

She needed to do something. But, as hard as she tried, she couldn't figure out what to do. God, she was tired. Unconsciousness tugged at her, its languid tendrils dragging her down. She knew what was down there, beyond her wall. She didn't want to give in, go there, but she was so tired. It felt good to let go and surrender. So she did.

****

"Why the hell in't my dinner ready?" her father slurred, two bloodshot eyes narrowing.

"It's almost ready," her mother offered, struggling

to keep her voice bright. Her beautiful, oval face bore a strained smile, an expression Cassie knew from experience was forced. "Only a few more minutes." Her voice lilted up.

The man took another step into the kitchen, stumbling slightly before catching himself. Cassie, playing with her doll on the floor off to the side, watched him, waiting, terrified. His gaze zeroed in on her mom and Cassie saw her cower, struggling to keep the smile in place. Then suddenly, he pivoted to Cassie and saw her watching him. "What are *you* looking at?" he hollered.

He took two quick steps—in his condition, how could he move like that?—and stood over her. The odor from his putrid breath belched down, almost making her gag. She shut her eyes and curled into a ball, knowing what was coming.

"Look at me when I'm talking to you," he screamed, his mouth inches from her head, spittle landing in her hair. "After all I do for you *females*, why don't either of you show me any respect?"

Still in a tight ball, she dared to open one eye. Her mom said, "Henry Richard, leave the young girl alone. She's only ten." Her mom's voice had a desperate, pleading sound to it. "Come sit down and I'll serve you some meatloaf. It's your favorite." She patted the old red Formica table.

Her father loomed over Cassie, massive and threatening, his eyes red, wild and huge. He straightened to his full six-foot height and turned toward her mother. "Woman, *you* don't tell me what to do," he got out between clenched teeth. He swiped one long, powerful arm at her. Cassie heard his hand connect with her mom's face, the smack loud in the small house.

She stared between the fingers covering her eyes. Her mom stumbled backward. Her head collided with the edge of the kitchen table, the thud ugly. Her mother's eyes closed. Her body collapsed onto the cracked linoleum. Her father moved across the space, stumbling again, and leaned over the still body.

"Caroline, that's enough." He had to lean against the table to steady himself. "Get back up here and get me my dinner."

Cassie scuttled over to where her mom lay, motionless on the floor. "Mom?" she cried, her voice sounding like a little kid. Cassie's gaze darted from the angry man looming over them back to her mom. The cut on the back of her mom's head turned red, and blood trickled from the wound, staining the worn white flooring red. She choked and mumbled, "Oh, Mom!"

Her father's toe nudged her mom's leg. "Stop playing possum and get back up. Come on."

Cassie rifled through the pockets of her mom's dress and came up with a small linen handkerchief. Her mom always kept one there. She pressed it to the wound. Immediately, the red overspread the white. Terrified, she stared at the oozing blood and then forced herself to look up at her father. "She's hurt. Bad." She had to choke the words out.

The man leaned against the table and stared at his wife on the floor, though it looked to Cassie he had trouble focusing. She pulled the handkerchief away, held it out to him, and quickly reapplied it. "She's bleeding bad. She needs help."

Both hands still on the table, he peered down at the

prone figure of the woman he married. His eyes narrowed in concentration. "Can't be too bad. She only bumped the table." He belched. "Give her a minute and she'll come around."

Cassie held the cloth tight against the cut, like her mom taught her. The blood still flowed, though the stream had slowed, she thought. She leaned in closer. "Mom?" Still no response. She glanced from her mom to her dad. He stood above her, a blank expression on his face. Cassie whispered, "She needs to go to the hospital."

"Naw, she just needs a little sleep time. A little nighty-night."

Cassie didn't know what to do. Unless she kept the handkerchief pressed against the wound, her mom's bleeding could get worse. But, if she didn't get help, her mom might not wake up. If she went to the phone, what would her dad do to her? He never liked other people in "their bizness."

She decided. "I'm calling for help," she announced. She expected a swift hand, but none came. She took a few quick steps to the phone on the wall and looked back. Her father stood there, staring down at her mom, head tilted to one side. She punched in the numbers her mom had scrawled on the pad beside the phone. She shot another glance at her father, who still hadn't moved.

"Caroline?" he said softly.

As soon as she heard someone answer, she blurted out, "My mom's hurt and her head's bleeding." Certain her dad would come over and cut off the line, she rattled off their address and said, "Send help quick."

She braced for the coming blow.

Chapter Fifty-Three

Darrell paced across the ER waiting room, his feet tracing the wide black line in the linoleum that ran in front of the five large windows. The daylight streaming through the glass was bright, blinding almost, but he didn't care. He kept on, using his arm to block the sunlight when he had to, ten paces across the room—he counted them—and ten back. As he walked back and forth, he stayed focused on the hallway where they took Cassie.

After the paramedics had rushed Cassie out of the restaurant on a stretcher, Erin had hurried after them, yelling at Darrell to grab the basket. He did and then once outside, he snatched Pogo's leash. They all ran down the block to his car and jumped in. He slammed on the accelerator and the car roared out of the parking space, tires leaving a black scar on the road. Speeding like a possessed race car driver, he swerved between traffic until he caught up to the ambulance. Then he kept on the ambulance's tail all the way to Burdette, driving in the wake of the flashing red lights and siren. He screeched into a marked space and threw the car into park, yelling to Pogo to stay. They bolted out of the car and ran through the sliding ER doors barely in time to see the EMT's roll the gurney back down the hallway. When he and Erin tried to follow, a security guard blocked them, despite Erin's loud protestations.

Darrell shifted his glance to the clock. That had been more than an hour ago. He returned his gaze to his feet and resumed his pacing. One, two, three, four. He couldn't help himself. Erin didn't even comment on his OCD behavior, and that worried him. Sitting forward in one of the blue cushioned chairs, she simply stared at the hallway where they'd taken Cassie.

A young doctor came through the door and asked, "Are you the nurse who brought the young girl in?" He consulted a clipboard. "A Cassie Davis?"

Erin shot up out of her chair and was standing beside the physician before Darrell could even stop his mid-pace. He hustled over and joined them.

"My name is Dr. Barrett. I was on call when they brought Cassie in," said the young ER doctor. "It's a good thing you got to her when you did," With his longish blond hair and dazzling blue eyes, Darrell thought he looked more like a young movie star than a doc. And with his boyish features, he could've passed for one of Darrell's high school students. "The girl's lucky you're a nurse. It was smart thinking to have the EMT's pump her stomach right away." He bore a solemn expression, which looked out of place on the youthful face. "What made you think it was poison? Have you dealt with many poison cases?"

Erin shifted from one foot to the other but held the doctor's gaze. "No, this is my first one. But I remembered the symptoms from my training—the white residue around her mouth"—she touched her own lips—"the rapid pulse and dilated eyes. And I didn't want to chance it."

The doctor glanced down at the floor for the first time. "Yeah, it must've been a strong dose, because she stopped breathing on the way here. Thank God, the paramedic knew how to intubate her."

"She's breathing through a tube?" Erin asked, her anxiety high.

Bringing his face back up, the doctor placed a hand on Erin's arm. "For now. Her respiration is back in the normal range. Now we want to give the rest of her body a chance to catch up." He swallowed. "I decided to put her in a coma."

"A coma?" Erin squeaked out.

The young doctor held her gaze. "Just for now. We need to give her system some time to try to fight off the toxin. I've already sent the stomach contents to the lab. As soon as we know what it was, we'll administer an antidote." He stopped and then added, "If there is one."

"Can we see her?" Erin asked, the sob evident in her words.

"In a little bit, yes. I have a few questions first. Are you family?"

Erin shook her head. "No, we're just friends. She doesn't have any family. At least, not around here. Do you need some permission for medical treatment?"

"No, she's stable for now," Dr. Barrett said. "But if she doesn't improve in the next few hours, we may need to airlift her to Philly Presbyterian. We'd need someone to sign off then."

Erin said, "If it comes to that, we'll see if we can contact someone."

The young doctor nodded. "Okay, do you know how she was poisoned? You had them pump her stomach, so you must have guessed she ingested the poison. Do you know how?"

Anxious to do something, Darrell answered first,

"We think it was in the muffin." He went over to a table and picked up the basket. The half-eaten muffin sat on top of the pyramid of baked goods and he pointed at it. "We found this next to her on the table. We figured she was eating this."

Barrett said, "I'll take that down and have it tested as well." He accepted the basket. Staring down at the colorful ribbons tied around the present, he shook his head, the long blond hairs flailing. "If it is poison, we'll need to notify the authorities."

Darrell said, "I already left a message with the Cape May Police Department. I'm hoping to hear back soon."

The doctor said, "I'll take you to see Cassie, but you can only stay a few minutes." He led the way, carrying the basket in one hand and holding the door with the other.

When they entered the cramped hospital room, Darrell was stunned at how small and helpless Cassie looked. A tube protruded from her mouth and extended to some kind of breathing machine as the mechanism pumped rhythmically. She lay there, eyes closed, her small chest moving slowly in and out. A line attached to her left arm led to a translucent plastic bag, and the liquid dripped into the line.

He studied the teen, wanting to do something, to reach out to her, but was afraid how their special connection might affect all this. Maybe Erin knew what he was thinking because she moved around Darrell and took the girl's free hand in hers. She whispered, "We're right here for you, Cass."

He glanced over at Erin, whose eyes were filled with tears. He fought it but could feel himself coming apart. Not in front of Erin. He bent over, shaking his head back and forth, back and forth, and felt Erin's palm on his back. He straightened up and faced her. "If anything happens to her..." He jerked his head toward the young girl. "If anything more happens..." He choked and finished, "If she doesn't come out of this okay, I'll never forgive myself." He felt tears trying to squeeze out and rubbed both eyes with a hand. "I can be so stupid sometimes. Why did I let her get mixed up with all this?"

Erin released Cassie's hand and grabbed both his hands. She tugged and forced him to look at her. "This is not your fault. Someone, some sick son of a bitch tried to poison Cassie. Not you." She sniffled and dropped one hand so she could use it to wipe her face. "Based on what Antonio told us, Cassie must've eaten the muffin not that long before we found her. Not much more than half an hour at most."

She turned her gaze toward the teen and Darrell followed. She said, "Cassie's one strong kid. If anyone can beat this, it'll be her."

They were so intent on watching Cassie, they hadn't even heard the nurse come into the room. She placed a hand on Erin's arm. "Dr. Barrett said that's enough for now. The patient needs to rest."

She guided Erin toward the door and Darrell followed. Before they stepped through the doorway, he turned back around and whispered, "I'm so sorry, Cassie."

Chapter Fifty-Four

Cassie heard more voices in the room. She dragged herself out of her stupor and concentrated. She thought she recognized them. Wasn't that Darrell? And Erin? She wanted to say something. Struggled to get some words out again, but couldn't. Her throat still had that damn tube. Straining, she caught bits and pieces, but not enough to understand what they were saying.

Again, after a few minutes, the voices started to recede, the room getting quieter. Then she heard Darrell say, "I'm so sorry, Cassie."

Sorry? Sorry for what?

She didn't want them to leave. Wanted to tell them to come back. She couldn't, and the voices died away completely. Then nothing, only the rhythmic beep of the machine. Instead, she felt herself being dragged back. Back where she didn't want to go. She fought it, but she felt so tired. She couldn't move anything, say anything. In the end, the blackness drew her under again. Unable to struggle any more, she gave in and surrendered.

****

She stood beside her mother's hospital bed, listening to the insistent beep of the machine. She wanted her mom to wake up, but the eyes stayed shut. Standing on her toes, Cassie stared at the dressing on the top of her mom's head. They had shaved away some of her mom's beautiful black hair! The scalp sat exposed, scraped red next to the white bandage.

Please, Mom, open your eyes.

A doctor, in a long white coat, came in. Cassie clutched her doll. He said her mom was going to be all right. He'd asked for her dad. Cassie didn't look at him. Told him Daddy went working in the mine. Wouldn't be done until late. The doc said her mom had a concussion and lost a lot of blood, but only needed time to recover.

It wasn't that Cassie didn't believe him. She needed to see those caramel eyes open. Maybe her mom could hear Cassie's silent wish, 'cause the brown eyes fluttered and then opened, staring at Cassie. A small smile broke across her mom's face. "Cassie, my little miracle."

Cassie jumped up out the chair and grasped her mom's free hand. Tears gushed down her face. "Mom, you're not dead. I thought Daddy had killed you."

Her mom gave a slight shake of her head. "Not yet." She tried to turn her head to the side and winced. She eased back against the sheet. Without moving her head, she asked, "Where is your father?"

Cassie gulped. "He said he had to go to work. He said we was making too big a deal out of a *little cut*. Said I shouldn't have called for help." Cassie stared down at the floor and said, "I knew he was going to hit me, but I called anyway." She looked back up. "He even argued with the EMT's when they said they needed to take you to the hospital. He yelled he wasn't payin' for some Goddamn unnecessary hospital visit for a bump on the head." Then she grinned. "They even let me ride in the ambulance with you."

"You did great, baby," her mom said, then coughed. "I'm going to be okay." She reached out and patted her daughter's arm. She stared at the clock across the room. "When did your father say he was coming by?"

Cassie's gaze went to the clock. "I don't know. He said something about stopping at Sharpie's after he got done."

"Good, then we got some time to talk." Her mom tapped a spot on the bed. "Come on up here, so I can see you without craning my neck."

Cassie climbed up onto the empty space on the sheet her mom pointed at. Her mom took a deep breath. "After this, I can't come back home."

Cassie's eyes filled with tears. "What do you mean? Are you going to die?"

Her mom patted her arm again. "No, I'm not going to die. At least, not yet."

"I don't understand." Cassie's tears rolled into her mouth.

Her mother adjusted a button on the bed and a motor whirred. The top half rose about halfway. She stopped it. "That's better. At least, I can look at you when we talk." She took another deep breath. "You remember I told you about my second sight?"

"You mean like when you told me we were going to have a bad storm and Bailey's house was going to have its roof lifted off? Then it all happened exactly like you said."

"Yeah, that's what I mean."

"Dad said it was all madness...and evil," Cassie blurted out. "He said people would call you crazy if they knew."

"He was partly right. People might think I'm crazy. That's why I've never told anyone but you…and your father." She met her daughter's eyes. "But it *is not* madness, and it certainly isn't evil. It's a gift…and I think you might have one too. Didn't you tell me you see some things and some people others can't see?"

"Daddy says it was crazy talk—"

"Don't listen to your father. He don't understand. Remember, you have a gift."

"What does that have to do with you not coming home?" Cassie sniffed, fear in her eyes.

"I saw something…in my second sight." Her mother's voice seemed to drift off and her eyes glanced out the window. Then she pulled her gaze from some faraway place to Cassie's face. "If I don't get away, your father…your father is going to kill me."

"No." Cassie shook her head hard. "No, I won't let him." She kept shaking her head hard back and forth.

Her mom reached out with both hands and grabbed her daughter's face, stilling her head. "I know. I saw, and that's the problem. If you try to stop him, he kills you too."

"You saw that." Cassie gasped. "Well, then, we'll tell someone. Tell them he hit you today. That he's going to hurt you. They'll make him stay away."

Her mom released her head and patted her hand. "No, baby. They'll all say I'm crazy." When Cassie tried to object, she stopped her. "Remember, this is your father's town. He'll say we were arguing and he's sorry about hitting me. He knows the cops and other important people. He'll tell them I'm crazy." She stopped for a bit and then continued, "And they'll believe him."

"But, Mama, what are we going to do?" Cassie tasted her tears again.

"Right now, I need to rest and think about this." Her mother offered a sad smile. "I want you to go down to the cafeteria and wait for your father."

"I want to be with you."

"I know, baby, but you can't. I need to figure this out."

Just then, a nurse came in and placed a palm on Cassie's back. "Your mom had a nasty bump on the head. Why don't we give her a little time to rest? You can come back a little later."

Reluctantly, Cassie released her mom's hand and climbed off the bed. The nurse continued, "James here will walk you down to our little cafeteria." She pointed to a man in white scrubs standing beside the doorway. "Maybe he can get you some ice cream."

As Cassie exited the room, she glanced back at her mom on the hospital bed. "I love you, Mama."

Her mom's weak smile returned. "I love you more."

That was the last glimpse she ever had of her mother.

Chapter Fifty-Five

Darrell sat in the waiting room, agonizing, hoping. No, flat out terrified. He stared at the faded, blue paint on the wall, with scuff and scratch marks making a jagged line at chair height, as if they were marking some flood line. Darrell felt like he was in the middle of that flood, surrounded on all sides by water. And he was drowning. Tears struggled through his ducts and stung his cheeks. Glancing across at Erin, he read the same miasma of emotions washing across her face, except she looked like she was holding it together better. She wasn't crying, at least, not yet.

They weren't alone in their misery. Two other individuals sat on the worn blue cushions in the ER waiting room, drowning in their own grief and anguish. The first was a man who looked ancient with shriveled skin covering his face and hands, a small wisp of white hair clinging to his scalp. He gazed desperately toward one of the bays, where Darrell'd seen two EMT's roll in a woman ten minutes earlier. The man simply sat, dull gray eyes glazed over, muttering, "Gloria. Gloria." The second, a middle-aged woman, rose from her seat and paced the space, like some caged tiger, much like he had before—though he noticed not along the black line.

Overhead, a ceiling fluorescent fixture sputtered, the neon blinking off and on in mind-numbing succession. The shutter effect of the light bathed the entire room in a surreal atmosphere, like some old-time movie.

Cassie was going to be okay. She had to be. He could not lose someone else. He *could not* be responsible for one more death.

But there would *be* another death, he knew. With the ghosts, it was simply a matter of time. And who.

He forced his gaze to the windows that lined one wall. When he and Erin arrived, it had been a brilliant morning, the sunlight dazzling earlier while they walked, hand in hand, along the beach. Was that only a couple hours ago? It seemed like ages. Now, even the outside appeared dreary, as if nature had conspired and stuffed gray clouds over their space. The afternoon had turned gloomy, oppressive.

A police car careened into the driveway and drove up the ramp. It jolted to a sudden stop. An officer vaulted out and strode through the doors, which swished open.

Darrell jumped up to meet him. "Officer Barnaby."

"I was out on patrol when they reached me," the cop said, removing his sunglasses. "They said something happened to Cassie."

Darrell gulped. "She's been poisoned."

"Poisoned? Really?" The officer glanced around the room. "Are you sure?"

Erin joined them. "They pumped her stomach and are testing the contents now, but from the symptoms she exhibited, I'm pretty certain it's poison."

"Was it something she ate?"

"Yeah, muffins," Darrell snapped.

"Muffins?" Confusion reigned in his blue eyes.

Erin said, "We think someone injected some kind

of poison into muffins that were delivered with a note to Cassie. The note was supposed to be a thank you from Vince's family, but we doubt it. Cassie had eaten most of one of the muffins and collapsed." She glanced at Darrell and finished, "We're waiting on tests on the muffins as well."

The cop glanced toward the bay, as if he was considering going back to ask the doctor, maybe checking on their wild story, but he didn't move.

After a beat, Darrell asked, "Have you found out anything about the car involved in the collision we discussed?"

Barnaby shook his head, as if he was bone tired. "I haven't had time to check it out yet."

"You haven't had time to check it out yet?" Darrell raised his voice. Erin placed a hand on his arm, but he shook it off. "How much more do you need? First, Vince gets run over and killed. Then someone drops a Goddamn timber rattler in our bed and tried to kill Erin and me." He jabbed toward the bays. "Now, someone just poisoned Cassie. What do we all have in common? We had the audacity to ask questions about the night Amy Palmer disappeared."

In a measured tone, Barnaby said, "You don't know they're all related."

"Tell that to the girl in there," Darrell called. "She may die and you're saying it's a damn coincidence?"

"I didn't mean it that way," the cop muttered.

Erin stepped in front of Darrell. This time she placed a hand on Barnaby's arm. "We're all freaked out about this. Cassie's a good kid, and we're afraid we got her into something ugly. Something we can't control."

The officer nodded. "Maybe, I can find out

something else from the doctors." He started toward the bays and almost ran into a young woman in a lab coat and a bun of blonde hair tied atop her head.

Though her face was pretty, her features bore a serious expression. Darrell's stomach knotted up. The woman glanced at the uniformed police officer and then at Darrell and Erin. "Are you the two who brought—" She consulted a clipboard. "—a Cassie Davis in?"

"Yes," they answered in unison.

She shot a look at the cop, as if asking if it was okay to go on. Darrell nodded and she said, "We got the tox screen back on her stomach contents and the doctor told me to inform you."

"What'd you find?" Erin asked, because Darrell suddenly found his throat went dry.

"It appears she had ingested hemlock. A good amount of it. We're guessing from the muffins, based on her stomach contents. They're testing the other muffins now, but we're pretty sure."

"Hemlock?" Erin sounded incredulous.

The lab tech continued, "It's a pretty common plant around here. Grows wild in some fields. Easy to get if you know what to look for. I've heard some crazies even cultivate it in their greenhouses."

Darrell glanced at Barnaby, who seemed to find the floor fascinating.

"What about an antidote?" Erin asked, her voice tight.

The lab tech now stared at the floor. "I understand they've flushed her system and pumped everything out of her stomach. Hopefully, that will completely leech the toxin out of her body."

No one said anything and Darrell glanced from

Erin to Barnaby to the lab tech. Finally, he repeated, "What about an antidote?"

The pretty blonde lab assistant never looked up. "There is none."

Chapter Fifty-Six

Cassie heard voices again and sensed, figured someone else was in her room. She tried to drag herself out of her stupor, maybe catch their attention. Could they help bring her out of this?

Nothing she did seemed to make any difference. Trapped in this twilight world and she desperately wanted out. Felt like she was swimming in quicksand, the walls of sand collapsing in on her, and the harder she stroked, the deeper she was sucked under. Her stomach cramped again, and the pain shot through her belly. She was going to throw up, but the damn tube down her throat stopped that.

She thought she caught Darrell's voice again. And someone else, a man she didn't recognize.

"Barnaby, she's in a coma." Darrell sounded angry.

"Do you have any idea how much longer she'll be under?" the other guy asked. "I need to question her. See if she knows anything about the person who dropped off the basket of muffins."

A quiet female voice responded, "Sorry, Officer, we simply don't know. It could be hours or it could be days. Sometimes, she seems to start to come out of it and then, for some reason, drops back into it. It's almost as if something is pulling her back under. We don't know. But the doctors believe she'll come out of it soon enough."

"Isn't there anything you can give her, maybe help wake her?" The cop sounded brusque.

Cassie tried to move, to make some noise.

"See!" the cop said. "She's trying to talk. Can't you take the tube out?"

The next words made Cassie's heart sink.

The quiet female, no doubt a nurse, said, "She's probably hallucinating. It's part of what the body goes through fighting off the poison. Her vitals look stable and we…"

The voice seemed to drift off, as if it were carried by some wayward wind. Cassie felt the pull of exhaustion dragging her down into the oblivion again. Heard someone crying.

Was that her?

****

A young woman stood sobbing inside a large tent with one flap open. Tears ran down her perfectly rouged cheeks, over the corner of trembling lips, and dripped onto a white lace collar. She shook her head again and again, tossing the golden tresses that had been gathered so carefully under the veil earlier.

"Amy, please, listen to me. It doesn't matter," a guy's voice pleaded.

"It can't be true," she managed, gasping. "You said your family has money. Big money. Your dad is the CEO of a large shipping company. My God, look at this place. It's a palace. And it's a *second* home." Her hands swept around the tent, the space crowded with more vases of pink and white gardenias—her favorite—than she'd ever seen in her life. The long white sleeves slid up as she gestured. "I heard what you and Jeremy were bragging about. Why would your family do…that?"

She stared at the young man, whose facial expression didn't change.

He was so handsome, she thought the first time she saw him, with the face you'd expect to see on some Renaissance painting—pouty mouth, deep, searching blue eyes, and small nose, slightly turned up. With the body of a Greek god. And on top of that, the family was loaded. When they met and fell in love, she couldn't believe it, thought she'd landed inside some fairy tale. Then, he asked her to be his wife.

Now this.

The corners of his perfect mouth turned up just a bit. "How do you think we became so rich?" He swayed a bit, but his cocky grin never left his face. "Look, we do okay with the shipping, and it provides the perfect cover." He leaned in closer, and the overwhelming odor of alcohol hit her. He whispered, "We've even adapted some of our trucks to provide a place for the girls to work their, um, magic. It's a secret compartment in the back of the trailers with a bed and air-conditioning and everything. Sh-sh-sh." He winked.

She couldn't believe it. "But you said the girls are young, even teenagers."

His grin morphed into a smirk. "Look, it's what these girls want to do. We're simply helping to prime the supply in a tough profession." His eyebrows went up. "The world's oldest profession."

Amy sniffed once. "Damn, why today? Why'd you decide to tell me today?" Her finger pointed out the opening to the vine covered arch through which they were scheduled to make their grand entrance to the reception. As man and wife.

The young man placed one hand on her arm. "Do

you love me?"

She sniffled and said, "You know I do, Travis." The tears came again, and she was unable to control the sobs between the words. "I've loved you since the day we met at the club on the beach."

"I love you, too," he confessed. But he wasn't done. "I thought you could handle it. And since we're married now—" He gestured to the large diamond ring on her finger. "—I figured you deserved to know. You know, since we promised to keep no secrets from each other. I'm not involved in that part of the business. But I get it. Someone's going to make money from that, so it might as well be us."

She started shaking her head again, more violently this time. The gardenias that had been attached to the edge of the veil came loose and drooped in front of her eyes. Her hand brushed them out of the way. "But it's wrong." She shook her head harder. "No, it's evil." She kept shaking her head, afraid to let it stop.

She couldn't look at him, couldn't stand to see that smile right now. She started to pull away, but he grabbed her. "I need to get away, to think about this," she said. "On my day, our day, this is too much."

She yanked away from him and ran out the opening, her hurried steps hampered by the long, flowing white dress. She heard her name called, first by him, then by some others, but she ignored their entreaties. She kept going across the Persian rugs covering the sand, over the wooden walkway, through the side yard, and down the circular driveway, following the trail of tiny twinkling lights edging the pavement. The noises of the party—their reception— flowed from behind the house, the music of the small

345

orchestra and the sounds of people laughing, talking. She turned to face them.

No, she had to get away, to think, so she whirled back around and kept going. She stumbled twice, her heels catching on the hem of the long dress. In frustration, she hurled the shoes onto the perfectly manicured lawn and kept going into the street. The roughness of the asphalt tore at her stockings and scratched the soles of her feet, but she ignored the pain.

How had she gotten herself into this situation? She always tried to be careful, to see all sides, to look at things from different perspectives. But she never even suspected anything like this. Not with that handsome face and that beautiful body. And Travis had been so good to her.

No, she couldn't think about that. She kept going, down the street and back onto Beach Avenue. As the music and party noise receded, the dark enveloped her. She slowed her pace to a walk, one deliberate step after the other. With each footstep, her decision became clearer. She loved him, but couldn't stay married to him, couldn't be part of *that* family. She used the silky fabric of her sleeve to wipe her eyes. She'd have plenty of time for tears later. Now, she needed to go back and tell Travis goodbye.

Behind her on the street, she heard the roar of a large car engine. She turned. A pair of bright headlights came directly at her. She raised an arm to shield against the light and tried to move away. Too late, she screamed.

Chapter Fifty-Seven

Darrell sat with Erin in two stiff, uncomfortable chairs beside Cassie's bed. At least, the nurses had let them in here. For a while, anyway. Through the narrow window in the room, the gray of the sky reached in and cast a pall over the room, only adding to his despair. Erin grabbed his hand and glanced at him, her eyes wet, and then at the still form of their young friend. He felt his own eyes moisten again and watched Cassie's chest make the slight rise and fall, in rhythm with the beeping machine. Erin squeezed his hand, hard.

What had the nurse said? Cassie could wake up anytime. Or it could be days. At least, she said the other signs were good. Her body seem to be winning the battle against the poison. Or so the doctors thought. They'd have a better idea when Cassie woke up.

How long had they been here? He glanced at his watch. Almost eight hours. He'd paced the waiting room one thousand, five hundred and fifty times. Erin had gone to the cafeteria and brought back a few highly preserved and processed items from the vending machines. But he didn't feel like eating. He'd wandered outside three different times, checking on Pogo, feeding him and taking him for a walk around the parking lot. For the most part, the dog had been content to gnaw on the small bone he'd found and to sleep. Once, Darrell tried to get a look at the bone, but the pug's paws huddled over it and Darrell couldn't see much. On the third trip, he waited and watched while Pogo did his business, then he cleaned up after him. He reasoned he wasn't doing anything else worthwhile.

Darrell knew he'd upset Barnaby when the cop had arrived earlier. Maybe even embarrassed him. He didn't care.

When Barnaby realized someone had really tried to kill Cassie, poison her with massive doses of hemlock, he flew into a rage, demanding to talk with her, to find out something about who did this.

It was almost as if, before, Barnaby could rationalize what had happened. Maybe the hit and run that killed Vince was an accident. Or about something else entirely. Drugs, maybe. And just maybe, the timber rattler had found its own way into Darrell's room. Or it was some stupid joke of someone else at the boardinghouse.

But when confirmation came about the poison, it was as if a switch had been thrown. Barnaby couldn't find another explanation. The square peg would not fit into the round hole.

When the cop finally grasped he couldn't talk to Cassie yet, Darrell convinced him to check with a few body shops about a damaged car from five years ago. To do something. Like he'd agreed to do earlier. And Darrell told him he'd call dispatch as soon as Cassie woke up. Barnaby left, muttering curses under his breath as he exited through the swishing doors.

Perched on the hard chair and still holding Erin's hand in his own, Darrell studied the girl. He sniffed back tears and whispered, "Cassie, I'm so sorry for getting you involved in all this." He stood and, leaning in close to the bed, watched as a tear dropped onto the bare skin of her arm. "You're a tough kid. You can beat this. I know you can." His gaze moved from her arm to her face. "Please wake up so we can see that pout of yours."

Cassie's eyes fluttered open, ever so slowly, so slowly he thought he was imagining it. He shut his own eyes and opened them again, staring. Cassie's green eyes were filmy, as if she couldn't see much, and they glanced left and right. Darrell nudged Erin, who had her head down, praying probably. "Erin, look. Cassie's waking up." He tried to keep his voice low, but his pitch rose.

Erin glanced up and shot up out of her seat. She leaned over the girl. Her voice trembled. "Hey, there's our Gothic Goddess." The words came out half as relief and half as exultation. She grabbed the girl's hand and squeezed.

Cassie's eyes opened fully at the sound of Erin's voice, and she pointed to the tube in her mouth.

Erin got the message. "Let me get some help." She released Cassie's hand and headed out the door. Thirty seconds later, she was back with help.

An older woman with short, brown hair bustled into the room, a big smile on her face. She wore a smock of brilliant, colorful flowers that seemed to brighten the room. "Look who decided to rejoin the living." She pulled a stethoscope from around her neck and put it to Cassie's chest. "Well, that sounds pretty good."

Cassie pointed to the tube down her throat and her wide eyes did the talking.

The nurse said, "Let's see what we can do about

that." She leaned over and removed the tube, being careful to pull it straight out and not hurt Cassie's throat any more. From the nightstand next to the bed, she grabbed a pitcher, still sweating with cold moisture, and poured a glass of water for Cassie. "Now, take your time and drink this."

Cassie pushed up from the bed and leaned forward into a sitting position. Using both hands, she grabbed the cup from her and drew on the plastic straw.

The nurse continued, "Be careful. Your throat's going to be really sore for a while. Don't try to talk too much yet." She patted the girl's arm. "I'll go get the doc. He's going to be glad to see you." She went out the door.

As soon as she left, Erin and Darrell crowded in next to the bed. Cassie looked at both, her eyes growing large, and took another slow slurp. Her hand went to her throat and she tried to talk, but her voice was so hoarse, she could only manage two syllables.

"Vish-ah."

"What?" Darrell could tell from the teen's eyes she was trying to say something important, but he had no idea what it was.

Cassie took another slow drink, swallowed, and tried again. "Vision," she croaked.

Erin pushed the button on the bed and the motor whirred, bringing the top even with Cassie's back. She leaned in close. "Did you say 'vision'?"

Cassie nodded and sucked on the straw again. When she stopped, she took a slow breath and whispered, "Ghost. Vision."

"I heard our young guest had decided to awaken from her beauty sleep," a male voice announced. A white-coated figure strode into the hospital room.

Darrell and Erin turned and then moved to make way for the physician they'd met earlier. When he saw Cassie, the young doctor broke out in a wide smile, shaking his head slightly. "I'm Dr. Barrett and we met earlier, though you were out of it then." His blue eyes actually twinkled, and he chuckled. "You look pretty good for a young woman who, a couple hours ago, was ready to meet the grim reaper. How do you feel?"

"Throat hurt." Cassie pointed to where the tube had been inserted.

Barrett leaned over Cassie and, with gentle fingers, he removed the last of the tape from where she'd been intubated. "Going to hurt for a while." His hand moved to her abdomen. "How's the stomach?"

"Cramps," Cassie croaked.

"Perfectly normal too. We pumped pretty much everything out of your stomach. You swallowed some nasty stuff."

Cassie looked puzzled. "Muffin?"

Dr. Barrett brushed a wisp of long blond hair out of his eyes. "Well, the muffin contained hemlock."

Cassie's gaze went from the doctor's face to Erin and Darrell, who had moved to the foot of the bed, her confusion evident. "Hemlick?" she tried.

The doctor's voice was calm. "Hemlock is a poisonous plant. Our lab tech told me someone put enough hemlock into the muffin you ate to kill you." Cassie's eyes grew wide in panic. "And they might have, too, if your nurse friend—" He pointed to Erin. "—hadn't found you when she did and got help."

Cassie looked to Erin and managed a raspy, "Thanks."

Dr. Barrett continued, "But we think you're going to be fine. We gave you some pretty heavy sedatives so you could fight off the toxins' effects. Looks like your body did the rest." He went through the routine of checking her pulse and listening to her chest, nodding as he finished. "Everything looks normal. We're going to want to keep you for a while longer, but you'll be out breaking guys' hearts again soon enough."

Cassie blushed again and picked up the cup, perhaps to cover her reaction. She sucked in more water and turned back to the doctor. "Hungry."

"I'm sure you are." The handsome doctor nodded. "But your stomach is pretty raw right now. Maybe we could try a little applesauce and some of our award-winning Jell-o. I heard the color for today is green." He smiled again and Cassie did the same. Turning to the nurse, he said, "Let's keep the saline solution going for a few more hours. I'll swing back and check on you before I leave."

Darrell stepped up to the doctor and reached out his hand. "Thanks, doc. Cassie is our good friend, and we appreciate everything you and the hospital did for her."

Dr. Barrett took the hand and shook. "You're welcome, but it looks to me like the real hero is Nurse Caveny here." He turned to face Erin. "Are you local, Miss Caveny?"

Erin released her brilliant smile. "It's Erin, and no. I'm an OB nurse in Maryland."

"Well, if you ever want to come to beautiful Cape May, you let me know. We could certainly use another quick-thinking nurse like you here." His gaze went from Erin and Darrell to Cassie. "I have other patients to check on, but I'll be back."

He left, consulting with the nurse on the way out. When they finished, she popped her head in and said, "I'll go see about some applesauce and some of our delicious green Jell-o."

As soon as she left, Darrell couldn't wait any longer. He glanced around to make sure no one was within earshot and whispered, "You had a vision from the ghost? From Amy?"

Cassie nodded and croaked, "Think so."

Chapter Fifty-Eight

"Ghost…Amy…wedding night," Cassie croaked, the words obviously painful. She grabbed the glass and let more water slide down her rough throat. "Hard to talk…ow…but need to tell you."

Erin said, "Then don't try to talk too much yet. We'll help you. We'll ask some questions and you can just nod. Or not."

Darrell took the lead. He got up, closed the door and came back to the bed. "While you were under, the ghost," then he corrected himself, "Amy showed you something?"

Cassie nodded.

"Something that happened on the night she was killed?" he asked and drew a more vigorous response from the teen. "Did she show you who killed her?"

Cassie shook her head slowly, as if she had to think about it, then a little stronger.

"No, hum." Darrell said and paused.

Erin leaned in. "Was the vision about Amy…and Travis?"

Cassie nodded hard. "Yeah," she rasped.

"But not about him killing her?" Erin pushed.

Cassie shook her head. "Saw collision," she managed. "Not who."

For several intense minutes, Darrell and Erin posed questions and Cassie responded, usually with her head and occasionally with a word or two. They stopped when the nurse returned with the promised plate, the green Jell-o shimmering when she took off the metal cover. The older nurse asked if there was anything else she could do and Cassie shook her head. The RN left the room, shutting the door again behind her.

Darrell and Erin resumed posing questions and Cassie did her best to respond. They asked and Cassie answered, between tastes of the bland applesauce and bouncy Jell-o. She nodded or shook her head most of the time but uttered a few more words. At times, Cassie got frustrated she wasn't able to simply tell them the whole story. It took nearly an hour to piece the story together, but it was worth it. Halfway through, Darrell remembered his promise to Barnaby and left to leave a message at dispatch and then returned. When the final details got puzzled out, especially about the secret compartment in the trucks, Erin and Darrell were stunned.

"And you saw the collision? Saw someone hit Amy?" Erin's tone revealed her horror.

Cassie nodded slowly and croaked, "Felt it too."

"Oh, God," Erin said, a tear in her voice.

A knock on the door interrupted them. All three turned to see Barnaby stick his head in the door. "Can I come in?"

As the cop entered the room, Darrell noticed his posture had changed. His bearing no longer carried the arrogance he'd shown earlier. Even his mirrored shades were stowed in a pocket.

Barnaby came over to the bed, and Darrell and Erin moved to the opposite side to give him room. Erin laid a hand on Cassie's arm, and Darrell caught a glance exchanged between her and Cassie.

The cop said, "I'm sorry for what you've gone through, but I'd like to ask you a few questions. To see if we can catch who tried to kill you."

Barnaby looked and sounded sincere. Darrell wondered if something had happened or the officer had discovered something.

The officer continued, "Some of these questions may be private or even uncomfortable. You might want them to leave." He indicated Darrell and Erin.

"Stay," Cassie croaked.

Erin jumped in. "We might be able to help. We've been trying to talk about what happened, but it's really hard for her. Her throat, you know. She was intubated and it takes a while to be able to talk normal."

The cop pulled a narrow notebook out of his pocket. "Okay, but it'd be better if I could get this information down as soon as possible. You know you ate a muffin that was poisoned?" Cassie nodded. "Where did the muffins come from? Did you bring the basket to Aleathea's?"

Cassie shook her head. "Was in break room," she got out.

"Did you see who dropped them off?"

Cassie shook her head again.

"I've already questioned Antonio and the other servers at the restaurant. No one saw who dropped off the basket. The receptionist at the front desk said a black-haired guy wearing a baseball cap left it on the counter and took off. She didn't get a good look at him." He consulted the notebook. "She said she thought he was a young guy but couldn't be sure."

Darrell and Erin shared a look and he wondered if

she was thinking the same thing he was. *Jeremey Tucker?* He didn't say anything. Not yet.

Barnaby was still flipping through his notes. "We already checked with the two delivery services in town. They know nothing about it." He redirected his stare to Cassie. "Do you have an idea why someone would try to poison you, Miss Davis?"

Cassie started to shake her head and Erin squeezed her arm, stopping her. "We think it might be because of what our witness told Cassie."

"Your witness?" The cop's tone carried his earlier incredulity. "Your mysterious witness who saw Amy Palmer get run down? The same one who's afraid to talk to the cops?"

Cassie nodded, a little more slowly this time.

"When did you talk to this witness?"

Cassie and Erin exchanged the briefest of looks. "Last night," she rasped.

"What did this witness tell you?" Barnaby's eyes leveled at Cassie.

Erin saved her. "That's what we've been talking about. Our witness told Cassie she has inside information that Armstrong Trucking is using their eighteen-wheelers to transport teenage girls to their gentlemen's clubs. And for prostitution. They've even outfitted some of their trailers as portable brothels."

"She told you all this, did she?" Barnaby asked, though with less skepticism.

"We're guessing maybe they found out Cassie knew about their enterprise somehow and targeted her," Erin said. She was doing a good job of selling the line.

"Who found out? Who do you think targeted you?"

"The Armstrongs," Darrell quipped.

"Uh-hum," Barnaby said. "How come these people haven't tried to kill this witness of yours?"

"Oh they have," Darrell snapped. "That's why she—or he—can't come forward."

For a while, the cop said nothing, only jotting down a few lines.

Darrell asked, "I'm guessing you haven't had any luck with the body shops yet?"

The cop grinned. "Then you'd guess wrong."

"Really?" Darrell and Erin said at the same time.

"Yeah. I thought, if there had been some kind of collision here in Cape May—like your witness claimed—then they would take any car out of town. Either Wildwood or even Atlantic City, if it was drivable." Barnaby consulted his notebook again. "But on a hunch, I checked with Marco's Body Shop here in town. Marco's son, Rusty, played football with me in high school and he now works with his dad."

"And?" Darrell raised his voice.

"As a favor he went and checked the company records for the week after the wedding, the week of June 28, 1993." He looked up from the notebook and met Darrell's stare. "And, exactly like your witness said, he found a receipt for a car brought in for front end repair. From a deer strike."

"Whose car?" croaked Cassie.

"A fire engine red Corvette registered to Travis Armstrong."

"That's great news." Darrell couldn't keep the excitement out of his voice. Maybe things were breaking their way. Finally. "Now you can search the car and find some evidence of blood, human blood, still in the front end."

The cop shook his head. "Won't work for two reasons."

"Why?"

"First, I'd have to have a warrant to conduct a search like that. And to get that, your mysterious witness would have to come forward and testify."

Darrell shot a glance at Erin. "That's not going to happen. You said two reasons."

"Yeah. According to their records, Rusty said the car was totaled." He looked at his notes again. "Rusty said he remembered the car and the damage, and he didn't think it was too bad. Didn't think there was any structural damage, but the Armstrongs put pressure on the insurance company and they agreed to scrap the car. It went to a salvage yard in Atlantic City."

Darrell felt like someone had sucked all the air out of the room. He glanced at Cassie and then at Erin. He muttered, "Well, that's another dead end then."

"Maybe not," Barnaby answered right away. "Rusty said, sometimes, with that kind of damage, the insurance company will let another body shop buy the salvaged vehicle and make the necessary repairs. He knows the shop who picks up most of those wrecks. He's checking to see if that happened and if he can track down the car."

"Still, that was five years ago. A real long shot."

"Yeah, but it confirms what your witness told you." The cop snapped the notebook shut and stuck it back inside his pocket. "It gives me enough to at least go talk to the Armstrongs. We can have a little polite conversation and mention a witness has come forward with information about the night Amy Palmer disappeared." He drew the shades from another pocket and slid them on. He smiled. "Shake that tree and see what happens."

Darrell asked, "Could I come with you?"

The officer started shaking his head, but stopped. He stood there examining Darrell. At least Darrell thought he was looking at him. Darrell couldn't see anything through the mirrored lenses.

Finally, Barnaby said, "Okay. You dug most of this up. And you being there might actually shake them up a little. Throw them off their game." He started toward the door and stopped, turning back. "You take your own car. I'm not doing any damn ride along."

Chapter Fifty-Nine

Barnaby strode quickly out the hospital exit. Darrell followed—right on his heels, hustling to untie Pogo and scoot him into the Corolla. One behind the other, the cars pulled into traffic, and in a few minutes, were headed north on the Garden State Parkway.

They had about a ten-mile drive on the expressway, so Darrell kept the police car in sight a few car lengths ahead and turned to glance at Pogo. As the car swayed through traffic, the dog's short, stubby legs balanced his body on the seat.

"Well, you weren't in there, but big news, Pogo. Cassie's okay and had a vision of the night Amy died."

Darrell looked over again to see if the Pug was paying attention and saw the dog's eyes wide in response. Sometimes, he thought the dog actually understood what he was saying, so he recounted what they'd learned from Cassie.

"Maybe Travis went after her, you know, to bring her back." He stole another glance at the pug who still stood at attention, listening. "I mean, he was drunk that night and, when he went after her, maybe ran her over instead? Then the whole family concocted the story about Amy committing suicide walking into the ocean."

Ahead of him, Barnaby pulled into the inside lane and Darrell followed as they passed under a sign that read "Venice 1 mile."

"It's Travis' car, so he's the most logical choice, but something doesn't feel right about it. Know what I mean, boy?" The pug gave a small bark. "That's what I think."

Since Darrell didn't know his way around Venice, he stayed on the black and white, even as he took in the estates they were passing. That's the word that came to mind—estates.

Each house they rolled past sat on a huge lot, one structure grander than the previous one with exteriors of fieldstone or fancy brick and siding configurations, and, sometimes, combinations of all three. Glancing from one side of the road to the other, he saw perfectly manicured lawns that would have put most golf greens to shame, all edged by sculpted shrubbery.

On the east side of the road, the emerald grass carpets spread behind the mansions and met the rising sand dunes. Beyond the houses, the blue of the ocean sparkled. From the opposite direction, the sun dropped in the western sky, burnishing the landscape to golds and reds and igniting the giant windows of the houses.

Ahead, Barnaby took a right down a side street that led toward the shore. A little way down, he pulled into a driveway next to a chiseled stone sign which read "Armstrong Acres," Darrell's Corolla right behind him. The crushed seashell driveway circled round in front of a palatial mansion sporting a massive front porch cornered by four tall pillars.

The Armstrong place made the other estates look like poor cousins.

"Would you look at that?" Darrell pointed to the house. "I guess that place on Poverty Beach is just a *second home*." He shook his head. "But you better stay here, Pogo. I'm not sure how they feel about man's best friend in there."

Already out of his car, Barnaby headed up the six large steps to the towering porch and Darrell hurried to catch up. A spur off the driveway led to a five-car garage, which sat off to the side about a football field away. Three of the garage doors gaped open. Inside one bay, an attendant buffed a bright fire engine red Corvette.

Barnaby rang the bell, sending melodious chimes ringing from inside. As the seconds passed, Darrell and the cop exchanged glances. He thought he read anxiety in Barnaby's features, though it was hard to tell with the mirrored shades in place.

The cop leaned over and whispered, "On our way here I heard from dispatch. Rusty at Marco's Body Shop came through. He gave us the name and address of the new owner of the refurbished red '93 Corvette, formerly owned by Travis Armstrong." A small grin emerged with the words. "When we're finished here, we can head over and talk to the gentleman. We still don't have a warrant, but we can ask."

The cop went silent again and, after a full minute passed, they heard the sound of steps coming to the door. When the huge wooden door swung open, a man in full black-and-white butler livery stood ramrod straight before them. He eyed them both, taking time to note the police uniform. In a pronounced British accent, he intoned, "May I help you?"

The cop pulled a business card from a pocket and offered it. "Are the Armstrongs in? I'm Officer Barnaby from Cape May PD and I'd like to speak with them."

The butler stepped aside. "Please come inside and I'll ask."

Darrell and Barnaby did as invited. The butler shut the door and strode down a long hallway, disappearing around a corner, though "hallway" was hardly an apt description. The corridor, more than twenty feet wide, looked more like some opulent hotel foyer with a polished marble floor and towering cathedral ceiling. The hallway opened to rooms on both left and right, and Darrell's gaze flicked from one side to the other. On his right, expensive period antique chairs and settees sat facing a stone fireplace large enough for a man to stand inside. At the far end of the room stood a large glass case with an assortment of guns—silver pistols, shining rifles and two gleaming black shotguns, both with gold engraving.

Barnaby followed Darrell's gaze. "I'd heard the whole family has quite a gun collection. Small example of it."

The room on their left was dominated by a huge dining room table with an exquisite vase atop, bursting with freshly cut flowers, their brilliant colors a stark contrast to the polished dark wood. Darrell counted twelve wooden armchairs around the table, each upholstered with some kind of crest. Underneath the table lay an enormous Persian rug in handwoven swirls of red and gold.

When Darrell's glance swept back to the hallway, he noticed the butler had returned, his approach almost silent.

"Mr. and Mrs. Armstrong are supping out by the pool. Please follow me."

Without waiting for a response, the butler turned

and led them down the long corridor. As they made their way, they passed more art on display. Atop one table, a blue and white ceramic vase sat under a spotlight. Darrell studied it and—thanks to a historical art class at MSU—recognized it as from the Ming dynasty. At the rear of the house, the butler stopped before a set of magnificent French doors with crystal etchings that opened onto a terrace. He went ahead of them, holding the door ajar.

They mumbled their thanks and walked onto a wide terrace, paved with precisely fitted red stones. The four corners of the terrace were framed by massive concrete planters, over four feet tall, each overflowing with flowering plants. Reds, yellows, and purples cascaded down from the tops, looking as if the containers were erupting. Beyond where they stood, the patio extended through a set of steps to two more levels. At the bottom, the Armstrongs—father, mother, and son—perched on cushioned outdoor chairs on the edge of a large kidney shaped pool, its blue water shimmering in the dying rays of the sun. Four more of the flowering, concrete planters marked the four corners of the pool.

"Officer Barnaby, come join us," called James Armstrong, his voice congenial. "We're just finishing. Can Harold get something for you?"

Even though Darrell knew why they'd come, he couldn't help but be impressed with the view. At the far end, the crystal blue of the ocean beckoned, its waves tiny ripples of white. In front lay a rolling lawn with precise rows of hedges forming perfectly straight, dark green lines running to the dunes.

"Thank you, no. We're fine," came Barnaby's crisp

response. He descended the steps toward the group, Darrell beside him.

James Armstrong said, "I'm at a disadvantage. I hear two set of footsteps. Who is that with you?"

Barnaby replied, still in a formal tone, "Darrell Henshaw. I asked him to join me."

"Coach Henshaw, welcome to our home," said the elder Armstrong.

The son, Travis, rose and came over and shook both men's hands. Andrea Armstrong nodded, saying nothing.

"Well, what can we do for you, Officer?" James asked.

"May I say first, folks, what a beautiful place you have here?" Barnaby offered.

"Thank you," James said, smiling. "Now, how can we help?"

"Sir, new information has come to light about how Travis' wife, Amy Palmer died," answered Barnaby, his tone almost apologetic.

Chapter Sixty

Barnaby removed his sunglasses and stowed them in a shirt pocket. "I apologize for disturbing you on this lovely evening, but a witness has raised some disturbing questions about the young woman's death. I thought you'd want to know what I've learned." He took his hat off and held it in his hands. "I'm not exactly sure how to tell you this, but we received an anonymous tip about how Amy Palmer died."

Darrell studied the reaction of all three Armstrongs to the cop's announcement. James Armstrong never moved a muscle below his shoulders, though he turned his head to face his visitors. His sunglasses blocked anything his eyes might convey, and the rest of his face gave away little. Darrell thought he saw a ripple of something—surprise, worry, fear?—cross Andrea's features, but only for a second. Then, the stoic mask slid back in place.

Travis was the one who reacted. Coming up out of his lounge chair, he uttered an audible gasp and cried, "About how Amy died?"

The Senior Armstrong shifted in his chair. "Nothing anonymous about it, *Officer*. We watched her walk into the ocean and take her own life. It was truly tragic and I'm not sure my son has ever recovered from the loss." His head turned to where his son still stood, frozen by the news. "I believe your department conducted an official investigation which came to that exact conclusion."

This time Barnaby shifted his feet and moved his cap from one hand to the other. Darrell glanced over. Was Barnaby cowed by the Armstrongs' ostentatious show of wealth and power? Then, when the cop lowered his head, Darrell caught a glint in the corner of his eye and got it. Barnaby was playing the Armstrongs.

"Yes, sir, yes, sir, I know that," Barnaby said without raising his head. "I wasn't part of the original investigation, but I read the report. Several times." His head came up and he stared at James Armstrong. "You and your wife testified you saw Amy walk into the ocean, but some others said they saw her head out to the street. Away from the water."

"Yes, yes, but that was earlier." James Armstrong's hand brushed away the contradiction as if it were a fly.

"This witness tells a different story—"

"Who is *this witness*?" Andrea demanded.

"I'll get to that in a bit," Barnaby continued, unrattled, any hint of deference gone. "A witness has come forward who claims she watched Amy die. When Mr. Henshaw first brought this information to me about a witness, I'll be honest. I was skeptical. But then, things started happening to people asking about the night Amy disappeared."

Before the cop could go on, Travis took a step closer. "This witness, this person knows what happened to Amy. How Amy died?"

Travis seemed genuine, heartsick, even after all these years. But maybe he was a great actor.

Andrea rose from her chair and came over to her son. "We know how Amy died, Travis. She walked into the ocean and took her own life."

Travis looked from his mother to the cop and then to Darrell. "Is that what this witness saw?"

Darrell glanced to Barnaby to try to figure how much he was supposed to say and started to shake his head.

The officer spoke up, interrupting Darrell's denial. "I only agreed to come today because things have been happening. First, this kid in town, Vince Rawlins, goes around asking a few questions about the night Amy died and he's killed in a hit and run. A witness said he saw a truck, a white eighteen-wheeler, drive off after the accident."

"Surely you don't think it was one of our trucks?" James Armstrong sounded incredulous.

Barnaby went on. "Then, after Darrell starts poking around asking the same questions, someone put a timber rattler in his room at the boardinghouse. Could've killed him and his girlfriend Erin."

Mrs. Armstrong's voice carried an imperious air. "You don't think those things have anything to do with us?"

Barnaby plowed on. "Then this morning someone poisoned and tried to kill Cassie Davis."

"Who? We don't know any Cassie Davis?" Mrs. Armstrong looked to her husband for confirmation. Darrell thought he heard a slight tremor in her voice.

Barnaby continued, "She's a friend of Vince Rawlins and was one of the waiters at your big party last night. And she was asking some guests questions about Amy. Now Darrell tells me the witness is too scared to come forward. I can't say I blame her...or him"

Andrea's words were laced with contempt. "How do we even know there is any witness? Because this...this football coach, this outsider *said* someone told him. Officer Barnaby, I don't want to be rude, but I think you should go."

Travis stepped up to Darrell and looked him straight in the eyes. "What did this witness tell you about how Amy died?"

Darrell met his gaze. "Amy left the reception after she had a fight with you about some, uh, questionable aspects of your family's company." Out of the corner of his eye, he saw the elder Armstrong shift in his chair.

"How would you know about that?" Travis seemed shocked.

Darrell ignored the question. "Broken-hearted, Amy walked out onto Beach Avenue. She loved you and couldn't decide what to do, so she took a walk. Then she was struck on the road by your red Corvette. And killed."

Travis staggered back as if Darrell had struck him. "What? Amy was hit by *my* car?"

Barnaby jumped back in. "Look, we know you had the car towed to Marco's Garage a few days after the party. Serious front end damage. Exactly like it had hit someone."

Travis seemed in a fog and staggered back to his chair. "My car?"

Mrs. Armstrong shook her head. "No, you struck a deer, remember. Messed up the front grill and fender, even the suspension on that lovely red Corvette. We had to total it."

Travis shook his head. "No, you told me you took it out for a spin the day after the wedding...and hit a deer."

Mrs. Armstrong moved beside her son. "No dear, you're mistaken. You were pretty foggy for a few days there. You probably don't remember." She patted his arm. "If you give me a minute, I'm sure I can find the paperwork from the insurance company which will clear this all up." She climbed the steps on the terrace and passed Darrell and Barnaby.

The cop turned to Andrea. "I'd like you to stay here please. I've already contacted the Venice PD and asked them to join us. They may want to search the house."

Andrea continued walking, as if she hadn't heard. Barnaby started after the woman, when James called, "Officer Barnaby?"

Darrell's gaze went from Andrea to Barnaby, trying to figure out what to do. When he heard the question, he turned. James was pointing a bright silver pistol at them.

Armstrong fired.

Chapter Sixty-One

"Gun!" yelled Barnaby.

Three explosions shattered the quiet air. Darrell dove behind the large concrete planter on the right. Barnaby did the same thing on the other side. The shots stopped. Darrell peered across the terrace. Sprawled on the ground behind one of the large stone vases, the cop had his sidearm in one hand, while the other held his thigh. Blood streamed through his fingers onto his dark blue pant leg.

In the distance, a large car engine started and revved up. Darrell stared across the yard at the garage. Andrea sat behind the wheel of the Corvette. She peeled out onto the driveway. Darrell's gaze darted from the cop to James Armstrong, still perched on the cushioned chair. Armstrong held the gun, calming waving it toward them.

Damn, the man was supposed to be legally blind, but he must be able to see some.

Figuring Armstrong was using sounds to help him aim, he whispered, "What do you want me to do?"

"Go after her. Damn, that hurts." He gritted his teeth. "I'll cover you."

Another bullet struck the concrete planter a foot from the cop. Barnaby turned and fired two rounds toward Armstrong. They struck the ground around the elder Armstrong's chair, but the man didn't even flinch.

Either Armstrong had a death wish or was just plain crazy. Then Darrell got it. He figured Barnaby could probably hit and kill Armstrong, if he wanted. He must be trying to keep him pinned until help arrived and they could get some questions answered.

At the first gunshot, Travis had crouched behind another planter next to the pool. Now, he stuck his head out. "Dad, what are you doing?"

Armstrong said, "Trying to protect us, son." He fired another round that hit the sandstone pavers halfway between Darrell and the cop. He yelled, "Look, Barnaby, I know you haven't contacted the Venice PD, 'cause I would've gotten a call."

Darrell glanced at Barnaby, who shrugged. The cop might be used to this, but he sure as hell wasn't.

Barnaby's voice was sharp. "Maybe Mrs. Armstrong's not trying to get away. Why would she leave James and Travis here? Maybe she's going after Cassie. To finish the job. And maybe get Erin." He gritted his teeth again. "Get going and call in the cavalry."

Darrell realized what he had to do. He called in a hoarse whisper, "Okay, cover me," and ran zigzag, until he got to the back of the house. He threw open the French doors and dove. One of the crystal panels exploded, raining shards of glass on him. He got up and ran, skidding around the corner and knocking into the Ming vase. The antique hit the hard marble floor with a loud crash. Darrell never broke stride, pleased to have cost the Armstrongs something, anyway. He bounded out the front door, running for his car. In the distance, he could barely make out the trail of dust the Corvette left on the long driveway.

How in the world was his little Toyota going to catch a Corvette with 350 horses?

"Hold on!" he yelled to Pogo. He threw his car in gear and floored it. When he got to the road, he looked both ways. No sign of the red sports car. Guessing, he steered south and stood on the accelerator. He shot a quick glance over to see the pug huddle on the floor against that bone. Practically bouncing up the ramp to the Garden State Parkway, he roared into the outside lane. He hoped there weren't any cops on the road. Then he realized he actually *needed* a cop. If they'd believe him. Peering through his dirty windshield, he thought he spotted a red car in the distance, maybe a half mile ahead.

He'd never catch her. She'd get to the hospital way before he could and would do what? It didn't make any sense. But damn, her husband had just pulled a gun and tried to kill a cop.

He pressed harder and glanced down at the seat. The cellphone. He could call in help. With one hand, he snatched the phone off the seat, while the other gripped the steering wheel. He took his eyes off the road for a second and stared at the open phone. He needed to call 911. His right hand hit the three keys. The left tires of the car caught on the berm and the car lurched. He dropped the phone.

Both hands back on the steering wheel now, he eased back into his lane. His heart pumped wildly. He couldn't catch his breath. Checked the rearview mirror. No cops. At least, none he could see. He glared forward again. He could just make out the speck of red ahead on the highway. He breathed hard, in and out, in and out. The mile markers sped past on his right. He checked the upcoming sign. Exit 10, the exit for Burdette Hospital, two miles ahead. For Cassie and Erin. The Corvette would reach the exit in less than a minute.

He concentrated and picked up the phone. He held it in his palm and used his fingers to punch the three numbers. "No Signal" scrolled across the screen. He cursed. Stared ahead. He waited fifteen seconds and tried again.

"911, what's your emergency?"

Darrell stuttered, "Uh, Um, uh." Then he blurted out, "Officer down."

"What did you say?" The operator barked.

Darrell took a deep breath. "He was shot."

"Who's shot? Where is this? Are you calling on a cellphone, sir?"

"Yes, and I'm driving following the suspect."

"What is the address, sir? We'll send help." When Darrell didn't respond immediately, skepticism crept into the speaker's voice. "Who is this?"

Darrell tried to collect his thoughts. "My name is Darrell Henshaw and I was with Officer Stewart Barnaby of Cape May PD on a visit to the Armstrong's house in Venice. He was questioning the Armstrongs when Andrea Armstrong took off in a red Corvette. James Armstrong started firing on us and hit Officer Barnaby in the leg. He told me to follow Mrs. Armstrong. Officer Barnaby, that is."

He climbed the slight grade, approaching the exit for the hospital. He strained to scan the mile ahead, searching for the red car. He couldn't see over the rise. "Damn. I've got to go. Please send help to Officer Barnaby." He punched the button and dropped the phone.

He was *not* going to let anything else happen to either Cassie or Erin, no matter what he had to do. He slid the car over to the inside lane, ready to exit. He came over the rise, hoping he'd catch sight of her. He stared ahead and saw it. The Corvette *didn't* take the exit and sped farther down the Parkway.

Where was she going?

He slid over to one of the passing lanes and pushed harder on the accelerator. He wasn't closing the gap, but he hadn't lost her. The miles sped by as his head spun, trying to figure out what Andrea was doing. With the lead she had, she could get off and, by the time Darrell could follow, she could be anywhere in the warren of streets. Ahead, he saw the blinking lights, warning about the end of the freeway.

The red sports car zoomed in between the other cars to find an open lane through the exiting traffic. Instead of slowing, the Corvette bounced through the far right lane and sped down the exit. He followed, zipping around cars to get there. He tried to pass through, but a car jumped into his lane in front of him. He hit his brakes to avoid a collision. But, instead of speeding through the far lane, the car, some fancy SUV, pulled to the side and stopped. He watched the driver reached across and come up with a map. Darrell hit his horn and she glanced back. Exasperated, Darrell gestured to the right. She finally got it, easing her car to the side of the road.

Darrell pulled his car a little forward so he could see around the bend of the exit. He stared through his windshield. The Corvette was nowhere to be seen.

Chapter Sixty-Two

Darrell slammed his fist on the steering wheel.

"Where is she? Damn, what am I supposed to do now?" he called to Pogo, who had climbed back onto the seat. As usual, the pug's big black eyes simply stared back at him. Looking past the pug, Darrell spotted the cellphone and picked it up. "You're right, Pogo, I should check on the girls." It took him a while to get the number for Burdette, then the hospital volunteer eventually got him over to Cassie's room. Erin answered and he let out a breath. She told him they were fine and Cassie was still improving. Then Erin explained they had another visitor.

Darrell's breath caught in his throat. "Who?"

"You'd never guess. Antonio." He could hear the surprise in her voice.

Then he told her what had happened at the Armstrongs.

"Are you okay?"

"I'm fine, but Barnaby was hit in the leg." He heard her gasp and continued. "I've called in help. They should be there by now. He'll be okay." He explained what he was trying to do. "I got to go."

"Be careful." The love in her voice warmed him.

After he closed the phone, he turned. "Antonio came to check on Cassie, Pogo. Maybe he's not a such an ogre. Now, where might Andrea be going? If she wasn't after Cassie or Erin, where did she need to get to in such a hurry?"

The dog simply stared up him.

"I see, you got no idea either. Maybe she had to find someone, to warn them? Or maybe she had to get something?" He shook his head. "I haven't got a clue. But we have one thing going for us, boy. There can't be too many gleaming, fire engine red Corvettes cruising the streets of Cape May. We'll have to poke around and see if we can catch sight of her."

Darrell put the car in gear again and slid back into the stream of cars heading toward Cape May and the beaches. The traffic was fairly heavy, and that suited him. As he drove, he had time to search the side roads for the Corvette. Having no real idea which way to go, he followed the line of cars. He rolled on, having to wait every half block for another car to turn off. His fingers beat a frustrated rhythm on the steering wheel.

Where was Andrea? Why was it so important she come to Cape May? Something Barnaby had said about the older Corvette and Amy's death had spooked Andrea. When he replayed the cop's words and thought about the wife's reaction, Darrell had noticed something in her face. He shook his head.

When traffic slowed again at the corner of Washington and Hughes, his gaze landed on a telephone pole. The same one where he'd stopped on his stroll with Erin last weekend. Was that only last weekend? Staring, he could still see the tiny purple remnants of the flyer about Josie he and Josh had attached. And someone had ripped off.

What had Amy's message said? IF YOU SAVE ME YOU RESCUE HER.

Based on Cassie's vision, Amy was killed because she overheard details about the Armstrong sex trafficking business. But that was five years ago? So, they've been tricking teen girls into that life—and then kidnapping them—for at least that long. What had Travis called it? A diverse stream of revenue. Maybe, if they could catch them, um…about Amy's murder, then Barnaby could flip one of them about the prostitution ring. Maybe that would help Josie?

But how were they supposed to do that?

Ahead on the right, he spotted a red car parked in a driveway, partially concealed by a tall hedge. When he pulled even with the house, he saw the car wasn't the Corvette, but a different red car. He let out another loud curse and hit the steering wheel again.

Darrell turned onto Ocean Street. Waiting at the stoplight at Beach Avenue, he was faced with a decision. Right or left. Right took him down the south end of Cape May Beach and left led him north to Poverty Beach. On impulse, he turned left. Once again mired in traffic, he took his time to check out every car parked. Without getting off the main road, he examined each car in the motel parking lots he crept past. He'd been right about one thing. He'd seen precious few bright red cars, but he hadn't spotted the Corvette.

Darrell had to stop again, this time to let a couple, arm in arm and laughing as if they hadn't a care in the world, dance across the wide road. God, how he envied the couple.

He glanced across the seat and saw the pug, paws up on the open window, studying the beach and the waves. "Well, Pogo, it looks like this is a wild goose chase. It's starting to get dark, and I'm not sure I'll be able to spot a red car then." The dog turned around to face him. "What do you say, we'll drive the rest of Beach Avenue and then we'll head back to the hospital to check on Erin and Cassie."

After more of beachgoers crossed, Darrell eased the car forward again. He kept going to the end of Beach Avenue, his gaze sweeping left and right, examining every parked car. No luck. Ready to head back, he made the sharp left turn. His breath caught in his throat.

There it was.

The red Corvette was pulled off the road, near the spot where Darrell had parked last night, next to the same copse of trees he'd taken Pogo into. The sports car sat, its throaty engine idling, both doors ajar. Both doors? She'd picked up someone? The trunk lid was also wide open. Darrell didn't see anyone around. He backed his car up and parked it around the corner, out of sight. He got out, Pogo bounding out right behind him.

He crept up along the shoulder, looking, listening. Some noises, grunting, and cursing came from inside the little woods. In a few seconds, a figure emerged holding one end of a long object. Keeping back, Darrell waited and watched, silent. In a moment, a second person emerged out of the trees, holding the other end. Both had their backs to Darrell and struggled with their bundle, trying to navigate their way through the nest of trees.

"Damn, hold onto your end," Andrea Armstrong's angry voice cut through the silence.

"I'm trying, but it ain't easy," shot back a petulant female voice.

He'd heard that voice before but couldn't put a name to it. Darrell didn't want to spook them, so he crept a little closer, keeping down. While he listened, he caught a few more sharp curses. The last one did it. "Jennifer Thomas," he whispered to Pogo.

The two women worked their way around the gnarly trunks and spindly trees and stepped out onto the shoulder, their backs still to him. In the fading light, it was hard to make out what they were toting. Then he got it. They were grappling with a large rolled up, dirt-covered rug, like the Persian rug he'd seen on the floor of Armstrong's dining room. Holding a body! Amy's?

Darrell came behind. "Can I help you, ladies?"

"Jesus!" screamed Jennifer and dropped her half. "You scared the shit out of me."

When Jennifer released the rug, the bundle landed with a heavy plop and Pogo ran forward, snarling at the parcel. The dog stuck his snout into a seam of the rug and, after a little rooting, came out with a bone. Andrea dropped her half and swung a leg to kick the little dog, but Pogo was too fast for her. He scooted out of the way, another bone clenched in his teeth.

Andrea pulled a pistol from a pocket and fired. Diving, Darrell scrambled into the brush, the needles and bark scratching his arms. He heard Pogo scurry into some overgrown bushes behind him. He went to raise his head and two more shots whizzed past. He kept down, his breathing labored. Andrea muttered some heated words, followed by more grunting.

A few seconds later, the car doors shut. He stuck his head back up. The Corvette's back up lights flashed on. The sport car accelerated backward, right toward where he lay.

"Let's go," he yelled to Pogo.

He got up and ran back down the road toward his car, the pug right on his heels. As he hustled, he glanced back over his shoulder. The back wheels of the Corvette got hung up on a downed tree, only a few feet from where he'd crouched. The giant engine roared as Andrea shifted the gears, rocking the car back and forth a few times. The Corvette shot out of the brush as if it were slingshotted. A shower of dirt and gravel sprayed out behind it. It hit the street and did a squealing one-eighty, heading back down Beach Avenue. By the time he and Pogo had jumped inside his Corolla, the Corvette shot around the corner and turned at the first side street. The last view he glimpsed was the rear lights of the red sports car disappearing around the corner.

"Oh, no. I'm not losing you again," Darrell yelled over the sound of his own engine as he punched his accelerator.

Chapter Sixty-Three

Darrell urged his car back down Beach Avenue and around the corner where he'd seen the sports car disappear. No sign of the Corvette. He figured she had to be heading out of town, so he followed the same path. He pushed the accelerator and peered down New Jersey Avenue. His luck changed. Several blocks ahead, the red car blew through one a stop sign after another. Darrell did his best to follow, but all his OCD would allow him was a quick rolling stop and then accelerating to the next corner.

The evening lights on the colorful houses lining the street—more modern, faux Victorians—became a blur in his peripheral vision. Up ahead, Andrea took a turn so sharply, he thought her left wheels would come off the road. The sports car's tires squealed, and she sped up Madison Avenue. A few seconds behind, Darrell made the same turn, though on all four wheels. Thankfully, because evening was setting in, he guessed, fewer people were out. He pushed the gas pedal and watched his little Corolla close some of the distance. He was half a block behind Andrea, close enough to see her turn and glare back at him.

They sped through the quiet streets, and he knew they had to attract attention. But so far, he hadn't seen any sign of a black and white. The town had only a few officers and they were likely close to tourist areas. If he was stopped, he'd have a difficult time explaining.

Ahead, the sports car swung wildly to the right, into the bike lane and parking area, and then back, speeding again. Then Darrell saw why. A mother, pushing a fancy baby stroller, had stopped in the middle of the road. Her eyes grew wide in his headlights. He stomped on his brakes. His car fishtailed wildly. He jerked to a stop less than five feet from mother and child.

For a second, no one moved. The radiator fan made a whirring sound. The woman scowled at him and hollered, "Are you people crazy?" and then took her time crossing. Darrell sat there, his heart pounding so hard he could feel it when he laid his hand on his chest. He heaved in and out, three huge breaths. He was trying to catch Amy's killers, but he sure as hell didn't want to cause another death. God! Especially a baby.

He sucked in a giant breath and hit the gas. He figured the incident would cost him the chase. But, when he rolled up to the corner of Madison and Lafayette, he saw the Corvette sitting there, stuck in the middle of five cars waiting for the light. Traffic both ways on Lafayette was steady. Apparently, even Andrea wasn't crazy enough to jump into the other lane and try to cut in between the cars heading back into town.

The light changed, and the line of cars turned onto Lafayette. His luck held because both cars, his and the Corvette, were stuck in the line of travelers going the speed limit. But as soon as the stream of cars passed the Lobster House sign and drove onto the four-lane overpass, the Corvette shot up the ramp. It swung in and out of traffic, switching lanes like a race car.

Darrell did his best to keep up.

The sports car exited the overpass, ran the light, and headed back onto the Garden State Parkway. Speeding up, he followed the same path. He shot onto the expressway, scanning the cars ahead. As dusk surrendered to dark, it became harder to locate the sports car amid traffic, its bright red color muted along with all the other car colors. Then he located it and, while he had the Corvette in his sights, he memorized the unique look of its rear lights.

Now on the Parkway, he squinted at the taillights in the distance and paid little attention to anything else. At one point, he glanced down at his speedometer, stunned to see he was doing close to eighty. He didn't know his little car *could* do eighty miles per hour. Traveling like this, they had to attract notice. He kept waiting to hear sirens.

He made a quick check of the pug, still huddled on the floor, his paws maneuvering the bone he'd grabbed from the rug. A human bone, Darrell knew, probably Amy's.

Darrell glanced from the road ahead—he had to work his way around two more cars to keep the taillights in sight—to the pug still clutching the bone. Darrell was a little creeped out but stayed focused on the highway and the four red taillights.

What were they going to do with the body? Maybe they were trying to dispose of it where no one could ever find it? But where were they going? And what was *he* going to do if…when he caught up with them? Andrea was armed.

He'd worry about that when he got there.

He pushed down harder on the gas and saw the

needle crawl past 90. His car inched closer to the Corvette, closing to maybe a quarter mile, both cars in the left passing lane. Then he heard them. Police sirens, in the distance, more than one, but well behind them. He guessed they were coming from Cape May. That's good. He glanced up, trying to gauge where they were on the parkway and saw the sign for Exit 13 pass overhead.

Right then, the Corvette jerked to the right and veered across three lanes onto the exit. Darrell tried to follow. He hit the brakes. He had to maneuver around several speeding cars. He didn't think he was going to make it.

"Hold on, Pogo."

Slowing his speed, he zigzagged between an SUV and a sedan in the inside lane as the exit came up on the right. He sandwiched the Corolla between the cars. He almost missed it. He hit the exit ramp sideways, bouncing over the left shoulder. He braked hard. The car skidded to a clumsy stop across the lane. His breath caught in his throat. Fearing someone would come barreling down the exit, he floored it again. The Corolla shot down the ramp toward the toll booth.

Up ahead, the Corvette, its bright red body gleaming now under the exit lights, sped through the third toll booth. The sports car joined the crush of cars exiting and Darrell kept focused on the taillights. He followed, this time zipping past the screaming attendant. When the police showed up, not paying the toll would be the least of his problems.

He studied the signature taillights as the sport car made a left turn onto Route 9. Darrell followed. Andrea swerved in and out, making her way through traffic in

Swainton, another small Jersey town. Where was she headed? He did his best to keep up, but Darrell, stuck behind a pickup truck, watched the Corvette extend its lead. Farther ahead, the traffic thinned and the sports car became the only pair of headlights traveling north. In the distance, the taillights disappeared left around a corner.

He concentrated on the spot where Andrea had turned. In a few seconds, he arrived at the same corner. He turned the Corolla and noticed the street sign, Highway 646. After he made the turn, he was amazed his luck held for the third time tonight. The county road in front of him shot out fairly straight and very dark. In fact, the only lights ahead were the distinctive four circular taillights of the Corvette. Andrea had been able to lengthen her lead, but, because the tall trees shaded both sides of the road creating a darkened tunnel, those rear lights formed a beacon. Darrell stayed on them, increasing his speed to match the Corvette. A section of the road curved and banked hard to the left. Coming around the bend too fast, the Corolla lost traction. He skidded onto the shoulder and then up the berm. He hit the brakes hard and stopped the fishtailing, but the car ended up sideways, its headlights lighting up the pebbled sticks of a hundred tree trunks.

His heart thumped inside his chest. He tried to breathe slow and long, working to control his panic. He was going to get himself killed.

Staring at the towering dark evergreens, he backed his car onto the asphalt and suddenly remembered. This was the road where the Haunted Bride had appeared. Where he'd driven through her. He accelerated again, this time on alert for the curves as they came up.

Rounding one bend, he didn't see the taillights. He went through another and out into a long, straight shot. He saw his quarry again. Well ahead, four small red ovals glowed in the darkness.

He pressed harder on the gas. The car surged forward. He held his breath. He was not going to lose her. He focused on the red lights. Then, the road ahead erupted with a silent, bright burst. A brief, blinding flash of white exploded in front of the sports car. He braced for the sound, some blast reverberating off the trees. It never came. The row of taillights swerved to the right and then quickly to the left. The Corvette skidded, losing traction, the squeal of wheels echoing off the trees. The car rocketed toward the woods. The front end struck the berm. The row of lights flipped, once, twice and then bounced and stopped.

In thirty seconds, Darrell closed the distance. He braked and pulled up behind. He turned onto the shoulder, angling his car toward the wreck. His headlights ignited a horrific tableau. He threw open his door and ran up to the wreck. Pogo padded behind, carrying the bone. The sports car lay on its top. Its huge engine still revved, the heavy car rocking slightly. The driver's door hung open. Andrea dangled there, upside down, halfway out of the car, head bloodied and eyes wide, perfectly coifed hair dragging in the gravel. An ugly red slash cut across her chest, blood streaming down her expensive outfit. She was trying to say something, so Darrell approached. He leaned down.

"It was *that bitch*. I saw her," she choked out, between bubbles of blood and saliva. "Can't be. I already killed her." Hard gray eyes stared at him and then closed.

Darrell reached in and turned the key, silencing the throaty engine. He fought his way through tangled and downed tree limbs around the front of the upturned car. The other door had flung open. No second passenger. Not good. He kept going around the twisted metal body. The trunk lid, popped in the crash, was wedged open against a tree. Spilling out of it lay the rug-wrapped bundle, partly unraveled and revealing human bones, white cloth decaying around one exposed limb. Pogo came up and dropped his bone. The pug crept close to the body and sniffed.

"Back, boy. Stay back." The dog obeyed but retrieved his bone again.

Amy Palmer. He lowered his head and blew out a sigh.

Darrell went back to the front of the car, searching. Using his arm to help shield his eyes in the glare of the headlights, he scanned the wooded area, looking for the passenger. Jennifer Thomas. He found her, just beyond the brightly lit space. She dangled from a large tree branch, her slender body impaled on a broken wooden shaft. A circle of blood bloomed from the wound, smearing the words on her tee. Darrell knew it was useless but stepped closer to check her pulse. Nothing. When he did, he glanced down and read through the widening crimson circle, "I'm too sexy for my shirt."

Not anymore.

Jennifer's long blonde hair draped around her head as if it were posed, her pretty face frozen in a scream of pain. The sickly sweet metallic smell of blood made him gag, and he backed into the lighted area. Darrell couldn't stand it. Leaning down, he vomited onto the ground. Wiping his lips, he came up and breathed through his mouth, loudly, over and over.

When he got himself back under control, he said, "Nothing we can do for these two now." He glanced down at the dog at his feet.

A light from across the street caught his attention. Darrcll jerked and turned. There she was. The Haunted Bride. Amy Palmer. She floated across the darkened road, her figure bathed in the white luminescence he'd seen the last time. And Andrea had just witnessed. An explosion of white.

She approached and reached out her hand, no longer bloodied. He took it. The electricity jolted from her hand to his, but he didn't pull away. Instead he stared, her face now only a few inches from his, the stunning beauty of her features obvious now. Shining azure eyes, a petite nose, and a perfect mouth forming a small smile. He never saw her lips move, but clearly heard a beautiful, lilting voice, "Thank you, Darrell. Now, go rescue the girls."

Pogo lumbered up to the figure and dropped the bone at her feet. Darrell looked from the dog to the ghost and saw her smile broaden. Then he heard the sirens. They must have been there all the time because they sounded close, though he hadn't noticed them until just now. In a few seconds, two police cars screeched to a stop behind him. Darrell turned and raised both hands, the red lights strafing him and the pug. As the cops yelled commands, he glanced back over his shoulder.

He and Pogo were alone. With three dead bodies.

Chapter Sixty-Four

Cassie couldn't believe her luck. The only luck she'd ever had was lousy. Her mom left. Her dad beat her until she ran away. Not to mention ghosts haunted her and she nearly died from eating poisoned muffins.

She'd come out of the coma, what, three days ago? Most of that time her stomach hurt like hell and she'd battled waves of killer headaches. Both not so bad now. Yesterday they poked her again. Said if the results came back okay, she could go.

It'd all been pretty shitty, but she'd never been alone. Two days ago, Erin had to leave to get back to her job, but Darrell had been here off and on every day. Of course, Troy never showed his skinny ass.

Maybe Darrell knew she was thinking of him—some sensitive thing of his—because right then, he walked into her room.

"How's my favorite Goth waitress today?" he called.

Cassie tried to give some smartass reply, but stopped. He wasn't alone. The young ER doc, the sweet one with blond hair and blue eyes, strode in alongside Darrell. The doc said, "Well, I just came by say goodbye to one of my favorite patients. Your tests all came back within normal range and you get to bounce."

He flashed her that perfect white-teeth smile. Cassie felt her face go red.

"I know I told you this before, but you are one lucky young lady," Dr. Barrett said, grinning.

Her…lucky.

She was dressed, ready to go.

She'd planned to slip back into her old life—shacking up at Troy's crib and hanging with the posse *and* working at Aleathea's. What else was she going to do? But the more she thought about it, the more she missed Vince. His death still ate at her.

At least they caught the guy.

"You have room for one more in here?" A cop stuck his head in the doorway.

Dr. Barrett placed a hand on her arm. It felt great. "I'm going to sign your discharge papers now and get Darrell a wheelchair to cart you out. Take care. I don't want to see you back here anytime soon." He gave a wave as he and Darrell exited.

Hat in hand, Barnaby sauntered into the room. "Going home, huh? Good. I came by to give you an update." He took off his shades. "After what you've been through, I figure you deserve it. You heard we caught the guy?"

"Yeah, Darrell told me. That asshole, Jeremy Tucker." She spat out the name.

Barnaby continued, "After we caught him on surveillance—even under a green Jets cap, we had a clear photo of his face while he was delivering the baskets of muffins. When we pulled him in and showed him what we had on video, Tucker freaked and spilled his guts. Said he was only acting under orders from James Armstrong. Even volunteered he was driving the truck that killed Vince."

"Really?" Cassie had suspected. Now she knew. It

didn't help much—Vince was still dead—but it was better.

"Yeah, with the confession, we got both Tucker and Armstrong. We have enough to put Tucker away for a long time."

That was something.

"Thanks," Cassie croaked.

Barnaby replaced his cap and shades. "I'll be in touch."

He left, leaving her alone with her thoughts. Of Vince. Of the jerk Tucker. Of the whole damn Armstrong clan. And of Amy, the Haunted Bride. Darrell had warned her that seeing the ghosts and helping them came at a cost. He sure as hell was right.

A knock on the door disturbed her thoughts. "You ready?" a deep voice called. The wheelchair rolled in, but not with Darrell behind it. Instead, Antonio straightened up, his grin wide beneath his thin black moustache. "I'm ready if you are." A second later, Darrell followed her boss in.

She still wasn't sure this was a good idea. Couldn't believe she let Darrell talk her into this. Hell, she couldn't believe Antonio wanted this.

Even in her stupor, she'd been surprised that her boss, the tyrant, came to check on her. She'd been even more amazed that he came back the next two days before and after his shift. Twice, she saw Darrell and Antonio talking in the corner and thought Darrell was asking her boss to cut her some slack. Or maybe they were discussing the medical bills.

When Darrell told her Antonio had asked if she'd like to stay with him and his wife…until she got on her feet, she thought it was a joke. When she realized

Darrell wasn't kidding, she started shaking her head.

In a quiet, kind voice, Darrell had asked, "Where else are you going to go?" She hesitated and Darrell explained, "Antonio's two kids have grown up and moved to California. He and his wife have two open rooms. They'd like you to have one." He'd repeated, "Until you get on your feet."

She thought of Troy's grungy place—and what she had to do to stay there. Shit, it can't be any worse. So she caved.

She slid to the end of the bed and mustered up a smile—not a fake one this time. She shot a glance at Darrell and Antonio and eased herself into the wheelchair. Maybe her luck had changed.

"Okay, let's get the hell of here," she rasped.

Chapter Sixty-Five

Darrell jumped out and tied up the rigging to the post, as Erin settled the sailboat next to the wooden pier. The gleaming teak of *Second Chance* shone in the sun, as the sailboat bobbed slightly in the wake of the St. Michaels harbor. Erin had piloted the boat over from Wilshire like the expert mariner she was and, while she handled the wheel on the short trip, Darrell savored the tranquility of the bay and inhaled the familiar brackish scent. The July morning was bright, with a hot sun overhead. But the breeze on the Bay felt incredible and Darrell smiled, recalling a few of their earlier trips in the boat.

Darrell reached a hand out to Erin as she climbed onto the dock and they headed past the restaurants and onto their destination for the day, the Chesapeake Bay Maritime Museum. After he paid, they strolled down the concrete walk onto the grounds, and the size of the place struck him. According to the brochure he'd received at the entrance, the grounds covered more than eighteen acres and housed docks, freestanding exhibits, and thirty-five buildings. The place looked huge. Staring ahead, he caught sight of the building he cared about, the jewel of the museum collection, the Hooper Strait Lighthouse.

It was great to be home. In his month at Cape May, he'd certainly grown to appreciate the town and found it possessed a beauty, intrigue, and enchantment all its own. After the crash of the Corvette, he'd spent several days answering questions and assisting Barnaby and the officers from several jurisdictions in the investigation. After that, the NYPD got involved and it became a multi-state affair. Last he'd heard from Barnaby, the FBI had muscled their way in.

Once the teens were released, he turned his attention to counseling a few of the kidnapped girls, helping them resettle. He even accompanied Josh and his mom for an intense, tearful reunion with Josie. She had been tentative at first, obviously embarrassed, but when both mother and brother smothered Josie with hugs, she caved, heaving big sighs and saying, "I'm sorry" over and over again. Darrell was thrilled to witness it. It *almost* made the struggles with his ghosts worth it.

Now, he'd only been back two days. It took him almost that long to clean out the fridge in his apartment and get his place back in antiseptic shape again. Add to all that the promising prospect of getting his old job back and he was starting to ease back into a comfortable life on the Bay again.

As it turned out, he hadn't missed much time with Erin, either. In fact, today was the first day she'd had off in two weeks. She'd missed several shifts helping out in Cape May—and agreed to make every one up—so it took her a while to get back onto any regular schedule. After everything they'd been through, both agreed on a fun, relaxing day and, since he loved history, they were here.

The best part was this whole day had been Erin's idea, which made what he had in mind that much sweeter.

They arrived early, and there were few other museum visitors about yet. Darrell was grateful. For what he had planned, he wanted a little privacy. Hand in hand, they ambled over to the first building, a large wooden structure covered with a bright red roof, which featured exhibits highlighting Bay history. Wandering around the displays, they examined the maps and primitive boats. The OCD side of Darrell's brain noticed the place was organized cleanly, with exhibits laid out in a symmetrical pattern. One more sign it was going to be a great day. With what was coming, Darrell was glad for the distraction. Together, they made their way over to a replica of an ancient dugout canoe Native Americans would've carved out of the indigenous tree trunks.

When they finished at the exhibit, Erin pulled Darrell over to a sketch on the far wall. She took a quick glance around and whispered, "Okay, I've been patient long enough and I'm dying to know. Weren't they supposed to indict the Armstrongs today? Heard anything?"

"I didn't want to spoil the romantic mood, but since you asked…I heard from Barnaby before I left. Both James and Travis were indicted at a nine a.m. hearing for the prostitution beef. It'll be on the news tonight."

"Not for Amy's murder?"

"No, James claimed Andrea took the Corvette and went after Amy that night to talk some 'sense' into her." He made quote marks in the air. "But she *accidentally* hit her and killed her instead. Then she and James concocted the story about Amy committing suicide, walking into the ocean. After everyone left, they buried her."

"What about Travis?"

"Both James *and* Travis claim the groom didn't know anything about his mother killing Amy. He knew Amy was really shook up and believed the suicide story." Darrell paused and then added, "But father and son were both indicted for prostitution, delinquency of minors, and about twelve other charges. Not to mention the attempted murder of a police officer for James."

"Knowing James Armstrong, I'm sure he's hired a stable of high-priced lawyers. Does Barnaby think they'll be able to make the charges stick?"

"Yeah. After James wounded Barnaby, the cops went ballistic. You know, one of their own. Venice PD refused to protect Armstrong. They got search warrants for the house, the office, and the Armstrong company trucks. They found the moving brothels and plenty of records dating back almost ten years on the whole operation. Going to be difficult to beat hard evidence. Besides, after the cops freed the teen girls and sent them home, several agreed to testify, including our own Josie."

"I'm so glad Josie is back home with her brother and mom. What about Jennifer, Travis' old girlfriend? I almost forgot. I never asked you about her."

Darrell shook his head. "Not guilty. Andrea needed someone to help dig up and lift the body. Jennifer's roommate said Andrea simply asked the girl to help out." He shrugged. "Said she overheard Mom promise she'd help get Jennifer and Travis back together. Turns out, Jennifer wasn't involved at all in Amy's death. In fact, from all accounts, she was flat drunk when Amy was killed."

Erin dropped her gaze. "Sad way to end."

Darrell was glad he never gave Erin a full description of Jennifer's gruesome death scene. That sight still haunted him. Erin had been through so much with him, he wanted to spare her.

They stepped outside into sunshine so bright it took a bit for their eyes to adjust.

"You're not the only one with news," she squealed. "I got news from the home front."

"I'm all ears."

"Last night Sarah called me at work around ten." Erin's green eyes sparkled. "She told me the School Board had just held a special meeting. Executive Session only, no public, no reporters, very hush, hush." She waited and smirked.

"You're killing me here."

"All the great press in Cape May didn't hurt. The vote was unanimous. They agreed to reinstate you." She paused a bit. "With all back pay. *And* give you an extended contract. Five years."

Darrell wrapped his arms around her and hugged. Staring down at Erin, he said, "That's great. I'm going to need the extra money. You know, I took this gal out to Cape May. Beautiful girl. We had a great time, but she has costly tastes. You know, fancy hotel rooms, expensive meals—the whole thing. She cost me a small fortune. I don't know if my credit card will ever recover."

She patted his cheek. "You poor boy."

As more tourists poured through the gate, Darrell scanned the grounds, watching the visitors spread out across the grass.

"Look at those two." Erin pointed to an elderly couple leaning on the rail of one of the boats on exhibit. "I think that's sweet." Darrell followed her gaze and saw the couple, watching as the man brought up his wife's hand and kissed it gently.

He followed the man's lead and took Erin's hand in his. But, before he could raise it to his lips, Erin asked, "Hey, why is your palm so moist?" She grinned at him.

He took his hand back and wiped it on his pants, casting another glance around the grounds. So far, it didn't look like any other visitors had made it to the vintage lighthouse. He decided now might be a good time.

"What do you say we check out the lighthouse next?" He indicated the structure at the shoreline of the property.

"Sounds great," Erin said, with a warm smile.

He *really* loved that smile. He hoped he'd get to enjoy it for quite a long time. Darrell reached a hand into his pocket, his fingers encircling the object. It was still there.

They crossed the lawn and approached the lighthouse, climbing the stairs to the first level. Hand in hand, they strolled around the structure, loitering on the harbor side, enjoying the breeze off the water and the peaceful view. Darrell leaned forward, elbows on the rail, and Erin followed suit. Together, they studied the channel, watching as a sloop maneuvered almost silently through the harbor to dock at a nearby pier.

"Did you get any more sense of our, um...our friend, Amy?" she asked, without taking her eyes off the water.

Darrell glanced around to ensure no one was within

earshot. "No, thank heaven. And I checked with Cassie. She hadn't sensed the Haunted Bride's presence either since…since then."

"Guess you helped Amy with her unfinished business."

Images leaped into his mind—visions of the twisted wreck of the Corvette, the dangling, decaying corpse, and the bloodied, lifeless bodies of Andrea and Jennifer. Darrell shook his head to dislodge them. Not today. He gave a dry laugh. "Yeah, I think that business is more than finished."

"And maybe." Erin turned and faced him. "Maybe, the most important thing is not only did you get justice for Amy, but you helped rescue those kidnapped girls from a horrid life. And you might not have made that final connection without Cassie's vision of the night Amy was killed. Without you two—and the ghost—the Armstrongs would've kept trapping teen girls in that life." She smiled at him. "Not bad for a history teacher and a teen runaway."

"Your favorite teacher?" Darrell baited.

"Without a doubt." She leaned forward and kissed him, long and hard.

When they came out of it, he said. "What do you say we take this up one more level?"

In answer, she grabbed his hand and led him inside the light keeper's cabin and past the antique desk, the ledger with the authentic hand-written entries still sitting atop the old desk. They crossed the room to the interior stairs, and he followed her up the twenty-five wooden steps. Nervous, he counted them in his head, as his feet tapped each worn tread.

At the top of the stairs, they came out onto the

narrow walkway, crossing in front of the lantern with the three-foot high Fresnel lens, and made their way to the railing. Darrell caught his breath. They were up thirty-nine feet in the air—he'd read the statistic on the plaque below—but it felt like more, much more. The view stretched out into the Bay for what seemed like miles, the channel with full, green trees lining left and right like verdant bookends. Above them lazy clouds floated by in a sea of perfect azure. Together they watched in silence as sleek sailboats crisscrossed the mouth of the harbor, the stretched white sails billowing.

Up here, at the top of the lighthouse, the breeze felt stronger and a brisk wind blew past them, cooling the sun-baked heat. Darrell's gaze went from the incredible turquoise water before him to the amazing woman at his side. She stood next to him at the railing, her emerald eyes sparkling and her lustrous hair being tossed crazily by gusts of wind. Seeing her red tresses dancing in the wind, Darrell smiled, remembering how she looked standing at the helm, steering the sailboat on their first date. In that instant, he knew he was making the right decision.

He got down on one knee and pulled out of his pocket a small box wrapped in deep blue felt.

Erin stared down at him and gasped.

"Erin Caveny," he said, "let's make our own history together. Will you marry me?"

A word about the author...

Dr. Randy Overbeck is a veteran educator who has served children as a teacher, as a college professor, and as a school leader. For more than three decades, his educational experiences have included responsibilities ranging from senior prom advisor to superintendent, and he's lived the roles of many of the characters in his stories.

An accomplished writer, he has been published in trade journals, professional texts, and newspapers, as well as in fiction, with his third published novel. As a member of the Mystery Writers of America, Dr. Overbeck is an active member of the literary community, contributing to a writers' critique group, serving as a mentor to emerging writers and participating in writing conferences such as Sleuthfest, Killer Nashville, and the Midwest Writers Workshop.

When he's not writing or researching his next exciting novel, he's spending time with his incredible family of wife, three children (and their spouses), and seven wonderful grandchildren.

www.authorrandyoverbeck.com